Ruffian Dick

RUFFIAN DICK

A NOVEL OF
SIR RICHARD FRANCIS BURTON

JOSEPH KENNEDY &
JOHN ENRIGHT

YUCCA

Yucca Publishing books may be purchased in bulk at special discounts for sales promotion, corporate gifts, fund-raising, or educational purposes. Special editions can also be created to specifications. For details, contact the Special Sales Department, Yucca Publishing, 307 West 36th Street, 11th Floor, New York, NY 10018 or yucca@skyhorsepublishing.com.

Yucca Publishing® is an imprint of Skyhorse Publishing, Inc.®, a Delaware corporation. Visit our website at www.yuccapub.com.

10 9 8 7 6 5 4 3 2 1

Library of Congress Cataloging-in-Publication Data is available on file.

Jacket design by Laura Klynstra
Jacket photo: Dreamstime/Tassaphon Vongkittipong

Print ISBN: 978-1-63158-102-1
Ebook ISBN: 978-1-63158-108-3

Printed in the United States of America

TABLE OF CONTENTS

FOREWORD

IT IS NOT EVERY DAY that the tedium of archaeology manages to unearth something truly spectacular, but I was on the receiving end of such an event last summer while kneeling in a cramped, meter-square excavation pit in the port city of Trieste. This was one of those typical urban archaeology projects that resulted in hundreds of artifact bags being filled with the humdrum slivers of shattered window glass, broken bricks and fragments of yesterday's domestic discards. However, what the earth gave up on that particular afternoon is something that will rock the world of letters and set our understanding of numerous historical events on their ear.

On that humid day near a diesel-fume-belching bus stop and from under the rubble of a ruined palazzo, a partially burned book came to light. After freeing it from the ground I slid my trowel midway into the volume and gently lifted enough to see that the pages were actually readable and gave the appearance of being a diary of some sort. I confess to not completely understanding the importance of what had happened until I returned to London, uncrated the book and began a detailed examination.

Once I got started and realized what was in my hands it was like being blasted out of a Victorian cannon and landing in a high-voltage world of 150 years past. The book offered a refreshingly blunt and ultimately convincing portrait of those times and is filled with the most unusual characters and fascinating situations imaginable. From the very beginning it ushered me directly into the contentious conclusion of one of the most celebrated and controversial travel adventures of the nineteenth century—the discovery of the source of the Nile—and the rest of the journal entries only ratcheted up further interest and combined to reach even greater heights.

Such extravagant claims call for quick explanation and substantiation and so I will get right to heart of these matters. We of course knew that our excavation was in a residential area of Trieste, but when the radiocarbon dates were obtained I was able to determine that we were digging in a palazzo dating to the late 1800s, and at that time this particular home was the residence of the local British Consul.

It did not take much checking to learn that the person who held that position at that place and at that time was the redoubtable Captain Sir Richard Francis Burton.

A preliminary but careful checking of dates and places in the book then sent me into a protracted and detailed study of Burton's life, for I was now fairly certain of what I had and wanted to know everything possible about the man, his work, and especially his movements.

I spent so many months in the British Museum on Great Russell St. that the staff began greeting me by my first name, and the patrons at the Museum Tavern across the street grew weary of hearing my excited after-hours talk about Sir Richard. I was somewhat careful about what I said, but then there was the exuberance, the setting, and so forth. I began requesting so much material that the librarian at the Foreign Office archives groaned each time I entered the door, and I also think they were beginning to tire of me at the Royal Anthropological Institute and the Royal Geographic Society. After a time, exasperated looks crossed the faces of the guardian matrons in each of these reading rooms. I was in there more than anyone else in recent memory and probably made them work harder than they were used to.

After a full year of research, correspondence, and cross-checking, it is my belief that the book is certainly one of Burton's private journals. What is contained in it comes from a carefully hidden and protected side of a mind belonging to one of the great adventurers and rogues in a time of unparalleled exploration and eccentricity.

The colorful, in-print parts of Burton's life are well known. As a lad he bashed his music teacher over the head with his violin, and as a young explorer had a spear thrust through his face by a native tribesman in Somali. Later, Burton discovered Lake Tanganyika, was the translator of the unexpurgated *Thousand and One Nights Entertainment* and numerous other erogenous Oriental texts. He penetrated the Muslim's holy Meccah in disguise at great risk, and once again using his verbal skills while in disguise, talked his way into the dangerous and forbidden East African city of El Harrar. He authored over one hundred books and articles, spoke twenty languages and dialects, and, more than a century after his death, he is still considered the world's greatest erotic anthropologist.

Burton served in the Crimean War as the commander of a cavalry unit comprised of Turkish delinquents and criminals known as the *Bashi Bazook*, and by the mid-1800s he was regarded as one of the finest swordsmen in Europe. Sir Richard rode sacred alligators in Karachi, chased sea serpents off the coast of Rio de Janeiro, mined for gold in Midian, founded both the Royal Anthropological Institute and something called the Cannibal Club. He kidnapped a Catholic nun in Goa (allegedly for prurient purposes) and served as British Consul in Brazil, Damascus, Fernando Po, and Trieste. It has been aptly said that Richard Burton led the lives of all Three Musketeers rolled into one.

Regardless of his many accomplishments, from early childhood until his death in 1890, Burton was a pariah in starchy Victorian society, if not a man who many considered on the verge of being dangerous. By his early teens he was consorting with Italian whores, was later kicked out of Oxford for placing bets at a horse race, earned a reputation for hashish use and romantic associations with women of color, and some say he even killed a man who discovered his disguise on his way to Meccah. Burton delighted in shocking people, whether it was by conspicuously reading *The History of Farting* at one of his wife's stodgy tea parties or his fascination with the bestial side of human nature. His furious and prolific writing, fierce looks and cabalistic countenance only added to his problems. The man who wrote *Dracula* said that Richard Burton had the darkest eyes he had ever seen, and to underscore this, Burton made it a point of concerning himself with the occult and things satanic and was actually working on a biography of Satan when he died.

It was these acts and other eccentric manias that troubled the Victorian world in general and his deeply religious wife in particular. In 1861, Richard Burton married Isabel Arundell, a devout English Catholic from a prominent family, and unwittingly set the stage for one of the greatest crimes in literary history. It was well known that Burton kept at least two sets of private journals that detailed the events of his colorful life. Those hidden feelings and observations contained within, along with his erotic texts and personal letters, were a constant source of embarrassment to his wife. They held the soul that she denied throughout her marriage and represented everything she feared and hated. At her husband's death in 1890, Lady Burton engineered a bizarre *post mortem* baptism of Sir Richard and directly afterwards sequestered herself for sixteen days of furious and destructive editing. She methodically gathered together every book and scrap of paper she thought objectionable, and then burned them all in the courtyard of the couple's palazzo in Trieste.

After the holocaust, only eighteen pages of one of Burton's private journals and in addition a portion of one complete second journal managed to escape her wrath. Those eighteen pages were rescued by Miss Daisy Letchford Nicastro who was a house guest at the time of Sir Richard's death. The eighteen pages were sent directly to Great Russell St. by Mrs. Evelyn Lindenmann Letchford and survive to this day. That other complete journal found its way into the hands of Sir Norman Penzer, Burton's official biographer, but like so many other Burton papers it too was destroyed by fire—this time at the hands of the German *Luftwaffe* during the London blitz of WWII. Before that, many Burton papers were incinerated in the Grindly's Warehouse fire in 1861, and there were also letter-burnings by his hated mother-in-law. After Isabel died, her sister even got in on the act and began a campaign of purchasing copies of Burton's erotic translations that were published abroad and burned every one she could lay her hands on.

As mentioned, these things are well known. But now Lady Burton and the fate of fires have been defeated, and with this private journal in hand the secret side of Burton's life can be brought back to life. It may be said with confidence that no one has laid eyes on this book for well over one hundred years, and it is entirely possible that until now Burton himself was the only person who knew what it contained. The first entry was made off the coast of Zanzibar in April of 1859 and the last on September 27, 1860 in Utah Territory. In an examination of just the first dozen pages we find, in surprising and shocking detail, the unexpurgated events which lead to the discovery of the Nile. This story is brought to light for the first time and is certain to ignite a firestorm of controversy. Burton also had a few things to say about Africa and its inhabitants at this time, and it is highly unlikely that one could gain such straightforward insights through any other published source.

From there the book allows us to follow Burton on a trip across America. Through the journal offerings, we are virtually in attendance at the Abraham Lincoln nomination in Chicago and get a glimpse into the birth of modern American politics. The book also brings us into the crowd at a crazy baseball game in New York City. We hear directly from an African slave about his unfortunate condition in the New World circa 1860 and visit with the Voodoo Queen in New Orleans. The reader becomes familiar with a variety of North American Indians, trappers, soldiers, and scoundrels, and we are even treated to an in-depth, Burtonesque interview with Mr. Brigham Young—and these may be counted as only the highlights, considering what this book has to offer as a whole.

The African episode will speak for itself, but from a letter I uncovered in the British Foreign Office we can get a glimpse of what was expected of Burton in America as a secret agent, where he was to go, and what he should and should not do when he got there. Even at this early date the British Government knew their man.

To: Dr John Steinhaeuser
    Civil Surgeon
    Her Majesty's Port of Aden in Arabia

From: R. Rafton Stiggins
    2nd Consular Officer
    Her Majesty's Foreign Office

King Charles St London
January 15th, 1860

Dear Dr Steinhaeuser:

It has come to the attention of our office that you are both pro-
fessionally and socially attached to Lt Richard Burton of the Bombay
Army who is at present ending his leave in Central Africa. It is our
understanding that you attended to Burton after some hard knocks
came his way in Berbera, and since then have cemented a friendship
of some depth with the man.

In consequence of the aforementioned we believe that you
may hold some considerable sway in the direction of his life.
I dare say that this is not an easy thing to accomplish, for our
records indicate a history of Burton's single-minded independence, which borders on insubordination, and a marked disincli-
nation to do as he is told.

While there is a recurring theme of indifference to authority in
his make-up, there is also an issue of conduct. For example, when
reprobates such as Rashid Pasha and the Baluchi Ramji weigh in
with complaints of his recent and scandalous actions, as I am afraid
they have recently done, one has to pause and take measure. We are
frankly at a loss as to how Lt. Burton manages repeatedly to find
if not manufacture trouble, associate with such shocking characters,
and get himself into sticky situations that are to our way of thinking
embarrassments.

Nevertheless, it has been decided here in the Foreign Office that
Burton is needed at the moment. There are reports that he may be a
bit chalked from Africa and in any case he could, given his authority
problem, resist a directive from this office. But as demonstrated several times in both India and Africa he is a plucky and daring traveler
who is likely to be able to navigate through a dangerous land, he
enjoys a reputation as being a non-political scientific observer, has
exceptional and quickly-adapted linguistic skills, and he is certainly
not behind hand in describing what he sees in an unusually direct
fashion. We have fears there will be an American civil war and we

need a savvy ear to the ground—not just in Washington, D.C., but throughout the length and breadth of that country.

Your orders are to begin in New York, move to the Conventions that will elect the new President of the United States, roam the heartland for more detailed observations, and finally cross into the Indian Territories West of the Mississippi River with the ultimate goal of reaching the Mormon settlements in greater Utah Territory, a place and a people we have grave concerns about. We suggest adding the enticing idea that Burton could penetrate still another Holy City—this time the polygamist Mormon citadel in Salt Lake City. The Director thinks this is just his sort of meat and will provide Burton with ample temptation to begin another one of the adventures he seems to crave so much.

Finally, please exercise great caution, Doctor, and be on guard at all times. This will not be a conventional assignment, I assure you— and it will not be an easy one.

God Save The Queen,

R.R. Stiggens

2nd Consular Officer

Her Majesty's Foreign Office

There is an unmistakable intensity and frankness attached to the writing in Burton's private journal, and the things he comments on are personalities and situations that only a special kind of individual can perceive. Burton had a genius for getting himself positioned as a participant at important and interesting events and was a virtuoso in turning the ordinary into the remarkable. He was a magnet for controversy and everyone who knew him or knows of him associates his name with one of the most colorful lives in history and links it to seminal and often surprising happenings.

Now that I have read his diary I can see why. What is in the journal surpasses even what has been written about him, and that is saying a great deal. This is Richard Burton unplugged and uncensored, and in a way it is probably fitting that his thoughts on so many matters make their debut in an era that can handle it.

What the journal has to say about his time and Burton himself is perhaps the most important part of what the book has to offer. Alexis de Tocqueville, Frances Trollope, Charles Dickens, and Oscar Wilde have all left lasting impressions of early America but combined they have not, nor could not, provide us with a portrait comparable to Burton's.

While this is indeed a new and significant look at a celebrated event in African exploration, it is a brief one. Much more important is the change in Richard Burton, and it is his transformed self that offers us a portrait of seminal America that was forged in a mud hut in Zanzibar. It is that place that this entire story is linked to and driven by. It was there in a spiritual divination that the raw power inherent in Burton's personality was unleashed and refocused by a tribal mystic who launched him on the hunt for himself and an unexpurgated explanation of nothing less than the human condition.

Introduction

A FULL APPRECIATION OF THE first chapter in Burton's journal cannot be obtained without some background information. By the mid-1800s, the greatest jewel of exploration in the Western world was the discovery of the source of the Nile. The Portuguese and Arabs had entered Central Africa over the preceding fifty years but neither produced any reliable maps of the region, and no one alive ever attempted to properly identify what had come to be known as "The Coy Fountains."

Richard Burton found this challenge irresistible. He managed to obtain a two-year leave from the Bombay Army and secured financial support from the British Foreign Office in order to solve one of the greatest geographical mysteries of his time. He proposed a twenty-one month journey of exploration that would begin at island Zanzibar, cross a treacherous straight to the continent and arrive at coastal Bagamoyo. He then proposed to move west with a substantial native entourage and into the African interior towards what the Arabs called the *Jebel KuMr.i*—the legendary Mountains of the Moon. Joining Burton on the trek was John Hanning Speke, a man who would later come to cause him a great deal of trouble. This association was doomed from the beginning through a number of significant differences. Speke, a Captain in the 46th Bengal Native Infantry, technically outranked Burton at the time, and unlike his peripatetic partner, who had followed his eccentric and money-strapped father throughout Europe as a devilish youngster, Speke was the privileged, obedient son of well-to-do rural British gentry and the brother of a high-ranking Minister in The Church of England. Speke's love of guns and hunting and dislike of books placed him in marked contrast to Burton who preferred sabers, the intellectual pursuit of human game, and a near addiction to the printed word.

But most significant of all, Speke had deep philosophical differences with Richard Burton. He was a model officer who did not drink or smoke, was a devout Christian, and aside from his mother, had no known associations with women. On the other hand Burton was already involved in a number of celebrated controversies with his superiors, and had developed a robust taste for brandy, cigars, plant intoxicants, and native women. He renounced Western religion and adopted the sobriquet *Shaykh Haji Abdullah* due to his associations with El Islam. His contemporaries complained that Burton had 'turned Turk' and referred to him as "Ruffian Dick."

After a grinding journey to the African interior, the expedition at last came upon a body of water more than 400 miles long; this was the Sea of Ujiji, which is now called Lake Tanganyika. All written sources concerning the actual discovery of the Nile source tell us that Burton elected to stay along the banks of Ujiji, while unaccountably, Speke left with a couple of guides to explore farther north and eventually discovered what would later prove to be the true fountainhead of the great river, Lake Victoria.

History has heretofore been silent concerning the reason why the adventurous Burton chose to stay satisfied at Ujiji—and what is even more perplexing, why the language-challenged and relatively timid Speke was motivated to continue north essentially on his own. As the reader will soon see, these questions have now been answered.

Midway through the journey Burton and Speke had learned to dislike each other thoroughly but remained together in deference to the goals and difficulty of the expedition. Speke left Burton in Zanzibar with a pledge not to go public with any information until they could do so jointly in London. He reneged on that promise and through the following journal entries we shall also see what really led to the discovery of the source of the Nile and the results of that episode.

Ruffian Dick

I

Africa and the Source of the Nile

April 1, 1859, off the coast of Zanzibar, aboard
the HMS *Dragon of Salem*

At last away from the Continent of Decrepitude and the land
where absolutely nothing can go as planned. Africa has nearly
taken my life. From my exposure to it I am sick to the bone and
through every fiber of my mind and body while Speke, damn
him, is up and gad-flying about as I lay rotting in my deck hammock. True to his lot, he is hallo-ing and cheerio-ing every Jack
Tar in sight, no doubt regaling them with his dreadful hunting
stories and vilifying me to the gentlemen officers. Already I have
heard whispering cowards misrepresenting the details of my brief
love affair with the daughter of Said bin Salim back in Ujiji.[1] To
compound my misery, I have learned that the gentle Col. Ham-
merton has gone to his reward since I was last there and has been
replaced at Zanzibar with Christopher Rigby. This cur has hated
me since I routed him on a Gujarati examination back in India.
Being both first-rate bounders, I suspect he and Jolly Jack Speke
will become fast friends.

I assume they will first compare notes on my social life as that is a
favourite target of the teetotalers and adult virgins I know them both

---

1 The same village where Stanley met Livingstone twelve years later. —Ed.

to be. Rigby's *bubu*[2] in India once confided to me that the man was horribly wounded while leading a charge in the Afghan Campaign, and that a devastating blow between the legs left him incapable of servicing women. She went on to say that he took the greatest care to hide his wound when changing trousers.

"My dear young girl," I said, "Lt. Rigby was no closer to Kabul than you were to Brighton when the Afghans staged their revolt. The idea of a man like that leading a charge is ridiculous and his effort to conceal his 'wound' can be traced directly to the uncommonly small size of his weapon."

She looked at me awestruck until I held up my little finger and wiggled it in the air. This simple gesture delighted her and she brought forth a genuine laugh. Like any woman would she later confronted Rigby with my story and demanded to know if this were the real reason she had been cheated in bed. Once exposed, so to speak, Rigby made a clumsy effort to purchase her silence in this matter.

Naturally, the girl solemnly accepted the bribe and then went about spreading this exciting news to relatives and soldier friends throughout the garrison. He has never forgiven me for the ragged doggerel I engraved on the table of the officer's mess:

Chris Rigby went to draw his sword
and found he had a dagger
he couldn't hope to thrust his girl
so instead paid pounds to gag her.

This catchy rhyme spread like a plague for Rigby and soon every *sepoy* in camp knew it by heart. I must be sure to scrawl it on the nearest wall the moment we reach Zanzibar and teach it to every prostitute in town. I am surprised to find myself comforted by the thought of returning to this filthy little island, but after what has taken place on the mainland, any sane man would have to agree with me.

---

2 A 'bubu' or so-called "native wife" was not uncommon for Englishmen in the Bombay Army. These were usually temporary relationships that terminated when the soldier's tour of duty ended. —Ed.

As dispirited as I am now, nothing could compare to those first days when we paused to rest at Tabora. After trekking back from the great lake (called 'The Sea of Ujiji' by the natives) both Speke and I were in a terrible way. As cruel fate would have it though, he was well on his way to recovery after a few days while I was still sinking. My own resurgence was hampered by a poor mental condition brought on by learning of the death of my father, the deplorable behavior of the Africans in my charge, and, most importantly, the overbearing compulsions of my *compagnon de voyage*.

As in every other place he has ever been, Speke was positively bored with the fascinations of the anthropology and geography of his present location and longed only for the hunt.[3] I will declare that any man, and under any circumstances whatsoever, who would happily kill and leave on the ground to rot 105 elephants (his contemptible total just so far) richly deserves a special place in hell. Might not Dante find an even lower level for this man's Eternity? I pray for this in a dozen languages.

His bothersome fascination with animal murder is just one of the many wedges between us. By the time we reached Tabora, there were only two men who would go along with him on his hunting adventures—both family-less natives who had participated in the lowest forms of capital crimes. The rest of the bearers shy from his fanatical recruiting. I could tell the natives harboured a dark secret about Speke's personality and tastes but I don't know yet quite what it is.

Speke was forever on edge and always ready to go. All that remained of his physical discomforts was an annoying whistle that accompanied the incessant blowing of his nose. An insect had gnawed a hole in

---

3 In the archives of the Royal Geographic Society there is a letter from Speke to Dr. Norton Shaw dated July 2, 1858. "Burton has always been ill; he won't sit out in the dew, and has a decided objection to the sun. . .This is a shocking country for sport. . .nothing but Elephants. There is nothing to write about in this uninteresting country. Nothing could surpass these tracts, jungles, plains for dull sameness, the people are the same everywhere in fact this country is one vast senseless map of sameness." —Ed.

his eardrum and air rushed through the wound whenever there was enough internal pressure. Worse, Speke could not conceive of anyone being ill when he wasn't. My first rumblings in the morning at Tabora were a torture of agony. My eyes burned when they met the light, and joints, stiff and swollen, would ache till the warmth of noon. He kept insisting that we "strikeout for some game" or "sharpen our eyes on a few targets." I once asked him if he would like to accompany me on a trip to meet some girls and he answered, "Oh no, that won't do, Dick. That wouldn't do at all."[4]

As I stirred to address this painful condition, I would look to the other side of the tent and see Speke, fully clothed and hunching towards me; he sat on the edge of his cot with his hands patiently folded by his knees. When he saw I was stirring from my hammock, he would begin beaming and talking at the same instant: "Well Dick, shall we have a go at it? I mean," he licked his lips. "Shall we load-up and really have a jolly good go at it?" His brows were arched and his fists now clenched in positive enthusiasm. I refused to move a muscle but continued to stare at him from my berth.

"I say, Dick, are you listening?" His idiotic smile disappeared for a moment and then quickly returned when he reported a wildebeest herd a day's journey to the west or the promise of "big game" just five hard miles south. I was too sick and disgusted to answer, so I continued glaring at him from my horizontal station. The prospect of even getting up to myself was a nasty notion, so one might imagine how I received his invitation to quick march off for twenty miles in order to do some sport shooting.

"Jack," I said finally, "you are a bloody ass and if you don't stop annoying me with this hunting business, I will take a spear from Bombay[5] and pin you to the wall like a ruddy bug!" This murderous threat shut him up momentarily and exasperated him so that he was forced to leave the tent. It was my first hint that I had the power to get rid of him without actually formalizing the request as a

---

4 Speke was such a prude he referred to his trousers as 'unmentionables.' —Ed.

5 Bombay (real name Sidi Mubarak) was head bearer, guide, and translator for the expedition. —Ed.

direct order. Any outright dismissal, of course, would be the subject of some tattle-tailing to the RGS[6]. Murchison and the rest will most likely find his hunting routine quite normal and suspect *me* of being the madman.

Later in the morning I ran into Speke near the tree where the bearers were staying. He was having an awful time trying to hang on to a cheap memento given to him by his precious mum. One of the petty chiefs of the village had taken a fancy to it and went so far as to inform Speke that it was part of his rent for resting his people on his brother-in-law's land.

When I arrived, the two men were actually tugging back and forth with the bauble between them. I could see that temperatures were beginning to rise and I stood by as a spectator with a group of young men from the village who had been attracted by Speke's cries of outrage. Of course, the villagers got into the tempo of the event at once and began jostling each other about in mock combat. Wagers were being made, and the level of horseplay began to escalate.

Two factions were formed along betting lines and began to out-shout each other. Voices became bellicose and I was quite sure that there would soon be trouble. Speke finally spotted me and said, "Damn it, Burton, can't you make this fellow understand that he can't have this? Doesn't he understand that it's *mine* and that I would rather *die* than give it up?"

I told him that by my calculations he should be getting his last wish in a few moments time. I suggested that he should try and strike a bargain as a general melee was about to break out and he surely would be involved. "Look, old boy," I said, "why don't you let me try and placate the chief here by offering him something else of yours? I really don't believe you have much of a choice at this point. Let me inform the chief who you are and see if that will strike the right chord."

As Speke could not understand the man's language, I was able to maneuver the conversation in a most direct and dishonest way. I suspect the ensuing interactions can best be written this way.

---

6 The Royal Geographic Society. —Ed.

JHS: By all means, Burton! Tell this clutching nigger who he's dealing with; tell him my *mother* gave this to me. Tell him if he does not desist I will beat him.

RFB (in dialect to the chief): My companion wishes to tell you that you are a great chief and a mighty warrior. He submits to you completely and wishes to formalize his defeat according to the customs of his people.

RFB: Quickly, Speke; unhitch your trousers and let them fall to your ankles. It is a sign of your virility and part of the important Unrecognized Male Greeting Ceremony. Do as I say or you may be killed.

The chief, amused at the spectacle of the white, thin legs before him, was a man possessed of a staccato, choking laugh that originated deep in his throat, and I can assure you it was at full force in this particular situation.

The chief: Tell your friend that his custom is a strange one. In Tabora when a man disrobes in front of another he is either about to bathe or else he is preparing for Arab love. I accept this apology, before he turns like a baboon and fouls the air. (Much laughter).

RFB: That's it Jack! He has forgotten about the memento from your mother and is willing to trade for something else.

JHS: Trade? Why, I'll do nothing of the sort. What could this savage possibly have that would be worth anything to me?

The chief had been chuckling with the other men since the time Speke's trousers came down. He interrupted his fun in order to share what he thought a clever joke. "Tribesmen from the northern villages make *this* kind of love with the Arabs." He slapped his buttock. "The Kowouli would be well pleased with your friend's apology and would be happy to give him forgiveness and plenty of attention." (Uncontrolled shrieks of laughter followed by hysterics).

RFB: Despite your sarcasm Jack, I believe this chap actually does have something you would be interested in. He has just told me that he can see that you are a great hunter and could be persuaded to tell you where the king of the village goes to secure his royal game.

JHS (Suspicious but interested; his trousers still on the ground): What does the blackguard want in exchange for this information?

RFB: He has indicated that one of your pistols and a few cartridges will be the price.

JHS: Another pistol? Does every black nigger in Africa want one of my pistols? This is the fifth time I've had to give up a revolver to save my life.

Poor Speke! He could not have known that I have been consciously suggesting his firearms as trade items from day one. My purpose is to lighten our load and, of course, not miss any opportunity to whittle his substantial arsenal down to reasonable size.

RFB to chief: I have convinced my friend that a powerful warrior like yourself would be better served by a gun rather than a simple locket.

The gun is exchanged.

At first stunned and then grateful, realizing he has been compensated as never before in his life, the chief thanked me and announced that, "This is the greatest day in my life. I must go and tell my wife." He motioned in the direction of his hut, the gun waving wildly over his head.

RFB: The chief said to travel north for five days until you reach the village of the Kowouli. When you arrive, demand to be taken to the "back trail" or the "royal road." And, Speke, if you value your life, be sure to let down your britches honoring the unrecognized male greeting ceremony. This will let them know your intentions and ensure friendly associations.

The thought of sending Speke off on a wild goose chase to the regional seat of homosexuality brought me a great deal of pleasure and comfort, but, as expected, there was a bit of devil to pay upon his return.

I was enjoying a glorious mid-day at Tabora until Jack and one of his men returned from their "hunting trip" up north. Earlier that morning, I had the opportunity to take some hashish with an Arab slaver, so the sight of their arrival proved even more amusing than I had anticipated. Speke looked horribly rumpled as though he hadn't slept since I last saw him and he was covered with dried mud. His bush *chapeaux*, usually fixed with military precision, was skewed and twisted over to one side of his head giving him a clownish appearance, his trousers were blown out at the knees and seat, and his socks had slipped from their garters and bunched loosely at the tops of his boots. This site brought an intoxicated smile to my face and I called out, "Hallo! Jack Speke. Is that you? Come over for some late breakfast. Why I hardly recognized you behind all that filth."

Speke interrupted a conversation with his guide and looked over at me. After a few last words to his man, he broke away and presented himself in front of my table. He stood there with a restrained look on his face and began brushing the dust from his sleeves and tugging on his jacket to smooth out the wrinkles. I spoke to him in a voice showing the greatest concern and interest. "Good heavens, Jack, you are a mess. Do sit down and tell me the most *intimate* details of your little trip."

He sat down without saying a word. Finally, after finding the wherewithal to compose himself, he said, "Burton, I suspect you of conspiring against me. You are a liar and a vulgar beast no different from your tribal friends at Kowouli: and like them, probably a homosexual as well!"

I later learned that Speke and two of his men arrived at the village in the midst of some sort of festival. Anxious to start things out on the right foot, Jack hailed the celebrants with a loud shout and after getting their attention, raised a hand in salute and performed the "Unrecognized Male Greeting Ceremony" according to instruction. This triggered a wild response from the Kowouli. Speke was mobbed, carried off and manhandled, so to speak, by adolescent boys clad only in their initiation markings. It was impossible to wrench any further details from the only other returning eyewitness. It is known that Speke's other companion elected to stay at Kowouli calling it, "the place of his preference."

Speke stiffened for a long bombast as he stood tall in front of me. "I have wasted ten days ration, left behind a once-decent and hard-working native, have been forced to surrender both body and soul, and have suffered the loss of all my Manton Brothers .70 calibers, which were stolen before my eyes in the first thirty seconds after

I arrived. Sir, you may be sure that the Royal Geographic Society will hear of this. If I am not mistaken, Sir Roderick Murchison will not take kindly to your wanton lack of seriousness nor your childish pranks. Why, had we not found the boat, there may have been a murder charge hanging over your head in addition to the grievous moral crime you have committed.

"Beyond these things, Lt. Burton, the dazed look on your face tells me that you are full of hemp smoke once again. Judging from past performances, I'd say you have a black wench procuring it for you, and no doubt performing other filthy duties as well."

"Jack," I said in an overly tender and calm voice, "Did you say something about finding a boat?"

Speke hung his head down for a moment and then rallied it up straight until his chin was pointed at my eyes. "Thank the good Lord we were able to launch the only available boat and make our escape by sea; and do not think for a moment that they weren't swimming after us or calling out the lewdest epithets: never in my life have I heard such. . ."

"Jack, does this mean that there is another great body of water in that vicinity?"

"Well, yes," he said in a startled voice that broke at the end of the final word. He cleared his throat and said, "Yes . . . yes. I suppose there is."

I could see the realization of what had happened slowly washing across his dull-witted good looks. He drifted off for a moment and then continued his stern harangue with a new confidence. "I plan on filing a full report of your actions and will not be at a loss for reasons why you failed to accompany me on my journey"—he cleared his throat and raised the octave—"to the . . . the *true* source of the Great Nile."

The bamboozled but now emboldened Speke stood up from the table in righteous triumph and with such rapidity that he knocked his stool off its feet. "I shall name the mighty sea Victoria after our Queen and mount another quest to this font so I may plant the flag of England."

This is the true story of John Hanning Speke's fumbling and accidental discovery of Lake Nyanza, which is also called Ukewere by the natives.[7] I dare not tell the tale for fear of the reproach which would be brought on me and the certain-to-be-fatal embarrassment to Speke. Not that I care so much of the latter, but one must always hope for the best in a hopeless world. History will likely administer reproach for being trapped by my own doings.

Speke and I have barely said a word to each other since that meeting at Tabora. There is no telling what papers he has been preparing in his cabin but I suspect the worst. He has been passing by my deck hammock and snickering for the past two days. Bastard! I know he is brewing some sanctimonious lie.

My brandy and cigar stores have been exhausted, new light promises a different day, and from here on the deck I can see the silhouette of island Zanzibar in the distance.

Tanganyika is a curiously bad memory.

Burton's letter to his friend Monckton Milnes, also known as Lord Houghton, dated January 14th, 1860, 14 Blvd. Haussmann, Paris.

My Dear Lord Houghton:[8]

Nothing can describe the present state of affairs. I am in voluntary exile in the land of the Frank, for life in England has become unbearable. As I'm sure you are aware, Speke has blundered into the limelight by accidentally discovering the legendary Lake Nyanza. It is a shameful and undeserved glory as it was I who suggested that he

---

7 Lake Nyanza was later called Lake Victoria and proved to be the true source of the Nile. Speke is remembered by history as the man who made this great find. A commemorative plaque at the place of discovery does not mention Richard Burton's name. —Ed.

8 Lord Houghton, real name Richard Monckton Milnes, was a wealthy, life-long friend and supporter of Richard Burton. The week-long salon parties at his country estate, Fryston Hall, were legendary, and, along with Burton, the guest list included some of the most noted eccentrics and artists of the Victorian Age. —Ed.

lose himself in that part of the continent. The details of his adventure with the Kowouli were received with great relish by our friend Hankey[9] and I must say that, to date, this small reward is the only one I have been able to enjoy. Everything else has gone Speke's way. Murchison and the rest have been completely gulled by the man's agent, Mr. Oliphant, and Speke is already preparing to return to Africa with a large purse.

Concerning himself, there is barely a scrap of truth in all that he has released to the newspapers. I am pleased to report, however, that all his veiled innuendo concerning my own actions are absolutely true; I can tell you, for example, that African hemp is plentiful and its powers formidable. While in Tabora a Twa from the kingdom of Rwanda brought me some of his native product. He called the cannabis *injaga* and pleaded with me to partake of it with him from a gourd water pipe.

You should know that the Twa are pygmoid types that are hated by their Hutu and Tutsi neighbors and are treated like quasi-domesticated pets by the ruling members of the Kinyarwanda-speaking people. This particular chap was exceptionally small but robust nonetheless. They have a peculiar method of packing the gourd pipe prior to smoking. The Twa packed the tube or stem of his pipe with *ingaga* and powdered charcoal and then filled the bowl with glowing hot pebbles from the fire. This act horrified an on-looking Arab who was accustomed to crumbling his narcotic in the bowl and then bringing over fire as needed. The Arab made some teeth-sucking sounds and shook his head. I could see that the Twa was nonplussed. The Twa paused to take an exasperated look at the objecting Arab but quickly returned to his task. He then proceeded to suck heat through the stem until the cannabis was ignited and great clouds of blue smoke were expelled from his mouth and nose. After a moment of rapid puffing he suddenly captured a quantity of the stuff in his mouth, held it in for a moment and then exhaled allowing his enormous pink tongue

---

9 Fred Hankey was an Englishman resident in Paris and making his living as a pornographer. The novelist Jules de Goncourt once visited Hankey's apartment and said it "contained every obscene object possible." —Ed.

to fall out of one side of his mouth. He then composed his face into a neat smile and said, "Now you! The pipe is ready for you." I began trying to draw the smoke and after dizzying hyperventilation, I was able to succeed. I tried to recreate my partner's ritual and knew I was ready to begin when I saw excess smoke running out of my nose. I pulled the smoke into my chest but was forced to send it out almost immediately. I began feeling the effects at once and reeled back against a tree for support.

I do not know how long I had been staring down at my boots but when I looked up I saw the Twa's watery red eyes fixed on the Arab. By this time the son of Al Islam had forgotten about his technical criticisms, was flashing an approving smile and showing interest over the obvious results. "Come over," the Twa said. "Now it is ready for you." The Arab touched his breast with the tips of his fingers and gave a surprised look.

"Yes, you! Come over as it is now your turn with the pipe." The grateful Arab quickly hitched-up his gown and joined our sitting. The Twa told him that he would begin the process again for he suspected his new guest "might not know how such things are done." As he said this, he glanced over at me with a mischievous look in his eye and I could tell that the Twa's offer to assist was paper thin. The tube was reloaded and new pebbles added to the bowl. The Twa now began puffing away with great enthusiasm and the glow from the bowl lit the Arabs anxious face. In between the puffs of smoke, he was showing all his teeth and nodding all around in appreciation. At this point the Twa motioned for the Arab to get a stick and stir the hot bowl to excite the fire. The obliging Arab responded immediately by leaning over the pipe and carefully poking at the coals. Just then the Twa gave a great blow into the tube and sent a volcanic shower of hot ash and cinder into the Arab's face. The Arab covered his eyes with his hands and he screamed out, "Allah, Allah! By the Prophet, I have been blinded by a dwarf!" He stood and groped for the curved knife at his belt.

With this, the drug-crazed Twa began circling the Arab and kicking at his shins and knees. All the while he was laughing and shouting, "Enemies of the Mwami—die, die, die!"

Old friend, I suspect that the hemp lent some extra drama to this event, but on my word, I have never seen anyone so inclined towards violence when intoxicated with that drug nor a person so enraptured with the sight of suffering others. Such are the workings of the Decrepit Continent. Ah, but that was then in what seems a more sane climate than the one I live in now. Back in England it was absolutely brutal watching Speke pretending to be what he isn't. Late one evening before I left, he arrived in a pub where I was drinking and was in the company of that simpering Lawrence Oliphant once again. They arrived to cheers, if you can believe it, and took up position at the best table in the house. What a pair the two of them made—Speke, tall, blond and breaking into his idiotic smile while attempting to field questions from the adoring patrons, and Oliphant behind him, nervously whispering in his ear like some smarmy solicitor on a bad day at the Old Bailey. I sat unnoticed in a darkened corner of the place and watched as long as I could bear it. Although I was aware of growing dangerous in my cups (and knowing like conditions in the past have given over to acts of violence), I nevertheless rose from my seat and started for the two of them.

Had not my adoring fiancée entered the pub at that moment, nothing could have prevented a dreadful catastrophe. Do not be misled into thinking that I was in any way restrained or calmed by my darling Isabel[10] for this was simply not the case. According to the way most events come to pass when she is involved, her assistance arrived in a rather oblique fashion. I quickly realized that my desire to avoid her superseded my murderous intentions towards Jack Speke and Oliphant (thereby sparing both an on-the-spot and sound thrashing) and to this end I bolted for the nearest door to make good my escape. In retrospect all was not lost, for I suppose it best that I did not administer a public beating and in the bargain managed to escape the resolute Miss Arundell. My actions did not go unnoticed, how-

---

10 Isabel Arundell was from a prominent English Catholic family and was smitten by Burton the first time she laid eyes on him. After a gypsy fortune teller advised her that he would be her husband she embarked on a long and determined pursuit of Burton that eventually ended in a most curious marriage. —Ed.

ever, and I enclose the following clipping from a recent issue of some London gossip rag.

> . . . for the heartfelt joy all about the
> table and surely in tribute to the verbal
> skills of Captain Speke. As we lifted a pint
> in honour and appreciation, a deranged
> madman rushed past our table at great
> speed, knocking it asunder and causing our
> toasts to the African hero to spill upon
> ourselves and the floor. That the proprietor
> of the Ram's Head should permit the entry of
> such drunken riffraff is a disgrace that will not go
> unnoticed by the readers of this column.
> Let it be known that those such informed
> did not fail to note the arrival of Miss
> Isabel Arundell at this notorious juncture.
>
> While officially a maiden's secret, this woman
> has 'let it out' and declared her marital
> allegiance to Lt. Richard Burton of the Bombay
> Army and recent companion[11] of Jack Speke in
> Africa. Can it then be too far afield to credit the
> resemblance between the madman who upset
> our table and the aforementioned Burton?
> It was our lion, Speke, who first uttered the name
> and then, after a correct pause, said, "Quite! The
> man has often acted like an orang-outang."
> This quip saved the day and we . . .

Speke disgusts me and so does the society that accepts him. I hope the beer will extinguish the fire of his lies. My Lord, how I yearn for

---

11 Burton, using a different ink, underlined the word "companion" and wrote in the margin: "Companion? Words of an ignorant ass, I assure you. As if he were anything but on my coat-tails the entire time. R.B." —Ed.

the freedom of the un-civilized world. I believe in that better place the collective attitude that is so much a part of traditional country life spares us from the artificial and solitary putrefaction of the city, a place where one feels terribly alone in a crowd. In our smelly metropolis we go about mindfully singular, falsely self-confident, and revoltingly self-serving. Our beacon has become a so-called complete man, at once puffed by and a slave to his corrupt society and too 'important' or 'busy' to care a fig for honour or truth. In short, a world tailored for the fatuous Jack Speke and his kind.

II

Zanzibar and Shihab

Next day: In review, I realize it is my curse to be struck with contradictory thoughts as I write and perhaps even more so the next day. When I am given over to romantic ideas concerning traditional behaviour, I need only report on the deportment of Gelele, King of Dahomey (a heroic dose of the aboriginal ideal *in vivo*) and my previous night's fancy is quickly brought to its knees. This Gelele's behavior is far removed from any Rousseauesque innocence and my sanctimonious ramblings concerning relative civility in the traditional setting. His conduct is dramatic proof that the beast is in the species, Milnes, and not particular to geography, skin colour, or religion. It is a disease of our kind. While I suspect I have made my point, I cannot resist a Gelele story now that his name has been brought up. According to all accounts, this African sovereign is more monster than monarch and the "Kingdom of Blood" over which he presides is in, no small thanks to him, well named.

The travel writer William Snelgrave tells of a lake of blood large enough to float a canoe and Archibald Dalzel reports the death of two thousand sacrificial victims at the hands of his Amazon army of she-monsters. It is my intention to travel to this place someday and actually meet Gelele.[12] I may need your assistance in order to bring this about. And as long as we are speaking of the denizens of the

---

12 Burton meets Gelele just three years after writing this. Here he encountered the Amazon army and received a human bone necklace as a gift from the king. —Ed.

Decrepit Continent, let us not forget the Wabembe, who prefer their men raw, and the Wadoe, who like them cooked.

Ah, Africa. For now, dear Houghton, I can only lament being in gray, dreary England, with the silly bravado of Jack Speke and the determined efforts of my fiancée. I have considered a return to Zanzibar and my beautiful girl-negress, Shihab, but just the sound of her name and that island are enough to bring forth a rush of confusion. I do not recall ever being so drawn by a woman that I would entertain a return to such a ghastly place. Some examples: when I first approached the island we passed a *dhow* crammed with slaves. Even though the Sultan of Zanzibar had outlawed this practice in 1845, there was no stopping the trade in practice nor the ends to which the slavers would stoop to "preserve" their cargo. A cool trimmer's mate on our ship told of how those who had contracted dysentery would be "sewn-up" by Spaniard slavers before being brought to the bazaar. We passed close enough to the *dhow* for eye contact with some of these unfortunate souls and I must report a collection of the most frightful and dispirited expressions can not be imagined.

Closer to the island a hot offshore wind brought the delicious smell of clove plantations, which for a moment gave me pleasant reminders of India. All this was lost as we neared the harbor for there is nowhere in India that can match the squalor and rot of this blistering, awful place. My first observation as we neared shore was that of a dog dragging a bloated corpse from the fetid coastal waters, and the hideous beginnings of a devouring. The situation only degenerated at landfall. We quickly learned that the Sultan had died seven weeks before our arrival and his two sons were engaged in a chaotic war to claim rights to this cesspool. The lawless, narrow streets are filled with human filth, and the thick well water is positively green and wholly undrinkable—the liquor, worse.

Atkins Hamerton was the British resident there at the time. Surely you remember this jolly Irishman from our sojourn to County Tip a few years back. Poor Atkins had become the epitome of the white man ground down by the tropics, and I found him a mere shell of the chap we knew back then. Zanzibar had done it, Milnes, there is no question about that. I called on Hamerton at the garrison shortly after our arrival and found him behind an empty desk. There seemed to be nothing more for him but to sit and sweat in the early morning torpor.

"Well, Burton," he said, "sit down and let me tell you what you've gotten yourself into this time." He opened a drawer, pulled out a bottle of Jameson's, and poured me a drink. "It's a bloody mess here, I'm afraid. Drought in the whole of the east has brought about famine, and the Sultan's pimp of a son over in Muskat controls what little food reaches the island. What does trickle in is very dear and occasions much fighting. Malaria, yellow fever, and hepatitis are everywhere." Hamerton managed a weak grin and added, "The good news, lad, is that the smallpox epidemic has just passed."

He was not quite done with his initial assessment of the situation, so he fortified himself with another drink in order to do so. Black flies were halfway down the inside of the glass before he could take the first sip.

"It's as dangerous a place as you've ever been and frightfully unforgiving. I can tell you a story by way of example." Hamerton stared down into his whiskey. "A young Frenchman by the name of Maizan attempted passage through here. I suspect it must have been ten years ago. I can't say exactly what took place between himself and the Mazungera, but they evidently didn't like something about him for they tied him to a tree and slowly dismembered him. Finally cut the poor devil's head off. Oh, naturally we raised a fuss about the whole thing but the results of our objections were scarcely less grizzly than the act itself. After some weeks the bastards delivered some poor chap from their tribe who they had designated as the scapegoat and fixed him up just as you see him today."

Hamerton motioned me over to his window and gestured down to the courtyard. There I saw a wretch who had been chained to a cannon for the past four years. His bonds had been arranged so he was unable to either stand upright or lay down. Needless to say he had gone completely mad many years ago and I could not understand how life still flickered in his awful body.

"Come away from the window now Dick," Hamerton sighed. "There is nothing anyone can do about the situation. A garrison marine named Michael O'Shaughnessy, an Irishman like myself from the same little town back in Cork, planned a mercy killing of the man in the yard after the first few months of his captivity. He told me of his plans over drinks one evening and I had later mentioned the possibility, in passing, to a Mazungera chief.

"'Oh no, Lieut. Colonel,' the chief said, 'that must never happen. It would be considered a big insult and an interference with tribal ways.' He looked at me very sternly and said, 'This would bring about many, many bad things to all the whites on Zanzibar; terrible things, Lieut. Colonel.'

"So, instead of killing the man, the softhearted O'Shaughnessy has been providing some shade and extra food and water for him over the years. He also cleans up the man's tiny area to keep the flies and dogs at a minimum. I'm afraid Michael himself has gone a bit mad from the task after all these years and I question if he is even fit for a return to Ireland. For the love of God, Burton, we can't even allow him near the munitions any longer." Hamerton's face twisted into one of resolve. "It's Africa, Dick. It's the breathless heat and the cruelty and all that's wrong with God's Children. And it's all right here before us.

"It will eventually kill the man in the yard and poor Michael, and me . . . and you if you stay here long enough." He gulped down the last of his whiskey and said "Jea-sus, let's get on with some better stuff, shall we?"

He led me out of the garrison and through the labyrinth of the city. The pestilential vapors of the streets were almost unbearable and the pervasive staring at us from every doorway always suggested trouble. "I am going to introduce you to someone, Dick, someone who is clean and decent . . . and indescribably beautiful. She is the daughter of my old friend Haj Siam; her name is Shihab, and I will ask that she take care of you." We pushed through the crowds on our way out of the city proper. "Her father has kept her away from the savages of this place, and if I weren't so old . . . well, you're not too old, are you Dick?" His laugh degenerated into a consumptive cough.

We found Haj Siam seated in front of his whitewashed mud home on the outskirts of the city. His wide smile on our arrival displayed only two teeth. He grasped Hamerton's hand and shouted "*Allah akbar*, God is Great" and "Peace be upon you, Armud Hammulsbad," then leaned inside the door and yelled, "Shihab, come Shihab. Now is time for Colonel Hammulsbad."

Milnes, I shall never forget my first sight of this woman Shihab. She was perhaps nineteen, tall, full and muscular, with perfectly brilliant white dentist's teeth and a drop-dead coquettish demeanour. Her house tunic fell slightly off her left shoulder and was cut low enough to reveal the tops of her *cafe au lait* breasts; she had blue stars tattooed above both nipples. Shihab was a Galla from Abyssinia and I had heard the stories about these famous and highly coveted creatures in Egypt long before I ever set foot in East Africa. For good reasons, Galla girls are said to fetch up to a thousand Spanish dollars at the slave bazaars, when available. Only a few Arabs could afford such a price but those who could readily paid when the occasion presented itself. It is claimed that their skin is always cool, even in the hottest of weather, and this alone would be sufficient cause for celebrity in this part of the world. But this is a trifle compared to their other famous talent.

The Arabs call them *kabbazah,* which means "a holder." You see, Milnes, the Galla women have learned to develop their constrictor *vaginae* muscles, so that when sitting on a man's thighs she can induce orgasm without moving any other part of her person. Needless to say, this has all the men wild and they have made the Galla girl into something of a goddess. It is a miracle that Haj Siam has been able to keep the hounds away from Shihab, even though his compound is well armed and she in the company of bodyguards at all times.

But there she was before me, fresh and happy and in no way undone by her surroundings. Her father and Hamerton were engaged in friendly conversation but I was so distracted I do not recall even being introduced. It must have happened for later the old man came over to us, placed my hand in Shihab's and said, "Hammulsbad's Raheed Burjom is guest of Haj Siam. You stay here for us, yes?"

"Yes, yes indeed," I answered.

"Good luck, Dick," Hamerton said. "This should help expedite your Kiswahili lessons. Oh, and Burton, I do beg you to be careful. Remember, the black lion often sleeps in a pretty nest." I had no idea of what this meant, but I thanked Hamerton and told him I would be on guard.

"*Bakooh Salaam*," he said, and I never saw him again.

I spent the next month with Shihab at a modest house in her father's compound. As I began learning Kiswahili and she a bit of English, we wasted entire days eating fruit in the shade and talking of Zanzibar, the coast, and about the lives of the people she knew. *Conter fleuretts* were expected throughout the day and evening.

One day she pointed out a woman who looked terribly ill and during a general discussion of her condition the term "black lion" was mentioned. I asked Shihab what was meant by this and she made a coy gesture which indicated that it had something to do with the genital area.

"Gonorrhea?" I asked.

"Oh, no Raheed Burjom, that is with everyone and is not even considered a disease here in Dhakilak."

Black Lion is their term for syphilis. They fear it most because the affected part will be destroyed. "In just three weeks time, no later," Shihab said, and she covered her mouth with the palm of her hand and giggled. "You lose your nose as well. You see, it is quite fatal."

The day eventually came when I had to leave, and I promised Shihab that whatever else happened I would come back to her again.

"You will never now, forever," she said sternly with what might have been a tear in her eye if her womanly constitution was congruent with the temperament of our own ladies back home. With this, she turned and disappeared into the shadows of her house.

I passed old Haj Siam on the way out and he asked that I wait for a moment. He came up, looked me over very carefully and asked, "Colonel Hammulsbad, what has become of your young friend, Raheed Burjom? You know," he whispered, "I believe Shihab like him. Maybe now is the time for marriage."

Just then Shihab ran from the house shouting my name. She rushed close and with a look on her face somewhere between sadness and resolve, hooked her finger in the belt loop of my trousers and said, "Raheed, I cannot let you go now; not before you meet someone—someone very important."

I told her it was best we break from each other now before things became impossibly complicated but she pressed her index finger against my lips and shook her head. "It is for your life, Raheed, for what is to come. You see, it is about your fate."

She had a few words with her father, who then promptly disappeared and returned a moment later with a sturdy-looking and well-armed native. I could only imagine this was the important someone I had to meet and that my life as well as my fate on earth was indeed being placed in his hands. With bandoleer crossing his chest, his rifle, knife, sword, and whip, this would be the man brought in to secure my lasting bonding with Shihab. He gave every indication of being one of those chaps who was far beyond any hope of reasoning with, and in fact every inch of his thick frame broadcast that there would be no possibility of debate on any matter whatsoever. It was rather a tense moment, as you may well imagine.

But nothing is as it seems in Africa, and perhaps even more so in Zanzibar. The assassin turned out to be one of Shihab's much-needed body guards and was summoned not to cement an on-the-spot marriage but to accompany us to an exceptionally dangerous place on an already dangerous island.

Any movement in Dhakilak is dodgy business, but with Shihab along it became an event. She was one of those women males stop to stare at, a woman whom even timid men feel bold enough to approach and a creature that bold and hungry men absolutely wish to consume. When people interrupted their routine to look at the Galla She-Goddess, the pedestrian traffic flow bunged on the already constricted medieval streets and from the clots of ragged humanity came hands that would attempt to stroke, pinch, and pet or purloin, needy hands, the greedy and grimy hands of Africa in heat.

Shihab concealed herself as best she could amidst cries of "Galla, Galla" and I fended off advances with nearly every step. But it was the body guard who kept us moving past the fruit stalls and shanty stores of Stone Town. He was not behind hand in clearing our path with the butt of his rifle or whip, and I noticed that just the look of him froze many who otherwise might have had designs on a biologically driven approach.

My god what a place this is. Bad behavior seemed to be on the ascendant everywhere as we pounded through this old Persian-built town. Amidst the riot of confusion, pushing and grabbing, a gang of joyful children followed not Shihab but most likely my newness, and they sang aloud what they had learned about the better parts of white men. With all arms up and down in rhythm, clapping, dressed in rags or barely at all, they skipped and danced without care or any trace of worry and began to sing, "Ink and paper. Ink and paper are the things we want. Give us paper, make the marks. Give us ink and paper, make us rich." Many just wished to hold my hand as we walked.

They were absolutely the happiest children I had ever seen anywhere, and nothing in the civilized West could compare; surely not the dispirited and mean street tykes in London or Manchester, who were no less grubby but entirely absent such unfettered jubilation. Old men at their beads and wearing skull caps watched it all, indifferent to the disorder and the delight. Perhaps in a way this can be considered an exemplary summation of the enigma that is Africa.

Our destination was still unknown as we passed beyond Stone Town, and as the press and insurgence attending to her presence diminished I was able to ask Shihab where we were going and who we were to meet when we got there.

"To a village where white men do not go, maybe even they cannot go there, even in times when there is not such a famous man who has come to visit." She stared ahead as she walked and continued, "The village is called Bububu and the man at visit is Laibon Mbatiany. He is Maasai. My father has asked if he will see you. It is a great favour because the laibon holds great powers, very great powers. It will cost my father many cattle. The Maasai like cattle.

"Laibon Mbatiany can cure sick people with plants. He speaks directly with Enk-ai, and he gives direction for the future because he knows about such things. My father said that is something you need—you need to know about the future, he could see that." I asked if this was about our relationship, and she answered, "It is about everything; everything there is."

It was straightaway apparent why Bububu was off the white man's road map. There is an air of general hostility about the place and by

the looks on some of the villager's faces it was almost certain that I
was the first white person they had ever seen. Probably my skin color
was equated with slavery for they knew of the great ships and their
unholy cargo and they all know who the masters of them are, and
that it was to these ships the Arabs delivered their sorry captives. No
one in Bububu wished to be a participant and so more than a few
villagers moved hand to knife as I passed. Shihab and the formidable
body guard were very helpful but I was still quite on edge.

Nevertheless this was all about a meeting with the Great Laibon Mbatiany and after a few begrudging directions we arrived at his temporary
headquarters. He was sitting on the floor of a mud hut dabbing at the
backside of a young goat. The man's skin was so black it was almost
purple but when he looked up at me I was startled to see that the pu-
pils in his eyes were as white as his hair and my first thought was that
the gods simply do not outfit ordinary gentlemen with these sorts of
physical astonishments. He commanded my full attention.

He motioned for me to sit and then in deference to his rank and
title went on at great lengths about the goat. Did I think he was a
handsome animal? Did I know that his goat father was a great breeder?
Does he not have fine testicles? It was a conservation he might have
been having with someone else in the village that had been temporarily interrupted and now resumed in mid-thought. I stumbled
through a few sentences of reply all the while wondering how this
had anything to do with my fate. The laibon then unaccountably got
up and left, leaving me in the semi-darkness with the wounded goat.
Shihab popped her head into the doorway for a moment but pulled
it back as soon as I caught her eye. My suspicions were running wild.

The great soothsayer returned after a moment and fumbled a bit
to adjust some buttons on his gown. When he saw me watching him
his *sui generis* eyes widened and he asked if I thought laibon was a man
who did not need to relieve himself.

He took back his seat on the floor and resumed dabbing at the
goat with a leaf. Without looking up he ask, "Do you know that black
is a lucky color?"

I had to confess that I did not.

"It is, believe the truth of this."

After more silent time with the goat he got up, stood over me and began running his long hands over my head and face as if he were a blind man searching for a tactile identity. Then he reached into his garment and threw some small polished stones on the ground before me. These he stared at with prodigious intensity and with something that might have been a muffled supplication. Then he looked at me with great passion.

"Haji Siam, he tells me you are in need of direction, the future, how you must act to acquire the wealth all men need. I can feel that he is right."

Laibon Mbatiany repositioned the stones with an elongated finger.

"You are forty years; that is easy to see, and you are a warrior. I can feel that too. Let me tell you something; it is at this time in life when a warrior, my people call them *moran*, finishes a cycle. Many show sadness at the loss of youth and wild adventure, some even cry at this time. But fools act even worse; they try to make the cycle longer, but it cannot be done by any man without bringing great shame upon him. You cannot hunt in the way of before and you cannot find your manly youth by being inside a young woman like Shihab."

I asked if adventure is over for me.

"Of a kind, yes, it is over. But your head also tells me you are not a fool and so you much recognize the kind of adventure that is suited to you."

I told him I like to travel for adventure and before being allowed another word he thundered back that I *must* travel. "But you also must lay down your sword and use your eyes and your pen to make adventure for all people. You no longer have to *do*, but you have to *be*. Do you understand?"

I confessed a bit of confusion. He looked hard at me with those albino eyes and said, "Leave what was before and be who you are from now until forever. This is the truth."

Laibon Mbatiany covered the polished stones with dirt, then carefully recovered one of them, clasped it with both hands and closed his eyes. Everything suggested a summary pronouncement.

"You must know that you have entered a new cycle and from this place you will take a journey, a very long one across a big land that you have never seen before. But this time it will be an expedition to find not a river or a holy city. This time you will find yourself. On the way along this journey you will find many kinds of people, very strange and different people, who have all come together in the big land for countless reasons. Here you will find Man, and he will reveal what you seek. Your fate is to tell people forever about who Man really is, and soon you will be able to see him as never before.

"Your journey begins here as a new man and in the end you will tell everyone about themselves and find yourself in the process."

By this time the laibon had me wild with curiosity. How did he know about the river Nile and the holy Meccah? Where I would be going, who I would be seeing and who is this new man I am supposed to be? Why will I find Man if I am already among them?

Laibon Mbatiany leaned close to me and began to chuckle.

"Use your eyes to see and your hand to scribe and do not be afraid to let your words flow as you wish. No king or earthly gods will ever be able to change or hide the truth in what you have to say. Speak of all men as they are, be they beautiful or befouled. Find Man—find yourself. This journey will allow you to do that, and from there another wiser one can begin."

I didn't know what to say beyond a callow asking about where another journey would take me.

"To the end—with your eyes and pen, my friend—until your fate is fulfilled."

This seemed all he wished to say on the matter, but he did allow a final comment. "Be alert for the sign that will launch this voyage. It will arrive by messenger in a packet from a friend. It will arrive when you are in your own land, but you will not be there for long. The final sign is that it will come when you are desperate for movement, but do not know where to go."

Laibon Mbatiany brushed me towards the door like he would a common fly and said, "Now move-on, and be careful not to disturb the goat."

Well, that was Zanzibar and a glance outside the window reminds me that I am still self-exiled in France. Surely this is not the place Laibon Mbatiany had in mind, nor is England or a return to India, Arabia, or Africa. I suppose I must just keep my eyes skinned and await the arrival of the so-called "packet"—if it ever should arrive. Fate is a coy mistress. In the meantime, I shall try and slip back for your party at Fryston Hall as I am most interested in re-meeting the Countess Maria Louise Ramee (Ouida)[13]. I will give Hankey your best.

With distant thoughts in mind

I am,

RF

---

13 The woman for whom the Ouija Board was named. She was the bestselling author of *Under Two Flags* and was a regular consort of Burton during his salon days. —Ed.

III

A Proposition, Several Letters, and Mr. O'Floyn "One Punch" Powers

March 15, 1860
11 Foubert's Place
London

Who is it in the press that calls on me?
I hear a tongue shriller than all the music
Cry "Caesar!" Speak, Caesar is turned to hear.
Beware the ides of March.
What man is that?
A soothsayer bids you beware the ides of March.
Drunk, and drunk again on the ides, but better binged than dead
I suppose. I have been at it heavily since my return from Africa and
now lie in bed deathly ill from last evening's alcohol poisoning. The
legendary twin vixens that Hankey sent over are gone, thank god.
They turned out to be Swiss, if you can believe it, totally unrelated
though both pure mountaineers and cold as frogs. I was ready to give
them a bash but soon learned that Hankey's claims for them are myth.
They were nothing more than ordinary bints, and the only really
nasty thing about them was their vulgar chocolate habit. I cannot

recall much of what took place past midnight but I find my flat a mess with books strewn about the floor and several large chairs over-turned. I do have a fuzzy recollection of chasing them around the flat with that ridiculously out-sized, tribal dildo I traded one of Speke's guns for back in Ujiji. It had them wide-eyed, on the run, and as animated as they were all evening, so at least there was some magic in that frightful thing. But today the sick smell of old cigars and spilled brandy is everywhere. Depression surrounds me.

This whole Speke thing has me going through a bad patch. The fool has been funded (£5000) and is off to the lakes again, this time in the company of the puppy dog James Grant—a man who would be a fit coMr.ade only in the eyes of someone like Speke's precious mum.[14] Even the missionary Livingstone has been given a purse and is away to Nyassa, and I lay in Soho reduced to a fugitive, constantly on the run from and only one step ahead of the excit-able Miss Isabel Arundell. This woman is fast becoming more of a problem than the entire African mess. I am certain she followed me to Boulogne and it has been a bit of a chore to conceal my where-abouts here in London.

Amidst the clutter on the floor were two envelopes delivered by messenger last evening. I had forgotten that. I have just opened the first and discovered a poem from Isabel.

Oh God, how did she ever find me here? I felt my stomach turn as I read this rat rhyme:

My brave soldier's heart
beats in far distant lands
a fortnight away from my sheltering hands.
His darling is HERE in old London's fold
awaiting his arrival
to give heat from the cold.
I am HERE my lord, come into my arms

---

14 Speke wrote to Norton Shaw on April 15, 1860 and said, "Mother thinks no end of our friend Grant and is immensely pleased with the idea of me having such a good companion." —Ed.

I shall find you, I shall hug you
and keep you from harm.

A postscript was added:

Loved one. I have obtained this address from the most charming two women. They are book publishers from Zurich and said they were sent by a Mr. Hankey in order to get a first hand exposure of the author. You! I shall let you take care of business with them, and good luck! I will arrive on the morrow so we can cuddle together as soon as possible.
Isabel

I think I shall be sick. But there is no time, for "the morrow" is now and she knows where I am. All thoughts turn to escape, all energy directed towards the next move. I suppose something was needed to break this cycle of depressed rage and drink and if it is another move, then I will owe something to my darling Isabel. The wandering heart needs no further motivation than that supplied by a closing, clutching woman, but even in the most urgent circumstances I'm afraid a destination is required. So the pressing question becomes, "Where shall I go?"

My question was answered magnificently as I began gathering things for my departure and in the process, and almost by accident, found that second envelope that was delivered in the haze of last evening. I was overjoyed to see it was a letter from old Steinhaeuser[15]. I opened it at once and realized that it was an invitation to join him on a trip to America.

I suddenly became as clear-headed as ever before in my life. My god, this is "the packet," isn't it? The big new land filled with dif-

---

15 Dr. John Steinhaeuser, MD, formerly Civil Surgeon stationed at the Port of Aden, Arabia. It was Steinhaeuser who nursed Burton after he was wounded in Somaliland in April of 1855 when a native warrior thrust a spear through Burton's face. The blow carried-away four back teeth and part of his palate before emerging on the other side and scarred him for life. Burton and Steinhaeuser became life-long friends, often drinking and travelling together. Steinhaeuser will play a significant role in these journal pages. —Ed.

ferent people, a place I have never been before (back in Zanzibar I imagined Cornwall), the arrival of the envelope by messenger, from a friend while I was in my own land, its direction for movement when I needed to move badly but didn't know where to go. It is all unbelievably flawless in its complete perfection and as true as I am sitting on this bed.

The delivery of Laibon Mbatiany's predicted and miraculous packet in but a few short months between augury and arrival gives one pause to contemplate the extraordinary, but surpassing that is the magic itself which forces the mind to accept what reason tells us we cannot. By god, the old man may be right that I can't hunt as before, but in my new cycle of adventure I can pursue these sorts of psychic mysteries until I die.

With Steinhaeuser's letter still in my hand, I heard the old man's voice in my head: "but this time it will be an expedition to find yourself," and I could almost feel his hands on me as they were in that mud hut back in Zanzibar. It struck me pure that through the observation of others, my goal is to define humanity and therefore myself as part of it.

When the darkest moment suddenly turns to light it is the greatest exhilaration of all, but when the unknown and unbelievable becomes truth before your eyes then you know that you have been touched by God.

This pursuit of Man is a frightful task in some ways. To see close-up the most dangerous animal on the planet and the sometimes horrific ways in which it goes about its business is strong stuff. But horror and beauty are curiously intertwined in the human experience, as are laughter and tears—opposites joined to each other through an inexplicable process—and in no other animal but man can these inter-doppelgangers be studied better.

The wisdom of the laibon also knew it would be America where the hunt for self and humanity must take place. It is nothing less than a call from man's oldest land to his newest—an ancient voice directing a modern mind to enter the future.

All of these things kept me thinking while still seated on the side of my bed; it was two hours that seemed like two moments.

I still had Steinhaeuser's letter in my hand and returned to it for completion. One part in particular left me in a merry pin. He said, "I'll drink mint-juleps, brandy smashes, whisky-skies, gin-sling, cock-tail sherry, cobblers, rum salads, streaks of lightning, and morning glory, and it will be a most interesting experiment. I want to see whether after a life of three or four months, I can drink and eat myself to the level of the aborigine, like you." There was also the mention of a Mormon Holy City where polygamy is practiced. Good stuff!

I must begin making preparations. Books must be sent to storage, notebooks to be gathered, other odds and ends. Above all, a correct wardrobe must be assembled for this trip, something fit and dapper for the United States, something rough and wild for the Territories of the Red Indian West. I really should stay to check the proofs of my *Lake Regions of Central Africa*, but I will not. This would be just one more reminder of the unctuous Jack Speke and all the rest that came about as a result of my bit of fun gone bad. Although, a second thought on the matter suggests that it may have been worth the cost after all. Knowing the Kowouli, I'll wager they gave Speke a sound and proper rogering back there. It was a full week before he could sit down without wincing. The loss of his priceless weapons, the ruination of his silly hunting outfit, the thought that he actually believed me and performed the fraudulent Unrecognized Male Greeting Ceremony before a bunch like the Kowouli—for God's sake, the price of high humour like this should be dear.

I would still like to know the other details of Jack's rough ride to Nyanza. Of the two natives that went off with Speke, one found his heart's content and stayed, and the poor devil that came back with Speke won't talk. Aside from the obvious, something very strange happened on that trip and someday I will find out what it is.

Before I leave for America, there is one piece of unfinished business I should like to take care of, and that is to deal with Mr. Laurence Oliphant. This weedy and exceptionally pale creature is reminiscent of so many other over-educated, sodding little Cambridge brats I have been forced to tolerate over the years. That time is over and now for a fitting *bon voyage* gift to myself.

Oliphant's penultimate desire (liaisons with homosexual men being the foremost on his aspiration list) is keeping the company of young girls between the ages of fourteen and sixteen. These he seeks out and cajoles in the most sycophantic way in order to gain their attention. I do not believe he has the sand to actually have sex with them, yet there is nevertheless something wrongly sensual that marks his behaviour whenever they are near. He presses close and lowers his voice to whisper pet names like "little boo" or "Elskins" (?) in their ears and will often greet them with tender kisses upon the lips. His fare-thee-wells are equally theatrical; a tragic expression crosses his face and he softly bids, "Well then, take care, little one." Then almost immediately, the sorrowful look transforms to a leer. I suspect Oliphant holds abeyant desires for these girls due in part to a cowardly fear of more mature women. Whatever the reason, his public displays are always repulsive and deserving of some bad turn. Now it seems to me that there was a small article in the back pages of the *Times* recently concerning a Mr. O'Floyn (One Punch) Powers, the Bare Knuckle Champion of England and Ireland. Powers has said that he fights solely for the memory of his sainted wife, who died in childbirth, and his daughter, little Maureen. Responding to the report that "little Maureen" would be attending the first social of her young life this Saturday in fashionable Mayfair, O'Floyn has been quoted as saying, "I'll be there alright, but will stand away and give the little dear space enough to think I'm not. Be sure that I'll be ready to tear the arms off any man who lays a queer hand on her, no matter how high fly'n a Mayfair gentleman he may be."

Mayfair? I say, isn't this Larry Oliphant's neck of the woods? And wouldn't it be wonderful if the great man had an invitation to meet "little Maureen" at a lovely social event? I do believe I have his address somewhere here and would be most happy to match-make this little assignation. As I write the following note to Mr. O, I imagine it being read over and over by an adoring, female adolescent before she drops it in the post.

Dear Mr. Oliphant:

Although I am only fourteen, I am a great admirer of your wonderful articles. While I know Blackwood's Magazine is usually unacceptable reading for a young girl, I will admit to you that I have obtained copies that I sneak into bed with me and read secretly at night. You are my hero and inspire me to bring forth all my confidence. With you in my mind, I have worked very hard to express some of my deepest thoughts. So then, may I present the poem I have written for you. . .Larry?

My brave writer's pen
speaks of far distant lands
he just minutes away
from my sheltering hands.
Next Saturday his darling will in Mayfair be
awaiting a man
her hero to see.
I will be there my Lord
come into my arms
find me, HUG me
and keep me from harm.

P.S. Dearest, I shall be at Willow Fork Hall, Saturday at seven o'clock: sweep me away from the dreary dance floor so we may cuddle together as soon as possible. You will recognize me by my red satin dress. In the meantime, I am
   Awaiting you,
   Maureen Powers

March 17th, 1860
Bloomsbury

Mon Cher Steinhaeuser:

Of course I shall be delighted to accompany you to America. A drinking tour it shall be. The details we shall have to work through quick post as I am wild about quitting this place posthaste. I must report another act of purposeful opprobrium when I was forced to sit through the stale opera *La Somnambula* w/ Miss IA two days ago. I'm afraid some bored young lieutenant who had spent too much time in Africa and India discharged a deafening fart at the precise moment Jenny Lind and Gardoni appeared for their stage bows after the final act.

An old hag seated next to this overseas Lt. almost fainted—although I cannot tell if it was the depraved act or its results which did the trick. In other news Sir R. and Shaw have turned their Royal Geographic backs on me, and even Livingston has rejected my offer of service. I am certain Speke will be killed this time around and the Man of God will need more than his King James to survive the test of East Africa.

Do you recall the famous "twins" Hankey wrote about? Well, he put them on to me here, to cheer me up, I suppose. A disaster at any rate; but after too many brandies I did end up chasing them about my flat trying for the hat trick.

I'm on the run from Miss Arundell but no matter how much she may deflate the limbic system, your mention of polygamy in the Mormon Holy City does excite the Captain back up on deck.

Do let us roam the American miles in high-style to reach the Great Salt Lake and all it has to offer. When I tell you of the African origin of your letter you will faint.

Believe me,
Dick

March 18, 1860
Bloomsbury
In favour of: Mr. Clive Tweed-Choat
Proprietor, St. John House
From: R.F. Burton

Sir:
I do not care if the condition of my now-vacated flat does not meet your final approval, and I will not pay a shilling of the proposed cleaning fee. Yours is a charnel house, unfit for the dead really, and a stinking mess when I first arrived. Your salacious reference to the visit of my two Swiss cousins is an insult to my moral self and was factor-less in the alleged damage or the reported screaming. For your

information, the "spilled fluids" encountered by your filthy-minded cleaning woman were merely drops and drizzles from a clam soup which was prepared by my cousins and were certainly not seminal. I am disgusted by the thought!

I also refuse to accept responsibility for the broken furniture. These pieces—and the bed especially—were obviously crafted by peasants in the last century and are not fit to bear the weight of a modern man. You may not charge my account, for I have none.

I will be out of the country for some months; if you wish to pursue this matter further, please ask for me at the Athenaeum in the fall and I will consider settling matters with a rumble.

The thought of ever hearing from you again depresses

Your former tenant

R. F. Burton

PUGILIST HELD IN ASSAULT ON JOURNALIST[16]

Mayfair. Popular boxing figure O'Floyn Powers is being held at police headquarters after an attack last Saturday on Mr. Lawrence Oliphant, a reporter for Blackwell's Magazine. It is unclear why these two public figures came to blows over the weekend but scores of horrified young people witnessed the bloody affair which took place at a debutante social at Willow Fork Hall.

A spokesman at St. Regis Hospital said Mr. Oliphant is recovering slowly from what was described as "a thrashing." Several broken bones are being attended to as well as numerous cuts and a severely bruised derriere. Inspector Grub of the district constabulary has indicated that Mr. Powers did not receive any injuries as a result of the fray and that the gentleman is refusing to speak with authorities beyond saying that he'd "do it again in an ace."

April 16th, 1860
Neston Park, Wiltshire
To: Richard Burton

---

16 A clipping Burton collected from *The Times* dated March 21, 1860. —Ed.

From: John Hanning Speke

Dear Burton:

The Blackwell cousins have been kind enough to send along your horribly bowdlerized manuscript *Zanzibar; and two months in East Africa,* and in spite of the recent attack and injuries upon his person, the resourceful Larry Oliphant has obtained for me a copy of your willfully scandalous, *The Lake Regions of Central Africa* from his friends at Longman, Green, Longman and Roberts.

I have taken the time to read this slouch and feel I must write to let you know that at least one astute critic lives to smother your lies and omissions. While no Christian could argue that there are many episodes which should be left out of your books, I find your wanton refusal to assign proper credit to certain events simply unbearable. For example, my rightful discovery of Victoria Nyanza was an event that not only changed my life and way of thinking, but one that will also forever be remembered by the rest of the civilized world.

Soon I shall be off to Africa again, and this time mercifully, without you. Through a route known only to me, I shall reunite with the great Kowouli and together we shall once and for all settle the matters of elevation and river discharge; these being the only remaining queries upon which you base your suppositions.

You scoffed at my sportsmanship, yet it was a hunting trip that ultimately led to the wonderful event, wasn't it Burton? You mocked me upon my return to Ujiji, not knowing the fullness of what had taken place in a manly land. Now you will rot in some Covent Garden brothel with filthy whores while I rejoin a valorous and plucky tribe on a righteous quest of rediscovery. Let God and history be the judge.

I pity you.
John Hanning Speke

IV

Arrival in America and Orders from Her Majesty's Foreign Office

May 2, 1860
Empire State Hotel
Manhattan Island

LABBAYK[17], AMERICA! And the hunt is on. After a rather un-eventful week aboard the SS *Canada* and amidst its dreary passengers (I confess to appearing in drag one evening in order to liven things) yrs truly has landed at Manhattan Island, the so-called civilized jewel of the so-called New World. After three days here at the prearranged meeting place I have finally managed to connect with John S. His delinquency was due, as usual, to overindulgence in spirits and he arrived looking and acting as one might expect after a weekend long bottle spree. His clothing was a fright from sleeping rough and he positively reeked of alcohol. As always, and even while detoxifying, Steinhaeuser was the perfect gentleman and delightfully friendly. Ours was a warm reunion that began with an over-animated, "Welcome to America, Dick," as soon as he burst through the door. I suspect there was still a goodly amount of alcohol surging through his system.

---

17 I am here. —Ed.

We chatted for an hour or more about old friends in the orient and I thought he was about to cry when I told him that Atkins
Hamerton had died. "Was it the drinking?" he asked, as if he might
be the next victim. I told him, "No, I believe it was Zanzibar that did
him in." He forced a hopeful laugh and his gaze drifted toward the
window.

He turned back to me after a moment and said, "Well, Captain
Burton, I am afraid there is some business we have to attend to."

I told him that I thought our business was to holiday through the
Republic. I reminded him of his letter talking about brandy-smashes,
mint-juleps, whisky-skies and polygamy. I said that business was
Speke, Africa, Oliphant, and Isabel Arundell, and that I was here to
get away from all that. I expressed my wish to pursue some pleasure
travel with an old friend, and told him about Laibon Mbatiany and
my quest for the human condition.

Steinhaeuser wrinkled his nose at the African story (the fool) and
informed me that there will be plenty of travel, but it would be at
the pleasure of Lord Palmerston and the Foreign Office. He pulled
a sealed packet of papers from his bag and slid them to me across
the table. "You can read these for the details whenever you wish," he
said, "but I know the general contents and would prefer that an old
friend break the news." I settled into my chair and motioned for him
to begin.

"Dick, the Foreign Office feels certain that the sectional controversy between the industrial Northern States and the plantation
Southern States is about to erupt into violence. Tempers have been
mounting, basically over the slavery issue, and Palmerston believes the
execution of this John Brown fellow in December may well have lit
the fuse. The F.O. recalled me from Aden in early March and as much
as ordered me to lure my friend Burton to America, employing any
means I thought may work. Once you arrived, I was instructed to
deliver the directives that are contained in the packet.

"I admit to being a party to something of a backhander's trick,
but I am away from Aden, we have a purse from the British government, and we are off on quite an adventure."

I opened the packet and discovered I was indeed back in the spying business. My instructions are to attend the Democratic Convention in Charleston, located in a place known as North Carolina, as well as the Republican Convention in Chicago which is situated mid-continent in a Franco-phonic sounding land called Illinois. At both locations I am to gather information regarding the country's political climate on what Lord Palmerston considers the eve of an all-American war. In addition, I am to wander about the States, both North and South, gathering information concerning relative strengths and weaknesses, preparedness of armies and militias, natural and man-made resources, etc., etc.

At the conclusion of these activities, I am to cross the Missouri frontier and enter the Territories of the West, my assignment there being to assess the intentions and loyalties, if any, of the various Indian tribes who have recently been displaced there.

If, for example, they were to unite against the Union, the secessionist efforts in the South would be greatly enhanced. My orders are to move about as Richard Burton, private citizen and travel writer, on my way to investigate still another holy city, this time the City of the Saints—the Mormon capital at the Great Salt Lake in the land of the Utes. I sent a silent prayer back to Africa and thanked the laibon for his comprehensive wisdom.

Most importantly, the Foreign Office would also like to know how the Mormon "Nauvoo Legion" might figure into any impending hostilities. It is rumoured that the Legion is six thousand to eight thousand men strong throughout the Territories and may be able to call on the assistance of thirty to forty thousand Red Indians in the event of war. I was told that all Mormon men between the ages of sixteen and fifty were drilled and armed and reminded that there were an additional thirty thousand followers of Brigham Young residing on British soil.

Steinhaeuser had to lie in bed as he heard me relate the details of my assignment. After a bit he sat up and asked for a drink to help with the vertigo. I poured some brandy from my pocket pistol and placed it in his trembling hands. John took the glass in a single gulp and regained a measure of composure before he spoke. "We have already missed the Democratic Convention in Charleston, Burton. You were a damn hard man to track down in London. It concluded two weeks ago in a victory for the diminutive Mr. Stephen A. Douglas. According to the press accounts here in New York, Charleston was not a very good host to the Northern delegates and was in no mood to participate in any Federal event. Just from what I've seen and read, Dick, I believe the Foreign Office is correct—war's alarm is in the air.

"The Republican convention in Chicago is just a week away, so we do not have much time to conclude affairs here in the East. I was told that you could easily obtain some powerful letters of introduction as a result of what's in the packet and that these would prove to be of considerable help in the months ahead." I rummaged through the papers and found a letter of introduction addressed to the Hon. John B. Floyd, Secretary of War in Washington, and another to Colonel Pierre G. T. Beauregard, Superintendent of the U.S. Army Military Academy at West Point, New York.

Palmerston left little doubt concerning his selection of these two men. I was informed that both were said to be admirers of my past exploits and writings and would gladly assist me in any efforts to reach the State of Deseret and investigate the Saints. In addition, Floyd was said to be an ardent Unionist, while Beauregard, a native Creole Louisianan, had a deep and chivalrous attachment to the South. Both men were very well connected in their spheres and both would likely speak freely to someone like me.

Steinhaeuser had fallen into a drunken sleep and was snoring loudly. He was best left undisturbed and I took the opportunity to stroll about the streets of New York for some preliminary flavourings.

My initial impression of the New World is that there is really nothing new as far as the characters in the streets are concerned. All Irish and German it seemed, with the brogue as common as Yankeeisms and the stench of garlicky schnitzel belching from a dozen eateries in the first city block. The number of establishments purveying bad beer and crude corn whiskey along the same route were uncountable. While there is a general air of industry, one cannot help but notice the number of barroom loafers spilling out from the many grog houses and gathered in happy but idle teams along the broad streets. The working class despair of grimy London is invisible, although I do not see how the glow of prosperity can shine in the faces of these leisurely and obviously unemployed immigrants.

It came upon me that perhaps this was a provincial holiday and I queried a passerby.

"No sir, no it is not."

He saw me gazing at the men in front of the bar and said, "If you are in need of a reason for a drink, sir, a Wednesday afternoon in New York is reason enough. You'll not be bound by London society rules on this side of the ocean."

May 4, 1860
U.S. Military Academy
West Point on the Hudson

John and I arrived yesterday and straightaway had our cards delivered to Superintendent Beauregard's office. A few hours later we were located by messenger in the lobby of our hotel and told that the Colonel would be pleased to host us for tea in his office at 4pm. We dressed accordingly and proceeded to the Academy at the appointed hour.

Col. Beauregard was a smallish man with a robust and oiled moustache, and as advertised, I was well received. "Why Captain Burton, surh, Ah am honoured. And, this must be Dr. Steinhmusher of Arabia. Gentlemen, please do come in and allow me to afford y'all some refreshments."

Beauregard was the very personification of etiquette and propriety and his English was in an accent unlike any I had heard before. His drawl, as it is called, was excessively polished, soft and slow, tended mightily towards the prolongation of vowels, and he often concluded phrases in the interrogative mode. I cannot resist a phonetic spelling of what he had to say.

A fine tea service was presented by a snappy cadet, who Beauregard acknowledged by saying, "Thank you Rawlins, that will be awl for now." We settled in comfortable chairs that had been arranged around an ornate cherry wood table. The Colonel spoke first.

"Ah welcome you both to this country and I trust yore junny here was a very pleasant one?"

I thanked the Colonel and told him that my journey was pleasant enough. Playing up my role a bit, I told him that I was bothered by neither lance nor spear.

"Well, that is fine, sur, very fiiine indeed. Ah know that you have been subjected to such inconveniences in the past and Ah am in debt to the forces that delivered a man of your fine accomplishments to this room. You see, Captain Burton, Ah have had the honour of reading your books concerning India and the junny to the Arab's Meccah and am a great admirer of these works. You are a man of great spirit and courage, fiiine qualities for a gentleman, sur, powerfully fiiine qualities, indeed." Colonel Beauregard touched the corners of his mouth with a linen kerchief and continued. "Ah have a sense that you have come to America in pursuit of still another adventure, Captain, and Ah wonder how Ah may be of survice?"

I stood and handed him the letter of introduction. I also had the good mind to execute a little bow and a "If you please, sir," which he seemed to appreciate a great deal. The Colonel opened the letter immediately and began reading.

"My, my, how impressive, Captain. Ah see hea a note from Lord Palmerston himself with a request that Ah assist you in your quest to another holy city and to facilitate your movements through the country, so that Captain Burton may avail himself of true samplings of the American charactah."

Beauregard looked straight into my eyes and said, "Captain, unfortunately, Ah must attend to some affairs heah which will prevent me from enjoying the pleasure of your cumpany for the next week or so. Normally, Ah would insist that you join with my wife and Ah for a social round heah in New York." He gave a sly look and added, "However, Ah have a much more agreeable suggestion."

The Colonel rose to attention and addressed me in a most formal tone. "Sur, would you grant me the personal pleasure and great honour of attending to you in mah native state of Louisiana? You see, mah sista is hosting a three day event for her daughter's debutante arrival in the city of N'Orleans. This will take place a few weeks from now and you would be a most welcome addition. Here, sur, Ah assure you, will be an opportunity, as your Lord Palmerston said to observe a sampling of the American charactah. In fact, Captain Burton, Ah must say that the very best of the American charactah has its roots in the South, and that no trip to this country could be complete without an exposure to some genuine Suthen hospitality."

As an afterthought he added, "Oh and please, Dr. Stienfeltza, won't you be mah guest as well?" Steinhaeuser grimaced after once again hearing a mispronunciation of his name.

Colonel Beauregard promised a general letter of introduction and another giving travel instruction to his sister's home in New Orleans. "They will be delivered to your hotel, Captain Burton. Now Ah am afraid you must excuse me. Allow me to arrange for Lt. Rawlins to escort you on a tour of our grounds, and Ah shall instruct him to answer any questions you may have. As a military man, Captain, Ah appreciate your interest. We shall meet again in N'Orleans, and a good day to you suh." For effect, he snapped his heels together after the Prussian style. I would later learn that Americans were often given over to such foolish pretensions.

John was in an agitated state as we left the grounds of the Academy. Since childhood Steinhaeuser has displayed an almost pathological obsession with the correct pronunciation of his name. Even simple misspellings could lead to bad results—and mispronunciations worse. Something to do with his family history would be my suspicion. There was virtually no chance that Beauregard's gaffe would go unnoticed. "God, Burton, that vainglorious little twig all but snubbed me the entire time. All that affected charm and courtesy. Why, I'll wager you'd see another little Napoleon with his guard down. He has the pomposity of a slave holder, Burton, and I do not like it."

But this was a simple preliminary for John's greatest objection. His face distorted into that of a pit dog and flushed with anger. "Did you hear what he called me? He called me Steinfeltzer. STEINFELT-ZER and STEINMUSCHER! Is he crazy, Burton?" He attempted to compose himself by changing the subject. "I'll say one thing, Palmerston was dead-on about Beauregard liking you and offering assistance. Wasn't it kind of him to deliver us into the hands of the obliging Lt. Rawlins who gladly provided answers to questions we should not have asked?" I agreed and commented on how shocked I was to learn that the United States Army was comprised of just eighteen thousand men. I may inform Palmerston that America simply does not have enough soldiers to conduct a proper civil war.

Steinhaeuser called for a drink. He has done nothing else but drink since he arrived three weeks ago, and I have to regard him as a bit unsteady for the experience. He was drunk in Aden but his surgery occupied eight or nine hours a day and kept him away from the bottle for that time at least. Here there are few limits.

V

AN AMERICAN BASEBALL GAME
IN HOBOKEN

May 7th, 1860
Hotel St. George
Manhattan Island

I would have to look as far back as Cairo to remember the last time
I was asked to leave a hotel as a result of unfavourable circumstances.
It was Rashid Pasha who orchestrated it back then, but who would
wish to sully the mind with recollections of that foul dog? The past
two days have been a series of swift embarrassments and as soon as
Steinhaeuser is well enough to travel we will quit this town under the
cover of darkness and keep moving.

Yesterday's mortifications unfolded in the following way. Once
reaching New York on our way back from West Point, John insisted
that we stop for drinks to, "take in some local colour for the benefit
of the Foreign Office." His pretense was that our intelligence work
was not done for the day. It was just after dark when we entered a
saloon called The Bat and Ball. Steinhaeuser immediately went into
action, using FO money to buy drinks for everyone who happened
to be standing near him. I took a table near the wall and watched
as he worked the crowd. Within an hour he had commanded the
attention of a large group and was engaged in highly animated dis-
cussions. He was going at the rate of three or four drinks to every
one of mine.

I should not have been surprised when he staggered to my table
with his arm over the shoulder of a man by the name of Frank Pid-

geon. "Rounders, Burton, bloody rounders! Old Frank here is the captain of a rounders team. Isn't that right, Frank?" Steinhaeuser's arm was now hugging the back of Mr. Pidgeon's neck and his grinning face was only inches away from his companion's. "These British fellows love rounders, Frank, so have a how-do-you-do to my friend Dick Burton from London."

Mr. Pidgeon was aglow from stiff drinking but nowhere near as drunk as John. He shook my hand with a very firm grip and introduced himself to me as Francis Pidgeon, dock builder and Captain of the Eckford Base Ball Club.

He informed me that the game isn't called rounders in America but rather, base, one-old-cat, or stool ball. His team was comprised of mechanics and shipwrights from the Henry Eckford shipyards and I was quickly informed that on the morrow they would be engaged in, "the grand match of 1860" over in a place called Hoboken.

Steinhaeuser lifted his eyebrows, interrupted and offered, "We are invited, Burton, as *honoured* guests. Frank, tell Dick about the match. Go and tell him what it's all about."

"Wall, ya see, Mr. Burton, our boys have been playing the game for a while now and we fancy ourselves in a perfect state of practice. Our first nine has beat the Knickbockers, the Excelsiors, and every club they've sent up from Philadelphia and Washington City. Hell, our second nine has defeated the Columbia Club in Bordentown and even our muffin fraternity beat the Red Riders who came down from Boston. We were beginnin' to believe there wasn't a team left to offer a challenge. That was until last week Thursday." He slapped me on the back and gave up an exaggerated wink. After Steinhaeuser ground his elbow into my ribs, I took the bait and asked Mr. Pidgeon what had taken place last Thursday to change matters.

"Wall, Mr. Burton, it's about our short fielder, Baby Palta. The lad was insulted by a group of the Bowrey B'hoy's from over in the Sixth Ward. They pushed him around pretty good, poured beer over his head, and challenged us to a high stakes game—two hogsheads of beer is the prize and there will be many side bets. Our first nine against theirs, for nine full innings—and may the best team win for all rewards."

Steinhaeuser asked who the Bowery B'hoys were and why the Eckfords had not played them before.

"This is a new and dangerous club," Mr. Pidgeon explained, "which was formed on Bowery Road over by Cooper Square, near Broadway. It is comprised of the criminals and derelicts that usually inhabit that part of the city and reinforced by a stock of genuine ball players that have been run out from other clubs.

"Ya see, in a match last year between the Shad Bellies and the Honey Bees in the Bronx, a gamer was murdered on the field. Five men were accused and kicked-off their teams as punishment. They were never formally indicted because in all the confusion, ya see, it was difficult to know exactly who did what to who. Now all five have resurfaced with this Bowery bunch.

"They call their club the Black Jokes," he said with a lifted eye that suggested dangerous and anticipatory competition. "The game is at three tomorrow afternoon at Elysian Fields and it is sure to be a corker. If you don't believe me, you can read about it here in these papers." Indeed Mr. Pidgeon was correct, for both *Beadle's Dime Base-Ball Player* and *Wilke's Spirit of the Times* featured long and lurid articles on the Black Jokes Club and their match against the unbeaten Eckfords in Hoboken.

Steinhaeuser had left the table and was now engaged in a loud rendition of the Eckford Club Fight Song. Once he memorized the refrain, his voice could be heard above all the rest whenever this part of the song came due.

> *So raise your glass to Eckford*
> *we've built a mighty ship*
> *in all the base ball matches*
> *we've never made a slip.*
> *So here's to mighty Eckford*
> *the heroes of the sea*
> *the greatest of the base ball clubs*
> *in A-mer-i-ca the free*

It was now almost nine o'clock and I could not tear Steinhaeuser away from his new friends and his bottles. Most of the ball players had left in preparation for the match against the Black Jokes the next day, and only the older club members were left to revel with John. I went to the bar and told him that I was going to take a long walk and then return to the hotel. By this time his starched collar had sprung on one side and his hair was fanned out all over his head. He gave me an unfocused look, smiled and said, "Have it your way, Dick. I'll see you back at the hotel."

As I walked the streets of New York City I was troubled by the fact that I had yet to meet or even see a single Indian of any tribe. With this thought in mind, I passed a theater house that was advertising their latest offering:

THE ORIGINAL, ABORIGINAL, ERRATIC, OPERATIC, SEMI-CIVILIZED AND DEMI-SAVAGE EXTRAVAGANZA OF POCAHONTAS.

At this moment I wondered if the new Americans had run all the Indians off this land, or if the Red Man had decided to just pick up and leave out of a sense of moral disgust.

I took a leisurely stroll home and stopped many times to examine merchandise in shop windows and exchange small talk with other pedestrians. In all, mine was a very pleasant stroll in the spring night air. As a result, I was unprepared for the spectacle awaiting me at the Empire State Hotel, but it should not have been entirely unexpected.

It seems that after being expelled from *The Bat and Ball*, John had invited the remainders of the Eckford Club back to the hotel for some additional drinking. When I arrived, the lobby looked as if it were in the middle of a rugby match. It was alive with employees shouting and cursing and chasing after Steinhaeuser and his friends.

John was eventually crowned with one of the hotel's framed oil portraits of somebody, and now his face protruded out of the canvas at the place where the original mug should have been. He was racing about with his pants off and a bottle in his hand, singing a garbled refrain of the Eckford Fight Song and keeping the frame in position with one deft hand. Other members of his party were struggling with employees or else actively bothering female guests.

I managed to get him back to our room by the time the police arrived. The door was wide open, and the floor covered with empty bottles and smoldering cigars. A naked club man was unconscious in the bathtub. They had apparently started here and then moved into society when the liquor effected its final erosion of their sensibilities.

Steinhaeuser had crumbled to the floor with his head still through the middle of the painted canvas. Somehow he landed with the frame perfectly upright and it appeared as if the artist had fitted a gigantic, mussy head atop a properly attired, tiny body. Then the manager of the hotel appeared at the door with several Irish volunteers from the Mutual Hook and Ladder Company No. 1, which was located across the street. He immediately rushed for Steinhaeuser and began choking him, screaming, "Get out of here, you no good son-of-a-bitch. I'll kill you. Get out I said."

The Irishmen held me before I could stop the manager's murderous assault. I begged him to let John go and we would pay all damages, leave at once, and he would never see us again. I suspect it was the scent of damage payment that broke the death grip, for it was at this moment that the manager turned to me and asked if we had two hundred dollars between us. It was an outrageous sum to ask, but I said, "Yes, yes we do." It was everything to get us out of there and away from more trouble.

"Well then, show me the colour of your money to the tune of two hundred and fifty and you've ten minutes to leave with your lives."

Steinhaeuser began coming around at this point. First, a weak moan, then mutterings of the Eckford Fight Song, then his arm appeared from the side of the portrait and attempted to give his head another drink.

"Come on, old man," I said to this framed, sad head. "I think we have about eight minutes to pay and pack." After delivering the ransom, we were assisted to the front door by the kindly gentlemen from the fire house and given a boot to our arse on the way out.

This is what brought us to the crusty Hotel St. George, where we took a room for the night and got some fitful sleep. At nine the next morning Steinhaeuser sat up in bed and sensed that something was amiss. "Burton, wake up! My left shoe is missing. I can't believe it. It's GONE!" I suggested that it may still be in the lobby of our last hotel or have slipped off when we were having our arses kicked at two o'clock this morning. He looked puzzled for a moment and the corners of his mouth turned down. He said that he may feel better if we had a drink before going to the game.

Elysian Fields held a crowd of perhaps four thousand souls who had arrived a full three hours before the match. There was a nervous air of anticipation among the men gathered around the numerous refreshment stands. Others pushed and shoved for position near odds makers who were yelling and waiving hands full of money over their heads.

"Bull Bathgate good for five bucks on the Black Jokes." And another rejoined, "Garth Woodside better for ten on Eckford."

Hundreds of others milled about drinking and debating behind the ropes that set the playing field from the betting and drinking areas. Dogs chased each other wildly through the crowd and fornicated openly without reproach. By game time the crowd swelled by another thousand or more and pressed against those hopeful ropes. Agitation was added to apprehension. This was followed by a huge roar as the Eckfords ran onto the field between two lines of men who had locked arms to form a passageway.

They were led by the valiant Frank Pidgeon and each had the silhouette of a steamship sewn onto the front and backs of their new, gray uniform shirts. They queued up along what's called the "foul line" and accepted the applause of the crowd. Betting intensified as the Eckfords began their synchronized pre-game gymnastics.

Then came a thunder of boos and invectives as the Black Jokes charged through the crowd forcing it to part before them. As might be expected, they wore black jerseys and matching pants, but I am at a loss for the reason why large, yellow question marks were stitched to their uniform fronts. The Black Jokes warmed up for the game by slashing their cudgels about in violent and menacing fashion, some managing three or four in their hands at the same time. A bold Black Joke man even charged the Eckford line in mock combat with a bat raised above his head. Others gestured to the crowd with a motion whereby a clenched fist is abruptly jerked upward with the arm bent at the elbow. At the same time the other hand is slapped atop the upper arm as if preventing its upward movement. There can be no doubt that this is a form of sexual derogatory relating to maximum intromission and was designed to send the crowd into frenzy. A drunk from behind the rope broke loose and charged the gesturing antagonist. I was horrified to see one of the Jokes strike the man behind his knees with his cudgel and then thump him on the back for good measure when he fell to the ground. When friends from the crowd came to drag the man off, the Black Joke attacker instinctively raised his club in defense. At this point the spectators went wild at the site and more than a few bottles were thrown onto the field. The Bowery B'hoys ruffians in the crowd in turn attacked the bottle throwers.

An Irish donnybrook was avoided when the crowd's attention was diverted by a man sitting on scaffolding who introduced the ball players by screaming their names into a paper megaphone. The crowd turned ugly again after the last Eckford player responded to his name and the Black Joke introductions began.

The general booing and jeering reached a crescendo when Mr. Nicey Horsie Vanderpole advanced and acknowledged the crowd with a raised middle finger, and there was almost a riot when Turnipseed Carrigan dropped his trousers at the announcement of his name. Bitchey Bob Turner and Jake Sampoon were hit with flying objects, including a dead cat.

In an attempt to restore order an umpire named Honest Jack O'Malley called for the captains of the opposing teams to meet at the strikers circle. There was a heated discussion, presumably over the ground rules, which ended with the Black Joke Captain simultaneously spitting and delivering a Neapolitan chin flick at Honest Jack and Frank Pidgeon.

While I am constantly being reminded that this game is not rounders, I say the two look very similar to me and I was able to follow the theme and action quite well. The first five innings were relatively tame by American standards. So far, all the actual fighting had taken place among the spectators. Nevertheless, every man there could sense that tensions were rising on the field and that the slightest incident could spark an eruption of volcanic proportions.

This came to pass in the latter portion of the seventh inning with the score tied at nineteen apiece. It began when an Eckford player was running between the first and second base in an attempt to "steal" the latter. Unaccountably, the Black Joke pitcher whirled and threw the ball at the base runner, hitting that man squarely in the head and knocking him into a state of unconsciousness. To make matters worse, he ran up to the motionless body, and shouted, "Yeer out!"

Honest Jack the umpire was mobbed by the Eckford team, who demanded he eject the pitcher from the game. Honest Jack was dishonest and claimed he didn't see it. He was obviously terrified that any disciplinary action would result in retribution at the hands of the Bowery B'hoys. Henry Eckford himself was one of those who helped lift the unconscious player from the field. He exchanged some unkind words with the Jokes' third baseman Burly Bob Sands who promptly picked up some dirt and threw it in Mr. Eckford's face.

During the Black Jokes' batting turn in the first portion of the eighth inning, Frank Pidgeon left his position at the first base and walked over to the feeder's circle. There the two were joined by the team catcher who had come out from behind the striker. After the conference had dispersed, the Eckford feeder proceeded to underhand perhaps twenty-five off-the-mark pitches in a row in an attempt to get the Joke's striker to swing at a bad ball. But Jake Sampoon would have none of it. After ten offerings, he called out to the feeder saying he was "yellow" and that his mother had conceived him with a chicken (although not in those exact terms). Then he acted bored and finally assumed a relaxed attitude at the home plate by leaning on his club, lazily watching the wide and high offerings pass by. As he was in this position, the Eckford feeder reared back and let go a beamer[18] that struck Sampoon right between the eyes. The crowd fell silent as the cudgel dropped from Sampoon's hand. His eyes crossed and he wobbled a bit before falling flat on his face, with his now unconscious mouth full of dirt.

---

18 In this case an overhand fastball. —Ed.

Then began a spectacle of vast disorder. Honest Jack O'Malley bolted for safety as members of the crowd crossed the ropes and ran onto the field. The horse pulling the wagon carrying the hogsheads of beer stampeded and made slashing turns and abrupt stops to avoid groups of fighting men. Bowrey B'hoys clashed with Eckford Club members. Frank Pidgeon engaged in a bat duel with Bitchy Bob Turner. And Nicey Horsie Vanderpole was rolling on the ground with Mr. Henry Eckford's wife. Baby Palta was seen urinating on the stone-still body of Jake Sampoon. When the beer cart finally overturned, both hogsheads burst open and the remainder of the rhubarb was conducted in a sea of foamy mud. The horse galloped off dragging broken pieces of the cart behind him and ran over several Black Jokes on his way out of the Elysian Fields.

But the real trouble as far as I was concerned was John Steinhaeuser. He had been drinking since before the game and had become a loud and active supporter of the Eckfords. By the fourth inning he had to be separated from an engagement with one of the Bowery B'hoys over a close play, and he disappeared from my side as soon as the fighting erupted. I caught a brief glimpse of him in the middle of the melee, fists clenched and face covered with mud, his eyes flashing back and forth in alcoholic alarm. He was delivered here at the St. George a few hours ago, eye blackened and sporting a vicious human bite mark on his cheek. He was out cold and I am yet unsure if he had been beaten into this state or had just been overpowered by the alcohol. When he wakes up we are off to Washington City.

NEWSPAPER CLIPPING FROM *THE NEW YORK BUGLE*[19]

May 10, 1860
GAMER KILLED IN TOWN BALL RIOT
Hoboken – A New York City baseball match ended in tragedy yesterday with the death of Mr. Percy Sampoon, a 31-year-old, unemployed resident of Manhattan. He succumbed to head injuries

---

19 Collected by Burton and inserted between the pages of his journal. —Ed.

and was pronounced dead at Belleview General Hospital early yesterday morning.

Dozens of other people were injured in a general scuffle that broke out after a recreational game between two ball squads. Among those admitted for care were Mrs. Julia Chase Eckford, wife of shipbuilding king Henry Eckford, and Miss Tessy Fenyatz, whose name appeared in these pages just one week ago in a story about using public restrooms for purposes of prostitution.

Dr. Muncie Chillsperth declined to be specific about the nature of their injuries other than to confirm that Mrs. Eckford suffered a broken nose and that both ladies had other feminine-specific contusions. Twenty-three members of the New York City Police Department were also among those hospitalized.

It appears that Mr. Sampoon was accidentally struck between the eyes on a routine play during the game and that efforts to revive him by concerned spectators were unsuccessful. The cause of the riot remains unclear but eyewitness accounts seem to agree that the game itself was a peaceful affair and the attending crowd very orderly and well mannered. There was no evidence of any alcohol use or gambling.

It is strongly suspected that a handful of outside agitators were responsible for most of the trouble. One man, identified as John Steinwasher, and claiming to be a visiting physician from Arabia, was singled out as one of those.

RICHARD BURTON'S LETTERS OF INTRODUCTION[20]

Favored Sir:

Will you kindly extend every courtesy to Capt. R.F. Burton of the Bombay Army. He is a guest in this country and a personal friend of the undersigned. To my friends in the Great South to whom Capt. Burton may become acquainted and likewise may request assistance, I make a special plea. Capt. Burton is no Yankee, but an overseas Gen-

---

20 One may wish to note the contrasting regional and political allusions in the different notes. —Ed.

tleman of great dash and valor. His safe passage is uppermost in my mind and I pray that God will see that you are empowered to render aid whenever possible.

Col. Pierre G. T. Beauregard
Superintendent
U.S. Military Academy

To Whom It May Concern:

Captain Richard Burton, a subject of her Royal Majesty, Queen of England, is favoring the United States and its Territories with a visit in order to pursue his travel writings. It is the desire of the United States of America that Captain Burton be allowed to avail himself of any and all offices under the lawful jurisdiction of the President, be it in the Northern or Southern portions of this great and sovereign land. By this letter, we wish also to inform our Indian brothers that the Great Father is well disposed towards Captain Burton and will, if necessary, provide much wampum for his safe passage.

Honorable John B. Floy

VI

BY RAIL TO THE REPUBLICAN
NATIONAL CONVENTION

May 12, 1860
Cincinnati City

Through Washington City in a blaze, and now a rush by hard rail West nearing Cincinnati. Here in Porkopolis, a delay affords the weary traveler time for a brief journal entry before swinging north to Chicago. I am still with Steinhaeuser but an ultimatum had to be delivered. A week of sobriety before another drop, and an end to his heart stopping misadventures or he will be sent to Coventry. His human bite wound has become infected and the left side of his face is badly distorted. One eye has closed and his upper lip is three times its normal size. Our driven schedule does not allow the rest needed for a proper recovery. He has been eating opium continually for several days and nights and consequently has rarely uttered a single word. He sits in his seat and stares straight ahead, his good eye glazed and watery with lid half closed. The route from the capital to here is all coal and zinc mines with lumber mills and tobacco plantations supporting smaller interests. I cannot speak for what lies beyond the rail lines for it is to these tracks that we are bound. One must express frustration at the lack of opportunity to meet with anyone save fellow travelers; and, I'm afraid, a great portion of these are convention-bound folks and therefore most conversations are centered around political matters. While their considerations are mostly baw, one does get an earful of current opinions, and our friend Palmerston will have all he cares to read once we are able to sit still and I can write.

Members of the Ohio Republican Delegation have boarded the train and are making quite a fuss. They are churlish, very loud, and consummate boors. One gaudy fellow from this group took a seat next to Steinhaeuser and has been rattling on for the past hour and a half about the merits and weak points of the different candidates and their platforms. Steinhaeuser's head moves only with the pitch and haul of the train ride. Except for his eye, which occasionally shifts ever so slightly, anyone who was paying attention may well have thought him dead and just propped up in the seat.

Our friend from the Ohio delegation was oblivious to this condition and continued his monologue as if there were a rational and responding human being sitting next to him. When his mates finally called him for a card game in the back of the car, the Ohioan grabbed Steinhaeuser's limp hand and began pumping it with forceful enthusiasm. "Been a great pleasure talkin' with you friend, but I have to go. Remember, a vote for Thurlow Weed is a vote for the Union. You'll remember the name Thurlow Weed, won't you friend?"

Steinhaeuser made a weak attempt to acknowledge this last remark by raising his good eye in the direction of the delegate. His head followed, and because he was unable to control the rotation, it soon rolled over until his ear was hard against the top of his own shoulder. From the unswollen side of his mouth he whispered something that sounded vaguely like "Thurlow Weed," and at this point the delegate let go of John's hand and gave him a hearty clap on the back which almost sent him flying out of his seat. He smiled broadly and thundered, "That's the spirit, friend. That's the American spirit!" I took Steinhaeuser's opium from his pocket and secured it in my bag.

May 16, 1860
Chicago

We are at rest now after straining every nerve to reach this city before the beginning of the convention. The train pulled into the station at 6am and it was all we could do to find accommodations, meager as they are here, in Mrs. Maggie Munson's recently vacated bedroom. This great city, hard by an even greater blue inland sea, boasts 100,000 citizens on a normal day, but due to the Convention, methinks 175,000 or 200,000 may be better figures. There is no single space that is not thick with convention goers and their entourages.

Our attempts to check in at the Tremont House were laughed at; the manager's expression turned from cynicism to fright as he described five hundred souls sleeping in quarters designed for sixty. He added that similar conditions, or worse, existed in the city's other hotels. "They are three to a bed and sleeping atop every billiard table in town." It was he who took pity on two foreigners and directed us to the kindly Mrs. Munson.

It was only with the assistance of Secretary Floyd's letter of introduction that we were able to secure tickets to the convention itself. I was told that under normal circumstances, these passes would not have been obtainable. The convention is to be held at the corner of Lake and Market Streets where a gigantic structure called "The Wigwam" has been newly built for this event. It is festooned with bunting, rosettes, and evergreens and equipped with gas lights for evening sessions.

After depositing our luggage at Mrs. Munson's, we headed straight for the Wigwam and arrived just before noon. A throng of perhaps twenty thousand people were gathered around the building, shoving and pushing each other about in a state approaching mass hysteria. In comparison, the Pilgrims at Meccah were much better behaved. When the doors opened, ticket holders slowly elbowed their way through the crowd and eventually passed the nervous doorkeepers. Then suddenly, in one great surge, the masses pushed aside all material and flesh-and-blood restraints and swarmed inside, producing a scene of Bedlamite confusion.

We made our way inside just as the opening gavel came down and a dull dog named David Wilmont began the proceedings with an uninspired speech accepting the post of Temporary Chairman. This was followed by an insufferably long and boring prayer by the Reverend Z. Humphrey. My formal initiation to American politics began with an offering by Mr. David Cartter, chairman of the Ohio Delegation—the same group that raised such a fuss on our train ride. Cartter began: "I move an amendment. I move to amend the proposition of the gentleman from Oregon or New York, I am not sure which [much laughter] Mr. Horace Greeley, that instead of each delegation presenting their credentials here, they present them to the Committee on Credentials." Mr. Greeley responded by saying, "I accept the amendment of the gentleman from Maryland or Rhode Island, I am not particular which [laughter and applause]."

Wilmont then called for a vote on Greeley's original resolution. Just then, a grizzled, homespun delegate named John Johns, a preacher from Iowa, rushed to the podium and proclaimed, "I have walked one hundred and fifty miles to ride a Chicago-bound train and I will be sent to damnation before I see anything proposed by Mr. Horace Greeley pass before this honoured body."

Someone else raised a fist and shouted, "Sit down, you old fool, Greeley has been amended." Preacher Johns responded he'd do nothing of the kind and leaped into the crowd at his tormentor.

The two were engaged in fisticuffs and in the process of being separated when someone grabbed the preacher's hair from behind and pulled off an unsuspecting wig. Howls of laughter filled the Wigwam as Temporary Chairman Wilmont beat his gavel for order.

When order was finally restored, a member of the Chicago Board of Trade stood and invited all delegates and guests to a boat ride on Lake Michigan at five o'clock. Sounds of approval and agreement were issued around the Wigwam. Mr. Cartter cried foul. "I came here to work, and am not going on the Lake, nor is any delegate who came here to work." This, of course was greeted with a chorus of booing. Someone from the Kentucky group stood and introduced a formal resolution that the boat ride offer be accepted, and this set off a deafening roar of approbation. Cartter then demanded that a platform committee be chosen at once and chided the crowd saying that the boat ride only represented a frittering away of time.

Ten speeches later, a compromise was reached whereby a committee was finally appointed. Unfortunately for Mr. Cartter, their job had nothing to do with platforms but was formed only to issue a formal apology to the Board of Trade and to notify them that the Conventioneers would be pleased to accept their offer on another day. Being exhausted after this grueling exercise, the Convention as a whole voted to break for a three and a half hour lunch.

At exactly 5:15 p.m., forty-five minutes after the extended lunch period had ended, Temporary Chairman Wilmont called the Convention back to order. The first business was a message from the Chairman of the Board of Trade. He solemnly reported that before the committee could reach them, his group had assembled what else but, "a perfect fleet of boats which stood at the ready." He added that if the Conventions affairs were that pressing, "they could conduct business on the decks of the vessels, if they desired." This triggered a violent debate where one side argued that the City of Chicago would be terribly insulted if the offer were not accepted and the other damning the City's feelings in favor of electing the "next President of the United States."

Wilmont lost control again, and then came a riot of calamitous noise and confusion. Several men pulled pistols and knives from their jackets as individual fistfights erupted in the unruly crowd. The moment was saved when the Hon. George Ashmun of Massachusetts was brought to the podium, was unaccountably declared the Permanent Chairman of the Convention, and was given an oak and silver gavel said to have been made from part of Commodore Perry's flag ship, *Lawrence*. Ashmun's presence, (or perhaps it was the gavel) gained the attention of the crowd and quieted it enough to be dismissed shortly thereafter. Thus ended the first day of the Republican National Convention. It would seem that absolutely nothing of consequence took place—that is if one was to discount the fisticuffs and threats of more imperative forms of violence.

But, hello, now I learn that the civic day was, in fact, far from over and one must look beyond the doings in the mighty Wigwam and into the crusty, dark night to appreciate fully the nuances of the American political system. It was into this night and the meretricious bars and restaurants of the city that the interested observer must repair in order to get a true feel for the complicated workings of the nomination process, for it is there that all the real work is done. They have a term for these efforts here. It is called "wire pulling."

Steinhaeuser and I left the convention center with the others and made the rounds of different establishments which are associated with the many candidates. Mr. Seward's people are centered in the lobby of Richmond House, and from there issues his splendidly uniformed brass booster band, free food, and many pretty girls with silk campaign ribbons pinned to their ample bosoms. Supporters of the wealthy and unprincipled Mr. Cameron have taken over two dozen of the city's whiskey houses, where the drinks, thanks to the candidate, are a mere fraction of their usual price, or absolutely free. Cameron's taverns have also been stocked for the occasion with ladies of dubious repute.

The simple-minded N. P. Banks has foolishly relied on temperance-themed street corner booths where nothing more than political tracts were handed to passersby. We agreed that the poor devil doesn't stand a chance.

A carnival atmosphere filled the streets. Surely the friends of "Old Abe" Lincoln had spread the word that if the people of Illinois wanted to see their man nominated, they should be on hand in great numbers and voice to insure the event. As this was his home state, one might expect a large representation, but their actual presence seemed beyond anything possible, and they made quite a racket. One supporter claimed he "could haller clear across Lake Michigan." Lincoln posters bearing his image are affixed to every wall, window, door and horse. Lincoln banners are stretched across streets and the sides of barns. And Lincoln "callers" roam the city, heralding his merits and even carrying lengths of boards to symbolize support for the "Old Rail Splitter."

While wandering about town this evening, Steinhaeuser stopped before one of the campaign headquarters and stared up at a large printed bunting over a door. It read, VOTE FOR THURLOW WEED, A TRUE AMERICAN. "Dick," he said, "I believe I know this fellow." I was about to launch into a retelling of events on the train but he interrupted saying, "No, look here, I'm serious, Burton. I know this man from somewhere." He flashed a smile and before I could begin again, the irrepressible Steinhaeuser rushed through the door and disappeared into the crowd.

As it turned out, Thurlow Weed was actually Mr. Seward's campaign manager, but Lord Thurlow's lackeys had made a show with this street nomination in order to gain favour with the great man and afford him the opportunity of graciously declining his party's call in favor of Seward.

This headquarters was clearly nothing more than a play to Weed's ego and a place where largesse may be distributed and deals done. The lean and white-haired Lord Thurlow had gained this appellation, and apparently a great deal of money, though a corrupt engineering of six street-railway bills in New York City. Mr. Proctor of Kansas said Weed reminded him of Byron's Corsair—"the mildest mannered man that ever scuttled a ship or cut a throat, politically, of course." The inside of Weed's dominion was better appointed than any of the other candidates. The girls were prettier, the food and cigars better, and, dangerously, the drinks flowed freer here than any place in town. Weed himself was present at this time and engaged in political banter with a score of well dressed men in the back of the room.

John was met at the door and at once fell prey to bottle after bottle of the liquor elite which were being liberally poured by the engaging hostesses. Their job was to identify the important visitors and soften any potential hostility with glasses of champagne. After an appropriate time, the visitor was to be brought to Lord Thurlow for a persuasive audience. The stage was set for some ugliness, but I imagined that John would quickly be relegated to obscurity by his accent and a failure to recognize his name as belonging to a person of political merit. I myself was approached by a young lady and was plied with carbonated wine.

While attempting to explain the difference between being a soldier of the Queen and working for John's Company, I kept an eye on Steinhaeuser and noticed he was getting on quite well with his hostess. Disturbingly well, for the entire Champagne bottle had passed from her hands to his. He was motioning for a second as the hostess brought her hand to her mouth to conceal a smile. "Why I didn't know you knew Mr. Weed, Doctor." I heard her say. "I'm sure he will be most happy to see you again, and I will arrange for this as soon as he breaks with Mr. Clay."

Oh God, by that time Steinhaeuser would be drunk again—especially with Champagne involved—and now face-to-face with Thurlow Weed. I feared the worst and attempted to get at John before something awful happened. Unfortunately, I was unable to rid myself of someone from the state of Kentucky who wished to impart his theory on the true source of the River Nile.

Contrary to my initial belief, it was Steinhaeuser's accent which eventually helped with his introduction. After hearing him speak and wrongly learning that the two were friends, the hostess must have assumed that Steinhaeuser was Delegate-at-Large Gustavus Koerner, an influential German/American member of the original Lincoln men. Before I could do anything about it, Steinhaeuser was being escorted towards the back of the room, where Weed was holding court. When I finally reached the scene, the following interaction was taking place.

"Why, I beg your pardon, sir, but you are not Mr. Koerner. The girls must have made some terrible mistake." Weed was very polite but almost jocular in tone, implying perhaps that a man as tipsy as Steinhaeuser could not possibly be a part of Lincoln's inner circle.

Steinhaeuser stiffened and looked Lord Thurlow in the eye. "And I, sir, do not believe that *you* are Thurlow Weed. Why . . . I have never seen you before in my life."

The two men stood apart and gazed at each other in disbelief. This went on for a long minute and I saw that Steinhaeuser was looking a bit woozy and beginning to turn pale. Suddenly, a great burst of vomit projected from his mouth and in an instant, the great power broker Weed was covered in bubbling sick. Steinhaeuser then dropped to his knees and let go another heroic volley that covered the tops of Boss Weed's shoes and spats and splattered across the floor.

A half dozen lackeys rushed to their mentor and began dabbing at his person with their handkerchiefs, and the enraged and temporarily blinded Weed began waving his arms in an attempt to push them away. His mouth was open as he staggered forward and within a step or two promptly tripped over Steinhaeuser, landing arse over tea cup in a pool of processed Champagne and Mrs. Munson's evening supper.

On our way back to Mrs. Munson's bedroom, John was sober and penitent. "It was the champagne, Dick, believe me, the champagne. I must be sure never to drink that stuff again, and not so quickly. It's no good, Burton, remember that. You see, the carbonation interacts with stomach contents in a way that often produces," he rolled his hands in front of him and frowned, "unpredictable results. But remember the Great Salt Lake, Dick, and all those Indians. That is what we're really here for. What happened tonight was nothing more than a bothering trifle along the way." He sent a playful punch across my arm and said, "Getting The Captain up on deck is what it's all about, right, Dick? Right, Dickey lad?"

Next Day
May 17, 1860

The Wigwam opened its doors at promptly 10 a.m. Rumour has it that several delegates will be missing from today's action due to a police raid on a brothel sometime last evening. Apparently, Chicago Mayor Long John Wentworth targeted a group of Lincolnites to exact a measure of revenge for not being selected as a delegate at the Decatur Convention. They are languishing in the Bridewell while their female companions were allowed out on modest bail. Opening day at the Wigwam produced at least one lesson that was quickly adapted by the masses. They soon discovered that all the chairs in the place were located in the balcony and that these were reserved for ladies and their gentlemen escorts. So when a ticket-holding gentleman found that he could not secure a seat without the assistance of a young lady, a booming escort business sprung up outside the front of the Wigwam. From the looks of the women offering their services, one might guess that they arrived directly after servicing the Lincolnites the night before.

This was a day of somewhat reserved American-style politicking, as the activities of the night before seemed to take their toll. There was noticeable absenteeism and the nursing of hangovers on the part of those still able to attend. Some platform business was attended to but the absolute highlight of the day was a performance by the Chicago Zouave Cadets. More importantly, it was decided to adjourn the Convention early so everyone could enjoy the much debated boat ride.

Despite the lackluster spirit that was exhibited today, one could not help but sense that this was merely the calm before a great storm. The general consensus is that "Old Irrepressible," William H. Seward will be the runaway choice of the Republicans. His name seemed to be on everyone's lips as we made the social rounds. As might be expected, we made it a point to avoid the places where Boss Weed might frequent, and this brought us to the camp of the Rail Splitter. Inside of the building were numerous hangers-on, newspaper reporters, and campaign planners all in a riot of activity. The Tribune was pro-Lincoln and their journalists were all about, busily crafting stories with the help of Old Abe's assistants. A dark horse, eleventh hour rally was on everyone's mind.

I had my fill of Seward's propaganda, and by God, I may box someone's ears if I hear his dreadful campaign song, *Isn't He Darling*, one more time. I found a reporter from the *Terra Haute Times* sitting by himself and asked him for his impressions of Mr. Abraham Lincoln.

"Well, mister, Old Abe's from these parts and we like that quite a bit. He used to live over in Spencer County, Indiana, you know. Let's see, he served well in the Black Hawk War, his grandpa was killed by Indians, and he's got more sense than schoolin. We like that too . . . well, not the part about his grandpa, you understand. But, hell, mister, there's no use in talkin' to me 'cause I gotta history of real bad luck." I asked what he meant. "Well, believe it or not, I was the feller who made the popular term, 'Go West Young Man.' Yep, that was me alright. But look at what good it's done me. Mr. Horace Greeley got all the credit, and he don't need a damn lick of it neither. If I tell you Lincoln's the man, then Cassius M. Clay will most likely win. I'm a man of real bad luck."

May 18, 1860
Nomination Day

Steinhaeuser and I agreed that we could feel it in the air as soon as we awoke. Mrs. Munson predicted it over breakfast, and every butcher, shopkeeper, and street Arab in Chicago had the word Wigwam on his lips. We could hear the roar of thousands of voices a full mile before we reached the convention center and the planks of the sidewalks positively rumbled as if moved by a growing earthquake. It was not a surprise then to find the greatest crowd to date surrounding the building. Steward's band, *The Irrepressibles,* passed us with their ep-aulets and snappy capes decorated with white and scarlet feathers, and marching behind them in military formation were two thousand pressure men.

To their horror, they were unable to fit inside the building because fifteen hundred seats, which had been occupied by the Seward forces for the past two days, were now in the possession of a noisy group of "Chicagoans for Lincoln," who had gained entry on forged tickets. A crowd of thirty thousand pushed in on the entrance doors, and all adjectives may be exhausted trying to describe the spectacle inside. Vulgarity was in the ascendant and there was a rumble of violence as a mighty shoving match broke out on the floor near the podium.

A flagrantly bogus group who pretended to be members of the Texas delegation was being ousted by regular conventioneers. The Texans were all dressed after the fashion of yesterday's hero, David Crockett, and looked ridiculously out of place in fresh buckskins and hats made from whole, dead raccoons. As they were being forced through the crowd, a member of the Texas group was recognized as one of the cowards that lynched an anti-slavery man named Bill Bew-ley down in Austin. A dirk was produced and the man was stabbed through the shoulder; blood gushed from the wound and soaked his new buckskin jacket. He was lifted over the crowd and passed hand-to-hand towards the door, all the while screaming, "Secession, seces-sion" and "all niggers must go to hell." A loud chorus then broke into chanting for Seward, and they were in turn shouted back by a rolling, deep cry for "Abraham Lin-coln, Abraham Lin-coln." There was a danger that bad taste may carry the day, but Reverend Green of Chi-cago seized the podium and delivered an impassioned opening prayer.

"Oh God, we entreat thee that at some future but not distant day, the evils which now invest the body politic shall not only have been arrested in their progress, but wholly eradicated from the system. And may the pen of the historian trace an intimate connection between that glorious consummation and the transactions of this convention."

President Ashmun thanked Reverend Green, hammered away with his gavel and quickly added, "The Chair feels it his first duty this morning to appeal, not merely to the gentlemen of the Convention, but to every individual of this vast audience, to remember the utmost importance of keeping and preserving order during the entire session—as much silence as possible—and he asks the gentleman who are not members of this Convention, in the name of this convention, that they will, to their utmost ability, refrain from any demonstrations that may disturb the proceedings of the Convention."

Rather than taking the words of these two men to heart, the crowd responded with prodigious shrieks, shoving matches, and often vulgar cheers that shook the Wigwam down to its foundation.

No sooner had the Texas frauds been expelled than Montgomery Blair of Maryland rose and instantly initiated another controversy. He asked for the accreditation of five new delegates at this last minute before the nominations began. These five were known to everyone in town as ardent supporters of candidate Edward Bates. Charles Armour, a Marylander for Seward, objected and denounced the five as outsiders. "We ain't outsiders," protested the prospective delegates. Armour threw a stack of loose papers in the air and exclaimed, "God almighty only knows where these men live." A noisy vote was taken and the Bates men were foiled in their plot. Nevertheless, a tone was set for this most important of days. The crowd grew restless and began agitating for the nominations to begin. Seward's and Lincoln's names were the first to be put forth and both were received with thunderous ovations.

Next were those of Dayton, Cameron, and Salmon Chase, who together did not command half the applause and cheers of the first two. Then, Caleb Smith of Indiana stunned the crowd with an early second for the nomination of Abraham Lincoln, and after that it did not matter that Mr. Bates, McLean, Clay, Banks, or Bell were mentioned at all. Seward's second occasioned a fury of hat waving and loud cheering, but when Columbus Delano delivered another and unexpected second for Lincoln, a thousand hats flew in the air and people in the balcony began stamping their feet and loudly shouting for joy.

Over the course of the next hour, Seward and Lincoln were in a horse race. Tally takers occasionally punctuated the deafening noise of the duel by shouting vote counts. "Mr. Seward 173 1/2, Mr. Lincoln 154," etc., etc. The anticipation became almost unbearable around two o'clock when Lincoln pulled within a vote and a half of the Republican nomination. At this point, David Cartter slowly rose, stood on his chair and addressed the anxious crowd. The Wigwam fell completely silent for the first time in a week, and Cartter began to stutter as he said, "I-I-I a-a-arise, Mr. Chairman, to a-a-anounce the c-c-change of f-four, four of my delegation's votes from M-M-Mr. Chase to Abraham Lincoln." There was a great collective heave as air rushed from a thousand lungs. A man with a tally sheet in his hand broke the silence when he called out to a sentry at the skylight, "Fire the salute! Abe Lincoln is nominated!"

The sound of the cannon blast on the roof was dwarfed by a vociferous explosion that was let loose by the crowd. It was worth a man's lifetime to hear. Someone later told me that, "A thousand steam whistles, ten acres of hotel gongs, and a tribe of Comanches might have mingled in the scene unnoticed." Women put their fingers in their ears to ease the pain, and many pistols were recklessly discharged into the air.

The news of Lincoln's nomination quickly spread through the large crowd outside the Wigwam, and their wild salutes added to the general pandemonium. The City of Chicago in general experienced a tremendous frenzy of enthusiasm that lasted for two days.

God only knows what the future holds for the American political system. If this spectacle is any indication it may be studied better as a case study in mass hysteria rather than as a proper system of the electoral process. Needless to say, there is also something profoundly disturbing about the presence of firearms at such events but these "irons" are seemingly as much a part of American dress as the very clothes they wear, and it does not take a great prophet to see that great trouble is brewing any time more than a few people appear in public. I asked one gentleman who had a pistol handle conspicuously displayed near the opening of his waist coat if he always carried that thing. "Oh hell no," he answered. "This is the one I call my dress-up gun. I use it for special events like this on account of the fancy grip and the nickel plating and all." He let me know he was just an ordinary chap most of the time by delivering a soft chuckle and adding, "I use a regular ol' six-shooter for things like shoppin', gettin' my hair cut, an' going about here and there."

The pistol seems to be the Chicago equivalent of the pocket watch in London, and it appears no decent fellow would think of arriving anywhere without one. If the man with his "dress gun" is just a regular citizen in a large city, then what will be in store once across the mighty river and into the "wild" territories? I will say finally that when men bring guns into convention halls, barber shops, and haberdasheries, one can only imagine the results when such hardware accompanies them into pubs and other venues that serve liquor. I fear it is already too late to even suggest disarmament or, god forbid, prohibition. Trouble brews in the New World, I say.

I have not seen Steinhaeuser since the announcement of the final vote. He ran off somewhere as soon as we left the Wigwam; I suspect he is horribly drunk by this time and out of control in some saloon. We are scheduled to depart for New Orleans in the morning and I am hoping better from America than I have seen so far. It is not just the lawlessness and pervasive violence. It is more about how such things are relished hereabouts.

Nevertheless, if the laibon could only see how apt his choice of hunting grounds has been he would be pleased, for here the game is varied, wild, and on display at every turn and on every occasion. No attempt at formality can veil it, be it sport or politic. There is no cosmetic strong enough around here.

VII

DOWN THE MISSISSIPPI BY PADDLEWHEEL STEAM SHIP

May 22, 1860
Rock Island

Away by train from the wildness of Chicago and today arrived at The Father of Rivers. With apologies to "Father Nile," this Mississippi, while perhaps not as long as its Egyptian counterpart, appears a full five times as wide and double the darkness. Its name is derived from a coupling of two Indian terms, *missi*—most likely a mispronunciation of the Chippewa *kitchi*, meaning great—and *zibi*, which is the common Algonquian or Ojibwa word for river.

We reached this river landing via the Rock Island Line, which is but five years old and represents the western reach of the American rail system. Here there is a pandemonium of excitement as stevedores and roustabouts prepare various cargoes for the arrival of our steamship. Dozens of barrels filled with oil, nails, molasses, and whiskey line the dock. There is livestock of every kind including a score of horses and several enormous oxen. A complete disassembled sawmill awaits the holds, along with stacks of hides, mounds of coal, rows of wheels, and runs of freshly cut lumber. I ask what manner of river ship could possibly swallow such a load.

Beyond the various hardware, liquids, and hoofs, there is a great deal of human cargo as well. Immigrants speaking a dozen languages idle along the shore. They are often young and single or grouped in small families with meager possessions wrapped in blankets and clutching the battered portmanteau and tin cooking pots. These plebes, while still no better off than they were at the place from which they came, seem cheered by just the promise of a future—something wholly unavailable to most of them back home.

John and I wandered the dock awaiting the coming of our ship. He met some Swiss from his native land and asked of recent developments at Berne or Biel, and I mixed with the Americans and searched for Indians. There were second generation Americans in a ratio of two or three to one with Europeans, and plenty of Negroes doing most of the work, but only a blink of the Red Man observing the goings-on from a distance.

Our ship will arrive from Galena to the north with lead taken from mines, once the property of the Sac and Fox tribes. These were the People of the Red Earth and the People of the Yellow Earth who were for years subjected to the outrages of both the French and Iroquois. Their sad saga finally ended some thirty years ago in the Black Hawk Wars, which resulted in the final loss of lands and eventual deportation. The involuntary movement of native tribes from their homelands to the Territories is a growing enterprise with the new Americans, and no place east of the big river is immune from these unholy uprootings. It is a diaspora worse than slavery itself. When I think ahead to my eventual shift into the territories where thousands of displaced and dissatisfied Indians have been forced onto the land of other tribes, and likewise made to deal with the bold and ferocious Americans already settled there I may well look back on Yankee baseball games and political conventions as models of civility. The traveler can only anticipate some appalling situations and so I must be ready.

Near sunset our ship appeared around a great bend in the river just above the landing. This occasioned much excitement with all parties coming alive and shuffling things about in preparation for boarding. She was enormous and looked like a floating city in silhouette, complete with steeples or minarets and peekings of lights from various portals. Her great paddle wheel slapped at the water, and the voice of the leadman calling depths was the only sound on the river in the failing light. As she gently turned for the dock, a screeching blast was issued from her whistle and this sent the Indians scurrying over the hill. After the landing was completed it became necessary to illuminate the dock with dozens of torches. It was then I first noticed that this lord of the river bore a most unlikely name. She was called the *Sucker State* and would be our home as far south as St. Louis.

The Captain, a religious man by the name of Ezekiel Bibbs, stood on the hurricane deck and closely supervised the loading of his ship. Ladies, of which there were few, and gentlemen were shown their cabins and others were condemned to far inferior quarters below. A cheaper ticket bought stuffy middle-deck lodgings and few comforts. Those less well-off were jammed far below with the sweat hands, Negroes, livestock, and machinery. Deck space was reserved for short term passengers and cargo.

Under the stern hand of Ezekiel Bibbs our journey on the *Sucker State* lost much of the legendary romance we had learned to associate with Mississippi paddlewheels. Bibbs had declared the vessel alcohol free, gambling free, and there would be no smoking, cursing, fighting, or spitting. Bible readings were offered and group prayers were encouraged.

The final barrels and passengers were put on board at midnight and we headed south into the darkness along the border of the American frontier. I spent my first four hours watching the stars, filling my lungs with the damp evening air and straining against the night to catch a glimpse of activity along either bank. The rest of the ship had gone to bed leaving only myself and the leadman on deck and Bibbs at the wheel. He looked ever straight ahead with the granite countenance of Ahab in Melville's *The Whale*, his posture stiff, and his grim face under-lit by a dim lantern.

It is no small feat to ply this great swirling river and learn its shifting hazards and currents. Sandbars form around every turn and sometimes lurk just below the muddy surface. The steam wheeler itself is a floating bomb with boiler always pressured for momentum, and explosions and fires are said to be common. An immigrant family I met on the dock told me they were following the footsteps of fellow countrymen who were blown off the *Sara Ann* near Hannibal in 1845 and never seen again. There are dozens of similar stories; however, I must confess to feeling a measure of security with a man like Bibbs at the helm.

Steinhaeuser was fast asleep when I entered the cabin. We are three days since leaving Chicago and this, I'm certain, is the longest he has gone without drinking since stepping foot on the continent.

We are another three days to St. Louis under the stern watch of Ezekiel Bibbs, and this may serve to dry him completely.

May 25, 1860
St. Louis

We have passed Nauvoo, the erstwhile home of the Mormon Saints, dropped off lead, and replaced it with cut stone. At Hannibal the oxen and some horses were traded for additional passengers. Other events on the journey of the sober *Sucker State* are mostly un-noteworthy. Bibbs was at the wheel on almost every occasion, watching the river and his charges like a hawk, and leaving me to wonder when the man slept, ate, or relieved himself. The only time I ever saw him away from his post was when the river widened broad enough to accommodate Nelson's entire fleet. When this happened, he would seize the opportunity to mix with passengers on deck and occasionally he found a group who would join him in long and lugubrious prayer.

Ezekiel Bibbs kept his ship as he liked it by refusing bookings to characters he thought undesirable. At both Nauvoo and Hannibal, he stood at the gangplank and turned away those carrying private bottles or weapons, those who were dressed too rough and those who were dressed too well. The former he suspected of being ruffians, and the latter gamblers. He made a habit of turning them back with the phrase, "God's ship for God's people, and may God have mercy on your soul." Routine and God's work were the food of Mr. Bibbs and our last three days must have nourished him well. The unending slapping of the paddlewheel and the monotonous callings of the depths from the leadman were our most entertaining companions. Always at the bow with his weight and rope the leadman called out incessantly to the pilot, "Ma-a-ark three, half twain, quarter less twain, mark twain. Ma-a-ark four, quarter twain, mark twain." At Hannibal I asked a young bushy-haired apprentice what this term meant. He told me it was "two fathoms, in English," and added something about a failure to understanding our common language. He gave me a wry smile and provided me with my first laugh on the river.

We came into smelling distance of St. Louis City about three miles before we could actually see any of its buildings, and this preview was not a pleasant one. The river was fouled and the early afternoon sun was almost blotted out by black smoke belching from dozens of mills and factories. Our docking was alongside a structure so dirty and dilapidated it looked as if it were constructed before the Revolutionary War.

As this was the final destination of the *Sucker State* we gathered our belongings and bid a religious adieu to Captain Bibbs and his church of the waters. It was now up to us to go ashore and secure passage on a similar but hopefully more exciting ship for the eight day journey to New Orleans. Our first human contact in this city was made by newsboys who bothered us to purchase two lurid publications, a shilling shocker called *Under the Gaslight* and a weekly rag entitled *Criminal News*. I had managed to brush them aside and was on my way down the dock when I heard Steinhaeuser call, "I say, Burton, have a look at this." He had purchased a copy of *Criminal News* and was reading the contents as he walked down the street. The first part of this publication featured images of professional criminals with their description, alias, and particular specialty described below. There was Edward Dinkleman, Bank Sneak and Pickpocket; Phillip 'Phillie' Vosberg, Sneak and Stall; Hugh L. Courtenay alias Lord Courtney, Swindler and Bogus Lord; Abraham Greenthal, alias General; Abe Goodie, Confidence Man, Skin Gambler and leader of the Sheeney Mob; James Wells, alias Funeral Wells; General Sneak, Bond Forger and Murderer after a Rough and Tumble. And so on.

It is impossible to describe the fascination these pages held for Steinhaeuser. He would stop every few moments and insist that I listen to the details of another felonious profile. I told him that we had no time for this and that our first duty was to find another ship heading south down the river and see if we could book passage to New Orleans.

He compromised by convincing me that we should stop for a drink. Let it be known that the St. Louis streets fronting the river are the filthiest I have encountered since my arrival, and the nadir of these is an unnamed alley between Washington Ave and Elm Street. Here was situated the first drinking establishment we came upon, and here is where Steinhaeuser demanded we stop. This public house bore its name on a sign which had fallen off its hinge on one side. The letters on the sign were uneven as if drawn by a child and simply said SALUUN. We entered into a dark, hot room that would hardly be fit for a decently brought up pig.

There was no bar. In its place was a supper table with three bottles of whiskey and some greasy glasses on one side of it, and a man seated behind sweating over what smelled like a bowl of last month's catfish parts. He sat with his head close by the horrid bowl and took a few slurps from his spoon before addressing us. Without looking up he said, "What'll it be gents?" Something must have gotten into Steinhaeuser, for he began to toy with the barkeep. In retrospect, I believe it may have had something to do with reading those entries from the *Criminal News*. He looked at me and said, "How about a nice cool beer, Burton? No, no, wait, I'll bet my friend would like a gin and tonic, with a slice of fresh lime if you please. As for me? Your best single malt scotch, my man. I believe it is a bit early for port or a brandy." He looked at me and was having trouble restraining his laughter.

The fellow behind the table interrupted his meal and wiped his chin with his naked forearm. His mouth hung open as he grunted, "Whiskey, we got whiskey." He fixed John with a look of distrust, but Steinhaeuser would not relent. "All right then, we've changed our minds—a bottle of chilled champagne, Herr Laden Miester." This time John could not control himself and broke out in a fit of giggling laughter. People seated at the tables behind us began to get up and leave.

Steinhaeuser took notice of this and asked, "Where are you going, my friends. I was just about to treat the house to a glass of champag . . ." That was as far as he got before a large bottle shattered over the top of his head. His hair was immediately matted with blood and whiskey and I dragged him out the door with muttering apologies. I was able to get his scalp stitched just a few blocks away at the upstairs office of a local surgery. The physician on duty drolly commented that, "Skull splitting doesn't usually begin until about four or five in the afternoon in these parts."

Steinhaeuser was able to leave the surgery under his own power but not before having a large section of his head shaved and a huge cotton bandage placed on the top, which was affixed by a gauze wrap that tied under his chin. I took his arm and directed us back to the docks in order to try and secure some tickets. We needed to quit St. Louis as soon as possible and hope that both social and physical conditions will improve as we travel south.

A return to the dock brought us to a ticket office, where after offering to pay double the standard price, an obliging agent secured cabin space for us all the way to New Orleans. He booked us on a steamboat called *The Sultana* and told us there would be but two stops between here and there. I was somewhat surprised to hear this and curious as to the reason. The agent sat back in his chair and returned to the business of applying a small knife to a piece of wood. He thought for a bit before addressing my question. "Wall, in the first place there just ain't all that many stops; one side o' the river's a slave state and the other's not until you hit Cairo, an' then you'll be in the South; you'll not encounter a single bridge across the river till you reach Baton Rouge, and . . . wall, fact is a lot of people just don't appreciate the *Sultana* puttin' in at their place. She's got somethin' of a reputation. You'll find that out soon enough." He looked up at me with one eye and commented, "Looks like your friend there already got hisself a *Sultana* haircut, so you're off to a real good start."

We found the *Sultana* in the process of loading cargo at the far end of the docks; she was off by herself and at first glance looked like any other boat of its kind on the river. Closer inspection revealed a marked decrease in the volume of below-deck hardware—they seemed to be loading only barrels of whiskey—and a waiting clientele who exactly fit the description of those who were denied passage by Ezekiel Bibbs. Men dressed in coarse dirty canvas with .30-caliber Fusils over their shoulders stood side by side with slippery-looking dandies wearing top hats and silk vests. Some others gripped bottles of liquor by the neck and drained heroic amounts while waiting to board, and then passed the poison to their scurvy mates. Blacklegs or turf swindlers mixed with drummers, the Barmecidean traveling salesmen of the New World. There is nothing the drummer will not attempt to sell, but nostrums are his most popular items. It seems Americans share with the rest of the world a love for being duped when it comes to their health.

Our Captain was nowhere to be seen at the scheduled departure time and when he rolled off the back of a wagon three hours later, he appeared to be drunk. He wobbled up the gangplank and began shouting orders in preparation for a quick departure. The centerpiece of the *Sultana* was a great salon and bar which occupied the better part of the upper deck. Here was the social hall for the passengers and the absolute center of all activity on board, which seemed to consist exclusively of drinking and gambling. The green cloth card tables were crowded with players from the moment we pulled away from the dock. Here one is afforded the opportunity of losing his money to a number games of chance. One may try his hand at poker, euchre, keno, rondo, three card monte, cutting the Jack, or the most popular of all, faro, which is also known as "fighting the tiger."

Steinhaeuser was still not feeling too well from his latest encounter and elected to stay in the cabin and rest. As a result, I felt able to roam the salon without too much fear of another rash incident. However much the world understands that spirits and gambling are a bad combination anywhere, here aboard the *Sultana* one has the feeling of exceptional volatility.

We were a good twelve hours out of St. Louis when it occurred to me that our captain, Lester Beach, had never once left his place at the faro table. He was drunk when he arrived, even drunker now, and in a mean spirit due to his bad luck with the cards. I walked out of the smoky hall to the open deck and took in the sights. The men with the Fusil rifles were lounging in a group by the bow where a leadman should have been. Some were either sleeping or passed out, I cannot say which, and those still with their wits were entertaining the music of a bandore. The pilot house was occupied by a nervous-looking boy of seventeen who gripped the wheel seemingly with enough force to crush it. I approached the lad and engaged him in conversation. He identified himself as the ship's cabin boy and said that he had been appointed Captain Pro Tem until such time as Mr. Beach's luck ran out. The good captain had provided the boy with a bottle of *Aunt Sally's Celery Tonic* to fortify him against the night air and make sure he kept his eyes skinned.

I later learned from the drummer who provided Beach with the bottle that Celery Tonic was in actuality a tincture of Peruvian coca leaf which is known to have strong stimulating effects.

The boy had been drinking this and bad coffee since St. Louis and the combination had his pulse racing and left him near a nervous fit of fear and confusion. Apoplexy was not out of the question. I spoke to him in gentle tones and reassured him that Captain Beach would be here to relieve him very shortly. The boy said that for some crazy reason he felt like he could take it for another full day, but he expressed concern that the approach to our first stop was among the most dangerous on the entire river and he didn't feel up to the challenge. I asked where this first stop would be, and he told me it was Cairo, at the convergence of the mighty Ohio and Mississippi Rivers.

May 27, 1860
Cairo

Lester Beach did indeed regain the helm just hours before we reached the convergence and just after what was at least, a twenty-seven hour debauch of alcohol and faro. The crusty Beach was in a dyspeptic mood. He cursed and spun the ship's wheel with great ferocity in order to avoid dozens of logs that now swirled about in the liquid mud. He seemed older in the sunlight, and the lines around his eyes and mouth appeared to be etched much deeper than just the day before. His hair was wild and he reeked of tobacco smoke and cheap whiskey. Nevertheless, he cut a defiant figure in the pilot's house and one sensed that he was enjoying this desperate tilt with Father River.

I will take back what I said about St. Louis, for Cairo is without a doubt the most foul dog hole on the river, worse than Zanzibar and Tobora combined. It is a humid and pestilential hell that is entirely covered in mud and mosquitoes, and I suspect the Pharaohs of old would burst their wrappings if they knew their namesake city was of such a low order. The Illinois natives even mangle the name itself, calling the place something that sounds like "Kay Row."

An unbearably heavy stench filled our lungs from the moment we arrived. Tar pots have been set off throughout the city and have been continually releasing thick black smoke into the air for the past seven days. This was the citizenry's answer to their most recent outbreak of Yellow Fever. Beach ordered the gangplank lowered and it immediately sunk into the mud. Greeters and stevedores had their overshoes clawed off by mud, wagons were paralyzed in the mud, livestock trapped in the mud were left to a slow death, and the very border between river and shore was blurred because of the mud. In fact, the whole of the convergence was nothing but mud, and the city of Cairo just a gloomy pile of sticks bobbing atop the ooze.

Steinhaeuser and I left the *Sultana* and managed to slog our way into a nearby shop. Fresh graves of Yellow Fever victims filled a lot next to the store and could be recognized by rows of gelatinous, quivering mud mounds that were a-swarm with flies.

The proprietor, a grubby man with a stubble beard and no teeth, saw me looking at the graves. He nodded his head and said, "Oh, Jack's been here again alright. Buried another one just this morning." Steinhaeuser inquired just who this Jack fellow was. "Yellow Jack, friend—yellow fever. Why do you think all them tar pots are a-smokin'? Folks here get used to lookin' into each other's eyes to see who's got it next." He rushed up to John and used his thumbs to pull down on his cheeks and expose the whites of his eyes. "Not yet," he snickered. His eyes flashed up to Steinhaeuser's head, "But you sure do have a funny lookin' bonnet on toppa that Sul-tana haircut."

Then in outright defiance of everything we had seen so far, he proclaimed that Cairo was the healthiest place on the river. Moving behind the counter he asked what "he could do us for," and I noticed that his shelves were stocked with every cure in the American pharmacopoeia. There were boxes of DR. CHARLES CHILLS AND FEVER MEDICINE, JESUITS BARK EYE WHITENER, PROFESSOR YANKOV'S FEVER DROPS, INDIAN CURE AND RELIEF PELLETS, CINCINNATI DIARRHEA CURE, OLD BOB'S STOMACH MIX, COMMODORE WHIPPLE'S

YELLOW AWAY, and INCA ROCA FATIGUE TONIC to name just a few of the many, many medicinal offerings. As it turned out, there was almost nothing else available on the shelves although the proprietor insisted that his was a "general store."

We left in hopes of obtaining basic stuff for the remainder of the trip and as soon as we took to the muddy streets again it began to rain. Now the stench of marsh gas mixed with the smoldering tar and forced us to tie our bandhnu over mouth and nose to prevent gagging. We passed a sickly young dog that had all four legs stuck in the mud for God knows how many days. It managed a pitiful whine as we passed by and Steinhaeuser stopped to rescue it. He took off his shoes, rolled his pant legs up above the knee and extricated the poor thing after much pulling and tugging against the sucking Cairo muck.

Steinhaeuser dried the dog with his coat and was rewarded with many grateful face licks and animated tail wagging. There was a nearby house and we approached it directly.

We reached Madame Gurnette's Boarding House in hopes of obtaining a brief respite from the driving rain and perhaps a bowl of scraps for Steinhaeuser's appreciative dog. We were greeted by Madame Gurnette herself, a cretinous old bag in her late 50s, whose operation was nothing more than a dank and swampy coffin with walls. She guessed that we were off the *Sultana* and made some disgusting comment which suggested that she and Captain Lester Beach were, or had once been, intimate. This thought alone was enough to send The Captain to his quarters with a shiver of revulsion, but what happened next was perhaps the *ne plus ultra* of Cairo opprobrium.

She told us to "come-on in" and lewdly battered the tarred eyelashes above her wrinkled cheeks. She commented that Lester Beach was not the only man off the *Sultana* that had gotten lucky with her after accepting a similar invitation. She also referred to me as "Sugar," which turned my stomach and made the Captain feel like bolting the door. John's dog was relearning to walk again on the landing in front of Madame Gurnette's door and was following Steinhaeuser everywhere he went. Just as I was about to decline her offer and beg a bone, she turned, pulled a pistol from under her apron and shot the poor dog off the porch, killing it with a sickening yelp and sending

the pitiful orphan back into the mud from which it had just been rescued. She refitted the pistol under a roll of fat and said, "Don't want
to get the floor any muddier than it is already. I like to keep a clean
house for my boys."

I had seen men shot and not felt as bad. Steinhaeuser stood with
his mouth open and then began shouting for an explanation of why
she would do such a monstrous thing.

"I already told you, handsome. Momma don't like mud in her
house when men come a-callin'." John ran out into the rain and
began throwing handfuls of mud against the house and at the awful
woman. He was crying and cursing and then began hurling rocks and
anything else he could lay hands on. Madame Gurnette was screaming for him to stop, but John was in no mood to obey her. While he
was searching for something else to pelt her with, I saw the old bat
reach under the apron again for her pistol.

At this point I produced my own gun, and placed the barrel of
one of Colonel Colt's excellent revolvers in her ear.

VIII

A Slave to a Slave in Old Louisiana

May 30, 1860
West Feliciana Parish, Louisiana

We have been on the river since Cairo and are soon to make port in the place called Louisiana. The feeling of being trapped on Lester Beach's *Sultana* has dulled the romance of the Mississippi and any friendly associations that may have once existed with this floating casino. Our landing will afford my first opportunity to get a glimpse of the South, its environs and inhabitants, and I am anxious to take full advantage of the two-day layover. Steinhaeuser has been in a funk since the episode at Madame Gurnette's. He has kept to himself and has been taking poison alone in the cabin, rarely talking when he is not asleep or passed out, and he is seemingly oblivious to all that surrounds him. I did not even inform him that I was leaving for a forty-eight hour off-board immersion because he has made ducks and drakes of all similar opportunities, so I left him in his cups and headed down the gangplank.

The entrepot here in West Feliciana is Bayou Sara, located on the alluvial flats just west of glacial bluffs which reminded one of the lower and more disagreeable portions of Switzerland. Ponce de Leon was the first European to see this area and it was he who gave it its present name.

Tonti, the companion of LaSalle, was the first white man to actually live here. Now, two hundred years later, my aim is to pay a brief visit to one of the plantation estates this area has become famous for and investigate the state of race relations under American slavery. And by God, I also plan on finally meeting up with the Red Man.

I have been reading Tucker's *The Valley of the Shenandoah*, and in these pages one is led to believe that the New World planter resides in a tidy, pillared mansion with manicured grounds and exists in the unlikely state of perpetual civility and gentlemanly good grace. Their women are both beautiful and chaste—a most improbable combination—hospitable to a fault, and matronly in the care of their charges. All about them are black field hands happy in their work, naturally given to lively outbursts of song and dance, unfailingly loyal to their deserving master and surrounded by joyous pick ninnies and fields of snowy cotton. What a cheery and unbelievable little world George Tucker has provided us. I understand that Littleton's *Swallow Barn* may even surpass *Shenandoah* in its incipient naiveté and capacity to offend.

On the other hand, it is impossible to turn a stone without having a copy of Mrs. Stowe's *Uncle Tom's Cabin or Life Among the Lowly* crawl out. In the eight years since its publication, methinks every literate fellow on the globe has had the opportunity to view the South with a jaundiced eye. Curious that nearly all the evil characters in her book are Yankees, and indeed one could make a case that the true villains are industrialism and enterprise, which are arguably Northern traits. Nevertheless, this work of mawkish fiction has left the South's reputation in low water. For some reason, this attitude has become so fashionable that a horde of imitators have appeared with hideously duplicative titles such as *Aunt Phillis's Cabin*, *The Cabin and the Parlor*, *Uncle Robin in His Cabin in Virginia and Tom without one in Boston*, and, I suppose, a host of others with which I am blessedly unfamiliar.

There is much activity around the dock on this morning as the *Sultana* is not the only ship in port, and a great many people are on hand either to take delivery of newly arrived goods or else deliver their home products for export. A small crowd pressed close and marveled around a shipment of Simeon Plows, and others excitedly took possession of long-awaited engine parts, tools, and factory wheels. A veritable market of cash crops was being readied for transfer to New Orleans and other destinations up river—bales of cotton stacked three times a man's height, tobacco, rice, sugarcane, flax, hemp, and indigo were all present.

Apart from the crowd was a Negro about my age, whom I overheard speaking to himself in a dialect unlike any other on the dock. In an instant I recognized him as a Kikongo speaker from Central Africa and seized the opportunity to greet the man in his native tongue. It is impossible to describe the look on his face when he realized that I was in command of his language and willing to engage him in friendly conversation. He began speaking very rapidly, alternately laughing and crying, all the while shaking and patting my hand and rubbing my shoulder at the same time. He said he has been unable to satisfactorily communicate with anyone for almost a full year. He became very agitated when he told me that his name was Kwomo! Kwomo, certainly not this name *Booster* that everyone calls him. He made a bad face when he pronounced his newly given name and then explained that he was Kwomo, son of Kwomo the farmer and was chasing a goat near his village when Arab slavers set upon him with an iron dray-pin. He let go my hand and held up two fingers to emphasize he suffered double-vision the whole journey while under guard to the coast. "Feeders on filth and carrion," he mumbled when referencing the Arabs.

From there he was forced into a cargo hold of the ship *Wanderer* and endured severe privations until landfall at Jekyll Island, Georgia. He was sold at auction and brought up the Savannah River by steamboat to work for a white man named Abner Stander, who had a crooked nose and owned a ceramic factory in South Carolina. "Another eater of filth" was the black man's evaluation of Mr. Stander.

I bid him to slow his narrative for he had run a gambit of powerful emotions in a very short time and was seemingly on the verge of infarction. When he regained his composure, I asked what circumstances had brought him from the East Coast of America to the banks of the Mississippi River in Louisiana. "Ooohhh," he groaned and covered his face with a long, slender hand. "That is a spider with many legs. But come walk with me if you will and I can try and tell you. I am bound to return to those who hold my freedom by afternoon. There must not be a delay or things will go badly for me."

I readily agreed for this was my opportunity to view first-hand the plantation owner/slave relationship that intrigued me so. I had already rejected the sentimental rubbish of *Shenandoah* and *Uncle Tom's Cabin* and yearned for the naked truth. Surely, the South had been forged from neither daydream nor libel, but if not so, then what?

But there was going to be no hints from Kwomo as he spoke only of his African home as we walked down the red dirt road. His lament was over people he was no longer able to see and familiar things he was no longer able to do. Perhaps his greatest complaints were the foods he was forced to eat in his new home, in particular "third grade shorts," which was the flour from which the Negroes made their biscuits. He also missed the prestige he once enjoyed in his village. He was extremely proud to tell me that he once owned seven animals, and one pregnant.

He thought his new masters physically repulsive and commented that there wasn't a woman among them over the age of thirteen to whom he would even consider administering *le patte de velours.* We passed many well-tended plantations in the first few hours that were indeed remarkable for their size and appointments, and I confess being disappointed as we moved on from one to another without stopping. Kwomo finally mentioned that we would be able to rest soon, and I looked forward to reaching his master's estate and getting on with my examination of the Southern agricultural and social systems.

Three quarters of an hour later we rounded a bend in the road and came upon what at first glance appeared to be a proper Southern "Big House." Closer examination revealed a false front masquerade before two structures no better than West Irish shanties with a dog trot between them. I asked Kwomo if this was his master's estate. "Oh no, no, not at all," he said. "This is where a slave may freely draw water and rest with impunity from the owners. This is a Yeoman farm, although the cotton snobs call them white trash because of some of the things they do and some of the things they do not have."

I was about to ask for a further clarification when a very poorly dressed gentleman approached us and offered his greeting. He was unaccountably eating a fist size chunk of consolidated soil. "How ye be, Booster?" He then turned in my direction, wiped his hand across the front of his grimy shirt and extended it to me for a friendly shake.

"Names Lee, Caleb Lee, and this here's my place. You're welcome to take water and some shade, Mister, just like old Booster. We don't make too much of a fuss 'bout strangers or Negroes round here. Just people all the same. Ain't that right Booster?"

Lee leaned in my direction and said, "Old Booster's a little retarded so he can't say too much." Under his breath in Kikongo, Kwomo mumbled, "filth eater."

Lee caught me looking at the dirt clod in his hand. "Oh, uh, y'all kin have some of this too if ya like. This here Feliciana clay contains natural medicines that fights all the lazy diseases. Gits rid of your hookworm, your malaria, pellagra, all those bugs what slows a man down." Mr. Lee sat to join us and this afforded me the opportunity of asking after his life on the farm. He told me that he does "keep Negroes," but that he is fair and kind, and offered for example, that he works along side of them and always takes care to restrict fasting as runaway punishment to only one or two days. Fasting? If I were a religious man, I would utter a prayer of forgiveness on behalf of this keeper of human beings.

He boasted that he hires Irishman for all dangerous jobs such as placing dynamite charges and further shattered the myth of plantation paternalism by pointing out that, "A man like Booster over there will work from kin to kaint and is worth more than a thousand dollars on the market, but a blowed-up Irishman's but sixty cents if he goes on the first day." I must have appeared startled at these supposed acts of fair play and common sense economics, for the nerveless Lee began retreating behind scripture for justification of his acts.

He began by reminding me that Noah cursed Canaan, son of Ham, from whom the Negroes were descended; and didn't I recall that it was St. Paul himself who instructed the servant to return to his master?

This was a disgusting and cowardly display of religion in the service of ignorance, although it is often difficult to determine which precedes the other. In Mr. Lee's case, these twin liabilities

seemed perfectly melded and it was not possible to resist exact-
ing some measure of payment for his lack of learning and spiritual
gullibility.

I said, "Brother Lee, I can see you are a man who lives according
to the Good Book, and I say unto you from Thessalonians in Chapter
3, Verse 10, 'If any would not work, neither should he eat'."

"Amen!" Lee said, thinking I was lending further support to his
practice of fasting runaway slaves.

"And as for my thoughts on the Irishman and the Negro, Brother
Lee?" He perked-up. "Ecclesiastes Chapter 9, Verse 4, teaches us that,
'A living dog is better than a dead lion'."

"Yee-haw, praise the Lord, brother," said an ebullient Lee. "'Wine
maketh merry; but money answers all things.' That right there's, Ecclesiastes Chapter 10, Verse 11."

"Ahh, Brother Lee, you are wise in the ways of the Lord." I took
a sip of water and then began looking at the soil clump in his hand
with great concern. I asked if he was aware of what the bible had to
say about the risks of getting involved in that sort of thing?

"You mean my Feliciana clay? Why, this is for my health, Brother
Burton." He chuckled nervously, "To chase away those ol' lazy bugs. I
discovered it my own self. Why I even got a number of my neighbors
usin' the clay and they say it suits them just fine."

I looked at him sternly and said, "Psalms, Chapter 106, Verse 39,
warns us by saying, 'Thus were they defiled with their own works,
and went a whoring with their own inventions.'"

Lee looked confused and a bit worried. He attempted partial
redemption by offering that he doesn't charge much for the clays,
"Only five dollars for a two-month supply."

I told him that wouldn't help in the eyes of God, and then I got
serious. "Brother Lee, I am a physician sent here in the service of the
Lord from England. I need to tell you that there is no merit in eating dirt. This is a false god you have placed before you and I will be
concerned for your spiritual and physical well being if you continue
this practice. Judging from other cases I have seen, you are most likely
already in danger of intestinal blockage, depending, of course, on how
long you have been at this practice."

Lee turned to me with a worried look and begged, "But Brother Burton, I have taken the clays for the better part of two years now and reckon it's been working just fine."

"I see," was my comment while rubbing my chin. "I'm afraid to report that there are no symptoms until just before the horrible end, which usually comes after approximately the twentieth month."

Lee wrestled with some base mental calculations for a long moment and said, "Why, near twenty months is what it has been."

"Oh my," I said. "Then it is my diagnosis that you have about used up your luck and must either be prepared to face the awful consequences, and soon after your maker, or else partake of the cure."

"There is a cure?"

"Yes," I said. "Yes there is, but I must caution you that it is not a very pleasant one."

"Well for the love of God, Brother Burton, what is it? I am not yet ready for my heavenly reward."

"Very well then, you must begin by gathering several kilos of droppings from a stooling cat and then cook this material in a covered pot. Shortly after a rolling boil is achieved the patient is to draw off the broth and drink a small glass of it twice a day."

"What?" Lee screamed. "That's cat shit y'all are talkin' about here. That's maybe the worst stuff that there is!"

I agreed but quickly added that it was not worse than a horrible death from intestinal blockage. I began describing how the body begins to bloat until there is a complete disfiguration and the pain involved with not being able to evacuate one's waste products.

"Hold on right there," howled Lee. "That's one of my favorite things!"

When I used the term "burst open" I was asked to stop, and he leaned against a tree to contemplate these two hideous fates.

"There's more," I said resolutely. Lee looked over at me with a look of anguish and absolute disgust. By this time he was holding his stomach and pulling at the collar of his dirty shirt. "More? What more could be asked of a man, even if it is to save his life?"

I told him that the paste from the pot must also be gathered and then applied to the patient's genitals as a poultice. As with drinking the broth, this must be done every day for at least one month. He looked exhausted and groaned, "Ughh. World-a-fire, doctor, are you sure about all this?"

"Absolutely drop-dead certain, Brother Lee. I beg you not to defer treatment as there is little time and I know this to be your only chance. You see, the feline intestinal tract possesses a unique chemical which, when taken orally, will act upon certain compounds that . . ."

"Stop, stop, Doctor Burton; my suffering will begin soon enough. The tracking of my wife's cat will begin immediately, and I will prepare and take on the horrid fluid to save my life." He placed his forehead against the top of his lower arm and began sobbing. I could see his shoulders heaving, but I had no pity for the man.

I related what had just taken place to Kwomo as we continued down the dusty road, for I know Africans love a good trickster tale. He chuckled very briefly and was unabashed in his comments. "Feeders on carrion. A filth-eater in the end, just as I told you. I hope he chokes on the cat shit and dies after the first treatment. I prefer a world lighter by even the weight of a single slave owner." He spit into his right hand, and for punctuation brought his left one down upon it in order to make a loud clap.

"When they all die, the world will be rid of so much grease and fat that it will take off from its place and lift up into heaven." He raised his eyes to the sky and laughed. "Go on all the way up into heaven."

I began pressing Kwomo for some sort of introduction to his particular situation. Was his master the likes of Caleb Lee? How big was the plantation he was associated with and what were the principal crops? How was he treated? What was his job? He thought for a bit and answered slowly and very carefully. "Well, I already told you that the women are very ugly," he shook his head, "very ugly, at least all of them over the age of thirteen." He then weighed-in on other related matters. He guessed that his master's land was only about three *arpents*, but, and he sneered, "They consider it much, much larger than it really is." He commented that they have adopted the manners and customs of the French, which he considered disgusting but allowed, with some degree of envy, that many of them did sport brass rings on their wrists, ears, and noses.

Needless to say, Kwomo's descriptions presented me with a most confusing image, for this was hardly the conventional likeness of an American Southern Planter. I was about to make further inquiries when he offered that we would be arriving at our destination very shortly and that I could make all further judgments for myself. We walked together in silence for an additional twenty minutes until we came upon a clearing that contained a dozen simple cabins, ten or twelve feet square each, which were constructed of pine logs and covered with bark. Inter-spaced among them were a few oval, palmetto-thatched huts.

Open fires smoldered about the camp, cur dogs sniffed at a gutted venison hung from a pole, and a dozen or more souls who were milling about stopped what they were doing and had a long look at me. It only did not take a moment to realize that there were no Negroes present, nor were there any whites. This was no southern plantation. I had been led into an Indian village.

"We are here," Kwomo said plaintively. "You should proceed with caution for they have some bad feelings for the English." Then he walked away and disappeared into one of the huts. Almost immediately I was confronted by a large stoic-looking chap wearing buckskin breeches and a calico shirt that appeared dyed with ochre. Cradled in his arms was an old firelock that may have been one hundred years old. He greeted me in French and identified himself as Zenon La Joie, Chief of the Tunica. I offered a handshake but he simply shifted the weight of the old musket and asked, "What has brought you to the land of the People?"

In common French I told him that I had arrived with Kwomo.

"Kwomo?"

"Well, Booster then, if that name suits you better. He is a friend of mine whose acquaintance I made at the dock."

"Booster?" He looked over at the hut that Kwomo went to and exclaimed, "Oh, you speak of Hoodoo Clay Maker." He looked at me with a suspicious eye. "You say you are his friend, but he is a slave and considered an outsider to The People who he has lived among for three of the *unakas* years. He speaks only a little Tunican and has not learned French. Hoodoo Clay Maker walks a single path, he has no friends."

I explained to the chief that I could speak to the man in his own African language, and this allowed us to form a friendly and very speedy alliance. A curious Zenon La Joie raised his head and said, "I would like to hear these words for myself, the language of this Afreeka."

So in my best Kikongo I called out, "Kwomo, son of Kwomo the Farmer, would you be so kind as to approach and allow a proper introduction to the Chief?" An instant later Kwomo emerged from the hut and presented himself before us. I said in dialect, "The Chief wants us to converse in Kikongo to prove it can be done."

Without missing a beat, Kwomo answered by saying, "You can tell the old man he can reach down and pull my *nana buluku*, just as his toad of a wife has been wishing to do for months." Kwomo bowed slightly and smiled at La Joie.

The Chief's first reaction was to suspect some sort of trick, but after Kwomo and I exchanged a few more words he accepted the fact that we could indeed communicate in this exotic tongue and shifted his concerns to a different area. "Hoodoo Clay Maker is not for sale," he said emphatically. "He was purchased by my wife's family and is of great value to The People. You may not purchase him for any price."

I turned to Kwomo and asked why he was considered so valuable to the Tunica.

"They call me Hoodoo Clay Maker because from crooked nose Abner Stander I have learned to craft a vessel of clay which is superior to the local version. With this I make hex jugs and luck balls which have come to be much valued by certain Shango cultists in New Orleans, who use them in their Hoodoo worship. Through me the Tunica have cornered the market in these pots which they ship to the great city and sell for a handsome profit. I see none of it you understand, but it is an easy life for me here among"—he shifted his eyes around and noticed Zenon La Joie was distracted at the moment— "The People. Can you believe that is what they call themselves?" he whispered. "The People, just as if there were no other people in the whole world. That is what that word Tunica means—The People. Feeders on carrion is what I'd call them." He blew air through his generous lips until they flapped against each other and made a sound which echoed contempt. La Joie turned quickly at the sound, and this in turn sent Kwomo on a hasty retreat to his hut.

I told the chief that I now understood Hoodoo Clay Maker's importance to The People and that I entertained no thoughts of attempting to purchase him. But I asked if I might be able to stay here for the evening and avail myself of their hospitality. Perhaps have a few last words with my new friend in his native tongue and leave in the morning?

Zenon La Joie looked me hard in the eye for a long and uneasy moment and said, "The People are much associated with the Five Civilized Tribes and are pleased to extend our hospitality to a fine French fellow in need of a night's rest and some food. Welcome, *mon amie* and be thankful that as a stranger you entered our camp as neither Natchez, Chickasaw, or English—for then I would be obliged to kill you."

He smiled broadly and led me over to his fire as the sun began to set in the direction of the Big River. That evening I spoke much of Boulogne and Paris and the women of Marseilles, all the while offering silent thanks that my restless father had raised the three of us children on the continent. My hosts told me of their ancestors who they called the Quizquiz and spoke of ancient, earthen temples on the lower Yazoo. Like Bedouin in the desert, their faces were periodically aglow, albeit here from their calumet smoking pipes in place of the Musaalam's *hookah*. We dined on the flesh of deer and opossum and after some corn whiskey was produced, listened to supernatural tales of men transformed into owls.

In time I was introduced to a fierce-looking Indian who had recently joined us at the chief's fire. His name was Volsin Chiki and was hailed as a paramount leader of the *indigene armee*.[21] His first act was to produce a large fishbone, and for my benefit he proceeded to soundly cut himself until a great quantity of blood flowed from his arm and down and about his clenched fist: an act, I suppose, designed to demonstrate his warlike disposition and manly indifference to pain. He then rose and reseated himself next to me whereupon he directly

---

21 The Tunica warriors. —Ed.

began to press his nose against different places on my blouse and trousers.

After much agitated sniffing, with his prominent nose invading the most embarrassing places, Chiki lifted his head into the night air as if to evaluate the odours he had just taken in. "This one does not have the scent of a French fellow. He is far too fresh." Volsin Chiki cast a hostile glare in my direction, circled behind me to snatch my traveler's bag and then dumped its contents on the ground. He pawed through my Patent Improved Metallic Notebook, my current reading material and my mail—some of which bore a HRM seal on the letterhead. He then leaned down and placed his head alongside my ear. Slowly and deliberately and in perfect King's English he said:

Fee, fi, fo fum,
I smell the blood of an
English fellow:
Be he alive or be he dead,
I'll grind his bones to
make my bread.

With no further warning he slammed the butt of an old Brown Bess into the side of my skull and I was conscious only long enough to feel myself hitting the ground next to the fire. I later learned that this practice was well known hereabouts as "the red nightcap."

It was sometime in the middle of that same night when I awoke in Kwomo's hut. I was having fitful nightmares of Shihab and Steinhaeuser flashing on Thurlow Weed's shoes. When my vision began to clear I was alarmed to find myself surrounded with the most horrible ceramic face jugs one would care to encounter under any circumstances, let alone someone in my present condition. Matters were made worse when the grotesque faces crafted into the clay seemed to change expressions in the flickering candlelight.

I'm afraid I let out a bit of a startled yelp for Kwomo came to my side to press a cool compress against my head and offer comfort. "Be settled now and still, my friend," he said in Kikongo. "Do not be bothered by the hex jars, they are just hoodoo pots for New Orleans and cannot harm you. You have taken a blow to the head but will be fit for work by first light."

"Work?" I sat upright on my sick mat and declared that I am bound for The Great Salt Lake. "I'll have none of that. I'm off to the dock as soon as I am able and then to New Orleans to be received by Col. Beauregard of the United States Army."

Kwomo regarded me with raised eyebrows. "Monsieur Chiki has announced other plans for you. He has spared your life so you may be Kwomo's helper. He said the English dog is fit to live only to dig the Feliciana clay from which I craft my pots. But do not worry, my friend, I have devised ways of easing my work load. I trick the filth eaters into thinking that I am working harder than I really do. I will teach you the tricks."

But Kwomo's words could not comfort me. They only confirmed the realization that the Tunica had decided that I was to become a slave to the man who is a slave to all men.

Kwomo bobbed his head approvingly and began rambling on in Kikongo. "So we will become good friends for a long time, yes? Oh, there is so much we will want to talk about my friend, and now so many days in which to do it. You do not appear to be more than forty years and that is my age as well. Why, that will leave us many, many evenings together until our hair turns white. I will teach you songs we can sing together and in time I shall instruct you to make the pots as I do. God has sent you here to improve my miserable lot in life, I am sure of that now. Praise be to him who sent you."

By this time Kwomo had maneuvered my head into his lap and began gently rocking back and forth and humming some God-awful tribal tune. He interrupted his contented melody to muse aloud, "A Kikongo-speaking white man befriends Kwomo in an Indian village so far from home and after all this time. Mmmm, mmm, mm." He shook his head in mock disbelief then raised his eyes towards the ceiling of his hut. "Makes Kwomo's spirit lift up to heaven; hee, hee; yes, go on all the way up into heaven!"

For the next week I was under the careful scrutiny of La Joie, Chiki, and every young man in the village. Their official purpose was to post a watch to make sure I wouldn't escape, but it seemed to me that they all secretly wished for an attempt for that would afford them the much sought after opportunity of killing me. For the time being, however, they appeared content with and derived great satisfaction from my status of being a slave to a slave. Even my friend Kwomo was a partner in keeping me from freedom, and doubly so, for not only did he enjoy and wish to hold-on to a person with whom he could finally communicate, but after only the first week of my captivity he had grown accustomed to having someone to order about and do all the heavy lifting.

In fact, any objective observer would have to agree that Kwomo's new-found powers had quickly transformed him into something of a slave-owning tyrant himself—probably now little raised above the likes of Mr. Caleb Lee. None of this of course was lost on the Tunica who worked in so many little ways to encourage Kwomo's authority over me, for my subjugation was a constant source of their entertainment. He was excused from most of his normal duties and asked only to administer my work. Kwomo still performed the final crafting of the pots, but I did all his labor and normal manual chores, plus a few others I'm sure, which tended to confirm my long-held belief that the dearest ambition of a slave is not liberty, but to have a slave of his own.

A stern word or harsh command from Kwomo would elicit widespread snickering from the women and children and a boot to my backside would all but cripple the entire village with howls of raucous laughter. The Tunican enjoyment of my predicament I endured for another week, but there were growing signs that the novelty of witnessing the *contretemps* of a slave's slave was wearing thin. Chiki especially was turning hostile, and I sensed that he wished to spill some blood as a final exclamation point to my sentence.

It was time for action. An escape to the docks a half a day's walk away may prove disastrous, as the *Sultana* had no doubt weighed anchor for New Orleans long ago and there may be no transportation available, plus I had no money. I needed to clear the territory altogether, and quickly, for the Tunica would surely be looking for me and I wouldn't be at all surprised if my "friend" Kwomo were leading the hunt.

Early the next day I managed to pinch some corn whiskey from Zenon La Joie's storehouse, and then doubled that amount with covert removals of the same stuff from three separate sources. Altogether I believed I had secured enough to get Kwomo quite drunk, and my plan was to do just that this evening and make my escape as soon as my master succumbed to the drink. I cannot say that I had a decent plan beyond that, but I knew that time was very dear.

After a day of digging and hauling under a blazing sun—I did all the work—master and servant returned to camp, were provided a modest meal, and remanded to our hut for the evening. Like most nights, Kwomo affixed a rope to my ankle and tied the other end to his wrist before going to sleep. As he lay on his mat I told him that I had secured a treat for us that he was to tell no one about. He perked up and asked what sort of treat I might have for him.

"It is spirits, my friend, obtained from the highest sources."

His eyes widened until the whites shone brightly in the darkened hut. "Spirits? What sort of spirits can be obtained by flesh and bone and brought to our house as a treat?" He appeared frightened and angered. "I wish for no white man's spirit to enter this place, it is bad *juju*."

"No, no Kwomo, I mean this kind of spirits." I held up the bottle of amber-coloured liquid and bit the cork from the neck with my teeth.

"Where did you get that?"

"As I said, my friend, from the highest sources."

His smile was so wide that even his back teeth became visible. "Well then, I do not believe I have ever been permitted to drink from the cup of Monsieur La Joie before, but as long as it is offered. Hee, hee." I brought the bottle to my lips but was interrupted by Kwomo who decided that by rank he was entitled to the first drink.

"Of course, my Lord, by all means, after you."

Kwomo held the bottle before him for a moment and then took a heroic draw, draining more than a third of the fluid in three exaggerated swallows. He paused, looked at me and then repeated the process. In his greed, I could tell that the effects would soon be even greater than I had expected. He groped about in the semi-darkness until he produced some corn silk, sumac leaf, and rolling papers, then prepared an enormous cone which he puffed away on with great abandon. I took a wee nip on the bottle and after holding it for a proper amount of time, handed it back to an already-affected Kwomo.

He looked at me with a strange, twisted smile on his face. "You know Burton, I like you," he said and then tipped his head back for another liberal drink. "I like you as a friend." He took a great amount of smoke from his cone and then held it to his face and stared at the smoldering tip. "I like you Burton," he began again, "but you are lazy."

He began to wax eloquent on the merits of hard work and industry, telling me that to make one's way through life one must not only devote full energy to his work but also to accept one's fate and place in the Grand Scheme. He explained that he was able to sense that I was not comfortable with The People and he urged me to overcome these feelings by a greater devotion to my tasks.

"The Great Father has brought you to The People," he said solemnly, "and we are grateful for that. You should be grateful as well." In his emerging drunken state, Kwomo was now one with The People and kindly lecturing their servant in hopes that he might serve even more. Washed away now were his former misgivings concerning slavery and the moral condition of those who perpetuated it. Gone were the much uttered phrases feeders on carrion and eaters of filth. Forget the tricks that make one appear to be working harder than one really was. Now that he was something of a slaver himself, and a drunken one at that, he fancied his advice avuncular and acted as if it should be well received. He continued on but his thoughts and speech began to thicken.

"You know, Buntrum, I once knew a lad in my village who did not like to work at any time. When the other boys went to perform their chores this one would hide behind the milk bush and waste his time thinking about a world that doesn't exist. That is not right. You take someone who knows what the world is really about, someone like Madame Marie Laveau, then you have someone who knows how it should be. Somebody who makes a difference and knows what things . . . somebody who is somebody and can do what . . . somebody OUGHT to do when some things need to," he belched, "get right."

I asked if this Marie Laveau was also from his village back home.

He widened his eyes. "Marie Laveau? Maybe you should not even mention that name."

"Is she a relative of yours?"

"A relative of MINE?" He looked around the darkened hut as if to make sure there was no one there to listen, then pulled me closer to him by the rope that was still affixed to my ankle. He lowered his voice to an exaggerated whisper and said, "Do you see all these hex jars around the room?"

He waited a long time for an answer.

"Yes."

"I make these things."

"Well, yes, Kwomo, I know you make these things."

"Well do you know who buys them?" He lowered his voice again to the faintest whisper. "Marie Laveau. That is who. She buys them, blesses them and sells them again for much money. She has the power to do that. She is the daughter of Damballa." He looked at me through unfocused and badly bloodshot eyes and insisted that, "She is the night."

"She lives in New Orleans?"

"Fool! She is the Voodoo QUEEN of New Orleans!" Kwomo seized the whisky bottle and drained off the last four fingers. He screwed his face into an awful expression that was not too dissimilar from the images on his pots and it appeared as if he may become sick.

"Look here," he said to me. "You leave off on this talk is because it's . . . dangerous to . . . and you think it's going to be alright but that's no matter, because . . . you don't know when anything . . . if it's. . . ." And with that he slumped over on his mat and fell completely under the influence of a much jollier god.

I knew this was my moment. I immediately undid the rope from my ankle and fastened it around Kwomo's other wrist. I then ripped up one of his shirts, stuffed a rag into his mouth and wrapped another around his head to hold it in place. I whispered to the moribund Kwomo that he had now really "gone all the way up into heaven" and patted him on the shoulder. "And good luck, old boy. You are going to need it."

Now what? Escape yes, but to where and how? I began ransacking Kwomo's hut looking for anything of value for I knew that some
sort of currency would be needed for quick transportation. There was
nothing in the poor devil's room worth a night's stay in a dog kennel
and nary a weapon with which I might threaten a passage. Then it
dawned on me—the pots, New Orleans, and Marie Laveau. I would
gather up all the hex jars and luck balls I could carry in a gunny sack,
and then beg, borrow, or steal transportation to New Orleans, and
then sell the cache to the Queen in order to replenish my money
stores.

I crawled out of the Tunica village while Volson Chiki and some
of his mates were telling stories around a fire. When I no longer heard
voices, I stood and ran as fast as I could, heading south along a narrow
footpath. I did not stop until I was quite out of breath and even then
slowed to a fast-paced walk as I knew every step of a head start would
be a valuable one. In an hour's time I came upon a road wide enough
to accommodate a wagon and simultaneously I was greeted by the
unmistakable smell of a horse.

"God bless you, stranger," called out two voices from the darkness.
In a moment I saw it was a man and his wife seated atop a run-down
cart. They were a plain couple, no more than twenty years old. He
wore a dirty old hat that rested on his ears, and his simple wife seated
next to him was wrapped against the night with an old blanket and
had on a pair of oversized boots that seemed best fit for the Yukon
Territory.

"Thought Faith and me were the only ones that travels by night
in these parts. Look it there, Faith. See, there's another man what
knows when it's cool and when all the dust settles. Night's a right fine
time to travel, don't you think, stranger?"

"Why it could not be better," I replied. "I am so happy to see
someone for . . . Well, it's a long story, but you see I am a passenger
on the Riverboat *Sultana* and through unusual circumstances I fell
onto hard times, and as a result have been held prisoner by the Tunica
Indians for a fortnight. I have endured many unwanted hardships and
have just now made my escape. I am in need of passage to New Orleans. Pilgrims, can you offer assistance?"

The husband and wife listened in silence until I finished, and then their dog began barking at me. "Hush-up, Maybelle," the man said. Then his wife looked over at him with sympathetic eyes and pleaded, "Oh George, that poor man has been held by the forest children. Just look at him. Can't we take him with us?"

"Git yourself in the back," he said while motioning in that direction with his head. "An' Maybelle, I don't want you to goin' at' him neither, hear?" He nodded at me after addressing the dog and said, "Last person that came on this cart got her mad as hell. Dog's got her a nasty bite, mister. Y'all mind your finger now. She nipped one off just last week."

IX

THE VOODOO QUEEN OF NEW ORLEANS, HER DAUGHTER, AND THE UNDOING OF MR. GEEK BABY JEM

June 19, 1860
New Orleans, Louisiana

Everyone in this bloody town seems to know Marie Laveau but no one knows where to find her. Many will add to this infuriation by asking if I seek Marie or her daughter, Marie II, and then proceed to tell me they do not know where either of them resides. It has also crossed my mind that they all have the information I need but are unwilling to pass it on to a stranger. A penniless traveler with a bag of hex jars and luck balls seeks a queen and princess lodged in a secret castle. Good Allah, what a strange predicament.

A trip to the docks, but no *Sultana*; and a check of a dozen pot-houses, but no Steinhaeuser. The directions to Colonel Beauregard's sister's house were left on ship with the rest of my possessions, wherever they may be, and there is no British Consulate in this Francophilic part of the world. What is a man to do when he has no papers or coin? But it costs not a farthing to see an *impromptu* street dance in New Orleans, and so this became my traveler's rest for the next half an hour.

The stage was simply the side of someone's house, and the occasion seemingly nothing more than a few open bottles of Jicarra. The happy performers were free blacks who were 'done up' in fine clothes and writhing to a perfectly delightful rhythm set forth from drum, violin, and a third instrument consisting of a simple serving spoon and a metal washboard. The movements of the women required no small talent for gymnastics as they heaved and contorted their bodies in answer to the music. Throughout the dance, or *conujaille*, the bosom is thrust out or moved from side to side in a most provocative manner, and one young lady's lascivious hip movements upended a nearby stool and knocked it into the orchestra. The bystanders laughed and shouted, "*Layotte, cessez le feu*" and "*Layotte, quitter vous habit.*"[22]

The woman smiled and covered her full lips with the tips of her fingers but did not miss a single beat. The dancing seemed to intensify, and her thin cotton top began to soak through with perspiration and cling to her well formed breasts. At this point, one of the drummers stood and sang along with the music.

I dun hunt dis settlement
all the way 'roun fum Pierre Sonait
Never see a yalla gal w'at kin
'Gin to lay 'longside sweet Layotte
Nevva see nothin' lak dis all day
Layotte she move in a sinful way
Yalla gal dance the *conujaille*
Yalla gal dance, *bon ton roulet!*
I been meet up wid John Bayou
Say to him, John Bayou, my son,
Yalla gal nevva meet yo' view
Got a face lak dat chahmin one.
Gullah Jack he know de way
an' Marie Laveau know what to say,
Layotte she love *conujaille*
Layotte tell the boys, '*bon ton roulet!*

The music ended with a flourish from the orchestra and the dancers collapsed into each other's arms laughing and sighing in contented

---

22 Cease fire and end your routine. —Ed.

exhaustion. I could not resist introducing myself to the one called Layotte. She was pinching the front of her wet blouse away from her moist body and fanning herself by moving the adhering garment back and forth from her chest. I greeted her in French and told her how much I enjoyed her dancing. She was suspicious at first but eventually responded with a polite nod and an announcement that she spoke perfect English.

Without letting my eyes off her I then asked if we could go somewhere and talk. She turned her head and looked at me sideways, as if asking what a country tramp such as myself could possibly want to discuss with a freeborn, *urbane* sophisticate the likes of Layotte. I looked as if I had been sleeping rough for a fortnight, which was in fact the truth of the matter, and before that a slave's life in a Tunican village afforded little in the way of proper toilet. The matter of appearance was complicated by the large sack I carried over my shoulder which seemed to hold all my worldly goods.

"Please excuse my appearance, Madame, recent misfortune has dictated my present situation and I assure you this is but a temporary condition. The reason I wish to speak with you is that I have business with Marie Laveau. I heard her name mentioned in the song just now and I thought that you might perhaps be able to direct me to her."

After hearing this, Layotte grew very suspicious and began edging away from me. I begged her to wait for a moment and began rummaging through the bag for one of Kwomo's jars. "I have this for her," I said proudly, and the look that crossed her face when she laid eyes on the jar I think almost caused her to faint.

"Turn dat thing from my face," she yelled and covered her eyes. "I don't want to see it no mo." After I replaced the jar she peered through her fingers to make sure it was once again safe to take a full look in my direction. "Where did you ever git such a thing? Do you know what such a thing is for?" I told her I had a good idea of what purpose such items played in local religious ceremonies and reminded her that what I had was for Marie Laveau.

"Well, I do not think your *juju* is enough for Marie Laveau, and if you mean to try and lay a trick on her, you will be the dead one, not her."

"No, please, I do not wish to hoodoo Marie Laveau, I bring these jars and luck balls as gifts. They are for her to use as she wishes. I bring her no bad *juju*, I only want to give her these in exchange for some help. She will look favorably on anyone who directs me to her, I am certain of that. I will also reward anyone who helps me make this delivery to the proper person."

She returned to the group of musicians and dancers, where there followed much whispered conversation and glances back at yours truly. I was re-approached after about ten minutes. "Alright *Blanc*, Layotte will show you the way and we will settle before the Queen; but I warn you, if there's any goddamn *mojo* goin' on it will be your skin."

We walked through a row of shanty shacks along the Rue Royale and on to a wide avenue named for either the rulers of France or, depending on one's pronunciation, the drink which seems to float this entire nation—Bourbon Street. Here at number 739, Layotte began making a series of polite knocks on a somewhat nondescript black door. She hid behind me when an elderly woman dressed in white answered and asked our business.

"I have merchandise for Madame Laveau from Booster and the Indians." The old woman glanced into the sack I opened before her then told me to come in and wait in the vestibule. Layotte did not wish to enter but was not shy about asking payment for bringing me to this address. The old woman scowled and took a few coins from the pocket of her dress. She dropped them into Layotte's hand and drove her off with an incomprehensible concoction of languages that would challenge the abilities of the greatest philologist. The best anyone might guess regarding the mix of this broadside would have to include words from the languages of Africa, England, France, Spain, and India; although Portuguese, Hindoo, Russian, and Chinese may be added with no surprise.

When the door closed behind me I found myself in a room filled with even a stranger and more varied assortment of items than tongues contained in the old woman's dismissal. Candles of differing sizes and shapes burned everywhere and illuminated both crucifix and dolls made of feathers which were wound with black thread. Unintelligible hoodoo markings on the walls appear to have been made with blood. There were human skulls and carved representations of the phallic Fon god *Legba* from Dahomey. Wooden images of Roman Catholic saints stood with offerings of what looked like cat bones piled around their base, and there were enough jars of powders and oils to fill a dozen British apothecaries. The old woman had slipped away without me noticing and in her absence I could not resist a closer examination of the labels on the many jars around the room. I took out a small notebook and began recording the fascinating titles:

BENDOVER MASTER LOVE OIL, POLICE STAY AWAY POWDER, MONEY OIL, GIT YOUR MAN OIL, GAMBLIN LUCK OIL, AUNT GINNY'S ZUM ZUM PENETRATION SPRINKLE, FIRE OF THE LOVE SNAKE ROOT, YOHIMBE KOOCHIE BARK, BABIES GRAVE DIRT, CONFUSION CAN-DLE WAX, DEAD MAN'S SKULL POWDER, WEASEL BONE, CHAMBER LYE STOOP WASH, WAR WATER, and DEVIL'S DUST.

I was startled when a tall woman dressed in black entered the room and said, "I see you have taken an interest in my preparations, Captain Burton."

"Why, yes," I cleared my throat. "I have . . . ah?"

"Madame Marie Laveau, Captain Burton." She extended a long gracious hand. "How good of you to visit my home; and what a lovely collection of gifts you have brought for me. *Je vous remercie beaucoup.*" As I bent to touch my lips to the top of her hand, I looked up and saw her admiring one of Kwomo's hex jars which she held in front of her face and rotated with her other hand. I never did reach her distinctive hand for I could not tear my eyes away from one of the most interesting creatures I had ever seen in my life. She was a qua-droon with green eyes, a long neck, and very high cheekbones. There was no doubt Indian blood mixed with the black and white, for her skin was vermillion. Her English was flawless and with just a twinge of French accent. Her age was an enigma. She may be an extraordi-narily handsome forty years old, but an exceptionally well-preserved sixty would not be out of the question either. No man could accu-rately guess. Her dark hair was parted in the middle with two blazoned streaks of gray descending down either side of her head. But it was the look in those green eyes and her very mysterious demeanor which set her apart.

"Excuse me, Madame Laveau, but I am afraid you have me at a disadvantage. I am puzzled how you know my name for I am certain we have never met before."

"Ha, Captain, of course, how thoughtless of me. You see I was recommended to a friend of yours, who asked for my help in locating you. He is a physician, from Switzerland I believe."

"John! Ahh God, how good it is to hear a reference to his name. Dear Steinhaeuser. Is he here, and where may I find him?"

"All in good time, Captain."

"I am astonished at my good luck, Madame Laveau, but I still must ask, how did you know the stranger at your door was me?"

"There was a description, of course," she demurred, "and as part of my method in such matters I always ask to touch something belonging to the person in question." At this point she reached out and stroked the side of my face. The feeling of her cool slender fingers on my flesh was positively scintillating. Her eyes seemed to look inside me.

Still admiring one of the horrid hex jars she said, "From the wonderful presents you have brought me, I can tell that you have had some recent dealings with the Tunica, yes?"

I proceeded to tell her of my fortnight of captivity, and through a process I cannot even begin to explain, my story began to include long passages that included the intimate details of my most inner feelings—thoughts that I have held dear for some time, secret thoughts I had no plans of telling anyone. I had to fight to pull myself away, *inshalla*, from this sudden and powerful compulsion. I cleared my head and looked over at my host. "I am sorry, Madame Laveau. I do not know what came over me."

"That is entirely acceptable, Captain. You see, I have developed quite a taste for men's souls. Yours is a very delicious one indeed and I look forward to dining at that table again very soon. But first we have to attend to some business. I would like to help you rejoin your friend, and I can make this happen very soon. But first I would like to beg a favour. I have asked my daughter to assist me by performing a small task, and I would feel much better if she enjoyed the company of an escort as she sets about this business. If you will do this, I would be very grateful."

"Of course, Madame, it would be my great pleasure to assist in any way I can."

"Very well then Captain, I will call my daughter. Her name is also Marie."

A moment later the positively stunning Marie II entered the room and immediately relegated her mother to the status of being the second most interesting creature I had ever seen in my life.

She was an almost exact copy of Marie I, except that her English was not as good. She was also fuller in the places desired by every woman and perhaps a bit more muscular. Her age was no enigma. Even Jack Speke would notice that she was not a day over twenty-one and shockingly beautiful. Like her mother it was her eyes, in this case bluish green eyes, that were *sui generis*, comparable only to those of Laibon Mbatiany, and haunting in a different way that was beyond belief.

Every inch of her was sex itself—all of femininity throughout the ages and in all races combined in one magnificent and mystifying package. She was the darkness of Africa, the mystery of the Orient, a naughty angel, a sainted demon, an Indian, and French and Black and Carib, and all of womanhood at once. My biology was excited the instant I saw her and remained so each and every second I was in her presence. She sat between us and allowed an introduction, all the while smiling and not letting go of my gaze.

Suddenly, I began feeling very heady, almost intoxicated, and the conversation in the room dimmed to a background murmur. For some unexplained reason I had thoughts of being in a graveyard at night and then a surge of erotica rushed through my body like a sheet of summer lightning and caused a noticeable quivering in my loins. This jolted me back to my senses. I rejoined my present surroundings by hearing the sound of Marie II's voice asking if I was alright.

"Yes, quite alright," I muttered. "Although I must admit to experiencing the most peculiar reverie."

Marie II looked at her mother before she spoke. "De mind command strange powers, Mr. Burton. D'ose with a strong sense can move with dere mind and go places forbidden to others. You can take a fearful trip to de other side of yesterday or reach into de uncertain luck of tomorrow." She paused for a moment and said knowingly, "Sometimes it is the powers of de one you are with that do the moving."

"Marie is right, Captain," said Marie Laveau. "The powers can come over a man from the outside, so it is important to choose your partners carefully—or pay very close attention when they choose you." She leaned over to me, placed her mouth against one side of my head and her hand on the other. She seemed to whisper in my ear, I distinctly heard the words but her lips did not move. "Normally I would have you for myself," she cooed, "but my daughter is very dear to me and I try to allow her what she desires."

Marie sat back and resumed her original position in the chair. "Take good care of my Marie, Captain. The task I have set forth for the two of you is not a very difficult one. When it is complete, Marie will lead you to a reunion with your friend John and you can continue on your way." She looked over at a strangely coquettish Marie II, "If that is what you still wish to do."

After this I was led to a room in the house containing a bed, a table with a basin and water pitcher on it and a fresh change of clothes. Although it was only four in the afternoon, I felt exhausted mentally and can think of no reason for this other than my brief hour encounter with those two very powerful women. I walked over to the table, splashed some water on my face, and when I looked up to the mirror on the wall in front of me, I saw a peculiar red mark near my temple. On closer examination it resembled one of the hoodoo symbols on the living room wall that had been made in blood. Marie must have placed it there while her haunting voice whispered in my ear. I let out an audible groan, stumbled over to the bed and fell into a deep sleep which held many frightful dreams.

It was just past eleven when Marie II entered the room and gently pushed at my arm. "Get up now, Captain Burton. It is time to begin our business." I questioned her about the time and commented that it was well past usual business hours. "Our business is not of de usual sort," she said. "Now is de time best suited to our needs."

After dressing, I met with Marie II in the living room of the house. She was sitting cross-legged on the floor with flickering candles and various jars of her mother's oils and powders all around her. She was mixing the various ingredients on a piece of paper and carefully transferring this amalgamation to a small red bag. Once this was accomplished we left the house through the back door and slipped into the night.

Our destination was a dilapidated shack just off the Rue Royale, the home of Mr. Geek Baby Jem, a notorious Negro, who, Marie II said, had caused, "much damn hullabaloo" by his transgressions against his many former girlfriends. It seems that after trading stories of his outrageous lies and infidelities, the girls had pooled their money and approached Marie Laveau to exact a measure of hoodoo revenge. The old queen decided that a younger woman should redress the honour of that particular age group, and who better qualified than her own talented young daughter, already a social consort of the offended parties and as such, someone extremely familiar with the many sexual depravations associated with Geek Baby Jem.

As might be expected, the attack was directed at diminishing, or probably eliminating, Jem's ample sexual powers, and to this end I learned that some of his semen (obtained I do not know how) had already been placed into a vat containing fighting vinegar, saltpeter, and twenty-five cents worth of mercury. Just in case this was not enough, Marie and I were dispatched with a secondary assault potion. We silently approached the three stairs leading to Jem's front door and Marie proceeded to cover the entire landing with the contents from the red bag. She had just begun making signs in the dust when a series of grunts and thumpings came from within. These were quickly followed by a staccato of high-pitched female shriek and a loud coupled groan of finality. Marie looked up from her work and cursed, "De bastard is at it again, but we fix him up real good dis time."

As soon as she finished, we ran from the steps down the darkened street and didn't stop until we were quite out of breath. "Well," I said panting, "I suppose that will take care of that. I do not want to get that close again. Like the man says, "Never get between a dog and his meat." From the look she gave me I could tell that this was not the best choice of terms, and I think I would rather face an angry *flagrante delicto* Geek Baby Jem than even one more of Marie's devastating glances. It was at this point I was informed that five visits to Jem's house on five different nights carrying five different mixtures would be necessary to complete the cure.

By the end of the fourth night word arrived that Jem's 'nature' was beginning to be affected. He had consulted a lesser hoodoo doctor concerning an unprecedented three consecutive nights of performance problems and had spent his entire last paycheck on HIGH JOHN THE CONQUEROR ROOT and WHAMBAM DO RIGHT OIL. Nothing seemed to be working.

As so often happens when a man and a woman share an adventure, Marie and I started to become close. Our familiarity grew with each visit to the shack off the Rue Royale, no doubt aided heavily by the excitement which was attendant to our task. She had guessed our victim had suspicions that a hoodoo hex was coming over him and the dangerous possibility that we would be caught by an ever emasculating and desperate Mr. Jem made for a very cozy situation between us.

The last application on the fifth night had to be delivered at exactly midnight and involved blowing graveyard dirt through the intended victim's keyhole. A strict provision of this formula called for fresh grave dirt which was to be obtained from the final resting place of a woman who had given much grief to her husband.

Those who would pooh-pooh the efficaciousness of hoodoo practices may note here that on this exact day was buried Madm. Edith D'ardent Sousette, a well-known local harpy who is said to have tormented her poor husband to the grave three years before. Since the time of her husband's passing she has become famous among New Orleans merchants and service people as one of the most vicious and bad-tempered shrews ever to don a skirt. Her burial was attended by no one save the parish priest and the grave diggers, who commented that, if possible, she would rise from her coffin and unleash at them a punishing fury of agitated directives.

Marie Laveau's complex network of spies provided information regarding Madm. Sousette's death and the exact location of her grave plot before this news reached a grateful public. As a result Marie II was well prepared when the time came to gather her final ingredient, and we set off from the house just after nine that evening to complete her mother's work.

Along the way Marie told me it was very important that the intended victim be home at the time the dust entered through the keyhole. For this reason she thought it best to wait in hiding until the victim arrived, make a dash to Madm. Sousette's plot, gather the necessary material and then return to administer the *coup de grace*.

We hid huddled together in a darkened alleyway until just past ten o'clock. The sounds of stumbling feet and some giggling alerted our attention to an obviously drunk Geek Baby Jem and his female companion—also drunk—who were arm in arm for mutual support and staggering up the front stairs of his house. "Neva seen that one before," sneered Marie. Her eyes blazed at Geek Baby's new girlfriend. "Well, you in for a disappointing time, sister. Jem gonna need splints from the doctor to make his man pay attention to you on 'dis night."

Once they were safely inside the house, Marie and I raced to St. Louis Cemetery #1 and weaved around tall, white-washed sepulchers on our way to the Sousette plot. In no time we came upon a mound of freshly turned earth with blades of the grave digger's tools still lodged in the moist soil. In semi-frenzy, I grabbed one of the spades and began digging. Marie looked at me and flashed a gorgeous smile.

"Calm yourself down now, Richard. We don't want to be meetin' up with Edith Sousette tonight. We just need a little teaspoon or so of her dirt." I leaned the tool against a nearby tree and Marie dropped to her knees and got serious.

She reached into her dress for several items and removed her long glass earrings. While still on her knees she carefully pinched a bit of dirt into a small jar and laid a coin on the grave. While doing this she leaned close to the soil and addressed the deceased: "Madame Edith Sousette, I ax for yo' help in makin' trouble fo' a bad, bad man. Dis Geek Baby Jem been round-eyein' five different wimmin at the same time, an' you know that ain't doin' nobody right. I lay money down for your dirt, Edith Sousette, an' want you to help me make his man act like a sick ol' garden worm what ain't got no strength." Marie placed another coin on the grave and removed another pinch of dirt. "Edith Sousette, make dat Jem's man soft as puddin' an' fall down his leg. I'm bringin' your dirt to his place to make dat happin."

Marie drew some signs in the fresh soil with her finger and then announced that we were finished. She stood, gave me a determined look and said, "Got to move with this hot batch and git de job done."

Back outside Jem's house, we carefully approached the window and peered inside. Our victim had by this time quit his regular street clothes and was now clad in only a scanty loin cloth that had been crudely hand-painted to resemble leopard's skin. He was strutting around the room with a whiskey bottle in one hand and the other lasciviously rubbing the front of his brief.

His face was angled into the most preposterous grin one could possibly imagine and with each of his stylized steps he uttered the words, "Here come, here come." Jem began circling his eager prey who had arranged her suggestively parted legs on a *chez lounge* so that her skirt was lifted to the ham area. She was unbuttoning her blouse to affect a shockingly low neckline as she sipped on her drink and watched Jem's courtship dance from the corner of her eye.

Marie whispered in my ear, "Sabrina told me 'bout him prancin' around in dem leopard's skin skivvies. Make de man look like a damn fool if you axe me." She turned back toward the window with raised eyebrows and said, "Sister's lookin' pretty good tho."

She tugged at my shirt and led me over to Jem's front door. Marie drew a hollow reed from her dress, loaded it with the dirt from Madame Sousette's grave and placed one end through the keyhole. She paused at this point as if waiting for a cue. After a moment we heard a voice from inside cooing, "Co'mon big cat, give your mama some of dat stuff." And, "Ooo-Wee Jem stud, I'm burnin' wet from your kisses and kaint wait no mo."

When Marie heard a creaking sound from a *chez lounge* attempting to bear the couple's weight, she let fly with a heroic blow into the reed and sent a load of Edith Sousette's grave dirt into the room. Following Marie's lead, I pressed my ear to the door and awaited the desired results. An unnerving silence followed and after a few moments in this atmosphere I became overcome with fear and a desire to cut and run.

Just then the quietude was broken by a sound only a woman can make when she has been wronged. "What the hell is that thing?" She shrieked. "What you think you gonna do with that? Man, git off me; an' while yo at it go take off that leopard wash rag. You ain't no cat, you nuthin' underneath, you hear me? I'm a full woman what needs a full man, not some little . . . garden worm!"

Marie's eyes widened with each invective and she nodded in absolute concurrence with the woman's last observation. Then came a flurry of activity from within, including glass shattering against the wall and the clanging of pots and pans. Marie and I quickly moved to the side of the house. The front door flew open, a naked Geek Baby Jem appeared, promptly tripped across the threshold and tumbled down the front stairs into the street. His leopard skin underwear followed him out the door and fluttered to a crumpled landing on his backside.

"Oh baby, it don't have nothin' to do with you," he moaned. "It's some kind of damn hex or something."

"Hex my ass, Jem. I believe you been doin' somebody else an' ain't got nothin' left for your nighttime woman. Don't you go tryin' to tumble me again, you drained snake!" With that she let fly a heavy iron skillet which found its mark with a ringing gong on the back of Jem's head.

Marie and I slipped away from the house and walked briskly down a back street. There was a possibility that Jem actually was exhausted from an earlier assignation, but in my mind there is now compelling evidence concerning the authenticity of the two Maries' hoodoo applications and the rapidity of their effects. None of this needed to be stated out loud. There was only the rumbling of thunder in the distance and the smell of rain hanging heavy in the air. Just as the first large drops began falling, Marie stopped in her tracks, felt for the lobes of her ears, and recalled that she had left something back at the graveyard.

"My earrings! They're still on Edith Sousette's grave, Richard. Ohh this is very bad, Richard. They must be removed at once before bad *juju* moves in on me. You saw dat Edith's powers at work and I don't want none of that on me. We got to fetch them back right now." By the time we reached St. Louis Cemetery #1 we were both soaked to the bone and found our way through the driving rain and around the sepulchers by the illuminating flashes of lightning.

When we reached Madame Sousette's grave, Marie dropped to all fours in the mud and began groping for the lost jewelry. The earrings were located at the next lightning flash, but when she attempted to stand up her foot caught the bottom of her skirt and ripped it away in front from where it was stitched to the top half of the dress.

Marie stood in the rain and mud with an exposed black triangle between her navel and the tops of her legs. She looked up at me, and with her free hand grabbed the top of the ripped skirt and tore it completely away from her body. The earrings were thrown into the night and she pulled me down on top of her by grabbing at my belt and pushing my legs out from under me. The lightning and thunder seemed to intensify as we rolled into the wet earth. My moment's reverie of a week past at her mother's house came to an ecstasy of reality on the muddy ground of St. Louis Cemetery #1. I now understood why I was allowed only a few seconds' preview back on Bourbon St. for this was going to be no ordinary sexual experience. The intensity level surged to several peaks over a period well beyond the capacity of any normal male. I felt as if sensory feelings were being time and again sent close to an echelon where one may no longer be able to stand the effects.

The experience was such that I sometimes felt positively crippled with ecstasy, yet coincidentally I was energized beyond normal limits. I have no idea of how long we were on the ground and wrapped around each other but when I began to regain my senses it had long since stopped raining and the clear skies were hosting a bright summer's moon.

As we were dressing before venturing into the street, Marie told me how exhilarating it was for her to see Jem's girlfriend on the *chez lounge* and how her posed body stimulated her womanhood to a boiling point. This goes a way towards proving my long-held suspicion concerning Sapphic arousal, tribidism, and the Eros of women brave enough to be excited by such sights. I continue to maintain that this form of stimulation can often produce the best reaction in women and advance heterosexual couplings as well. As proof, on this night The Captain was not only standing tall on deck as never before but energized and willing to springboard into the warm sea and bounce back on deck to do it again and again.

When we returned to the house, Marie Laveau was there to greet us at the door. She congratulated us immediately on effecting "the cure," although I have no idea how she could have possibly known what had taken place across town only a few hours earlier. There was also an undeniable reference to the episode in the rainy graveyard. She could read the astonishment on my face and said, "I cautioned you that the powers of the mind are very commanding, Captain Burton, and that they can be moved by someone who is close." She looked at her daughter and smiled. "And do not think that the mind's eye cannot read a lover's story that is frozen for an instant in the brilliance of a lightning flash."

I slept for nearly all the next day, as an exhausted man should after a hard week's journey and a Herculean conclusion. At five in the evening I was hosted for tea by the two Maries. "You have completed your portion of the bargain, Captain, and have made us very happy in the process." Marie Laveau placed her arm across her daughter's shoulders, "Very happy indeed. Now I am obliged to return the favour by asking Marie to escort you to the place where you may be reunited with your doctor friend from Switzerland. What you wish to do at that point is your option as a free man, and God only knows that the wishes of a free man in this country are something that needs to be respected."

She turned and disappeared from the room without saying another word, leaving Marie II to take control of my ship. "Are you ready to leave, Richard?" I told her that I should take this opportunity to rejoin my companion whom I had not seen in almost a month. Marie looked at me carefully and said, "I understand. I know where to find him and I think we should leave for dat place now so's we can meet up with him 'fore it gits too late."

I think I knew what she was getting at, so we left straightaway and headed for our destination, a place Marie called Congo Square. As we strolled through New Orleans town at sunset, Marie passed comments on a wide range of subjects, but it was the people of this city who commanded the majority of her attention. "Dese damn Keskydee's." (I later realized that she was referring to French speakers, who were always asking, *Qu'est-ce qu'il dit?* What did he say?) "Dey think a Negro woman jus' dere for de takin'. Think dey can jus' show-up at de Placage an' take their pick. Negro woman jus' as fussy as anybody else when it comes to pickin' out her man, Damn Keskydee don't even know dat.

"Another thing—white man thinks every Negro in New Orleans is his slave. We got mo' free blacks here dan the whole rest of the South ever had, ever. Makes it hard for decent folk to git by in this town. At's why hoodoo so important—ain't no man black or white kin mess wit that. No sur, lay some hoodoo on people an' dey start to know what it's all 'bout."

X

DIFFICULTIES AT THE
DEBUTANTE BALL

I HAD HAD ENOUGH OF racial injustice and hoodoo for the time being and wished to change the subject. My thoughts were of rejoining Steinhaeuser and how soon before we would be at that place. I began asking her questions about Congo Square.

"Congo Square is where de' culled folk go to have fun an' be social with each other. We go dere to dance the *calinda* an' the *pile chactas*"— Marie whirled around as she walked—"and the *conunjallie*, the *bamboula*, or the *carabine*, anything you wants to do. It's where a man an' a woman can git together and fool around. . .maybe have a little drink."

I slowed my pace when I heard these last two words and put them together with thoughts of Steinhaeuser. I must have appeared rather distracted.

"Did I say something wrong, Richard?"

"Oh, not really, Marie. It's just that past experiences sometimes give me reason for pause. I'm sure it's nothing, let's just carry on." It was well past sundown when we reached Congo Square, and already there were groups of people congregating about in lots of fives and tens. That is save for a mass of activity involving perhaps sixty or seventy people located near the center of the grounds.

As we approached, the sounds of wild hand-drumming and laughter became louder and louder, and it was apparent that the participants, who were all writhing in synchronized contractions to the music, were near beyond themselves in an ecstasy of rapturous delight.

The carrying-on was infectious and we found ourselves being drawn towards the celebrants and their music. On closer inspection, it was clear that the excitable gathering was arranged in a large circle around the object of their uncontained enjoyment.

Marie and I weaved through the crowd of dancers and peered over the shoulder of one of the sweaty participants to catch a glimpse of the main attraction. It was Steinhaeuser, hopping and shaking his body around in awkward response to the rhythm of the drums and violins. John's efforts to dance were positively spasmodic. His head jerked up and down in defiance to the beat, and only the Creator knows whether his step was a hyper-activated nervous reaction or some sped up and grossly modified Germanic folk dance.

In any case, Steinhaeuser's bizarre gyrations, however inappropriate, seemed to delight the crowd to the extent that different women fought to enter the circle and pair themselves with this pale dervish. In front of the madly dancing physician and all around him, the girls displayed their best moves and strained every nerve to outdo one another in an attempt to capture his attention. The drumming and clapping increased to a fever pitch when one of the largest women I have ever seen danced into the circle and began to jig towards John. She was uncommonly tall and were it not for her womanly clothing, hips and bust line I would have thought an exceptionally well-conditioned male athlete had entered the contest. She began swinging her powerful arms about according to the music and moving in rhythm towards a seemingly mesmerized John Steinhaeuser.

Upon reaching her target she reached up, pulled her blouse down from off the sides of her shoulders and while quivering in place, stuffed Steinhaeuser's head between her massive breasts. She then flung her arms out to their full extent and began shaking her hands and upper body. Her head fell back and she uttered a deep, masculine "Ha ha ha" before she leapt up and locked her mighty legs around the small of his back. Steinhaeuser began staggering about the circle. His head was completely buried in flesh with only a shock of wiry hair erupting from the twin mounds and reaching just below the woman's chin. I fully expected his knees to buckle under the weight of his Amazon cargo, but somehow John managed to remain upright and keep dancing.

"Take a ride, Billiette. Ride de man down, Billiette," shouted members of the delighted audience. And ride Billiette did. Steinhaeuser wobbled her to one side of the circle and back to another. Women screamed and covered their faces as the couple approached their position and others stiffened their arms in anticipation of a bone-jarring collision. At last Billiette's great mass bested poor John, and the two of them crashed to the ground, with Steinhaeuser flat on his back and his face still lodged between her breasts.

He began thrashing his legs about and there was a muffled attempt at communication coming from beneath Billiette's chest.

Marie and I rushed into the center of the circle, recovered Steinhaeuser's body from the wreckage, and got him to his feet. His face was covered in perspiration and although he was mumbling something about not being able to breathe he wore a cockeyed look of supreme satisfaction across his face. It was a moment or two before he turned and recognized his rescuer, and when he did his eyes widened and he began to chuckle. "Dick! My God, man, I thought you were dead. Where the devil have you been?" His laboured breath was heavy with the smell of alcohol.

Steinhaeuser began to describe the lengths to which he had gone to try and locate me. When he reached the part about recruiting a hoodoo priestess, he did a double-take and fixed his eyes on Marie II. "My God, Burton, however do you come up with such exquisite women companions? Don't we know each other my dear?" He groped in her direction for an introductory handshake, and then in a fit of jealous rage Billiette rushed up, clamped her arms around John, and pinned his appendages to his side. She leaned her head down and began kissing him on the side of his mouth. I explained that this was the daughter of the woman he had hired to find me, and, for the benefit of the imposing Billiette, I hastened to add that Marie and I were enjoying a splendid relationship, thank you, and that we have been staying together on Bourbon Street.

"Well, Dick, I'm afraid that I must put a damper on your good luck. You see, in a panic I sent a telegraphic dispatch to Lord Palmerston, informing him that I had lost track of your whereabouts, and, of course, I also told him that we needed more money."

I commented that London would most likely find his note a most disturbing combination of fact and request.

"Precisely, Dick. Just this morning word reached me that the Foreign Office is most upset and suspects that you may be having one of your adventures at their expense. They want to know just what we are doing in New Orleans in the first place and have also requested a projection as to when you will reach Salt Lake City. I was instructed to find you at once and in no uncertain terms they demanded that you break off from whatever you are doing and continue moving west into the Territories towards the goal."

Marie II squeezed my hand when she heard this last directive and looked up into my eyes. She pulled me over to a place where no one could hear what she was about to say. "Richard, you be leaving N'orleans soon, I know dat now. Do you remember what happened on de first day we met, how you thought of de graveyard before anything happened there, an' dat feeling you had when it got into your mind? Dat came from de power my mother and I have, same powers what made your man stand up, same ones that made Jem's lay down. Same powers what brought you here, same ones that lets you go. Dat way it all makes sense, Richard. Makes sense for you an' makes good sense for me. Lot of people goin' to be needin' you to roam so's you can tell 'em what you seen. You goin' to be famous Richard Burton, an' you can't git there by stayin' here."

It was impossible not to reflect back to Zanzibar and I clearly heard Laibon Mbatiany's words in those of Marie II. Thousands of miles away and months later the message was identical; the mission now even more unmistakably defined and reinforced. The mind wants to entertain impossible thoughts of a physic telegraph between them. The rational mind rejects the notion, but the extra-sensory self[23] demands some sort of explanation. It makes me wonder if such things are not a buried yet connective facet of Man's religions. No doubt the quest for solution is part of this new-cycle undertaking.

I managed to interrupt my reverie to acknowledge my remarkable companion. "And what about you, Marie? What do the powers have in store for the daughter of the Queen?"

---

23 Richard Burton coined the term Extra Sensory Perception. —Ed.

"I got a whole lot of livin' to do, Richard. You were my first but cannot be my last. De powers say I will become my mother and the Marie Laveaus will live as long as there is hoodoo and people to say our name. You see, Richard, in dat way my mother and I are goin' to be together with you for a long, long time. We all be history. Now go back to your friend an' finish up your business. I'm goin' to go tell my mother that this part of de song is finished bein' written. But she'll already know that by de time I git there."

Marie disappeared into the crowd just as Steinhaeuser approached and asked what was going on. I told him I was just watching the tail end of history pass out of sight.

Steinhaeuser was soon joined by Billiette, who immediately began to administer a series of crushing hugs and kisses which was her wont after even the briefest separation. While still in her grasp, John suggested that we leave Congo Square and begin resting up for tomorrow's engagement. After I gave him a searching look, he informed me that Col. Beauregard would be hosting his niece's debutante ball beginning at four o'clock the next afternoon. John gave me instructions to the flat where he was staying and told me he would join me later after he attended to some business. He raised smiling eyes up to Billiette and made disgusting little smooching gestures with his lips.

When I awoke the next morning in Steinhaeuser's flat, he was sprawled across his bed stark naked, and there were deep purple bruises on the tops of his upper legs and his sides. The entire room reeked of alcohol. He began to stir and groan and then sat up in bed and began hacking. I asked if he had been attacked and beaten last evening after we parted.

He glanced over at me with a cat-that-swallowed-the-canary look on his puffy face and shook his head. "No, Burton, nothing of the sort." He noticed the bruises on his body and acted pleasantly surprised. "Oh my, that Billiette is quite a woman, don't you think, Dick?"

By four o'clock that afternoon we were sipping punch on the manicured lawn of Col. Pierre G. T. Beauregard's sister's mansion in the most fashionable section of New Orleans. Ladies and gentlemen of the highest social order were gliding between polite engagements around the spacious grounds, dressed in proper waistcoats and lacy crinolines and nodding in refined approval to the sounds of French chamber music.

At dusk, uniformed attendants asked that all guests repair to the reception hall in the main building for introductions and dancing. Inside that immaculate room, young debutantes from the finest families in New Orleans were excitedly rushing about checking that each other's outfits and accoutrements were arranged just so and that each hair was in its perfect place. I could not help but wonder what was taking place on the other side of town in Congo Square.

After all had settled in the great room, the orchestra broke into a triumphant overture signaling a pair of servants to open double white doors at the top of a long staircase. There appeared Col. Beauregard himself in full dress military uniform and on his arm a blushing young woman on the verge of her social arrival. They smiled at each other then descended the steps with the aplomb of gods, which indeed they considered themselves to be. At the foot of the stairs they stopped and offered a short bow. The Colonel stood perfectly erect and said, "Ladies and Gentlemen, Ah have the great honour to present mah niece, Miss Vivian Beauregard Chouinard of N'Orleans."

After a round of polite applause the guests were asked to queue-up for introductions. John and I stood side by side and eventually reached our brief audience with the guest of honour.

"Why Captain Burton, surh, Ah am de-lighted that you were able to make the trip all the way from New York. Ah trust yours was a smooth junny through this great land and that our natives treated you kindly." He turned to his niece and made soft chortling sounds. Realizing a potential *faux pas* he quickly said, "Oh, Ah am so terribly sorry, Captain Burton may I introduce Miss Chouinard, and Miss Chouinard, this is Captain Burton of the Bombay Army. You may recognize his name as being the author of some of our great travel books and the doer of various acts of daring around the globe?"

"How do you do, Captain."

"Charmed, I'm sure."

"Oh, and with the Captain is, ah, Mr. Steinquencher here, from Sweden isn't it, sir?"

Steinhaeuser was doubly stunned before becoming furious and then controlled, but only through affecting a cynical and exaggerated Scandinavian accent and a purposeful verbal reduction of Beauregard's rank. "Yaaa suuure, Lieutenant. Sveeden it is, ver ve don speak English so guud."

As Steinhaeuser looked away there was an unmistakable mark of contempt on his face. The innocent debutant was the next to speak. "I am pleased to meet you, Mr. Steinfulcha, thank you so much for coming all this way."

Steinhaeuser's eyes widened at the young girl, and in an effort to control himself once again, he flipped into low caste, London cockney accent. "No trouble a'tall, missy. Me ol' mate Bilaricki Dickie 'ere, an me, maybe just lookin' to pinch a bum or too while we're 'ere, eh Dickie? Ain't that ryght Dickie?" His cockney accent was worse than his Swedish one, but I suppose it served its purpose by confusing and upsetting his hosts.

Colonel Beauregard looked hard at Steinhaeuser and narrowed his eyes. He was certain that John was attempting to register some sort of complaint but was not exactly sure of the gravity of his intent or what would come of it. Decorum and civility dictated that he issue a benign dismissal and push on to safer ground. "Thank you very much, sir. And now, Miss Chouinard, may I introduce Reverend and Mrs. Craighead of the Church of Christ in Plaquemine?"

As soon as we were out of earshot I turned and snapped at John, asking what on earth he was trying to do.

"Did you hear what he called me, Burton? Steinquencher, that's what. And his primpy little niece called me Steinfulcher. It is HERR DOCTOR STEINHAEUSER to these self-important colonial bumpkins. Doctor Steinhaeuser from the medical school in Bern, Switzerland and Herr Director of the Clinic in Arabia, goddamn it!"

I made the mistake of telling him to calm himself by having a drink and for the next hour he stood alone in a corner of the room emptying glass after glass of rum punch spiked with whiskey from his oversized pocket flask. When the introductions were completed, the orchestra conductor tapped his podium and the sounds of genteel dance music filled the air. Middle-aged couples whirled about the floor and were soon joined by the debutantes themselves who were coaxed from their seats by young gentlemen who had registered their intentions well in advance.

After a few spins with the cream of New Orleans, I approached Steinhaeuser and asked how he was getting on. His mood had brightened considerably from the alcohol. He said he was feeling much better, but was suffering some pangs of embarrassment as a result of his earlier actions. "Don't be silly, old boy," I lied. "Nothing was made of it. In fact, they've probably forgotten all about you in the process of those interminable introductions. Why don't you just sign up on the card of a pretty girl and have yourself a lovely dance? Come on, John, forget those pompous aristocrats. Put the drink down for a change and have some good fun."

"I suppose you're right, Burton. I could only make matters worse by getting drunk at a place like this. The things I tend to do when I get going. My God, do you recall what happened when I drank too much and returned to the Empire State Hotel with those base-ball players? What a bloody mess I made of that."

"Don't even think of that, John. Look, there is no need to sign one of their little dance cards. I'll introduce you to a nice girl straightaway and you'll be on the floor in no time."

"Really, Burton? Well, I suppose that will be a 'bit of alright' as you say in England." He perked up and began straightening his collar. It did not take long to re-meet one of my former dance partners and arrange for a sidestepping of protocol. Much to the consternation of the many chaperones, I pulled one of the debutantes over to John and after a brief introduction sent them off to the dance floor.

I enjoyed seeing Steinhaeuser stepping around with normal people; although he had been drinking quite a bit, he was not yet drunk nor in any immediate danger of causing the type of incident I had grown to fear so much. I turned from this happy scene in order to locate a young lady who had caught my eye earlier this evening. She was standing near the wall next to the other girls and my pace quickened when I caught her already looking at me and smiling.

Just then there was the sound of a horrific crash; I whirled around in time to see the garden doors explode into the room with such force that wood splinters and shattered glass were sent flying on to those unlucky enough to be standing nearby. Women screamed and grown men took a step backwards as an enraged Billiette charged into the room and began making her way towards the dancers.

Her first act was to grab Steinhaeuser's dance partner's face in her mighty hand. With one remarkable thrust Billiette pushed her down to the floor and sent her skidding across the waxed surface with her legs up in the air. She then seized John by tucking him under her muscular arm and held him like a small animal. This completed she began fighting her way out of the room. The Amazon was able to use her free arm as a club and she bashed away at those few brave souls who tried in vain to stop her.

A last attempt to thwart the kidnapping took place at the shattered doors where Col. Beauregard and another man had taken up positions. Armed with lengths of the broken entrance frame, they braced for the final confrontation. Billiette stopped before them with Steinhaeuser still under one arm. She wiped her forearm across her mouth and took a deep breath which expanded her already gigantic chest. Somehow John managed to extract his pocket flask at this point and held it up to his mouth for a long drink. Some of the whiskey spilled down his face as he began a crazy, maniacal laugh.

Beauregard's companion brought his stick down hard against Billiette's free arm and shattered his weapon on impact. At the same moment Steinhaeuser spit a mouthful of whiskey into the Colonel's eyes as Billiette promptly blasted him on the side of the head. Beauregard was spun around from the impact, his face smashed against the door jam and he collapsed to the ground.

Billiette jumped over his motionless body but not before Steinhaeuser let out a wild war whoop and threw his empty flask at the astonished crowd. He could be heard screaming "STEINHAEUSER, DR JOHN STEINHAEUSER" as they disappeared into the night.

I slipped out a side door and have to repair at once to a safe hiding place where I shall stay until securing passage to St. Jo. This is the last straw. I will leave a note for John, wishing him well but insisting that the rest of my journey must be solo.

LETTER FROM THE FOREIGN OFFICE TO BURTON C/O STEINHAEUSER

Capt. R. F. Burton
c/o John Steinhaeuser M.D.
Theobald's Boarding House
416 Rue Lafayette
New Orleans, Louisiana USA
June 26, 1860

Dear Burton:

Dr. Steinhaeuser has been kind enough to send us a brief communiqué regarding your whereabouts, which is more than we have received from you since landing in America more than two months ago. He has reported you "missing," which gives us great cause for concern.

As you are fully aware, your assignment is not to get lost and remain incommunicado but rather to subscribe entirely to the instructions outlined in the documents which were hand delivered to you in New York City. Tensions are rising and we need you at the Great Salt Lake to suss-out the whole Mormon situation.

We at the FO strongly suspect that a man possessed of your great travel skills is not really "lost" but rather "off" and attending to one or another of the dishonourable stunts for which you are becoming famous. However, in the interests of fair play, we shall not consider an official sanction or recall until providing you with an opportunity for explanation. Specifically, would you please consider telling this office what has brought you down to remote Louisiana, so far from the former Colonial States we have interests in, and equally far from the Territories which are also the loci of much desired information? Also, may we ask for a proper elucidation of what has taken place so far? Your ports of call and observations gleaned from conversations with pivotal personages are of special interest to us. As you may recall, this is the very purpose of your trip.

As far as your request for more money is concerned, we are begrudgingly forwarding an extended purse to the deport station at St. Joseph,

Missouri, a Western gateway we expect you to be passing through in the very near future. We fear that an accounting of your expenditures to date would only serve to detail the reasons for your failure to communicate and the quirky travel route. Please work on a palatable and believable presentation of receipts before returning to London.

And, Burton, do take care not to use your special talents to offend anyone while on this mission. The last things we need are reports of excessive drinking, brawling, or miscegenistic trysts with local women.

God Save the Queen,

Lord Palmerston

Her Majesty's Foreign Office

BURTON'S THREE RESPONSES TO LORD PALMER-STON'S LETTER OF JUNE 26, 1860[24]

My Dear Lord Palmerston:

Deepest apologies for the delay in writing. I have been hard at work on a number of sensitive issues which I have hesitated to post for reasons relating to privacy and secure delivery. Suffice it to say that a wide range of important individuals have been contacted and I have acquired a great deal of information on topics which I'm sure will be of great interest to all concerned. I thank you in advance for extending funding for this valuable project. . .

Lord Palmerston:

I regret your concern over my failure to report to the Foreign Office but circumstances have prevented taking time to attend to routine matters. Movement to Louisiana was necessary in order to cement good relations with Col. Beauregard of . . .

---

24 These three draft responses to Palmerston's letter were all written on a single sheet of paper in Burton's tiniest handwriting. Note the degeneration of his salutations and the corresponding reluctance to contrition or convention. —Ed.

Palmerston:

I'm afraid that I have been hard-pressed to dash off a note on spying in America for there have been a number of bothersome little distractions. Let's see, there was the game ball riot in Hoboken, and being booted out of a hotel, a saloon, a campaign headquarters and a debutante ball were also very time consuming. In between, my spare time was occupied by being kidnapped by murderous savages and falling in love with a voodoo princess. I'm sure you understand.

These tribulations notwithstanding, I have managed to assemble some important travel notes which are presented as follows: American electoral politics may be likened to bad circus, and one is in more danger of being killed attempting to enter a convention center than an Indian encampment. I would recommend strongly against taking a holiday in the southern section of Illinois, and one must be sure to carefully preview Captain and crew before accepting bookings on any Mississippi river boat.

Steinhaeuser's conduct has been abominable throughout (thank God he's not British) and I have been forced to cut him loose. No sign of a civil war yet, but I shall keep my eyes skinned and let you know as soon as I see one.

Meanwhile, drink first and believe me,

Ev. Yrs. Sincy.

RF

XI

PREPARATIONS FOR THE
RED INDIAN WEST

July 22, 1860
St. Joseph, Missouri

Eccomi qua[25] across the mighty river and at the frontier of the great and wild American West. I am alone now and this is probably the condition that best suits me, but considering dear John, the alcohol and the problems that surpassed its pleasures overtook him—the embarrassments, the wasted days, and so forth. Curiously, he always advised me when entering the realm of Bacchus that it is all about "control, control, control." I cannot suffer many men who would turn their back on one of the world's best remedies—and why did the learned Arabs of old ever abandon the pleasures that would have continued their advancement?—but America is a different world, where "control" is hard to come by and a land where certain kinds of attractive freedoms constantly dare to challenge the sensibilities of what drink has to offer. There is the newness here and a certain exhilaration that seems to fuel excesses of all sorts. Ah, well. My best to him, but now a different stage of the hunt begins.

At first sight, the dry land port of St. Jo appears to be under siege, for hundreds of white tents surround the city and the crackling of gunfire can be heard any time of the day or night. This later condition may be explained by the scores of bivouacked would-be pioneers and their preposterous preparations for the journey West—to wit, every

---

25 Here I am. —Ed.

dirt farmer and shopkeeper inhabitant of this tent city has recently armed themselves against all perceived trail hazards and are becoming acquainted with their unfamiliar possessions by shooting apart every stray dog, tree stump, and glass bottle in sight. One finds it nearly impossible to enter the city proper without running a gauntlet of "tenderfeet" playing with their new toys.

Once past this dangerous free-fire zone, the traveler may gain some understanding of how this situation came about. A sign posted on the first frame building in town warns:

BEWARE OF CONFIDENCE MEN AND BAD ADVICE, DO NOT LEND YOUR MONEY TO STRANGERS, and finally, WELCOME TO ST. JOSEPH, GATEWAY TO CALIFORNIA.

The so-called pioneers swarm here at St. Jo and then leave like columns of ants heading West in lines of wagons. These are no real pioneers, of course, because all available literature demonstrates that the land had already been nicely pioneered and was well-known to those Indians who came long before them. It may be allowed that it was not populated or exploited enough to suit European tastes, but herein rests the core of the problem—half of the "wildness" of "The Wild West" is based on the resistance to the wagons, their passengers, their designs, and the suffocating feeling that they were never going to stop coming. The other half may be measured by the personalities of the new-comers and the fact that many of them were headed West because they were sacked by the society they came from. Here is fertile ground for the opportunist, for those who have committed capital crimes elsewhere, for hunters such as Speke, and for the takers and the re-makers who want to bring their ways to a new land and have others conform to it. Among the wagon people there are surely passive farmers, the unfairly oppressed and the benignly hopeful, but from what I have seen so far they are outnumbered five to one by a more destructive breed.

Aggressive local merchants have convinced the newcomers that the trail is so dangerously thick with murderous Indians, "rattlers" and "b'ars" that they must arm themselves to the teeth, and it is said that some have paid more for their guns and ammunition than they have for their wagons and food stocks.

The noisy streets are lined with shops catering to the thousands of immigrants wishing for new luck in the promised lands; however, it is difficult to see how the trumpery being sold to them can assist in their quest. At the first "provision" store I happened upon several men who were struggling to hoist a piano aboard a prairie wagon which was already loaded with trunks of women's clothing, a heavy cast iron stove and what appeared to be part of an ornate staircase. The proprietor was assuring his client of the value and appropriateness of her purchase while biting down on a Partagas and counting her money. I fully expect to see these unnecessary items littering the side of the road by the time we reach Turkey Creek.

There is a pandemonium of excitement on the streets as people rush about in the heady atmosphere of confused hope and anticipation. This is an America quite different from any I had previously encountered, for here tempo and tumult approach the Arabesque. St. Jo may be likened to a great wooden bazaar with the intrigues and clamor of the Orient configured in a bold and raw new way.

Arrangements are made on every street corner. There are holy pilgrims with blond hair, buckskin sheiks, assassins wearing cowboy hats, harems of dancehall girls unaccountably singing "Oh California, that is the land for me," and black-skinned Nubians who pride themselves as being "pure sang." Everyone is off to somewhere and no one passes through these parts without being touched somehow by the Grand Vizier, Joseph "Joe" Robidoux, who is the father of this city—and no less than sixty-seven children sired with various women both red and white.

Robidoux's St. Jo here in the Blacksnake Hills marks the beginning of the wild America one imagines back home and is the turning-back point for the genteel, careful women, and the faint of heart. This is a town of hard swearing, stiff drinking and relentless, unmerciful spitting. The aforementioned gun mania that is being promoted to the immigrants is enhanced by a healthy population of weapon-toting regular citizens who bring their imperative tools with them into the town's many saloons, gambling establishments, and bordellos. In this America, no man can separate another from his "shootin' iron" without a fight, and it is of course with guns that most of the fighting gets done.

As one might imagine, this is also a town where physicians skilled in the treatment of gunshot wounds prosper as quickly as undertakers and regulators. All these professionals, like everyone else in St. Jo, double their rates as soon as the sun goes down.

Not to be undone by my new surroundings, I purchased a Bowie knife, a LeMat nine-shooter I picked up in New Orleans, a .70-caliber Hawkins, a double-barrel 12-gauge, two Colt dragoon revolvers, and an air rifle to astonish the Indians. A bit overdone perhaps, but I now feel at home and in league with everyone else in this town. My laibon would surely understand that the pen is surely not enough in this land.

In order to thwart scalp hunters both red and white, I have shaved my head. This act, as foolish as it may appear, might actually save me some trouble in the upcoming journey, for the town is still a-buzz over Major Ormsby's loss of forty militia men to Washos, Pah Utes, and Bannacks at Honey Lake. In addition, the Comanches, Kiowa, and Cheyenne are said to be "out" in Nebraska. The good news from trail scouts is that the Potawatomies are busy trying to kill off the Fox and Crow, and one need not worry too much about the Sioux for they are currently occupied in their efforts to "rub out" the Pawnee. It is to their credit that they have neither overpopulated this land nor exploited its resources, but like everyone else on Earth they are at each other's throats and now can redouble the excitement by adding the wagon people to the mix.

I have taken up residence at the Dipesto Hotel, which is a frowzy dog-hole of a boarding establishment for those with just enough money to forgo the rigors of tent life. This place is owned and operated by a husband and wife team in their mid fifties who are no Darby and Joan. Forever at odds with one another, they nevertheless combine to make a living from pilgrims waiting for convoy or ambulance west. He does everything but cook, and she complains and collects the money.

The drinking establishments in St. Jo are interesting but dangerous, especially after dark, so it was the dining table and sitting room of Chez Dipesto where I made most of my introductions and gathered information regarding the upcoming trip. Mrs. Dipesto looked askance at my brandy and cigar sessions in her parlor, but the love of money reduced her complaints to sharp looks and the noisy handling of kitchen equipment whenever I was within earshot. I'm afraid it was her poor husband who mostly felt the point and edge of her wrath, because she harped after him as he went about his many chores, stomping her foot for attention and punctuation and leaning in close to him for the deliverance of shrieking admonitions. A near perfect example of why I maintain that there is nothing on this earth more fiend-like than a menopausal woman.

On the second evening I dined with a U.S. artillery officer named Lt. Dana. He and his wife were on their way to the newly established Camp Floyd, which was situated within easy striking distance of the Mormon capital at the Great Salt Lake. It seems the United States has come to fear and distrust the Mormons and have sent 2500 men to Utah to keep an eye on them—and perhaps more—should the Nauvoo Legion become restless. Little wonder Palmerston keeps pushing me there.

Lt. Dana recounted some very nasty business that happened a few years back at a place called Mountain Meadows, when a Mormon gang disguised themselves as Indians and attacked a wagon train of settlers. "Nearly everyone was killed," Dana said as a matter of fact. But he did lean away from his wife and softened his voice to inform me further that, "Some of the corpses had been insulted."

He raised his eyebrows at my reaction and continued on secure in the knowledge he had captured my full attention. "They also set fire to Fort Bridger. You knew that didn't you?"

"Why no, Lieutenant, no I didn't. Please feel free to provide the details."

"Burned it to the ground and plundered its stores. I cannot say much beyond what I learned before leaving garrison in Ohio, but the story goes something like this. Mr. Joseph Smith of New York, who by all accounts was a wilder kind of blinking idiot, fancied himself a prophet of God and gathered a following. It all has something to do with golden tablets and multiple wives. At any rate, the number of converts began to grow and as it did the congregation was chased from every place they attempt to settle. People don't like the Mormons. Smith is eventually killed in Illinois and his successor, a fellow named Brigham Young, moves the "Saints"—that's what they call themselves—lock, stock, and barrel to Utah Territory and starts his own nation."

"This is all very fascinating, Lieutenant. Please continue."

The somewhat dapper and clean-cut Dana seemed gratified to deliver this synopsis and eagerly resumed his narrative. "Well, the nation is called the Imperial State of Deseret and is occupied by a large group of followers that is doubling every day. The worst part of the story, and the reason why I am on my way to Camp Floyd, is that the Mormons have become aggressive.

"They are suspicious of outsiders and their leaders fear assassination. Now here is where matters start becoming dangerous. They have assembled a wild bunch of triggermen who call themselves the Danite Band. They are the guardians of Brigham Young and the destroying angel of those who they think pose a threat to the nation. These are the same ones who killed those poor settlers in Mountain Meadows, and the same gang that burned down Ft. Bridger. They are desperadoes and bigamists, Captain Burton, and the United States Army must stand ready to uphold the moral and civil laws of this great country.

"We have targeted three of these criminals in particular, for they are the leaders of the Danites and some of the most ruthless men in the territories. Ephe Hanks is one, and the lawyer turned killer Bill Hickman is another. Though by far and away the worst and most dangerous of them all is Orrin Porter Rockwell. He is the one who shot Governor Liliburn Boggs in the back of the head, shot and killed Lt. Frank Worrell of the Carthage Greys, hunted down Moses Clark, and ended the lives of Joachim Johnson, John Gheen, and the bullwhaker Martin Oats. And that's just to name the most famous of his victims. This Rockwell is a villain of the first water and devilishly accurate with either pistol or rifle. There's not a living soul west of the Mississippi, white or red, who doesn't know and fear his name. Some call him The Son of Thunder."

At this point the door to the Dipesto Hotel burst open and a thick man, clad in buckskins and furs, boldly walked in and placed his hands on his hips. Like everyone else in St. Jo he was well armed, although this particular gent had set himself apart from the others by sporting a great number of glass trade beads about his person, as well as a very conspicuous bear claw necklace, an enormous fur purse, and two large bird feathers which had been affixed to his hair and the side of his very bushy black beard. The smell of old campfires and danger filled the room.

He surveyed the parlour with blazing eyes and a maniacal grin on his face. Finally his booming voice called out and echoed off the walls. "Did I hear mentioned the name of O. P. Rockwell?" He looked about for a moment and growled, "Wal, speak up whoever it was."

The young artillery officer got to his feet and courageously replied, "I am the one sir. Lt. Dana of the United States Army, Mr. Rockwell, but I am unarmed at the moment and ask that you take this into consideration before you. . . ." Mrs. Dana interrupted at this point with a plaintive howl, "George, George, I am too young to be widowed and on the frontier." She dropped to her knees, clutched at the leg of her husband's trousers and turned to the imposing desperado. "Please, I beg you Mr. Rockwell," she sobbed, "we are just beginning our lives, my husband is a good man, I beg you."

This menacing man rested a meaty paw on one of his pistols, then picked a piece of gristle from his teeth and spat it on the floor. He finally grinned down at her, then threw his head back and let out a laugh from deep in his throat. "Why you Gord domned fools! I ain't Rockwell. The name's La Mash, Gaston La Mash, but everyone east of the Rockies knows me as Lord Kill B'ar. Rockwell? Oh that's a good laugh. I know how to fix a rifle alright but I ain't never ended the life a white man, no, just rabbit, deer, b'ar, and such. Had some bad run-ins with Injuns—w'al, bad for them I reckon 'cause I still got my hair." He lifted his cap to reveal a greasy black mane. "No, I just asked to see if ol' O. P. might be in these parts. That would mean some serious damn fireworks if he crossed back into Missouri, yes sir. He had to git up an' git after what he did to Governor Boggs. Wouldn't want to be on the streets around here if he was back 'cause old Port would be takin' a few men with him if the shootin' started. Yes sir, he's one of the best shots in the territory, I'll tell you that. Don't care if he's one o' them Morans or what, he kin shoot to kill and does a-plenty!"

Lord Kill B'ar La Mash flopped down on one of Mrs. Dipesto's parlour seats and began another protracted monologue. "Why don't you git yourself up off the floor, Missus." He pointed to Lt. Dana and said, "An' you better grab your seat again, sonny. Ain't no sense you both actin' like that in front of an ol' mountain man the likes of me. I ain't goin' to hurt ya."

He reached into his fur purse and produced some "fixin's" in preparation for a smoke. Mrs. Dipesto looked on in horror as he swung his muddy boots up on the coffee table then rolled and ignited a crudely made cigar. He casually tossed the spent match over his shoulder and onto the floor behind him.

"Anybody want some of this here kinnekinnick? It'll blast hell out of yer lungs an' give yer head a spin until you settle in with it. How 'bout you young lady, feel like fixin' yourself up some Injun smoke after the start I gave you?" He blew a thick blue cloud into the air and quizzically looked around at the three of us. "I'm just fresh in town and looking to move west, maybe Californie. Hear tell man has room to move around in those parts, not shut-in by weather or what you might call socially confined."

As if to punctuate his last statement he leaned far to one side, lifted a haunch off the seat and let go with an awful fart that whistled and growled in the direction of Mrs. Dana. She screwed her face into a look of outrage and immediately brought her kerchief to her nose and mouth. The officer's wife knitted her eyebrows and grumbled from behind her mask. "Mr. La Mash, pleeease. If you are ill, I recommend you see a physician at once!"

"Oh don't you go worryin' 'bout me, Missus. I feel just fine, haven't been sick since I got fed that Gord domned Shoshone stew. I'll be teetotally rumflumuxed if them savages weren't tryin' to poison me." He began to tilt to one side again and gave a wink at Mrs. Dana. Her eyes widened as she realized it was probably too late for an escape.

Brraaap!

"I fixed them Shoshone up real good later on. Yes sir, you can believe that. Besides, La Mash has a strong meat bag." He patted his stomach. "I've eaten near everything the world's got to offer, both cooked and raw. Why just this afternoon I ate me some cow brains and hoof soup an' washed it on down with last week's goat milk. Didn't bother me one bit, 'cept for a little gas. Nah, an ol' ba'r hunter like me's got to have a strong meat bag, wouldn't last long in the territories without one, you'll see."

He readjusted himself on the couch. "I used to be a trapper up in Colorado Territory 'till the beaver give out—then it was griz. Huntin' ba'r ain't all that easy neither. Them mountains are damn cold, yes sir, you can believe that. Oh, I suppose the cold weren't the only thing. You see I got into some trouble with the Flatheads over a squaw. She was a pretty little thing but wasn't worth a good Gord domn beyond that, couldn't even pull jirk if you kin believe it. That ain't like an Indian gal but it's true, so I took her on back to the chief and told him so, told him I wanted my trade rifle back too.

"Wal, the old chief wasn't too keen on returnin' my rifle, an' he also seemed reluctant to take the squaw back, bein' probably happy to git rid of her in the first place. Things were startin' to git pretty heated so I figured I best prepare for some trouble. Just then the squaw's brother comes whoopin' towards me with a big knife in his hand an' lookin' angry as a train wreck. I reckon he didn't want to see her come back neither.

"There was nothin' left for me to do but pull my revolver and let go a ball at the young brave. Problem was that my aim was off in all the excitement 'cause the ball only caught him in the hip, ricocheted off the bone and came bustin' out the side of his waist. I'll be dumfouzled if that same ball didn't go on to hit the old chief over his left eye and killed him dead right on the spot.

"Wal, the other two braves what wuz there stood still for a moment wonderin' just what the hell they wuz to do? I couldn't believe they wouldn't be angry as wasps when they come to their senses, so I shot them both in the legs before they had a chance to think about it. Shootin' 'em in the legs was a charitable thing to do but it left 'em alive to tell the rest of them Flatheads what happened, an' as you kin expect, the entire nation like to lift my hair right about now, and in that neck o' the woods a man's left to just count the days 'fore that happens.

"So, now you know why La Mash left them mountains and come to Missouri and why I'm lookin' west to start over again." His face lit up when he made the pronouncement, "This time I'm going to hunt buffalo—the Boss!"

XII

BY STAGECOACH INTO THE TERRITORIES

August 7, 1860
Big Muddy Station
Kansas Territory

I cannot say that I was unhappy leaving St. Jo, an altogether disgusting little town where the law is openly and boldly defied everywhere. Further reason was provided by La Mash who took a room at the Dipesto Hotel until he could secure passage west, a move which redoubled Mrs. Dipesto's dyspeptic temperament and brought about still worse service and food. This strained and ever degenerating situation did not seem to bother Lord Kill B'ar in the slightest but was surely having a dramatic effect on everyone else. Mrs. Dana refused to dine at the same table as La Mash, and two other boarders bought a tent and elected to camp out with the pioneers rather than listen to any more of his stories. Mr. Dipesto ran away from wife and home leaving hundreds of little things undone and no one but us for his wife to direct her bitchery.

So, it was with great relief when word reached me and the Danas that our coach was finally ready for the journey to Utah. Mr. Walter Withrow, the contracting agent, appeared in person at Chez Dipesto to make the announcement that fresh mule changes were at last in place at all stations along the trail.

He apologized to the three of us and even rested his small hand on Mrs. Dana's arm to assure her that the journey would be a safe and comfortable one on the Utah Coach. He looked into her eyes and said, "The Withrow Ambulance Co. forbids drinking, profanity, gambling, and travel on Sundays, Mrs. Dana; I trust you will be comfortable with these regulations."

The young woman smiled while nodding and then shot a daggers drawn look at La Mash who had just entered the room.

"Ahh, Mr. La Mash," Withrow said, "just the man I was looking for, I have some good news. There has been a last minute cancellation and the fourth seat on the Utah Coach is now available. Would you still be interested?"

La Mash roared rhetorically, "Whoo-weee! Wal, does a fly land on shit, Withrow?" He turned to Mrs. Dana with widened eyes and asked loudly, "Does spit hit the ground?" He clasped her on the shoulder leaving a filthy handprint and said, "You bet your sister's vent I'll buy that ticket, yes siree Bob."

A greatly satisfied La Mash looked around the room, nodded his head and screamed out. "This here St. Jo's a great little town but it can't hold the likes of me, no sir, you can believe that. No siree, I'm on my way west in high comfort now."

I need not point out that Mrs. Dana was completely devastated by this development and seemed suddenly weak and very pale. In the rush of excitement to share his good news with someone, the hirsute La Mash unnecessarily brought his face within inches of Mrs. Dana's and hollered, "Whoo-wee, Missus! Looks like we're all headin' out together! That'll be just fine with me, I got no particulars 'bout who I move around with just as long as they're decent folk and don't expect no kick-shaws."

Mrs. Dana managed a weak cough and again placed her kerchief over her nose and mouth. Her husband intervened at this point and said, "That will be enough, sir." To which a wild-eyed La Mash responded, "I'll just get a little road stake together and meet everyone at the stables."

Within a half hour we were all crowded aboard the Withrow Ambulance company's Utah Coach and headed into "Bleeding Kansas." We crossed the Missouri River by steam ferry and traversed five miles of bottomland until reaching the rolling prairie. On our way to the first resting station we passed depressing, lonely little shanties at places with names like Cold Spring, Kennekuk Station, and Grasshopper Creek, which are all populated by equally depressing little families trying to wrest a sedentary life from a land best suited to nomadism.

Big Muddy Station was, as its name implies, a swampy and mosquito-infested pigsty of an outpost set against a vista of flatness. Here a lonely proprietor keeps a few mules and hogs but precious other stores. We were only able to take on what is called "cold flour" which is nothing but parched maize pounded into the consistency of meal. This was supper after it was mixed with a little flour and gagged-down as a beverage.

August 11, 1860
O'Fallon's Bluff
Nebraska Territory

Upper Kansas and across southern Nebraska presents mile after end-less mile of scrub grassland or vacuous emptiness. We have been bumping along at the rate of three miles an hour through a vast, dry sea of still texture, burnt earthy smells, and measureless swarms of flies and other biting insects. Praise Allah for the relief of opium over such a stretch for neither Warburg Drops nor the holy weed nicotine could surmount such drudgery.

Reading and writing are out of the question while confined to the Concord coach, for the ride is rough enough to cause nasal hem-orrhage, and annoying bladder and kidney hyperactivity which occa-sions many unscheduled stops along the way. This is of course for everyone but Lord Kill B'ar who manages to contort his person in such a way as to relieve himself through either window or door while on the fly.

Mrs. Dana pretends not to notice this and other stunts, but I can tell that her patience is wearing thin. Gaston La Mash is like a two-year-old child in some ways, forever scrambling in and out the win-dows, toying with and sometimes breaking whatever little gee-gaw he can lay hands on, and most lately bothering our driver or "ripper" who he plies with stories from his past. I overheard him telling the story of the Flathead squaw for the third time last afternoon.

I have long ago exhausted the company of La Mash and the Danas on this just the fourth day out. I try desperately to stay awake long into the night writing by firelight and when the wood burns out, contemplating the stars so sleep may come easy in the coach the next day. To this end I have taken to making nightly camps by myself some distance away from the rest station and the banality and outrages of my cabin mates. They all think I am queer and some have even whispered that I must be mixed with Indian blood to want such a nightly existence. Well, all the better I say.

It was earlier this very evening that I made my fire in a wooded area a good distance from the others at the so-called inn and experienced a most unusual event. While writing notes in the fading campfire light, I had the most peculiar sensation that someone was watching me. I turned quickly and saw nothing, but when I looked again no more than two seconds later I saw the face of an Indian illuminated by the flickering orange of my campfire.

I was quite a distance from my many guns so I concentrated instead on searching his taciturn face in hopes of ascertaining his intentions. And I must say I believe he was doing the same with me. This unblinking engagement lasted far longer than any other of my life. At last he stepped forward from the shadows and exposed himself fully to the light. He was extraordinarily tall and well-made, and his face was painted with two broad horizontal strokes of green and red from cheekbone to cheekbone. He wore a snakeskin band across his brow and had what appeared to be a fox or wolf tail tied to the back of his head. This giant was wearing an un-collared shirt with the tails cut off, a loin cloth, and was unaccountably carrying a pair of trousers.

The tall Indian slowly raised his hand open-palm towards me which is a universal sign of friendly greeting. I responded in kind and uttered the word "*how*," which I have been told means "good" in most Indian languages and is an appropriate and friendly greeting.

"*How* are you doing this fine evening?" he said gravely.

"You speak English."

"Yes. Now I would like to know, how is a white man getting along on the ground and away from his bed and his roof? Other white people do not act this way. Are you an outcast?"

"No I am not. I prefer my own company over that which I have been forced to travel with." He turned a corner of his mouth into a reserved but knowing smile and grunted by way of approval.

"Mmmm, I know what you mean. Other people—bad medicine."

"Would you care for a cup of tea?"

"Yes," he said in a slow, deep voice. "I have had this tea before and it is good. I will sit with you."

I placed another log on the fire and poured him a cup of hot tea. He looked into the cup for a bit before carefully probing the liquid with his finger. "I like to make sure there is not any tea at bottom," he explained. "Makes the last drinks very bitter." He turned the corners of his mouth down and nodded in affirmation. "I also prefer Earl Grey."

"Yes, I understand." Although in truth I did not understand the incongruity of the looks and language abilities at all.

He lifted his head from the cup with a somewhat puzzled look on his face. "You ride with the others but do not make camp with them. This is very strange. And you sleep on the ground when there is good shelter nearby. This is also very strange. Do your people think you are crazy?'

"Well quite frankly some believe I am crazy, others think I do it because they imagine I am part Indian." He looked startled. "No Indian would do something like that, not even a Pawnee. Have the others turned you out because you want to sleep with men?"

"Well no actually. You see I much prefer women."

"Mmmmm. Yes, women are much better to sleep with than men, softer, easier to move." He looked into the fire for several minutes and then addressed me without taking his eyes from the flames. "The reason I have come to you is because my people have a custom. They take a young man from the tribe, make him feel unwelcome and drive him from the tent into the forest where he is forced to camp alone. They do this in the hope that the young man will meet a god who will take pity on him and give him power. With my people, this is how a boy turns into a man."

His eyes left the fire and looked me up and down. "But this happens to only boys when they are young. You are too old for the power quest, I saw that right away. Then I thought maybe you were a god. There is a look about you that is different from the others."

The big Indian let out a soft sigh. "But I know now that you are not a god, just a man like everyone else." His eyes slowly returned to the fire and we sat in silence for the next several minutes.

When he spoke again he asked, "Tell me, man, what do they call you?"

"Richard Burton."

"Mmmm, Richard Bur-ton." He thought for a moment. "Then you are an Irish-man."

"My, you not only know the white man's language but you also seem to be able to recognize the different types of Europeans."

"Yes, but it is a very difficult thing. Mostly they all look the same, especially the bearded ones. To my eye they appear like dogs running away with squirrels in their mouths. It is the sound of the white man's second name that makes the difference. It does not take long to part the O'Boyles from the Beemsterbobers. But I always wonder, what is the meaning of these strange names? It is a cause of much talk around our fires."

"What is your name?" I asked him.

The corners of his mouth turned down and he stared off in the distance. "Never ask an Indian what he is called. Misfortune falls on a man who tells this to a stranger. If there were another here to ask, then he could speak the name."

"Very well then. I will wait for that time, if we should ever meet again."

"Our paths will join again soon. We are travelers to the same place."

"What do you mean? How do you know where I am going?"

"The white man's wagons move along a single path from one horse station to the next. This is the only way they can survive on the land. None of them stop for very long until they reach the salty waters near the land of the Sioux." At the naming of that tribe he frowned and made a slashing move across his throat with the palm and fingers of his open hand. "Bad people, the Lakota. Everyone just calls them Sioux because that is the Ojibwa word meaning enemy."

I asked him if this was where he was going. Is he also traveling to the salty waters?

He stood and looked down at me. "I am going to my fire for the night." My visitor surveyed the immediate area before taking a step and issuing a final statement. "Look out for Indians," he said. "Next to white men, they are the most dangerous thing along the trail."

I did not have any trouble staying awake for the remainder of this evening because I could not get the encounter with the big Indian out of my mind. His version of English was almost a parody of what I was told it would sound like, but who would dare point out such a thing to a specimen like that? What was he doing out roaming about at night, and whatever was the reason for carrying a pair of trousers over his arm? He had obviously spent a great deal of time around whites, but under what circumstances? Why was he wearing ceremonial paint on his face, and what is his business at the salty waters near the land of the Sioux? It was obvious that he was not a returning member of that tribe, and it was well known that Indians from one group were in more danger than white men when it came to crossing into foreign territory.

As the first hint of the new day appeared in the east, I was still sitting in front of the embers wondering about last evening's curious visitor and his prediction that our paths would cross again.

XIII

Fort Laramie

August 15, 1860
Box Elder Creek Station
Wyoming Territory

The first evidence of buffalo appears, although merely in the form of what is called "chips" here on the prairie. These dung piles make convenient fuel in the land of precious few trees and are used just as *argul* is in the Tartary deserts. La Mash has been quite excited by these droppings and today insisted on bringing a disturbingly fresh load into the coach for further examination.

"Yes siree Bob," he explained to Mrs. Dana while squeezing apart a pie. "If'n you expect to hunt the Boss you got to look at his *bois de vache*, there's no gettin' around that. This here will tell you what they et and how long it's been since they wuz around." He brought the steaming mess up close to her face and begged her to take a closer look. "Lookie here, Missus, see them little seeds in thar and them tiny bug carcasses? That means Boss has been down by a stream." Just then the coach must have hit a deep hole or rolled over a large rock, because La Mash lurched forward and smeared Mrs. Dana with buffalo excrement from bosom to nostril.

She gasped with fingers spread wide apart on both hands and then began screaming her husband's name. "George, George, do something, please. Oh, I never, uggh, George, Geooorge!"

Lt. Dana began fumbling around in her bag for something clean in order to attend to his wife, but before he could manage a penitent La Mash began to wipe at her chest with the sleeve of his greasy flannel shirt. This was the limit. Mrs. Dana began slapping him and throwing her hands about as if in an epileptic fit. Her screams became incomprehensible and it was all the Lieutenant and I could do to keep her from leaping from the coach.

The ruckus brought the ambulance to a halt and our ripper, Mr. Mahoney, jumped from his station and appeared wide-eyed at the window with a shotgun in hand. Mrs. Dana freed herself from our grasp, blew out the door past the astonished driver and ran crying on to the prairie.

The young artillery officer caught up with his wife, and in the distance I could see him trying desperately to comfort her with hand motions and offers to help clean away the mess. She fell to her knees, buried her head in her hands and was apparently sobbing.

She eventually calmed down and was persuaded back into the coach but only after being assured that La Mash would ride on top with Mr. Mahoney and not speak with her the rest of the trip. Fortunately we were just six hours from Fort Laramie, where we thought it would be possible to bring her into surroundings not too unfamiliar for an army wife.

As things later turned out, the fort itself was not exactly appointed as one might expect a U.S. Army post to be. In fact, it may be said that Fort Laramie was the last insult to the memory of proper military discipline, order, or any kind of a defensive installation. To begin with, there were less than two hundred uniformed men posted to Fort Laramie, a number that was easily doubled by the variety of Indians and civilian desperadoes who freely mixed with the soldiers. I had imagined a timbered stockade with a proper gate and cannon the likes of what we had seen at Fort Kearney, but here was just a rough assortment of outbuildings and a large stable. Had these structures not been arranged around a flagpole there would not be the slightest hint that one was in a military garrison.

After approaching and freely entering the wall-less fort without challenge from sentry or day officer, Mr. Mahoney unhitched the team and immediately headed for the first tavern in sight. This was a small task for I counted no less than three such establishments scattered among the eight other log buildings on site. Lt. and Mrs. Dana made directly for the Commanding Officer's residence, and La Mash and I wandered into the fort's trading post.

Just inside the door we were approached by an eager Indian wearing a blanket and a felt Rocky Mountain hat with broad brim and tall, steeple crown. "*How* friends," he said. "It is good to see you again. I have been waiting for you for five cycles. Now we can talk and exchange many presents. My wife is just outside. She has meat and some coffee. How was your trip?" I was certain that I had never seen this fellow before in my life and I asked La Mash if he had made the man's acquaintance sometime in the past. He shrugged his shoulders.

Inside the establishment we approached the counter, but he followed us and wondered aloud again about our trip after leaving St. Jo. "Seen any Indians?" he asked. "The trail is very bumpy isn't it? You must be happy to be here and rest. I'll go and make sure that my wife will make the coffee to your liking." There was much hand-shaking before he turned with a giggle and bounced out the door.

The man behind the counter shook his head. "That's just Ben Acts-Like-He-Knows-You. Crazy little fellow does this to everyone in camp. Not just white folks or new arrivals either—other Indians, soldiers, Mormons. It don't make no difference. He likes to strike off towards California with different groups after he meets them, sort of tags along after the wagon trains trying to do this or that and hoping people will take him in. Usually don't make it past Greasewood Creek before he's right back here an' doing the same thing all over again."

"What about his wife," I asked. "Does she go along too?"

"Ben Acts-Like-He-Knows-You ain't got no damn squaw. People around here can't even tell what tribe of Indian he belongs to. The Irish soldiers treat him as kind of a mascot and look out for him. Don't know how he'd get by any other way."

We purchased a few items at the fort's store and decided to join Mahoney in a cup of kindness. As we walked through the commons we passed Ben Acts-Like-He-Knows-You who acted like Ben He-Never-Saw-Us and entered the Fort Laramie Saloon. This establishment provided the first glimpse of military life as one is accustomed to seeing it—the enlisted men were all crowded around the bar while their officers were comfortably seated in a better section of the room near the fireplace. Everyone stopped talking and turned to look at us as we entered the room.

At last one particularly haughty officer called out to us. By his accent I could tell he was of southern extraction, and from the cut of his uniform and neatly trimmed moustache and hair patch under his lip, it appeared the man fancied himself something of a cavalier. He assumed a fashionable pose and addressed his fellow officers.

"Ahh, by the look of things gentlemen I'd guess we are finally being visited by a well-bred traveler and," he paused for a moment and flashed a look of disdain towards La Mash, "perhaps his body-guard or meat hunter.

"Well, sir, join us for a drink of pure Cincinnati, and have your man wait over at the enlisted man's bar. Ah believe they are serving Indian liquor at the moment, but they may even pour some mescal brandy before the afternoon is over." His fellow officers chortled at the segregational allusions and pulled over an empty chair from a nearby table. La Mash took a hard look at the young officer and for a moment I thought there may be trouble; but instead he threw his head back, roared one of his unmistakable laughs, and elected to join the regular soldiers, which I believe would be his want in any case.

It did not take long for the officers to determine that I was English and a military man of rank myself. Once these two important distinctions were established, the men around the table felt free to speak to me as they would among themselves, and in this way I was able to be privy to many interesting anecdotes. Squaring with my initial impressions, I quickly had it confirmed that the officers considered themselves aristocrats, if not medieval knights within their limited circles. They were almost exclusively from the South and went out of their way to distance themselves from the mostly German and Scotch/Irish troopers whom they considered peasants.

They told a joke at the expense of a fellow officer who was conveniently absent. It seems he had recently been charged with conduct unbecoming a gentleman for beating his Scandinavian wife while drunk. But at this table additional charges were brought by his peers who accused him of conduct unbefitting an officer for marrying the woman in the first place.

And they did not like the Mormons, not one bit. They considered them murderous fanatics and pined for an opportunity to join with the forces stationed at Camp Floyd to drive the Saints into the Salt Lake. Part of this is due to the fact that all the men were wildly fond of Col. James Bridger—affectionately called "Old Gabe"—who shares with Christopher Carson of the Wind River the honour of being the best guide and interpreter in Indian country. The officers took personal offense when Rockwell and the rest of the Mormons decided to burn his fort and destroy his stores.

The Mormons claimed Bridger was the cause of their Indian troubles. No one in the Territory but the Mormons will have a minute of this—not even the Indians themselves. The men at Fort Laramie were also furious about the Mormons providing the local tribes with Albright Percussion Rifles, with which they did regular and deadly damage. And the Mormons' refusal to supply provisions to passing travelers was seen as ungentlemanly.

By this time La Mash was well on his way with the enlisted men. He was regaling them with his trapping and bear hunting tales and, yes, I believe I overheard a retelling of the Flathead squaw story at least twice. Each time a great howl of laughter and obscenities came from the soldiers at the bar. An officer looked over at the men and commented that one could not expect all the cardinal virtues for thirteen dollars a month.

I took my drink over to the bar and attempted to bridge the payroll gap. La Mash was in mid-proclamation when I arrived—"I would just like to see a man try 'n make me do what I don't want to do. Why that's all I live for. I'd burst any varmint that tried, yes sir, you can believe that. I'm the first cousin to Beelzebub, an' that's a fact."

One of the soldiers raised a glass and in doubly-Dublin brogue shouted, "I'll give a Kilkenney hurroo to that."

La Mash offered to refill the man's cup and asked what he was drinking.

"Missouri White Mule!"

"Tarantula Juice," yelled another.

"Make mine a Leg Stretcher," offered a third.

A soldier with an intelligent face approached me and said that some of his friends tend to become quarrelsome and dangerous when they get going like this. He warned me that the last step in the process happens when a drink called "Tangle Foot" is brought out. I was almost afraid to ask what sets "Tangle Foot" apart from the other poisons and I believe the young man anticipated this because he launched into a description straightaway.

"They call it that because a man can't walk but ten yards before he begins to wobble 'n falls down. The record is twenty yards. Sergeant Buck made it that far back in April. Man's a legend for it, maybe more like a hero. Most people just have to stay put where they drink it, 'lessn they want to fall down. Can't really blame a man though once you consider what they put into it."

"Alright, private, what do they put into Tangle Foot to make it so potent?"

"Well, sir, to the best of my knowledge it's made-up of pure diluted alcohol, chili and regular pepper, tobacco, gunpowder and," he swallowed hard, "nitric acid."

"Lovely. Sounds like it could destroy the constitution of an ostrich. I'm surprised it doesn't kill you after tangling your legs."

The young private thought for a bit and said, 'Well, sir, I believe it's done that too."

I walked out of the drinking establishment and a few of the other men followed after me claiming they did not want any part of what they were sure was about to happen. From the looks of him they were certain La Mash would call for the strongest drink in the house and they all were aware of the results. One of them ventured further on the subject of my companion. "Your friend Mr. La Mash surely has ol' grit to him. He will fit very well in Wyoming Territory, I can tell you that. Both red and white men seem to be cut from a certain cloth in these parts. Very tough people, very rugged, men willing to roister about with trouble at a moment's notice. You take that Indian right over there, but for God's sake don't be lookin' at him. He owns a reputation for being the most feared man in the territory, cut a man to pieces in a knife and hatchet duel just last month, and nobody around here's about to do anything on account of it neither. Oooh, he's someone to be reckoned with alright, and everyone from St. Jo Mo to California knows it too.

"He's a Delaware. Col. Parker swears that they're sure as a Colt's revolving pistol when it comes to trailing and tracking, and that one there's about the best of his kind." The soldier lowered his voice even more and said, "He's killed everything there is, man and beast, and he's second to none in a rough and tumble as well. Name's Rifle Shot. They say he can shave the eyelashes off a wolf as far as a shootin' iron can carry a ball and put an arrow through a keyhole a hundred yards away. Used to be a scout for Col. Parker but he up an' quit one day. Nobody really knows why 'cause he only speaks in pantomimic signals—you know, sign language—and even then he don't say much. Some maintain he can't speak nor hear a word."

Just then the object of this conversation unaccountably turned and fixed us with a very severe look. The young private began to tremble and he immediately looked down at his boots in an obvious effort to show submission. On the other hand, I was not able to release my eyes from his stern gaze for I realized that the man called Rifle Shot was the big Indian who had visited my campfire five nights earlier.

The soldier began to shuffle away and for an instant I thought I saw a corner of the Indian's mouth turn into something approaching a smile. He slowly raised his hand with open palm towards me and then moved on.

At this point a trooper staggered out from the Fort Laramie Saloon, wobbled forward a few steps and then collapsed into the dust. La Mash and the others were crowded at the doorway and watched him intently until the crash. Some money was exchanged and I overheard my companion bellow, "Why I'll be in-tire exflumicated! Hee hee, you fellas were right all along, an' it was worth the dollar to see it too. That ol' Tangle Foot's powerful as a mule's capriole, you can believe that! I got to git some in me right away an' fix a few more bottles for later on. Yeee-haw, com'on boys, we got a heap of drinkin' to do." They all disappeared back into the saloon leaving the poor soldier still on the ground; he was now pointing up into the sky and jibbering on about some place in Kansas and a girl named Clemmy.

Mrs. Dana was still in the Commanding Officer's residence, and as I passed the window of that building I could see Col. Parker's wife comforting her with a grave look of concern on her face and offering the shaken young woman another cup of hot tea. Could there be any doubt that Mrs. Parker was hearing first-hand the horrors of being confined to a coach with a man like Gaston La Mash? I do not know, but surely this was not the first poor feminine soul unnerved by territorial life who was in need of a woman's soft touch and some kind words. I offered a silent salute to Mrs. Parker as I passed, knowing that this would not be her last refugee nor the extent of her extra duty on this rugged frontier.

A few paces past the Parker residence I ran into Mr. Mahoney who had stumbled out from one of the fort's other pothouses. After taking a moment to recognize me he asked if I would be "sleepin' Injun style" again this evening. My answer was that tonight I would be enjoying my solitude more than ever because of what was taking place at the Ft. Laramie Saloon.

"And just what would that be?" he asked.

I explained that La Mash was taking on a drink called Tangle Foot with some of the regular soldiers and that there was sure to be some sort of outrage as a consequence.

He considered this for a moment with a dazed look on his face, then smiled and staggered over to join them. I went to the coach, gathered my belongings and resolved to make tonight's camp even farther away than usual.

For this purpose I secured a mount for the evening and slipped out the back of the stable in order to avoid Ben Acts-Like-He-Knows-You. He was obviously shopping the grounds for general affiliation and perhaps even someone to accompany on a move somewhere else. I headed off from the fort for over an hour until discovering a wooded area by a stream. Here I unloaded my kit and began preparing for the night.

This day's sunset was magnificent in this delightful and secluded little spot. It is a pleasure to enjoy the splendid topography and fresh evergreen aroma of the Medicine Bow range after the relentless, horizontal tedium of the prairie lands and its smell of burnt grass and roasted buffalo chips.

Just after the last light slanted through the trees and faded into early darkness the temperature began to drop and I was having second thoughts about being this far from the warmth of the fort and a hot meal. I was gazing into the campfire, listening to its cracks and poppings when I thought I heard something else off in the darkness. I turned to the direction of the noise and gripped my pistol in anticipation of some trouble. Sitting motionless, I listened hard in complete silence for several moments until I was reasonably sure that the odd noise was just a random, natural sound and not associated with an unwanted intrusion. I relaxed after a few additional moments of anticipation then almost experienced heart ossification when I turned back to the fire and saw Rifle Shot sitting across from me.

"Wah, you look frightened Bur-ton. Did you think I would attack you?"

"No I did not, but I must say you gave me quite a start. Do you always sneak up on people like this, Mr. Rifle Shot?"

"Mmmm, you have learned my name from someone else. That is good." He nodded in approval. I was still a bit upset and warned him that a man could be fired upon when he sneaks up on an armed camp and that there was a danger I might have killed him.

The big Indian looked at me matter-of-factly. "I do not think so." He pointed off into the darkness, "You were looking in the wrong direction until after I joined the fire. That is no way to prepare to kill a man, looking where he is not."

It was, I believe, out of consideration that he wished to change the subject. "Rifle Shot has thought of Bur-ton many times. It is fine that you do not wish to camp with the others. They smell like the hogs they keep and they drink the devil's water. Make plenty noise," he shook his head in disgust. "Bad medicine. But you are not fit to camp alone Bur-ton, you may be killed by Indians. They will take your boots. Wah, Bur-ton, you must spread your blanket with me and share Rifle Shot's fire. We will have the women prepare food. Then we will take the big smoke. It will be good."

I did not wish to disagree with the man, especially after learning of his reputation. I suspect there is no debating that I'd feel safer in his company, and this would be an unparalleled chance to see first-hand the workings of an Indian in a domestic situation. I do not count my slavery with the Tunica as anything but a fortnight of misery and impressed labour.

I was settled at Rifle Shot's camp within a half hour. There was a conical bivouac similar in shape to the ones employed by Captain Rhodes' regiment in the Punjab, a half-faced affair covered with gutta-percha cloth that seemed to be for more informal resting. Two squaws busied themselves about the camp; both had difficulty keeping their eyes from me and I confess that one of them had my almost full attention in return. She boasted that *beaute du diable* with faultless, dentist's teeth, bovine brown eyes, and satin long black hair.

Rifle Shot immediately went to the fire and pulled a piece of roasted flesh from a small animal on a spit. He bit off a chunk of meat, began chewing very purposefully and motioned to the carcass with the portion still in his hand. I was to join him in a meal. I was made to feel right at home, alternately eating and accepting his pipe. It was in this relaxed atmosphere that I asked if I could quiz him on a number of issues that have been puzzling me since we first met. He kept eating but nodded in approval.

"Well, the first thing that comes to mind is this business of carrying your trousers. It seems so much easier to just wear them. After all, you do wear a button shirt, so western clothing cannot be the problem."

He turned his head to face me and said, "No, there is no problem. I like the white man's robes; fine colours, soft." He closely examined the piece of food in his hand. "I prefer to carry the trousers because of the marking."

"Marking?"

"Yes, you see, when I was a young man I once shot a rattlesnake that was crossing a river; just one bullet. None of my people had ever seen such a thing before and for this fine shot I received the honor of having a serpent drawn on me." He stood up and proudly opened his shirt to reveal a tattoo of a blue snake coiled around his waist. He then lifted his breechcloth and displayed the lower half of the body decoration which wound-down to the pelvic area and terminated with a depiction of the serpents head upon that part of the anatomy which the ladies especially will be able to guess.

The squaws interrupted their work and grinned broadly at the display. I wanted to pull my eyes from his private part so I made an inquiry about the prettier of the two young women. "They are both my wife." He said indifferently. "Sisters. Keeps the tent quiet. They are less likely to fight. He looked over to see if they were listening and finding them occupied, continued his story in softer tones. "I had to make it that way after coming back from hunting one day at the end of the last snows. I had just one squaw then. When I come home one day she says, 'Rifle Shot, I know you not off hunting, you off seeing another woman.' I told her I was at Three Trees hunting for fox, no other women there."

"She throw dinner on ground and cry for two days." He gritted his teeth and shook his head. "No other women near Three Trees. All make up in head.

"Wah, Bur-ton, for Delaware people, when a man and a woman eat together too much, the man's hunger begins to weaken while the woman's hunger grows. Hungry woman think man is eating from another bowl, maybe not bringing enough food to her. Hungry woman go crazy, on war path with words. Make sure man's life filled with many sorrows. This is the cause of much fighting." The big Indian turned to me with palms lifted toward the sky and in an exasperated voice asked, "Tell me, Bur-ton, is this the way among white people?"

I told him that unfortunately the Delaware were not the only ones with these problems. "It is the same story wherever I have traveled, my friend. There is no escape and no known cure."

"No, no cure," he said. "But marry two squaw and get sisters, big help."

I asked if this solution would not eventually result in them joining forces against him.

"That is one thing Delaware do have cure for." He grabbed a nearby rock the size of an orange and brought it to eye level for our examination. "Squaw-husher," he said with a malevolent grin. "Work good!"

"Quite so, old fellow," I said nervously. "But now may I ask you about some other things that have been puzzling me?"

He tossed the rock aside and resumed eating. "You have many questions, Bur-ton, but I do not mind. A man must speak straight with another when they sit around the same fire."

"Very well then, you told me that we were traveling to the same place—the city by the salty waters? That is where the so-called Saints live. I wonder if I might ask what business you have with them."

"I am going to use-up the Big Mormon."

"I'm afraid I do not understand. You mean you wish to *kill* Mr. Brigham Young?"

Rifle Shot looked hard into the fire and said, "Rub him from the earth."

It seems the Delaware had long expected wergild compensation to the kindred of a slain person. Apparently, someone of great value to Rifle Shot had been murdered by a Mormon, and now payment was due in the blood of a man of equal value and Rifle Shot had elected to go for the very top.

"I will use him up for Yellow Bear. They are no saints and he is no god," he said bitterly. "Yellow Bear had no scars on his back before meeting Mormons. Then he was shot from behind like a coward who was running away. This is not right. Yellow Bear did not run from any man."

"And this is why you quit being a scout for Col. Parker?"

Rifle Shot's mouth was a straight line across his face. "Mmmmm."

"Look, Rifle Shot, this assassination business may not be as easy as you think. Have you ever heard of Orrin Porter Rockwell? He is Brigham Young's bodyguard and is said to be a man second to none with a pistol and rifle. They call him the avenging angel." Rifle Shot cast great doubt on this pronouncement and was perhaps a bit offended. He gave me a look that I hope never to see again in my life and after a long pause said, "Wah, I do not think so. This Rock-well is the one who tried to rub-out the Great Father in Missouri, the governor Boggs. Shot him from behind like Yellow Bear. He is a

coward and I will use him up too on my way to the Big Mormon."
He once again cast that look of ultimate severity and commitment.
"A hard rain is going to fall Bur-ton. They will both die." Then there
was some hushed chanting.

Thank God the women appeared at this time with additional
food. Rifle Shot seemed to be entering a state that I did not think
healthy. It was as if he were reliving the death of his friend in his
mind's eye and steeling himself for the upcoming battle.

He caught me exchanging purposeful glances with the prettier of
the two sisters and asked if I knew any sign language. I said I did not.
"Just cross hands over your chest in front of the one you prefer. Every
squaw know what that means."

"Oh, I am sorry, I hope you are not offended that I showed interest."

"There is nothing wrong with showing interest in a woman.
Which do you prefer?"

"Prefer? Why, I do not wish to pretend to either of your wives,
sir."

"Why not? Does it hurt you to look at them? You must pick one
for companionship this evening, it is our custom."

"Oh, I see," was my response while ogling the one possessed of
the splendid smile and superior limb development. "If that is the custom."

The warmth of the squaw and the buffalo robe made for a most delightful evening. I had dreams of Shihab in Zanzibar, and later Marie
Laveau appeared riding a stallion alongside the Sultana. I was deep
within the realm of mighty Morpheus and cannot recall a more re-
warding evening as I woke several times in answer to the squaw and
then drifted back to sleep with her in my arms. Her hair smelled like
wood smoke and honey.

I awoke with the first light of dawn and was alone under my
kit blanket. Except for my bag and horse, everything from the night
before was gone. There was not even a trace of the campfire. I do not
know how it was possible for the three of them to break down such
a camp and disappear without my knowledge, but this is exactly what

happened sometime on that most memorable night in the Medicine Bow.

Burton's letter to Mockton Milnes, Lord Houghton, August 19th, 1860

My Dear Milnes:

I write from the land of many rough knocks where hemlock and wild onions is the antidote to scurvy and where your scalp may be danced over the return of an unsatisfactory squaw. Just last evening I witnessed a regular trooper who had been "pole-axed" after a drink of something called Tangle Foot.

If you think the continental French are bad, you would positively stare at what they have become just a generation removed over here in America. One of my companions, a Monsieur La Mash, claims to be the son of a soldier in *Le Grande Armee*; however, I doubt even the rattiest of Napoleon's little folk could have sired such a creature, even if mated with a grizzly bear. The man has found the most ingenious ways of torturing the poor soul of a soldier's wife who is trapped with him in our carriage. He has already managed to pass wind close to her face, urinate out her window, and befoul her bosom with buffalo feces. The hilarious details are best provided in person and shall be upon my return. I have been refrigerated by rain and nearly bled to death by an atrocity of mosquitoes, which are twice the size of anything like them in Africa. Food along the trail west is nothing short of a disaster of fat and sinew. Wolf mutton made from coyote is bad, but old bull buffalo meat is a match for elk when it comes to being dry and gamy.

The coffee is weak and vile, and the dented tin cups in which it is served are positively slippery with grease. Mawkish green and poisonous fritters are served along with doughnuts at every stop. The truth is they are only fit for the herd animals that are penned next to these foul doggeries of restaurants and should never be offered for human consumption. Nomadic Arabs eat better in the desert and maintain better sanitation on their left hand. I shall not even go into what happens here with firearms and associated violence save to ask if you have heard of an outlaw named Orrin Porter Rockwell. Probably not. He is the talk of the frontier west of the Missouri and is called the Mormon Avenging Angel for the number of his celebrated assassinations. I anticipate there is soon to be a confrontation between Rockwell and a tall Indian of my acquaintance who also enjoys something of a reputation in these parts. It shows all signs of being a very bloody affair and there is a chance yours truly will be on hand to witness and report. I shall keep you posted. Speaking of that, could you have a word with Palmerston on my behalf? He is likely beside himself with anger at not hearing from me.

Adieu por le moment and my lonely salaam's to Mrs. Houghton.

I have the honour, Sir,

Your obedient servant,

Richd F. Burton, Capt.

Bombay Army

A Second Letter to F.F. Arbuthnot

Caro Bummy,[26]

It was so good to see you again while on furlough in London. Could it really have been five years since India? And speaking of that place, what of Lumsden, I forgot to ask.

Your fascination with Balzac interests me but not as much as our discussion regarding a translation and publication of the *Ananga Ranga.* The Methodists have done to Oriental writing what Bowdler has to Shakespeare, and what better rejoinder than to shiver those tender and sententious prigs with an un-castrated English version of an East Indian marriage manual with all its frank recipes for love philters, aphrodisiacs, and orgasm?

We will talk more later on this and with Ashbee—should make for a few nights' entertainment. As for now, I am at camp in Wyoming Territory, which is filled with personages that would satisfy your

---

26 This letter was almost certainly written to Foster Fitzgerald Arbuthnot, a close friend of Burton and a collaborator on the translation of the Anaga Ranga and other erotic Oriental texts. —Ed.

Maupassantian love for low-lives and the acts which give them form. This is the case across the land as a general rule, but I have noticed that the human character declines considerably as one pushes west from the Mississippi. Here truly is *La Comedie Humaine* where one may meet virtually everyone who either could not or would not fit in the conventional society of Europe or the American east. These are the whites who have pressed themselves hard up upon the unsuspecting American aborigine, and may I point out that these same Euro-American ambassadors easily surpass the red man in every category of barbarism and raw savagery.

This is not to say that our red brothers, especially those peripatetic Plains Indians, are without human failings. While I think their intertribal warfare is laced with more horror than that which is directed against the whites, it is a certainty that the careless pioneer can easily lose both scalp and cod over a variety of misunderstandings. Most of these have to do with possessions. The Indians are daring and expert kleptomaniacs who for some reason see the liberation of whatever is not bolted down and heavily guarded perfectly justified against the loss of their own possessions—namely their game, their self-respect, and their traditional homelands.

Along with Southern slavery, the uprooting and movement of the American Indian is a national disgrace. Nevertheless, there have been no shortage of hostile Indian changes to the tribal map over the past thousand years, and one of the worst turns administered to me so far was being "done up," as they say in these parts, by a black slave who attempted to pass down his misfortune to one who had caused him no harm.

Remember, Bummy, the disease lies in the species; it is not particular to time nor skin colour. It might be argued that whites are better at these treacheries than shaded people, but I have seen too much around the world to award the title just yet.

The prairie ambulance is a paroxysm of *ennui*, the food along the route is unfit for a wild dog, and the deportment of my fellow travelers has, on a nightly basis, sent me to the society I most desire—my own. I have seen the American *de lunatico* over a sporting event, an election, a home cure of simple dirt, a hoodoo curse, and a drink.

This is a large, diverse and very strange country. My reason for being here has to do with a prophesy made by a laibon in Zanzibar. It is a complicated story, but for the moment suffice it to say that I am here changing cycles, hunting for the meaning of Man, and trying to fulfill my fate.

We first met between my pilgrimages to Meccah and Harrar, and this letter finds me a pilgrim once again now headed to the Mormon City of the Saints where a man is said to be able to enjoy the delights of multiple wives. Please do not worry about me, Bummy. I have brought along a copy of the *Stage of the Bodiless One*, our guide to preventing sexual satiety in a relationship and the book which instructs the husband to vary the enjoyment with his wife so he may live with her as with thirty-two women. With this in hand and five able Mormon maidens, I expect 160 carnal episodes in my scheduled five-day visit. Oh well, Bummy, *militat omnis amans*[27] and it appears as if I am going to war once again.

On the hunt of Man

I am

RFB

---

27 Every lover is a soldier. —Ed.

XIV

THE PONY EXPRESS AND THE
TRAVELLERS' TRAVAILS

August 21, 1860
Simpson's Hollow
Wyoming Territory

We endure wasted mile after endless mile of wild sage in between pools of alkaline waters which are dangerous to both cattle and man. The last station was run by a hopeless family of Canadians who could provide little more than second-rate blacksmith services. We dined on a supper of cold and glutinous peas, and later, instead of salt, we sprinkled a little gunpowder on tough, overcooked mule stakes. These are *mauvaises terres* and may be likened to Tartarus in Virgil's *Aeneid*. Dead cattle lie in different states of decomposition beside the trail along with the hastily prepared graves of would-be settlers who found premature and unhappy ends to their search for an earthly paradise. We are among dead men.

As predicted, this way west is now also littered with much of the superfluous trumpery which I saw being purchased in St. Jo. Things that seemed so needful in relatively settled Missouri are now merely roadside decorations here in Wyoming after being discarded to lighten overbearing loads. They have become nothing more than ominously out-of-place carcasses that have been picked apart by Indians. The red man must do this work at night and has managed to salvage every useable part down to the very last screw.

A notable break in the monotony came at midday when we were overtaken by a single rider who passed us at full gallop then unaccountably stopped just ahead and waited for us to catch up. Mahoney, who I suspect was still drunk from the night before, pulled our ambulance to the side of the trail and began fumbling under the seat for his "scatter gun."

When we approached, we could see that the rider was a very young man, covered in road dust and in appearance did in no way seem threatening to us. He wore a boyish grin on his face and kept moving his hand up and down before his mouth. Mahoney was beside himself. He apparently couldn't locate his shotgun and was now tugging on the handle of his side arm trying to free it from its holster. Now both hands were on the pistol grip, and with one last frantic heave he managed to pull himself completely off the buckboard and down headfirst into the rocky ground. His gun discharged immediately upon impact and blew the heel off his right boot.

The young man dismounted and rushed to Mahoney's side. "Holy Saviour, mister, you damn near blowed your own foot off. I wuz just trying to ask for a drink of water, that's all." He began laughing and addressed the passengers in the coach. "Did ya see that everybody? The damn fool almost blowed his own foot off."

Mahoney made some growling and groaning noises and began trying to untangle himself and get up from the ground.

"You smell like you dun took a bath in rye whiskey, mister. Yup, yezzsir, that's what that smell is alright, rye whiskey."

Lt. Dana stepped from the coach and offered the young man a drink from his canteen. He commented what an unusual thing it was to see a horseman riding so hard and alone in this forsaken part of the country. The young man took two swallows of water and spit out a third. "Well, that's my job. Don't tell me you ain't never heard of the Pony Express? Poster on the stable over in St. Jo said they's lookin' for wiry young fellows not over eighteen who's willin' to risk death—an' that they prefer orphans—an' I say, well hell, that's me! Father died of fever three years ago, an' I took care of momma 'till she passed last month. Nobody left now, so I took that job because they offered it to me." He looked about at the rest of us and gave a genial nod. "And I took the twenty-five dollars a week too." He took another swig on Lt. Dana's canteen and thanked him very politely. As he walked back to his horse he patted the dazed Mahoney on the shoulder. "You take care old man, an' don't be drinkin' so damn much. There's wimmin a-ridin' behind you that needs carrin' for."

He remounted, flashed a carefree smile and tugged his horse around. He waved his hat over his head and shouted out, "Missouri to California in ten days or less. U.S. Mail on the move!"

I noticed that the Danas were holding each other's hand as they watched him ride off. It were as if they were looking together into the future and imagining a boy of their own who they had success-fully brought to the brink of manhood, a good boy with a cheery grin and a whole world to look forward to. La Mash began hacking and spit something awful into the dirt. "Ten days to Californie? Naw, I can't see it. Too much that can go wrong, you can believe that. Why, I knew a fella once that tried bringin' a packet of letters from Denver City to Durango all by hisself. Said he wuz a Messican Var-quero or some damn such and that he could ride like the wind. Wal, he didn't make it, got an arrow stuck right in the middle of his fid and froze to death while he was tryin' to crawl away."

Using himself as a model, La Mash rumbled over before Mrs. Dana and took the time to point to the exact place the arrow entered the man's body. "Right here, squar on the fid, can ya believe that, Missy? What a shot that Injun must have been. They only found him by trackin' the frozen blood in the snow. I'll be in-tire rumfluxed if I know why they think some runny nose kid can git to Californie all by hisself, just don't make no sense."

He thought for a moment, threw his head back and roared a wild laugh. "If he would've lived one sure fire thing he wouldn't have to worry about is gettin' hit in that same spot with an arrow. Nope, that there was one shot in a million, you can believe that." La Mash fin-ished off the sentence by reaching deep into the front of his trousers and unabashedly scratching himself.

Mrs. Dana lost control. "Oh for John's sake, Mr. La Mash, can't you find a good word about anything? Every time you open your mouth all that comes out is some vile story about death or filth or suffering . . . or spit." She brought her hand to her mouth and quickly turned back for the coach.

La Mash seemed positively astounded at her behaviour. "Now what do you suppose got into her?" he asked to no one in particular. "Damn wimmin's as unpredictable as a dust storm. One minute they's just fine, an' another they's at your throat." He clapped Lt. Dana on the back. "Suspect you know all about that, the way they'll turn on you with no warning. You can believe that can't you, general?"

Lt. Dana glanced over at his wife and back at La Mash with a defeated and sick look on his face. This in turn prompted Lord Kill Ba'r into still more dialogue. "Man's got a right to express hisself in this country ain't that right, Capt. Burton? We ain't got no king around here what says what a man can and can't do, an' that's a fact." La Mash looked out at the horizon and said, "Why I just live for the time a man's gunna try an' tell me to do somethin' I don't want to do."

Mr. Mahoney took this opportunity to add his own appraisal of the Pony Express system. "The boys riding this route need to look out for Mormons more than Indians. The firm of Magraw and Hockaday been handlin' the mail from Independence to Salt Lake City until just recently. Now it's the Brigham Young Express and Carrying Company that's gettin' all the work—the YX is what they call it. You know why they're carryin' all the mail now don't you?" No one spoke and Mahoney carried on. "Anybody think it might have somethin' to do with ol' Bill Hickman and Orrin Porter Rockwell? Who do you think killed Mr. Babbitt? That wasn't no Indian—that was Port Rockwell disguised as an Indian is what it really wuz. And Captain Gunnison and those seven other Pacific Railroad surveyin' boys? Weren't no Pahvant braves. Was Port Rockwell again, 'cept that time he didn't bother with no disguise."

I asked Mahoney if we were getting near Mr. Rockwell's headquarters.

"Last I heared he opened a place called Murder's Bar over at Buckeye Flat. He was usin' the name James B. Brown 'cause when he had that halfway house on the American River him and Boyd Dixie got into to a shootin' match which occasioned the wildest whiskey fest ever seen in the gold fields. That there wuz an ugly mess if there ever wuz one. Troopers should've been called in to end it but they wuz nowhere to be seen."

We re-boarded the coach and pressed on toward the next station. Mahoney called into the passenger section and said that we were running past schedule and would be driving into the night and hoping to reach Dry Sandy Creek by midnight. That afternoon seemed to drag on longer than usual and the passengers' attitudes were noticeably affected. A completely bored La Mash twisted and turned about inside the coach, forever shifting his person and in the process sometimes coming dangerously close to Mrs. Dana. She in turn sucked at her teeth whenever he came near, put a hankie up to cover her mouth and nose and clutched her husband's arm very tightly. Lt. Dana felt his wife was too confining sometimes and when he wished for more freedom by changing positions, she felt insulted and abandoned and threw herself into a dyspeptic fit.

Relief came at sunset when we came upon a caravan of wagons that had left from St. Jo almost one month earlier. We stopped briefly to rest the mules and allowed them to feed on the tolerable grass available near the campsite. This also provided a few hours' rest for our human party, but I must say the mules were much luckier in terms of nourishment.

These particular pioneers were from Indiana and had placed their fate in the hands of a wagon master by the name of Johnny Cotton. I should have instantly recognized Mr. Cotton for the scoundrel I later discovered him to be, for he sported that distinctive look in the transverse diameter between the parietal bones where destructiveness and secretiveness are placed. An additional bad sign was that he and Mahoney appeared to be old friends.

These forbidding twin indicators were soon matched by a discourse which may have led one to believe that a band of Gypsy wagons had been encountered and that their chief swindler had stepped forth to see what could be gained from the unsuspecting visitors. The Danas left the carriage and repaired to a locale as far from La Mash as possible while the great Lord Kill B'ar promptly cornered the first group of settlers he could find and began worrying them with his stories of frontier hardships and atrocities.

This left Mahoney and I to be entertained by Mr. Cotton. Almost immediately he admitted that he had taught his charges to play two card games known as "Old Sledge" and "Chihuahua Red Dog" and commented with a sly grin that Indianans weren't much when it came to gambling. He boasted that he had already bled several of them into bankruptcy and forced them to turn back before the wagon train hit Wildcat Creek. Johnny Cotton thought this positively hilarious, and I am afraid that even the physical telling of this terrible story also produced some equally dreadful and very disgusting results. You see, Johnny Cotton's mouth seemed to produce an overabundance of saliva and when he got too excited the excess fluid would either have to be periodically gulped down or else sprayed in the direction of his unfortunate audience. When he mentioned to Mahoney that he had mulcted the hat from a tag-along Indian called Ben Acts-Like-He-Knows-You he exploded in a mocking laughter that threatened to soak the front of my shirt.

Mahoney confronted Cotton and said that the last time he saw him he was working as a tent pole setter for Herr Driesbach's Travelling Circus and was curious to learn how Cotton had come to be a trusted scout in the Territories.

"Well, this is America, ain't it? I just went ahead an' started me a business after conferin' with Texas Jack."

Even Mahoney seemed startled at this. "Texas Jack! That snake's never been west of Yip Hop's laundry in his whole life, an' I don't think he's even been outside of Crystal's Saloon and seen the daylight in three years."

Johnny Cotton's eyes widened. "It ain't like that, Mahoney. Jack's a good businessman and that's what it takes. He taught me everything I needed to know from right inside Crystals."

As might be expected, Cotton's charges were in terrible shape. The lucky ones had been swindled early at parlour games and had been forced back to St. Jo. Those unfortunate souls who managed to hang-on wore the haunted look of shipwrecked sailors who had been adrift for weeks in leaking rafts. They were dreadfully unprepared, low on supplies, and their prairie ships were nothing more than rolling wrecks. Families who had lost poorly outfitted wagons to the road were forced to double up with those whose wagons were still up and running. As a consequence, the remaining oxen were straining to pull twice-loaded carts while the wretched humans were left to trudge alongside.

Everyone in the party seemed racked with disease or despair, except a robust and exuberant tyke identified to me as "Little Boy Cotton." This lad was seated on a pail behind a crate that was being used as a gaming board. On the other side were a group of bewildered Indians who were examining and conferring over what appeared to be a poker hand. Little Boy Cotton could not have reached his tenth year, yet he manipulated the cards with an *eclat* that might have impressed a hardened veteran aboard the *Sultana*. He was sitting among a pile of pelts, jerk meat, and other aboriginal goods that had recently been forfeited to his talents, and he squealed, clapped, and rubbed his hands together when the Indians threw down their cards and realized that he had triumphed over them once again.

We watched as the lad scooped up another set of pelts and threw them on his winning pile. "He is an unnatural child," Mahoney said while shaking his head. "He was just like that back in the circus days an' he wasn't but seven years old at the time. Trained by his father I suspect, an' maybe Texas Jack."

The Indians began to grumble. Some spoke Hunkpapa and others used sign language, but by any means it was clear that they believed they had been cheated. Little Boy Cotton was completely unfazed by this, then tied one of the Indian's forfeited bonnets around his head and began to prance around the crate in a mock war dance.

One young brave became completely outraged by this. He was not that much older than Little Boy Cotton but his physique looked as if it were chipped out of granite. The young brave stepped forward and made a very threatening gesture. Little Boy defiantly imitated this gesture right back at the young brave, stuck his tongue out at the group and intensified his awful taunting. I am sure it was only through the intercession of an elderly chief that bloodshed was avoided.

The unhappy Indians gathered up the playing cards and disappeared into the darkness. The brat brought his loot over to show Cotton, Sr., and it was an unholy sight to behold, father and son gloating over such things. They were *taeter ex colei*[28] if ever any existed, but it

---

28 From Latin one can only translate this as "a disgusting pair of testicles." —Ed.

was all made much worse when Johnny instructed his son to store the goods in with the other things in their supply wagon.

The little demon went to the only wagon in the group that was in a state of good repair and deposited his winnings in various trunks that held ample food supplies and a great number of personal possessions that were no doubt once owned by both the Indians and the Indianans.

Johnny smiled and shook his head from side to side in mock disbelief. "What a boy, I'll tell you. He could charm a snake and make him pay for it. Can you believe his mother wanted to send him to a reform school back in St. Louis? Shows you how much she knows, that stupid bitch." Then Johnny Cotton floated a tender note. "She hurt the little guy's feelings too. Poor little guy naturally come to his daddy after that and now look how good it all turned out."

I turned and saw Little Boy Cotton racing around the sick and dispirited pioneers with the oversized feather bonnet on his head. He paused to agitate an already rattled Mrs. Dana and then attempted to stir up a chase with some of the other children, but they were too weak to respond.

Mahoney asked if that little girl back in St. Jo ever fully recovered.

"You mean the one that was burned?" Johnny seemed a bit defensive. "Yeah, she's OK. She's fine, just fine. All the bandages came off before we even left town. She's like new, brand new."

He looked over at me and grinned. "Little Boy kind a got wild with a box of Lucifer Matches. His mother hid that sort of thing from him, an' the poor little guy didn't know what they wuz all about. Wasn't none of his fault, and besides the stupid little bitch deserved bein' lit-up. Nobody tells my boy he's got a bad breath problem. Poor little guy, it hurt his feelings. Don't they know it ain't right to be hurtful like that?"

Mahoney thought that the mules had sufficient rest and food, so he said good-bye to Johnny Cotton and called for the rest of us to get back to the coach. For the first time since the trip began, I was able to assume a positive attitude towards our driver for I sensed that he despised Little Boy Cotton and his father as much as I did. Before we left, the Danas and I distributed some buffalo meat pemmican to the worst off of the Indianans and even La Mash parted with a few of his hardened corn dodgers to a group of hungry children who began to *queue* up in front of him.

The grizzled trapper almost couldn't believe his eyes when Little Boy Cotton appeared in the line with his hand out. La Mash looked around to see where the child's father was, and after confirming he was nowhere about, he took the hellion's legs out from under him, knocked him to the ground and kicked some dirt into his face. Little Boy fell with a thud and almost began to cry—although I doubt if he has any of those fluids in him.

But instead, the diminutive tyrant got to his hands and knees, spat at La Mash and then administered a long and vicious bite to the side of his calf. It took two hard leg kicks to make the beast let go. Undaunted, he chased after our coach as we pulled away and hurled rocks at Mahoney. He finally caught up with us and pulled some Lucifer matches from his pocket with an eye on the mules. His father appeared and yelled after us, "What did you do to the poor little guy, Mahoney? I'll square up with you later, you stupid son-of-a-bitch."

It was near a full moon and we followed a silver ribbon of trail for an additional five hours on our way here to Simpson's Hollow. The station keepers were already down for the night when we arrived, so the three other passengers and Mahoney sought shelter in the adjoining stable and fell asleep on a mat of wild sage.

I made a small fire and began to set all this down on paper before it was forgotten. I am exhausted and will not last another ten minutes, but I will go to sleep thinking that my laibon may vomit after learning of the Cotton family, and sometimes I wonder what the worth of their exposition may be.

XV

TROUBLE ON THE TRAIL

August 23, 1860
Fort Bridger
Wyoming Territory

Mahoney forced an unusually early departure from Simpson's Hollow because he did not want to be charged for sleeping in the stable. It was still quite dark when we re-hitched the team and started back on the trail.

Dawn displayed to us the valley of Green River which boasts good grass and fresh water one hundred yards across. It was an unusually crisp and clear morning featuring an ideal temperature and our first interesting landscape in two weeks. Cottonwood trees and yellow currants shone in the sun and I can't recall a better start to any day so far. The climate inside the coach was also much improved on this day as I think a night's sleep and the memory of a common revulsion to last evening's events went a ways toward easing some of our internal hostilities.

La Mash was in an exceptional mood and offered to grace us with a song he learned in a bar in St. Jo.

Have you heard of Porter Rockwell, the Mormon Triggerite
They say he hunts down outlaws when the moon is shining bright
So if you rustle cattle, I'll tell you what to do,
Get the drop on Porter Rockwell,
Or he'll get the drop on you.

Lt. Dana burst into applause after the last word and I thought I noticed that even his wife was holding back a smile.

"Wal, if'n ya liked that one, general, I'll go right ahead and sing you another." La Mash cleared his throat and began:

Old Port Rockwell looks like a man
With a beard on his face and his hair in a braid
But there's none in the West but Brigham who can
Look in his eyes and not be afraid.
For Port is a devil in human shape
Though he calls himself Angel say
vengeance is sweet.
But he's black, bitter death, and there's no escape,
When he wails through the night his dread war cry
Wheat, Wheat.
Somewhere a wife with her babes kneels to pray
For she knows she's a widow and orphans
are they.

Lt. Dana laughed and began clapping again but this time his wife spoiled the mood by reminding him that there was nothing funny about widows and orphans.

"Of course not, dear. Now, Mr. La Mash, what's all this about his war cry, *Wheat, wheat?*"

La Mash explained that Mr. Rockwell was given over to using this term on a number of occasions and that it had become his signature. "Wheat" when he toasts a drink. "Wheat" when he gets angry. "All wheat" when he means it is good.

"You know, ol' Port's not an educated man. Kaint even read or write a word nor sign his own name. Might be that he's at a loss for fancy words an' says wheat to mean a lot of different things."

Just then Mrs. Dana let loose a blood-curdling scream. "Oh my God, my God. Look over there!" She burst into tears and buried her head in her husband's jacket.

It was the young Pony Express rider. He was tied to a tree, shot through with arrows and was a bloody mess from having been horribly scalped. He was already dead but his eyes were still half open and his mouth no longer wore that innocent smile. These empty features combined into an expression suggesting that his last act was to try and let his murderers know that they had made some sort of terrible mistake or that he was embarrassed such a fate had befallen him. La Mash and Mahoney went up to the young man and released him from the tree. They identified the arrows as belonging to the Hunkpapa and when they began cleaning away the blood they discovered one of the arrows pierced a handful of playing cards that had been placed on the boy's chest.

"This is for what happened last night." Mahoney rubbed the top of his hand back and forth across his mouth as he looked down at the young rider. "The Hunkpapa's a people what won't kill a child or the sick or defenseless no matter what they done to them. But they're a proud folk who won't sit still for being taken advantage of neither. This poor young boy here got chosen to deliver the message." Mahoney took a flask from his pocket and retreated to the coach. Lt. Dana and I helped La Mash scrape a shallow grave on the side of the road and we lifted the rider into it and covered this likable lad with a goodly number of silently sad rocks.

We each sat by ourselves for a while, lost in thoughts of the unfairness of what had taken place. The evil child who caused all this, who at age ten can only be considered a rotten product of his time, place, and equally repulsive father; and the Hunkpapa who butchered an innocent man because they are too noble to exact such measures on those who they consider feeble. And the dead orphan in a lonely grave at seventeen. It is a discomforting and unsatisfying thing to have no villain, or all villains. To be in a land at a time when survival takes on such grotesque shapes and where the notions of justice blow the mind apart with storms of contradictions.

Johnny Cotton and his putrid child are bloated ticks, alive right now and living off the blood of those who pay them for protection. An innocent boy lies dead on account of these two, and his hair hangs on a pole above some *wikeap* that belongs to some pitiable savage who had to do something to help assuage his indignation. Something that made perfect sense to him, but which seems utterly cruel and senseless to the foreigner who has invaded his land and was taking everything he ever had.

Lt. Dana placed a reassuring hand on his wife's shoulder and La
Mash and Mahoney shuffled around the coach acting as if they did
not know whether to stay and try to do something or else get away
from the scene as soon as possible. After a short time, everyone realized that there was nothing that could be done save more brooding,
so we rejoined the trail and pressed on to the next station.

Ham's Fork, if not the most dangerous station along the route, is certainly staffed with the surliest and most treacherous attendants of all
the rest stops encountered to date. Our first act upon arrival was to
inform the station master that a man was murdered ten miles back
and buried along the side of the trail.

"So what you want me to do? Say a fuckin' prayer?" He said this
with cruel indifference and then spit an evil-looking mess of tobacco
juice on the floor. "Somebody's gettin' killed all the time around here.
I just hope he was an Injun or a Mormon. Neither of them is worth
a goddamn and one less of either is reason for a drink." His crusty
friends laughed at this, but when their little joke was over, a pervasive
air of hostility hung in the room. They sat in grim silence and followed our every move with suspicious and antagonistic eyes.

Finally, a man who was sitting backwards on a chair and resting his chin on the side brace addressed us. His tone was as cutting
as a barber's razor. "Any special thing you ass-sucking faggots want
around here?" He pulled his lips back tight against his teeth as he
looked down and cleaned his greasy fingernails with a large knife.
Then lifting his head up with a threatening look on his face said,
"Some little thing we can do for you before you git on your way an'
clear the hell out of here in the next five seconds?"

Mahoney said that he had hoped to feed and water his animals
and perhaps find some food for his passengers as well. "Besides," he
said, "this here's a rest station and we plan on doin' a little of that too.'

The men in the room looked at each other as if to affirm among
themselves that Mahoney's last comment should be considered a
challenge. One young man, about nineteen years old and menacing
beyond his years, stepped forward and said, "Just what the hell you
mean by that, stagecoach driver?"

A deferential Mahoney in a failing voice said, "Well I don't mean to make much of it. Just here on a routine stopover, and, well, just lookin' for a little common help." Mahoney sensed the tension and strained to break the present course. "Say, you boys thirsty? If you got a bottle and some glasses I'll buy us all a drink."

A protracted silence, and then, "We don't drink with no damn Mormons."

"Well then, that's not goin' to be a problem boys 'cause we ain't Mormons."

Lt. Dana and his wife entered the room at this point, and the intense young man loudly announced, "And we don't drink with no candy-ass East Coast soldiers neither." And after eyeing Mrs. Dana he said, "But we could make some room for a whorey slut, right boys?"

Another man rose from his seat. He approached Mrs. Dana and began touching the edge of her blouse then salaciously slipped his fingers inside between the buttons. Lt. Dana was frozen in terror, and there descended on the room a hazardous silence with all parties sizing each other up in anticipation of some trouble.

La Mash spoke for the first time and commented that it seemed like the gentlemen in the room didn't want to drink with anyone. An older, pock-marked desperado threw a toothpick from his mouth and sneered, "That's right, you sloppy fat man. We especially don't want to do no drinking with your greasy ass."

La Mash turned to the man and an instant later pulled a Bowie knife from his waist band and whipped it under the man's chin. "Wal, that's too bad, son. Cause I been in a foul mood all day long an' sometimes when I git like that, I want to do some harm 'less I have a drink or two to calm myself down."

The man's eyes strained down in their sockets to see the knife at his throat and he began sweating profusely. La Mash kept the knife in the same position and began laughing. "You know, boys, I once ran into a old *coureurs des bois* who didn't have no time for his fellow man, as cantankerous and contrary a man as you could ever imagine. And, wal, there came a time when he crossed the wrong trapper, a feller who wasn't lookin' for nothin' but a kind word and a friendly drink after he buried a friend earlier that day. That trapper had a bad mean streak in him too, you can believe that. He could turn a man inside out with a knife if he came across someone that was just out lookin' to bring trouble his way." La Mash lowered the knife and began slowly cutting the buttons off the man's shirt. "They found that old *coureurs des bois* with his cold heart cut all the way out of his chest. It was just layin' there on the floor wishin' it was back where it belonged."

One of the other men in the room began to reach for his gun and La Mash turned the blade of the knife against his captive's chest and drew more than a little blood. As the front of the terrified man's shirt quickly reddened, his eyes flashed over to his friend.

"Don't do nothin', Stewart. He'll kill me for certain sure."

La Mash ordered the others to put their guns on the floor and instructed them to prepare some feed and water for the mules. He told them he and his friends would be resting inside until the animals were fit to continue.

As they passed by him on their way out the door, one of the men stopped and snarled at La Mash. "We'll be lookin' out for you, Frenchy." He jabbed his finger in the trapper's face. "And when the time comes, we're going to pull down on you and finish things."

Without a moment's hesitation, La Mash lashed out and severed half of the man's right index finger with a savage swipe of his knife. Lord Kill Ba'r threw his head back and roared a wild laugh. "You're going to have trouble pulling the trigger now my friend, you can believe that. Look there, your finger's lying on the floor." La Mash continued to stare at the man until he ran out the door clutching his bad hand with his good one.

Mrs. Dana stifled a gag reaction.

We spent almost an hour inside the station at Ham's Fork. La Mash retrieved Mahoney's scatter gun from the coach and supervised the care of the mules from a chair on the front porch. Needless to say, we were all relieved to continue on, but our driver did complain for the first ten miles saying that he could never pass that way again. He was drinking hard from his flask and grumbling as he drove the team faster and faster.

"Crawford brothers humiliated like that . . . guns taken away from 'em, an' George Oaks' finger twitchin' on the ground. I don't know, I don't know. I might require federal protection. Damn Kill Ba'r don't care. He don't have to drive this route again."

Mrs. Dana appeared to be a different woman at the end of this long day. Her usual nervous temperament had disappeared, and she sat stone motionless with something that could be described as a cold smile on her face. At first, I thought she may have been stunned into a state of shock by the double dose of horror inflicted on her by the murder of the Pony Express rider and the confrontation at Ham's Fork. But that was not a satisfactory explanation for what I saw in her. I then thought she may have stopped being bothered by La Mash, whose recent actions could have been considered heroic. But even that could not account for the demeanor of the new woman sitting across from me.

I later learned that any hint of temerity in her had been evaporated by the American West. She looked older and wiser in a way, and determined. Nothing could stop her now—no murder, no buffalo chip, no horror of a severed body part. And there was no longer any thought of turning back. She had melded into this great national mania for Western movement that needed to press towards the Pacific like a massive and relentless insect storm. She was now going to be a problem for the Indians and the Crawford brothers, George Oaks and La Mash, and anyone or anything else that got in her way. She had become a real American.

Later in the day we entered Ft. Bridger just as the sun was going down. It is comprised of two double log houses about forty feet long with a horse stable between them. Not far off to the east we could see the remains of the old fort which had been attacked and burned by the Mormons a few years past. Like Ft. Laramie there were Indian lodges set up so close to the stockade that it would be impossible to distinguish one encampment from the other. White and Indian children played together and raised a cloud of dust as they raced about the premises using sticks as imaginary guns and engaged in a mock combat that was too close to reality to be considered charming.

La Mash headed straight for the fort's only saloon while Lt. and Mrs. Dana began to inquire about safe shelter for the night. Mahoney put up the animals and vowed to sleep with a gun for fear the Crawford brothers and George Oaks might catch up with him in his sleep. There was some wisdom in Mahoney's fear, and I took special precautions to make my camp this night in a place far from the others, and one which might easily be defended should there be an attack.

I located my spot in a wooded area about twenty minutes from the fort. The first order of business, as always, was to make a fire and assemble a lean-to of some sort for protection against the elements.

It is fortunate that these precautions were taken for as the sky darkened, the stars and moon became periodically hidden by fast moving black clouds. There was some wind-blown rain and loose bits of vegetation began to skip across the ground in front of me. I gripped my Colt Dragoon and pointed it in the direction of a noise. I cocked the hammer back and then whirled around and pointed it in the direction of another disturbance. Nothing, but I prayed this was still another preamble to an appearance by my formidable Indian friend. As I was about to return the gun to my side, an enraged George Oaks burst from the shadows with a bloody bandana wrapped around one hand and a pistol blazing crazily in the other. Stewart Crawford was directly behind him.

Coincidental with a shot from my pistol came a larger caliber rifle discharge, and a fraction of a second later an arrow pierced Oaks' neck. Blood gushed out of his mouth as he staggered forward clutching his throat. He fell into the edge of my campfire and newly-spilled blood hissed as it rushed across the hot rocks and embers. His eyes rolled back into his head and his hair began to singe. The sight and smell turned my stomach.

The next thing I saw was Rifle Shot. He was wearing a wooden helmet and cradling a still-smoking breechloader in the crook of his arm. His expressionless face looked past me and I made a half-turn to see Stewart Crawford sprawled on the ground with a hole matching the size of a one-ounce Yager ball through the middle of his forehead.

There was a moment of confusion when I thought of Oaks and the arrow through his neck. That is when my squaw appeared with a long bow in her hand. She was grinning broadly at the sight of what she had just accomplished.

What can be said about the beauty of those smiling, perfectly matched white teeth, set against the alarm of knowing their owner had just dispatched another human being in such a violent and bloody fashion? There was further consternation as she rushed next to him and began extinguishing his burning hair in preparation for lifting it from his skull.

Rifle Shot removed his wooden helmet and walked over to Stewart Crawford and nudged him several times with the barrel of his breechloader. He seemed pleased there was no reaction, although for the life of me I do not see how anyone with the back of his head missing could have been expected to move a muscle.

The squaw finished with her ghastly work and hopped up and down while yelling a staccato chant and holding Oak's bloody hair and scalp in her hand. She was wild with excitement and began running back and forth between Rifle Shot and myself displaying her trophy.

The wind blew a rain squall to us and the tall Indian suggested we repair to his fire for the evening. He gave not a minute's thought to the two dead men on the ground preferring instead to worry about how his fire was doing in the rain. To Rifle Shot and the squaw it was simply another day in the American West with its accompanying little episodes of joys and sorrows.

To: Norton Shaw
Royal Geographic Society
14 St. James Sq.
London

My Dear Shaw:[29]
You would be astonished at America. That the Roy. Geog. Soc. has yet to promote a formal expedition to this raw place is a cheat to those members whose tastes run to the savage and most foreign

---

29 Norton Shaw was a friend of Burton and Secretary of the Royal Geographic Society. —Ed.

parts of our globe. Do not think for a moment that Father Civilization has completely spread his seed over this land, for the sword and
shield horrors of our own darkened past are played out here on a
regular schedule, often after drunken disputes and sometimes for simple sport. And nowhere in the world may a traveller witness so many
guns, let alone an armed grease-drinking contest!

One has the feeling that the newness and freedom of the place
has caused the white man to go berserk in his efforts to spoil it, and
the Negroes, as Thomas Jefferson warned, are just waiting their turn.

The only thing that is somewhat settled is the society of the red-
man, although it is being torn asunder at an alarming rate, and bringing forth the very worst elements in their character. In my humble
opinion, the only chance for salvation would be a mass conversion
to pacifistic Buddhism, but this would be as likely as wild and naked
John Speke performing the saber dance in a Turkish whorehouse.

As for what has happened east of the Great River, I was a month
before sighting any Indians, and once I did have the honour, was held
as a slave to them, by a slave of Shem and Japheth, in the land of slavery. A most undignified experience, I assure you.

The American West surpasses Africa and the Orient in its collision of competing human agendas. Here, Canadian trappers clash
with local tribes and European immigrants do battle with the sons
of earlier arrivals from the same place. The Southern whites are in
action against the Negro, and in the North, the English and French
have combined to nearly clear the land of every aboriginal soul. The
Indians are at constant war against each other, and have been for years,
and now have the whites to deal with as well.

Homesteading farmers have hard feelings for the open range
hunters; ranchers have an aversion to the miners; the Mexicans dislike
the Americans; the North detests the South; the Blacks despise the
Whites; the soldiers deplore the Indians; the Indians resent them all;
and everyone seems to hate the Mormons. America—it will probably
bloom into one of the most cohesive and powerful nations in world
history, with the Mormons leading the way.

Has Speke been killed yet? And what of poor Grant? I do not
wish to think what will become of him after JHS's first experience

with the Kowouli. *Entre nous*, I'll wager Speke will spare them both the moment and keep him hidden in Ujiji.

I am sick to death of bad food and semi-civility. I would prefer starvation and pure barbarism any day.

I subscribe myself. etc., etc.

Yrs. very truly

R. F. Burton

August 24, 1860
Utah Territory

Back at Rifle Shot's *wikeap* we parted company with my squaw who rushed to her sister with George Oak's scalp in hand. There were screams of delight over the trophy and some excited conversation as the engagement was relived in words. Rifle Shot was busy with his big smoke but did take time to motion in their direction and comment how such a small thing can bring so much pleasure to the girls.

Now once again in control of my senses I had to ask how he found me earlier that evening. I mentioned that his timing was positively amazing.

"Wah, Bur-ton, your camp was so noisy that every animal within one day's ride could hear you like thunder, and every nose below the wind could smell you like a skunk. Do you think the Delaware have no ears or nose?"

"Yes. I mean no, but I cannot believe you arrived when you did. And considering the distance since the last time we met—how, I mean how?'

The squaws interrupted their celebration and giggled at my repeating of the word "how."

Rifle Shot endured my query with great patience and then calmly explained the situation in review. "You missed both men with your pistol. Bad shooting, and you were about to die. So we helped. That is all. I did not like them from before, so it was an easy thing. Back at the place you call Fort Laramie, we spoke then of the salty waters and my journey to the Mormon camp. Like I told you, we were on our way there and stopped to see you. The squaw wanted this."

I nodded.

Rifle Shot continued. "Wah, this is the path I am on now, to the Mormons for Yellow Bear."

"Yes, but your arrival just in time to dispatch those two assassins and save my life—it's remarkable!"

Rifle Shot seemed perplexed. He shook his head at me as if there were some communication problem. "So the men from what they call the Ham's Fork were used-up at your camp. It was a natural thing, and so long in coming. I will use-up the Big Mormon the same way. It is not a big thing. We are on the same path and you are a friend of Rifle Shot. You camp alone, away from the other white men. It is good." He paused and looked over at the two women. "Besides, squaw wishes for more bundling under the robes."

Bundling? Good god, I thought. Does the man think we were practicing Fanny Wrightism[30] the last time we were together? Given his reputation, I was not sure if I wanted to confess that there was no hand fasting on that particular night.

I proceeded cautiously. "Well, yes, of course, if that our next time together meets with your approval."

"Yess, Bur-ton, but we must speak." He said something to his wives in dialect and they both stood and left the tent. Rifle Shot stared into the fire and spoke softly but very gravely. "We must speak as men, Bur-ton. Wah, it is about you and my wife. I must ask you plainly about your time with her."

I was very nervous for I did not know how to, or even if I should dare, discuss the intimate details of my last night with the squaw. After all, he said it was alright to sleep with her, and what does he expect a man to do under the circumstances? I didn't think Indians even knew what bundling was.

"Bur-ton. My number two wife like you, I know that. And now she has killed a man who was about to do you harm. This makes big difference."

"What sort of difference?"

---

30 Fanny Writism, which was also known as Free-Loveism, Bundling, and Hand Fasting was the practice of unmarried couples sleeping together without undressing. —Ed.

"It mean that, well, you owe her a life, or maybe some big thing. So maybe you can keep her so that man and woman who like each other can be in tent together, and woman can cook your food, and so you not camp in dangerous land alone."

Then the big Indian disgustedly threw a small stick into the fire. His tone of voice changed to one of frankness and confession. "Wah, Bur-ton, I must not shoot a crooked arrow, I must tell you true. It is my first wife; she has new problem now. She doesn't want her sister in the tent anymore, doesn't want to share time. Jealous. Now she tell me to go to Three Trees and hunt so I will stay away from her sister."

He turned to me with a look of absolute exasperation. "Hunting at Three Trees is what cause sister to come in the first place."

Poor chap. He was in a bad way over this thing and wanted me to help out. I reckoned it may be considered extremely poor form to say no, and the woman was very attractive; however, getting married to a Delaware Indian squaw was not exactly on my dance card at the moment. I had to think fast.

"I am extremely flattered, Rifle Shot. It must be very difficult for you to give her up because your second wife is a beautiful woman."

He pursed his lips, raised his eyebrows, and nodded. "Better than first wife, I can tell you that."

"I accept your generous offer, sir. For reasons which I cannot discuss at the moment, I must ask that you keep my squaw with you during the days when we travel. Now I must ride in the coach with the others. At night I shall come to her and we shall make our home together in a tent separate from yours. Will this please your wife?"

Rifle Shot took a deep breath and blew the air out very slowly. "It is hard to say what will make her happy. Separate tents mean that sister sleeping with other man. "Mmmm, that might end biggest problem."

He threw his hands into the air in frustration. "Wah, Bur-ton, I cannot say what will bring peace to my camp. Maybe the man you call god can understand squaw. For me, it is like trying to look past the edge of the earth. It cannot be done."

The next morning I rose early, returned to Ft. Bridger around dawn and found Mahoney still asleep in the stable. At the first hint of a sound he jumped up from the straw with a pistol in each hand and blinked hard to wrest sleep from his eyes.

"Damn you, Burton. I hardly got a wink last night for fear of them Ham's Fork boys arrivin' here for some revenge. I near blasted your head off. Should be more careful when commin' up on a man in my condition." I apologized to our driver and said that I did not think Crawford or Oaks would be causing us any more trouble.

"I dunno 'bout that. Maybe not in England where you come from, but 'round here you can pretty much count on some sort of re-taliation. All of 'em are crazy from takin' that Apache whiskey root,[31] an' with Oaks' finger cut off and all . . . wal, you better quit goin' off by yourself at night and stay close to the fort for protection. I'm ready for 'em, though, by crackie, you stick close to me, Burton, and you'll be alright."

Here at Fort Bridger, Colonel Gardner has garrisoned two companies of foot and horse under the banner of the 10th Regiment. Since we are but 125 miles from the City of the Saints, every soldier here has had dealings with Mormons and none seems to like them very much. My meeting with Col. Gardner in his office may be offered as but one of many examples of this. Gardner, like most officers in this country, is originally from the South and as such considers himself an aristocrat rather than simply someone with a purchased commission. He was rather tall and gentlemanly and seemed to take great pleasure in reading my note of introduction from Colonel Beauregard. He held the document in his hand and admired the signature while shaking his head.

"P.G.T. Beauregard himself. Well my, my, Captain Burton, you do seem very well connected. How may I be of service to you, sir?"

---

31 The "whiskey root" was *Lophophora williamsii,* commonly called peyote. The effects of taking this drug have been called "fantastic and unworldly" and Spanish chroniclers reported those who took it saw "frightful visions" and remained drunk for two or three days. —Ed.

"Your hospitality here is greatly acknowledged, Colonel, and I do appreciate your reconstruction efforts of cedar and pine. It appears you experienced quite a fire here sometime in the near past."

"The Mormons were responsible for that, Captain Burton, like so many of our other problems here in the Territory. You see, the fire of religious cultism burns in their veins, and because of this they are given over to acts of fanaticisms which are directed against Indian and Gentile alike. Have you had any experience with religious fanaticism, Captain Burton?"

"Maybe once or twice."

"I see. Well it is not an easy thing to deal with, I can tell you that. These are people who wish for fundamental change in society and believe God almighty has sanctioned their actions."

The Colonel then proceeded to define his troubles with the Saints. "All the problems of New York and Nauvoo have now been pushed onto my shoulders. The Mormons are administering their own brand of vigilante justice, breeding like polygamist flies, and building their own Babylon just three days' ride from here. Now I realize I am an American speaking to a continental gentleman, and you must think this whole country is filled with people just like the Mormons. Problem is they have this special ability to churn the temper of everyone they've come in contact with, a most remarkable ability, and this is what sets them apart and has occasioned their many solicitous movements across the continent."

Gardner stood and paced across the room, searching for examples to prove his point. "Sometimes I say to myself, Why should these seekers of religious freedom be such outcasts in a country founded by those who sought the same thing? As a Christian, I have given this a great deal of thought."

He came to an abrupt halt and pirouetted towards me. "It is their damnable self-righteousness that makes the gorge rise most, but the secretness, materialism, and relentless industry of the Mormon also makes the blood boil. I'll tell you, Captain Burton, I have seen this process in action and it is not a pretty sight to behold. Things become unglued when Mormon meets Gentile. As I said, it is a most remarkable phenomenon." He regained a measure of

composure and cleared his throat. "Of course, it is my duty to protect the peace in this territory, and that responsibility extends to all
the citizens in the territory be they red, white," and he made a bad
face, "or Mormon."

It was revealing, if not amusing to me, that Colonel Gardner felt
he needed to make a distinction between white people and Mormons. It were as if he considered them a race unto themselves and
completely foreign from everyone around them. Moreover, one got
the impression he assigned them to some foul sub-group which
should be considered inferior to the others due to their remarkable
and ubiquitous abilities to offend.

"On my word, Colonel Gardner, this Mormon settlement seems
to be something of a thorny patch hereabouts."

"Oh yes indeed, sir; a most difficult situation. I have all I can do to
keep the men from giving vent to their anger. If they had their way,
the City of the Saints would closer resemble the Roman Vulcan. It is
my prediction that someday soon the 10th will couple with the men
at Camp Floyd and crush the Mormons in a fatal pincer action. Mark
my words well, Captain; by the year eighteen hundred and sixty three,
there will not be a single follower of Joseph Smith alive in Wyoming
or Utah Territories . . . or anywhere else in these United States. You
can trust me on that, Captain.

"Now, I am afraid you must excuse me, sir. I am expecting Lt.
Dana, an artillery officer on his way to assignment at Camp Floyd."
Gardner paused for a moment and flashed a look of modest embarrassment. "Oh my, how forgetful of me. You must have arrived in the
same coach."

"That is quite alright, Colonel Gardner. I thank you for your time
and our insightful conversation. I shall leave now in favour of your
next appointment."

Gardner began to arrange some papers on his desk. "One last
thing, Captain Burton. Do take care not to associate with the Indians.
You are new in this land and cannot be expected to know much of
their ways. The Indians are a treacherous lot and will take your life in
an instant for a pot of beans. I do not want to be the one writing Col.
Beauregard that you were killed on my watch."

"I will be on guard against all villainy and mistruth, sir."

Gardner looked down at his papers and drew little circles in the air with his pen. "Goood, very good, Captain!"

I left Gardner's office at roughly nine in the morning which is considered midday at the typical western military garrison. The sergeant majors "break out" at four thirty and rouse the enlisted men. A half hour later, the officers are having their morning eye-opener, which is a cocktail of whiskey, water, bitters and sugar. This is followed by a call to roll and orders in the parade ground just as the sun is rising. While the U.S. Army is far from the Dorado of military decorum and drill, I must say that all the men were uniformed and almost looked smart in their blues, yellows, and reds.

For the camp Indians this was surely one of the high points of each day. The notion of warriors made to stand still in lines and then march around like schoolboys was hilarious to them, and near every member of the red community suspended their morning activity to witness this spectacle. Indian children formed ranks in ragged imitation of the soldiers, and young braves bumped into and saluted each other in mocking parade.

Curiously, they all stopped clowning and stood in awe as the morning bugler delivered his salute to the raising of the flag. Here was something that struck a solemn note; something worthy and deserving of serious attention. For the life of me, I cannot understand what inspired them to act in such a way, unless it was the sound of the music or the resplendent colours of the flag. Perhaps they had never before seen a man-made object hoisted that high in the air. I believe it must have been something of that nature for they surely ascribed no allegiance to the nation or society that was inexorably devouring their own. Some of the more foolish troopers actually believe they have become patriotic.

I spotted Mrs. Dana as I crossed the grounds. One might have expected her emerging from the home of the KOW—the euphemized abbreviation for Commanding Officer's Wife, because obviously the more correct spelling just wouldn't do—but rather Mrs. Dana was in fact resident in the farrier's section of the stable.

I watched her as she studied the smith, and then unaccountably, she took his hammer and began driving nails into the back hoof of a horse that was in need of shoeing. I almost could not believe my eyes. Her blouse was unbuttoned to a shocking level and she had somehow obtained and was sporting a pair of trooper boots.

In no time, a small crowd of soldiers and stable boys gathered to witness this unusual event. Mrs. Dana occasionally glanced at them with a maniacal grin on her face and then pounded harder and harder until even the taciturn horse became alarmed and had to look around to see what was happening. The smith was finally obliged to take the hammer from her. "Whoa there, Missus. You're going to drive the shoe clear through ol' Brownie's hoof if you don't ease-up."

Mrs. Dana was sweating and appeared preoccupied, maybe anxious to find something else of equal intensity. The hammer fell to the ground in the exchange and she left the stable without saying a word, but not before nodding and taking one last hard and defiant look at the gathering.

La Mash apparently also witnessed this extraordinary episode, because it was all he could talk about at our noon meal. "Wal, did ya see that, the general's little wife inside there with them blacksmiths? I'll be dumfouzled if'n I can figure that one out. I know'd a woman once who could ride and shoot like a man, chewed tobacco like a horse, and drank rye whiskey, lots of it too. She was Jake Blake's daughter though an' I suppose that would account for it. But that one in the stable, she ain't the same one we hitched-up with back at St. Jo. No siree. Somethin's gotten into her, you can believe that." Lord Kill Ba'r then broke off his narrative when he discovered, captured, and then ate a louse which was crawling on his chest.

XVI

GRIPS TIGHTEN ON THE APPROACH TO THE GREAT SALT LAKE

August 24, 1860
Carson's House Station

We are in the land of graves. The trail winds along a ridge to Quaking Asp Hill and down a tricky descent into the deprivations of Sulfur Creek Valley. This rocky stretch is trying to wheels and animals alike, and the skeletons of many a lesser coach and mule lie rotting along either side of the road. Here there is no good water or grass and the swampy valley floor positively smells of death. Shade is dear and the heat excruciating.

Mahoney was mad to get through this land, correctly noting that it was one of the worst parts of the trail and famous for claiming lives. He did slow down as we passed a burnt and ravaged wagon that was a porcupine of arrows, and from the number of spent cartridges scattered on the ground next to it, one could imagine the terrible struggle that must have taken place here in the not-too-distant past. The odour of carbonized wood was still in the air a hundred yards away. We soon came upon four stone piles with crude wooden crosses over them. These undoubtedly marked the end of the trail for the hapless pioneers from the wagon. Some Christian passer-by buried them here and included a personal touch atop each cairn; a cottage bonnet, a single shoe, a slingshot, and a child's doll.

"*Mon Dieu*," sighed La Mash. "It's probably a whole family. This must have happened in the last couple of days. The damn wood's still warm on the wagon. Where wuz Gardner's troopers when all this killin' took place?" He drew his .44-caliber Walker revolver and loudly cursed the sky. "No all-fired red belly's going to take out Gaston La Mash, you can believe that. I'll be chewed up before I'm going to let myself git kilt like them settlers."

He was answered from inside the coach by an icy feminine voice. "Maybe they deserved it."

Everyone in the coach turned to Mrs. Dana in disbelief. Her husband was the first to speak. He gave his head a small shake and with a cautious smile asked, "What did you say, dear?"

I said, maybe they deserved to be killed. Maybe the damn fools did something to the Indians first."

Not another word was spoken for the next several hours until we came upon another wagon that was broken down along the side of the road. I think we were all relieved to find the owners alive and somewhat comfortably camped next to their disabled ship.

He was an old Cornishman, on his way to Salt Lake City in search of polygamy. Unfortunately, I believe he had reached that time in life when perhaps the responsibilities of such a happy situation may quickly overwhelm his abilities. He was in the company of a full-blooded Negro woman, half his age and perhaps twice his size, who was introduced to us as his "girlfriend." After this revelation, she blushed as only a Negress can, and swung her arm around his shoulder.

"J. T. Twiggs is the name. Welcome to my new, temporary home. And will you stop and have a sip of tea with a fellow the likes of me? I've plenty."

Mahoney stared at the couple with his mouth open and then allowed that the animals could use the rest. We stopped and offered some verbal comfort to the shipwrecked couple. There was really nothing more we could have done.

"Me mates said I was crazy, joining the church and coming all the way out here. Not at all, sez I. The delights of plural marriage will transcend the hardships of this journey and leave me a contented man. It will make Deirdre contented too. Isn't that right girl? God has come to me in a dream and declared that I will have three wives—one black, one white, and one red. So when I learned of Mr. Joseph Smith in America, I knew I had to join with him in his heaven upon the earth. While still in Cornwall, word reached me that Mr. Joseph Smith had been martyred in Illinois, and that Mr. Brigham Young was moving the Saints west into the land of the red man. Well, that did it right then and there, my dear, as I knew for certain then that the prophesy would be fulfilled. I need only bring a black woman with me and the white and the red ones would be provided at the Great Salt Lake. It's God's will, and the Perpetual Emigration Fund did us no harm either, isn't that so, Deirdre?"

I asked Mr. Twiggs if he was aware that the Daughters of Ham are not admitted to the communion of the Saints. He looked at Dierdre and told me that was not possible. "That's not part of the dream," he insisted, "and besides, the Saints would never do anything like that."

We left the star-struck Mr. Twiggs and his girlfriend on the side of the trail after they refused passage to the next station. I wondered what the Mormons would think when they laid eyes on Dierdre, and how they would view her use of Perpetual Emigration Funds.

"Just tell Mr. Young that we are on the way, and he will send the Saints to our rescue. I have faith that he knows who we are and what we need."

The last words I heard from him were ones of consolation to Dierdre. "Don't you pay no mind to those people, woman, you'll be welcomed in the communion of the Saints, you can trust me on that."

Colonel Gardner said I could trust him that the Saints would be completely eliminated from the territory in three years. He also believes I will be killed instantly the moment I associate with Indians. The most feared Indian in the territories is frightfully worried by his own squaw, and the most timid army wife on the trail is now becoming more dangerous than Gaston LaMash ever was. Mahoney believes I have a better chance against two dead men by staying with him rather than camping alone. Some of the troopers actually believe the Indians gather in the morning to salute the flag. And Mr. Twiggs tells his Negro girlfriend that she will be readily accepted as a Mormon. Alas, in the land of freedom, it seems everyone is free to be an idiot.

We reached Carson's House Station at five o'clock this evening. A sign was stenciled on the front of this establishment which read, 'Maud Carson!!! dispenses comfort to the weery! feeds the hungrie!! and cheers the gloomy!!! at her well-stocked and famous!!! station. Don't pass by me!!!'

The inn behind this painted lie featured only its overbearing filth and its relative nearness to civilization. Situated in these mean lands between Ft. Bridger and Salt Lake City, Carson's House managed to merge the worst of all three worlds.

Something is terribly wrong with the semi-civilized state. It is as if one world vitiates the other in a vicious and unending exchange of corruption. We were immediately driven out of the so-called dining room by a thick swarm of biting black flies and found ourselves back outside and in the company of the worst hung-dog Indians and criminal-looking whites I have seen so far.

The flies were beaten off after a rag was wrapped around the end of a broom handle, soaked in kerosene, and ignited. The old crow of a cook paraded around the room with the torch over her head until a greasy black smoke settled over every surface, including the horrid food, and every spoon, knife and cup. What must have been Maude Carson herself appeared in the doorway and gave an exaggerated bow. "The room is now purified, your royal highnesses. Youse don't have to fear the man-eating housefly no more." She cackled like a witch and extinguished the stinking flame in a barrel of drinking water. Needless to say, our rancid food and water was now sharp with the taste of kerosene, and black soot stained both flesh and clothing each time anyone made contact with anything.

After dining—if it can be called that—my coach mates set about attempting to find decent quarters for the evening. As it turned out, Carson's House Station provided just a single, filthy room for such purposes, and that meant the Danas and Mahoney would be forced together into this close quarter piggery, along with La Mash and two other miscreants who happened to need lodging at the same time.

As was my usual custom, I would set off for the evening and look after myself. There had been no prearrangements with Rifle Shot and my new "wife" regarding a time or a place to meet, so I carried on as usual and suspected that wherever in the Territory I might decide to settle for the evening, they would most likely find me in the first few minutes after dismounting.

I was not disappointed. My squaw came to me and indicated in sign language that I follow her back to camp. As I might have guessed, there were now two tents erected and other indications that I would soon be performing *le danse l'amour* with my new mate on another night. Once settled I joined Rifle Shot at his fire. He was busy with the care of his breechloader, bow, and many arrows, and I was afraid he was making final war preparations as he drew nearer to Salt Lake City.

I attempted to broach a few issues with him but he seemed pre-occupied. When I mentioned passing the burned wagon and the four graves earlier on the trail, he stopped cleaning his rifle and looked into the fire. "Yes, I know about this. That is too bad for the wagon people—but not under this sky. The little white boy should not have acted as he did to the Shoshone. The brave was called Looking Bird. He had been killed the day before by another group of white men, for stealing one hearty-choke."

"You mean he was killed over the theft of an artichoke?"

Rifle Shot formed his hands into a ball. "Small plant with sharp points on leaves? Look like green bird lodge?"

"Yes, yes, that's the one. But what exactly did this little white boy do?"

"After he was killed for taking the plant, Looking Bird's people placed him on his blanket for the death journey near the wagon trail. The boy from another wagon came to him and took a necklace from his body. It was a beautiful necklace with many coloured beads."

Rifle Shot looked at me plainly and commented, "White men angry when Indian just take scalp from dead enemy, then don't care when boy take beautiful thing like necklace. There is no sense in this. Boy make Shoshone very angry, more angry than before. If Shoshone boy does wrong his mother pours water down his nose. Shoshone do that when child is bad, teaches good lesson. It is the way of this earth. If grown man had done same thing, they would have taken skin off while still alive. White men don't see," Rifle Shot searched for the right words, "don't see clear to do this right thing.

"White boy's father comes and argues with Shoshone after they see boy with Looking Bird's necklace. Boy's father does not know how to speak with them. They show him necklace but he does not understand everything that has happened. Big fight happens, many arrows, many cartridges spent. Many people killed."

He turned from the fire and looked at me. "All that blood worth one hearty-choke? I do not think so. One hearty-choke not same as eleven people. More Shoshone dead, all white family rubbed-out . . . plenty more hearty-chokes." He almost laughed but didn't and shook his head instead.

He concluded with some thoughts that left me wondering about a number of issues. Rifle Shot pointed his finger at nothing in particular and said, "When you are not part of this real earth, and you come here, you bring pain from somewhere else that cannot be understood. You bring trouble into a land not made for rolling tents or children who are allowed to take necklaces from dead warriors. People from this earth sometimes rub them out to make their land real once more. With the cleaning of death everything can begin again." He returned to the care of his weapon.

I asked if he still intended to carry out his plan of killing Brigham Young.

"Mmmm."

I took this to mean yes, so I questioned if this wouldn't just be more killing and this would only continue the cycle of violence.

Rifle Shot held his weapon to the sky and looked through the barrel. "Mmmm. Yess, Mormons will hate Delaware after I use him up. Like I said, this is the path that is taken when different people meet in this way. We are in a land wet with the blood of many tribes. Like the wagon people, the Delaware and Mormons come from other places too, and bring their own pain and trouble to this real earth. I do not know what to say about it all. Maybe the spirits can understand." He looked at me with a pensive and timeless expression. "But is it not the same in the land of the white man? Has it ever been any other way?"

What can I say about the land of white men and the paths they have taken? Shall I tell him that the Anglo-Saxons and Franks scalped each other, and everyone else they could lay hands on, until AD 900?

That there have been feudal-clerical wars that have ruined whole countries or that illiterate and brutal baronages travelled thousands of miles for two centuries to kill neighbors of a different religion? Should I say the white man hacks away with swords designed to maim and invented lapidary machines to sever men's heads? And that it continues to this day not only among the whites but everyone else, everywhere in this troubled world? Should I admonish Rifle Shot and say Indians are savages and that his proposed murder of Brigham Young will only promote a world of unending violence and tribal hostility? It is a headache just to think of these things.

This hunting of Man is a tiring and confusing business, but I can see why Laibon Mbatiany chose this continent for the stalking. It would be too delicious if Rifle Shot and the laibon could sit together and help straighten things out for me, and it might not be a bad idea to ask Marie Laveau to come over and lend a hand. But at this relatively early stage in my new cycle I doubt if I could fully understand their wisdom on the matter, and besides it is my job to make some sense of mess, and in the end probably find myself squarely in the middle of it like everyone else.

At this point I would not even be surprised if my three sage counselors got into a fistfight among themselves while trying to explain matters.

The only sane and decent thing I can think of at the moment is to retreat to the tent with my handsome squaw and heartily embrace those dear moments of peace, romance, and harmless adventure. Fate can wait.

XVII

A Member of the
Dangerous Danite Band
Encounters Rifle Shot

August 25, 1860
Valley of the Great Salt Lake

It was not an easy thing this morning to untangle myself from the delicious, dark olive limbs of my new wife. Our evening was so amusingly playful, and she so anxious to please, that I shrink from the thought of ever again engaging the waxy, cadaverous Englishwoman with her petted attitude and constitutional frigidity. I do believe I am suffering from *squaw mania*—a disease for which there may be no cure.

Nevertheless, I was able to return to my *compagnons de voyage* by seven, and after a cup of tea and a hard biscuit we set off on the last leg before attaining Zion. The morning's first chore was to follow the rocky course of Bauchmin's Creek for several hours and then assault "Big Mountain." This was no small task as the eastern ascent took every minute of five hours and, as evidenced by the many roadside burials, the grade was steep enough to end the lives of many a thousand-mile pilgrim here at the very doorstep to Eden.

The crest of Big Mountain provided our first look at the Valley of the Great Salt Lake, a sight which cannot be viewed without considerable emotion after nineteen hard days in a mail ambulance. We were now just eighteen miles from the Holy City, and one cannot help but remark that Independence Rock bears a remarkable resemblance to *Jiwe la Mkoa* in Unyamwezi and the Devil's Gate to the *Breche de Roland* in the Pyrenees.

An equally difficult descent brought us to the gorge of Big Kanyon Creek and a mid-day rest at a small station situated between the trail and a narrow ribbon of water running next to it. The proprietor was none other than Mr. Ephe Hanks. I recognized the name from Lt. Dana who back in St. Jo named Mr. Hanks as one of the triumvirate Mormon leaders of the Danite Band, along with Bill Hickman and O.P. Rockwell. Mahoney said he knew him and I begged an introduction.

"How dee do, Captain," were his first words. "Are ye almighty terrified to meet up with your first desperado Mormon?"

I told him no indeed. "Danite or Damnite, it was pretty much the same to me."

"Well fine then. Will ye come in and have some victuals?"

I thanked him and entered the station. There we sat and were served by his "Old Lady," who turned out to be neither old nor a lady, but one of his four teenage wives, who from her mannerisms and speech had obviously not spent a single day in the schoolroom. Mr. Hanks himself was a decent enough looking fellow of average height and build, and appearance-wise not near the demon I imagined after hearing some of the terrible stories. Over dinner he told me of his seafaring days out of New England, and in his conversation he covered a variety of other quite ordinary topics.

He expressed a child's interest in my air rifle, but this was simply an excuse to clear the way for him to make an ostentatious display of his collection of high-caliber weapons.

"Yes siree, these come in handy if'n ye meet-up with ol' Ephraim when yer out on the trail. Griz with a cub like to claw yer guts out, 'less'n ye git to her first. Gotta have yer killb'ars ready for business, there's no gittin' round that. I've fixed mine many a time and have done deadly damage." Hanks heaved a laboured sigh. "There's no countin' the number or the ways. A man of the west just gotta do what he's got to do, and have the right means to do it."

When I gave a knowing nod, he looked at me and burst out in a derisive laugh. Perhaps it is because I am British and have the look of newness about me, but I also suspect he thought the air gun my sole means of defense, or worse, the only shooting tool I could command. I could not bear to let this mockery go unanswered, for I had already seen too much in these forty years to allow such an event to take place. Why, if the man were at Berbera five years ago, it would have been naked sword against native lance, by god, and no quarter given. Something had to be done.

"Mr. Hanks, it is one thing to face an unarmed bear in the wild, and I am sure it takes a marksman's nerve to get the job done. However, it is something altogether different to engage the true king of beasts at equal strength and come out on top."

This surely caught his attention, for he interrupted his chewing, and with a mouthful of food garbled out, "What the hell ye mean by that, Captain? Is it another man ye are speakin' of?"

"Well, yes, actually. Where I come from, the true measure of a person's mettle is always gauged against his success in manly combat, and nothing short of that is worthy of a boast."

"Izzat so? And a boast is it?" He abruptly scraped his chair across the floor and stood over me. I had apparently touched a nerve for he snatched away his bib, glowered down and shouted, "We can gauge between the two of us on this very afternoon if it's a boast that's stuck in your craw, Captain. An' if you're feelin' the manly need to act as ye would where ye came from . . . well, we can settle that today too."

"Now, now, Mr. Hanks, I do not think it is necessary to have an American style shoot-up between us. Might not a better idea be to tangle with the Indians? We could go out together and try and settle with some trouble makers. You do have Indian troublemakers in these parts, don't you?"

He paused for a moment before telling me that there were some Gosiutes who had become "a bother." There had been some raids and some horses missing, and as he thought about it, I could see Hanks smiling and warming to the idea of taking care of several matters at the same time. "You gots yourself a deal, Captain, although I'd recommend bringing something more manly than your air gun over there. The Gosiutes may be a lowly, half-naked race, but they'll have your scalp if'n you go in unprepared. 'Sides, how'd we sort out who's got boastin' rights if you went and got yourself killed?"

He suggested that at sundown we should make a camp some distance away from the station and that a few extra ponies be brought along as bait. As a further enticement, Hanks asked that I make myself conspicuous by the fire. He, on the other hand, would wait in ambuscade close by until the renegades came, and at that point he would rush from hiding and we would together engage the savage Gosiutes to see who the best of us was.

I had difficulty keeping from a derisive laugh of my own, for I could guess what might happen if Mr. Hanks followed me to a separate camp.

We made arrangements to leave the station at five that afternoon and the self-confident Hanks casually hummed a sailor's tune as he prepared himself and the horses. He would occasionally look over at me and it seemed all he could do to keep from laughing. Once on the trail he intensified his campaign. "Ever seen a Gosiute, Captain? They be small devils and ragged, but what they can do to a man is horrible . . . less'n ye knows how to handle them. Any Gosiutes over there in England, Captain? I suspect not. Ye know, they can come up on a man sudden-like, take ye by surprise if'n ye don't know the things to look and listen for."

Hanks was relentless. "When the shootin' starts, lad, best lay ye flat on the ground so's not to be hit by one of my balls, for they'll be a-commin' fast and furious. An' take care that a dead Gosiute don't fall on ye and break one of yer bones. I'd hate to have to leave a man in the wild, but in these parts, a man that can't ride gots to be left. Course then they is prey for the wolves and the other Gosiutes that'll come at night for their dead."

And a short while later, "Do ye have next of kin, Captain? Someone who we could write with the bad news? Ye know there was a tenderfoot Englishman through here some months ago, boasted that he knew what it took to live in the territories. Some little-bitty Gosiute tore him up real bad and we didn't even know where to send the pieces. It was a pitiful shame."

After an hour or so of almost uninterrupted harassment we came upon a well-known clearing near a creek and made a rough camp. The courageous Hanks bid me sit next to the fire while he settled into some knee-high brush not twenty feet from my post. All the while he chatted away through the bushes.

"Ye gots to know the sights and sounds if'n you expect to be top dog in these parts, Captain. The filthy beggars fancy themselves expert stalkers, but Mr. Ephie Hanks has taught them a trick or two I'll tell ye and made 'em pay dearly for it as well."

I turned to look at Hanks as he prattled on and saw Rifle Shot begin to slowly and silently rise up from a bush located not three feet behind him. When he straightened to full height, he simply listened with a taciturn face as Hanks worsened the situation.

"Sometimes a scroungy little Indian near the animal stage can overtake a fully armed white man that's lackin' the necessary skills, so ye have to watch close for that and always be prepared. I'll tell ye lad, I can smell the dirty mutts a mile away."

Just then my squaw came into the clearing at the far side of the camp. Hanks finally spotted her after she took a few steps into the light and he let out a loud yelp, "There's one of the dirty curs right now! The primitive bitch is tryin' to sneak up on us whilst we weren't lookin." He began fumbling with his rifle. "Clear the way boy an' I'll drop her like a sack of shit."

At this point Rifle Shot reached down and wrapped his massive hand around the barrel of Hank's weapon. He lifted it over his head while turning it, and then brought down the flat side of the butt hard against the top of Hanks head. Rifle Shot then took the gun and snapped it in half over his knee. The big Indian stared down at the unconscious Hanks then looked over at me with a quizzical expression on his face.

"Was he your friend?" He shook his head. "Why he sit in bushes when so much better by fire?" Then the squaw came over and took a look at the crumpled body. She said something about how deranged white people were and how typical it was of them to be doing something strange like that and reached for her scalping knife.

While still looking at the motionless Hanks, Rifle Shot addressed this issue with his former wife. "Wah, hold-on, hold-on. I do not think they are the only ones who are crazy. My mother's sister's son, Lazy Horse, he used to sit in bushes too. No one knew the reason."

Did I understand him correctly? Could my ears have failed me? I asked Rifle Shot if he meant "*Crazy* Horse" (in Standard Lakota Orthography Tȟašúŋke Witkó) literally, His-Horse-Is-Crazy" or His-Horse-Is-Spirited. Could my formidable friend also be the cousin of the fierce warrior, Crazy Horse?

"No. *Lazy* Horse. Crazy Horse is Oglala Sioux, name Tashun-ca-Uitco. Lazy Horse is Delaware, part of my own clan." Rifle Shot grimaced. "Sometimes he put fish on top of head and dance *tout nu*[32], very strange."

August 28, 1860
Salt Lake City

We have at last descended into Immigration Canyon, and now the entire Holy Valley of the West and the Great Salt Lake lay before our view. It is a magnificent sight. After a short time the city itself was revealed, all laid out before us in the distance as if upon a map. The Metropolis of God was arranged in neat rectangular blocks each containing dull, gray adobe dwellings. Only the Prophet's house was whitewashed. Next to Mr. Young's residence and the courthouse, I am afraid that the most prominent structure in the entire town was the arsenal.

The agricultural fruits of Mormon industry were apparent in well-tended fields surrounding the city. Rows of corn and sweet sorghum accompanied orchards of apple and peach. There was nothing to compare with this west of the Mississippi, and I can easily see why pilgrims consider this God's own land.

Noteworthy on our approach to the city was a moat which was dug to provide material for an equally curious structure—a Romulian

---

32 Totally naked. —Ed.

wall made of puddle and stone, which was nearly six miles in length and twelve feet high throughout its course. I later learned that this worthless expenditure was built in 1854 to dissuade the Lamanites [Indians] from attack. My guess would be that despite all the effort put into building it, this laughable barrier could not hold off a half dozen Utes for more than fifteen minutes as they would quickly flank it and get on with their business.

As we rolled through our first properly civilized town in nearly three weeks I could not help but stare out the window of the coach and marvel at the order of things and the abundance. This was no Cairo, St. Louis, or St. Jo, but rather an Athens from a distance and up close, a budding Paris with wide, tree-lined boulevards and the feeling that everything in the city had been carefully planned well in advance.

There was also a distinct air of calmness and civility that obviously did not sit well with Gaston La Mash. He was unusually quiet and sat frozen in his seat shifting only his eyes to take hesitating looks out the window. He once leaned in that direction as if to spit, but caught himself and swallowed hard; I believe the apparent absence of barbarism actually frightened him. Mahoney waved to a few people as we passed, and Lt. Dana waxed enthusiastic to his wife. "Look dear, a dry goods store with calicos, and over there is a theater house of some sort. Why, they have in-door plumbing and bake shops. Isn't this wonderful?"

Mrs. Dana gave her husband a surly look and appeared much more interested in his Colts' Dragoon that lay wrapped in its issue belt on the seat between them. Since back at Ham's Fork, the woman's attitude had soured and hardened more with each passing day until now. Like La Mash, I feared she may not be fit for civilized company. Her hair, once wrapped in a neat bun, now hung in greasy strands down her face. Dark circles had formed under her eyes, and there were outbursts of wicked laughter that responded to no apparent stimulus.

After some turns through the city we pulled up to the Salt Lake House, the best hotel between Chicago and California. This would be the end of the trail for Mahoney and, for all practical purposes, the Danas as well. They would be off to Camp Floyd after a two- or three-day rest and Mahoney would book passage on the next coach back to St. Jo and begin the ride all over again.

My own plans are to stay here for two weeks in the hopes of exploring and perhaps even experiencing Mormon polygamy. After unpacking and taking a bit of decent food, I wandered the streets for an initial, firsthand impression. It did not take long before one was able to tell which citizens were Mormon, which Gentile, and who among them represented the dedicated anti-Mormon contingent.

As for the Mormons themselves, disposition is the first indicator. They appear stoic if not severe but with a surprisingly sunny disposition, and if this is not enough, the stranger may also identify a Mormon by looking towards those many citizens sporting blond hair and pale blue eyes. One also has the distinct impression that there is a *subrosa* element in all affairs of the state. This secretive attitude seems to spill over into even the most routine matters and breeds an atmosphere of suspicion directed towards the newcomer. "Smiling deception" may be the best way to characterize the Saint's demeanor.

The Gentiles, and there are but four hundred of them in this city of nine thousand, seem somewhat less secretive and are conspicuous by their groupings around the saloons of Whiskey Street. This is the section of town where the soldiers take their leave and seemingly the only place in Salt Lake City to get a drink. I did not know that semi-temperance (at least in public) was the rule of the day among the Mormons, and I was chagrined to learn that the devout take nothing stronger than lager beer. I am naturally suspicious of those who turn their back on the occasional drink, but I shall try not to allow this to colour my impressions.

The anti-Mormon presence is most apparent by the select literature that is available in several stores about town. One is certainly able to patronize a few non-Mormon shops, and in some of these establishments the reader may peruse titles such as: *Friendly Warnings on the Subject of Mormonism, An Exposure on the Errors and Fallacies of the Mormon; Les Harems du Nouveau Monde*; and perhaps the longest and most inflammatory title, *Fifteen Years Among the Mormons, being the Narrative of Mrs. Mary Ettie V. Smith, late of the Gt. S.L. City, a Sister of one of the Mormon High Priests, she having been personally acquainted with*

most of the Mormon leaders and long in the confidence of Brigham Young by
Nelson Winch Green.

Soldiers in Camp Floyd also print and circulate *Valley Tan*, a vehe-
mently anti-Mormon tract. It is a testimony to Mormon tolerance
that such publications are allowed anywhere in the city, for they could
surely suppress such literature without too much trouble.

There was much to think about as I took my stroll through the
streets of Zion. As this was the first real pause in my trip across the
American west, I could not help but reflect on some of the characters
and events of my journey so far. The apparent collapse of Mrs. Dana
is certainly noteworthy, if not troubling, and I fear that events may
come to a hard end very soon. Can there be any doubt that she is but
one of the many psychological casualties of the way west? I think not.

It is difficult to determine if it was murder of the young Pony
Express rider, Little Boy Cotton, or the incident at Ham's Fork Station that snapped her into this new and dangerous self. Perhaps it was
the rapid combination. Only god himself knows what role La Mash
played in this, but there can be no doubt that he helped set the stage
with his early barrage.

And what will become of La Mash? I do not think it is possible
to say. He claims to be here for the buffalo, and if this is true, I believe
he may be in the correct element. These creatures of the plains also
inhabit the mountains, although they are being eliminated at such a
shocking rate methinks they may all be gone by the time he leaves
the coach.

Lord Kill Ba'r seems best suited to a place like Fort Laramie, but
I do not think he will retrace his steps and move back east. It is my
hope that he will swing north to Canada, but he has made mention
of California so we may be together for a while yet.

Then there is this business with my new wife, and more importantly, Rifle Shot's intention to kill Brigham Young. Now that we
have reached the city of his residence I suppose that there will be an
attempt on his life, and because of my associations, there is a chance
I too will become involved. This is not a happy prospect. And what
of this Orrin Porter Rockwell fellow who is Mr. Young's bodyguard?

His reputation seems as formidable as Rifle Shot's and a confrontation between them is sure to be bloody business.

There are many things to contemplate here in the City of the Saints but none more intriguing than my desire to sample the Mormon harem. How one gains *entree* to this garden of delights is a mystery at the moment, but I shall be pursuing a solution with great diligence. As for now, it is a return to the Salt Lake House for a much needed rest and a drink. This will be my first proper bed in nearly a month and I cannot say that it won't be welcome. I suspect the brandy in these parts will be both dear and bad, but no matter, if I can find a bottle, I'll see it through in a heat.

ANOTHER LETTER TO LORD HOUGHTON, DATED SEPTEMBER 9TH, 1860 FROM THE GREAT SALT LAKE

Carissimo Milnes,

Yrs. truly has the melancholy satisfaction to report that I am now a week deep in the pervasive gloom of Mormon religiosity. It seems that I have travelled near one thousand miles just to dwell in the odour of sanctity, and a pretty strong one it is too.

It is a fact that Salt Lake City is as safe as St. James and that the entire town requires only a handful of police to maintain order, but that is also part of the problem. I had a chat yesterday with the Chief of Police, a brass-fronted and copper-bottomed Scotsman named Mr. Sharp, who took great pride in informing me there was not a loafer rich or poor, an idle gentleman, a drunkard, gambler, or a prostitute in the whole Mormon community. What a pity I say!

These professionals, membered now exclusively by a few Gentiles, were once a numerous if not unanticipated and underappreciated item in these parts. It seems that Mr. Smith's vision did not foresee the gold fever that would bring hordes of such characters to isolated Utah Territory. It was not until Denver and Carson City effloresced and lured the crusty miners to this isolated part of the globe that the Mormon Jerusalem was effected, and that in turn helped to settle this place into the dreary and sanitized little monastery that it is today.

It is worth mentioning that America's general response to the chaos of freedom-emboldened miscreants is a corresponding hardening of religious beliefs and structure. This dichotomy, if it continues, promises a future land torn between two extremes leaving little ground for normal citizens to enjoy a balanced life.

A word or two on Mormon polygamy, for surely one would think that such a practice could enliven even the most common and cheerless town. Not so! To begin, Mormon polygamy lacks the sensuality of Islamic harem life. If you can believe it, Mr. Young expressly forbids pleasure in the married state beyond that single episode which is requisite for ensuring progeny. He has therefore created a state of Puritanical Polygamy, and what good is that? Good god, man, given this somber mandate it is no wonder why multiple wives are a positive necessity for all healthy young men. The rest of America must recognize this Mormon tragedy and forgive them.

Jollification hereabouts revolves around the church. The many religious events are always *coram publico* and involve mighty speeches designed to leave the audience in a rapturous state of spiritual ecstasy. Never mind the pleasures of physical love or the imperial numbness of a stiff drink. What could be more satisfying than to hear Jedediah Smith rail against filth and whores or the vascular A. O. Smoot run on about the joys and gladness of being filled with the Holy Ghost? Nothing is the correct answer for there is no genuine satisfaction in that.

Just as the love-making is regulated, so is almost every other aspect of Mormon behaviour. Unlike Turkey and Egypt—which we recognize as the twin mothers of municipal misadministration—the Imperial State of Deseret runs like a Swiss clock and governs the Saints with a mandate that transforms romance and reverence to religion and the church. Therefore, it is for the church, to the church, and all about the church, that makes the Mormon world.

There is, for example, much tithing to the church, which is done without so much as a whisper of complaint. This practice is especially hated by the Gentiles. I believe it offends their New World sense of independence and recalls a time when paying tribute to a king was the order of the day. This is but one of the reasons why the Mormons are considered "downright un-American."

In an act of courage, I sat down and attempted to read the Book of Mormon and Maroni the Prophet. This was a painful and brutalizing effort that left me utterly exhausted well before the halfway mark. Those wishing more may be in need of *sal volatile*[33] and perhaps something to quell a rising stomach. The Holy Bible did me, but this book did an extra do.

One must admit, however, that the Book of Mormon has done something for America that America could never have done for itself. It has created a fantastic non-Indian history for the country, a miraculous past related through a most improbable saga. This tale informs us that the Indians, or "Lamanites," are really Hebrews whose skins have been darkened by apostasy. More dangerous is the declaration that upon their conversion they will become once again a "white and delightsome people." The world should brace for a new plague of missionaries, and a special caution issued to dark-skinned people everywhere.

I suppose it would be impolitic to mention Mr. Smith's extraordinary translation of those unique golden tablets upon which the Book of Mormon is based, or their remarkable resemblance to the decorative copper plates that are so abundant in Indian graves throughout the state of New York. Likewise, there shall be no mention of the same Mr. Smith's history of violating those final resting places in search of loot. If faith were money, Milnes, the Mormons would be millionaires. But enough of the Saints for the moment. Have I told you of my marriage to a Delaware Indian squaw? Her name translates as "Love Eye." Not a word of this to Miss Arundell, if you please. You see, ours is just an "over the broom," frontier sort of wedding that would in no way be recognized by the One, Holy, and Apostolic Church of Rome. In consideration of this, Miss Arundell's deep devotion and fragile mindset, I say why trouble the poor dear with something of such small consequence?

---

33 Smelling salts. —Ed.

Regarding the squaw in general, suffice it to say that the female aborigine is not petted and spoiled as her Anglo sisters tend to be back home. Because of this she is not frail and less likely to be possessed of the highly nervous temperament that causes so much domestic trouble. The squaw is also well-conditioned because she is a willing and acrobatic bedmate, her sturdy and muscular frame being both the cause and effect of her vigorous and profound love-making abilities.

As happy a union it may be, I am afraid mine is not destined to be a long one. "Love-e" as I call her, would not fare well in England for a variety of reasons. I can just imagine what the Arundells would think if I walked off the boat with her, not to mention the reactions of Palmerston, Murchison, and the rest. It is a delicious thought, but one probably best left as just that.

No, it appears that we may even part ways here in Salt Lake City. Her ex-husband and brother-in-law (they are one in the same, and were once both at the same time) has brought her this far so she may assist him in the assassination of the Mormon leader, Mr. Brigham Young.

This big Indian is a very able warrior and determined, and I think I have told you before that it makes some Indians "feel good" to eat a bit of their defeated enemy. This could get very messy. For their part, the Mormons have a history of not being behind hand in responding forcefully whenever they think their best interests are being threatened. One can only imagine what would happen if someone were discovered trying to "do-up" Mr. Young in the same fashion that Mr. Smith was "done-up" some years past.

I shall be here at least another week trying to find a woman for myself, but so far it appears the blasted Mormons have them all. Another trip to a Holy City and the practitioners of polygamy, Baw! I must be contented to once again pay the penalty of ignorance.

Tout a vous,

R. Burton

XVIII

THE BIG MORMON, THE SON OF THUNDER, AND A CASE OF AMERICAN JUSTICE

Sept. 18, 1860
Camp Floyd,
Utah Territory

At last a few quiet hours to write after an eight-day trip to Camp Floyd, and later, American Fork in search of the vaunted Mr. O. P. Rockwell. I left on horseback under the supervision of a Gentile guide named Tree Jimboy, whose appellation no doubt comes from his extraordinary size and reluctance to undertake any superfluous movement.

Mr. Jimboy was a first-rate hand in shirking anything that resembled work, and being a life-long product of the high plains and completely uneducated, he spoke a type of English so mangled and perverted that the home reader could hardly distinguish it from High Dutch. In spite of these handicaps, Tree Jimboy was placed in charge of the convoying and delivery of ten Mormon horses which had been purchased by the adversaries of the Saints at Camp Floyd.

It is a curious interplay between the soldiers and the Mormons here in God's land. There is no secret that the Saints dislike the troopers for their wild and reckless ways, and the very existence of the military garrisons stands as a testimony to the government's distrust of Mr. Young and his charges. The soldiers at Camp Floyd have a favourite aphorism that says simply, "They hate us and we hate them." The

popular Mormon rhyme which serves as a counterpoint is known by
every blond child in the street:

> *If Uncle Sam's determined*
> *On his very foolish plan*
> *The Lord will fight our battle*
> *And we'll help him if we can*
> *If what they now propose to do*
> *Should ever come to pass*
> *We'll burn up every inch of wood*
> *And every blade of grass*

Yet it is the Mormons who deliver the U.S. Mail, produce much of
the soldiers' food, provide the very lumber from which the fort is
built, and many of the horses which may someday be used in raids
against them. The only possible explanation rests in the materialism
of the Saints, a doctrine which is so leveling in its unauthorized de-
ductions at home and so prominent in its dealings with the outside
world that even the materialist must reject it.

This situation exists because Mr. Brigham Young, like the Imam
of Muscat, is both the chief merchant as well as the High Priest.
In such situations, spirituality and material interests are inexorably
mixed to such a degree that empire building becomes the highest
form of Godliness and it is even acceptable to aid one's enemy for the
right price.

I had the opportunity to meet face-to-face with Mr. Young on
the day before my departure. This meeting was arranged at my request
by Gov. Cumming and took place in Young's private office. No one
enters the room of the "President of the Church of Jesus Christ of
Latter-Day Saints all over the World" without passing a number of
body guards and engaging in a certain amount of smiling.

Once inside, I was approached and greeted by a handsome man
whose demeanor was characterized by an air of utmost civility and
regal calmness. I knew from earlier readings that Mr. Young was
born in Vermont in 1801, which would make him fifty-nine years

and some days at our meeting, but one could easily lose a wager guessing his age, for the man appeared to be not a day over forty. If just appearance is the reward of clean living, then you can have it for what it's worth.

The Prophet, son of a Revolutionary War soldier, had the appearance of a gentleman farmer. He was stately and even and there was a total absence of pretension in his manner. As an ultimate compliment I would say that he was so used to power that he cared nothing for its display.

After exchanging the usual pleasantries, Mr. Brigham Young, with few words and a gentle eye, let it be known that he would be pleased to know the exact reason for my visit. I told him that I had heard much about Utah and wished to see the place for myself.

"Oh, is that so, Captain? Then by all means allow me to describe for you our soils, methods of agriculture, and animal husbandry." And this the Prophet did in detail with all the acumen of a highly accomplished estate manager.

After an uninterrupted half hour of desultory monologue he looked at me with a twinkle in his eye. "Are you interested in our methods of water harnessing, Captain? Or perhaps the influence of climate and elevation on timber growth. We have developed quite a complete chart on these matters."

I began to squirm in my seat.

His Excellency President Mr. Brigham Young had adequately succeeded in demonstrating his abilities to deal with someone who was being less than direct with him, but he felt compelled to punctuate the matter in a most straightforward way.

"Captain, are you not the same Richard Burton who has investigated and written extensively on the forbidden cities of the Orient and Africa? Kurrachee in Scinde, Meccah, Hurrar, Zanzibar—places like that?"

"I am the same, sir."

"Then you are the same Richard Burton who is famous in some circles for his social and anthropological commentary, the man with the great interest in language, world religions, and," he smiled, "harem life? Oh, come, come, Captain Burton. We mustn't be coy in such matters. You have travelled to Salt Lake City in order to investigate the Saints, to see what sort of men we are, what we are made of. There is no crime in that Captain."

Mr. Young removed himself from behind his desk, clasped his hands behind his back as he paced the room, and he spoke with a smile on his face that communicated a perfect confidence in what he had to say. His words were careful and well chosen, and while it is often difficult to discern a great spirit at first impression, I felt strongly and at once that this was no common uncommon man.

"I'm afraid you'll find no demons here, Captain Burton. The Saints are a God fearing people, lovers of liberty, and benefactors to our fellow man. There are no secrets in these matters, no exposé to be written in a popular travelogue. We are simply hard-working servants to our creed, a people who wish nothing from others, nor want anything but respect in return."

Brigham Young's hands were gesturing in the air as he moved about his office, and like all good preachers he could sense that he was now warmed-up and gaining narrative momentum with each new thought. "You fancy religions other than your own, isn't that so, Captain? You see, I have read your books and know your love of spiritual adventure, of penetrating holy cities." He forcefully thrust a forefinger towards the ceiling. "You are a seeker! And I like that!"

He placed his arm around the back of my chair and lowered his voice. "Mr. Joseph Smith was a seeker, just like you. And he was murdered for it. Murdered by men who could not tolerate the seeker, men who have not the Spirit of Zion within them."

The Prophet straightened before me and nodded. He then walked to his desk and expectorated into a spittoon which was discreetly placed behind a floor safe. I believe he realized that a sermon was perhaps not the best approach in my case, and being the man that he is, naturally composed himself and redirected the conversation. "I am a practical man, Captain. I understand yours is an academic interest in our community, and as a scholar you are welcome here, as are all men who lead decent and intelligent lives."

I told him that my interest was not wholly academic and made an inquiry as to what conditions are necessary in order to join the union of the Saints.

Mr. Young chuckled. "You wish to become a Mormon? Oh, I am afraid your reputation precedes you in that respect, Captain. I think you have done that sort of thing before." He gave me a knowing and somewhat sly look. "No, Captain, there is much, much more to being a Mormon than to be sealed to a number of wives."

I glanced down at the floor momentarily and said, "I see. If that is the case and you do not find me a fit candidate, then may we at least speak freely on the subject of polygamy?"

"Plural marriages," he corrected.

"Very well then, plural marriage, if you like."

Brigham Young reseated himself behind his desk and displayed a comfortable if not serene disposition. "Normally I would not consent to probing inquiries from the outside world, but in your case, Captain Burton, I shall make an exception. The answer to your question is yes; feel free to ask what you will."

"You are most kind. As President and Prophet, may I ask if you personally are a practitioner of plural marriage?"

Young gave a slight nod and said modestly and slowly, "Yes, I am sealed to over fifty living women. But I would like to add, Captain, that I am a conservative man, I sleep with none of them."

"But, you do . . . ?"

The Prophet spared me the indelicacy of finishing the sentence by answering very patiently. "I had nine children born to me in the past week, Captain. I refer to sleep in the literal and not the biblical sense. I take my sleep in solitude for reasons having to do with quietude and health."

"Then your wives are kept elsewhere?"

"I do not know that *kept* is the best term, Captain, but they are together in a place apart from my quarters."

"It has been said, sir, that Mr. Heber Kimball has from the pulpit, referred to his young wives as, 'little heifers.' Grouping your stock together away from the main house is what one does with cattle. Is it possible that the Gentiles derive anti-Mormon fodder from these acts and Mr. Kimball's words?"

"What I do know, Captain Burton, is that plural marriage has abolished prostitution, concubinage, celibacy, and infanticide. In Salt Lake City there is no such thing as an old maid."

"Thank God for the last blessing, Mr. President."

"Thank God for Jesus Christ and the Book of Mormon, Captain Burton."

"Sir, since my arrival, it has come to my attention that the Mormons take nothing stronger than lager beer and also disdain the use of tobacco. Many people of the world will disavow one or the other, but both sir? It seems a bit strict."

"Captain, may I inquire of your travels in this land before your arrival in our *strict* city? I have in mind specifically if you have encountered any episodes where the use of spirits has encouraged social collapse or engendered any other acts of public opprobrium?"

I instantly thought of Steinhaeuser at the baseball game, but then there was the episode at the hotel, and at the Republican Convention and Congo Square, and then Lester Beach and the Sultana, and the Tangle Foot session at Ft. Laramie, and the saloons in St. Louis and St. Jo, and so much more I will never forget.

"I see that I may have touched a nerve, Captain. I'm sure you have noticed that America is something of a lawless land filled with adventure-seekers and firearms. Do we really wish to have alcohol added to this mix? No, Captain, no we do not. The State of Deseret is far better off without it, and tobacco for that matter." The President's eyes widened. "Have you ever suffered the smell of someone who has both evils on their breath at one time? It is the height of revulsion," he contorted his face and shook his head, "the very height. As for me, Captain, a baked potato with a dollop of buttermilk is as exhilarating as the Gentiles' brandy. A glass of water to wash it down and I have my earthly intoxication. Nothing more Captain, nothing extreme, nothing in excess."

"Except women?" I added.

Brigham Young almost gave in to expressing outrage at my comment but quickly composed himself and calmly reminded me that,

"The Lord has instructed us to be fruitful and multiply and replenish the earth. He has said that it is not good that man should be alone."

"Quite right, Mr. President. I trust the wisdom of the Lord in this matter but must tell you that as a Gentile in your city, *Je meurs de soif en couste la fontaine.*"[34]

Mr. Young flashed a smile and began to chortle. "Oh Captain, ho, ho, you are a card. I'm afraid that in this instance the Lord's words are meant for the Lord's people, and while your passage from Mr. Charles D'Orleans is amusing in this context, I do not think you would be a very good fit in our society. Perhaps you should explore some other avenues to satisfy your secular desires? Have you considered conventional marriage to a loved one back home, or perchance in your case bonding with a Laminate squaw?"

This last suggestion naturally brought me to thoughts of my Delaware wife and her revenge-minded ex-husband and my current brother-in-law. My familial respect and obligations notwithstanding, I felt honour bound to alert Mr. Young that his life was in danger.

"Sir, not that I wish to change the subject, but there is another topic which must be addressed at once: I must inform you that there is an agent close to the city who wishes you harm. Someone quite formidable and very dangerous whose desire it is to end your life."

"If you are referring to those silly French assassins Jules Remy and Julius Brenchley, they have not succeeded and have been sent on their way for almost a year now. And I would hardly consider either one of those two *formidable.* You would think the French could manage better than that."

"They are not who I had in mind, sir. The individual in question is fully capable of the most extreme forms of violence and should not be considered lightly."

"Do you mean Joachim Johnson?"

"No."

"Not that bullwacker Martin Oats?"

"That is not the man."

"Lot Hunnington then, is that the man?"

---

34 I am dying of thirst at the fountain's brim. —Ed.

"It is not."

"John Gheen! Is it John Gheen you are referring to?"

"I have never heard of a John Gheen."

"Do not tell me that Martin Brewer is posturing once again. Another alcohol victim, Captain, always full of vinegar when he is at the bottle."

"I do not refer to Mr. Brewer, sir."

Brigham Young then came the closest I had seen to losing his composure. "Well, who then? I could run this list to Carson City if I be forced to list all mine enemies. Utah Territory is filled with people who do not like the Mormons and would die for a chance to try their revolver on the Mormon leader."

"It is an Indian, sir, and I can say no more about him."

Young walked around behind his desk, leaned forward and rested his knuckles on a stack of papers. He studied me for a moment and drew a long breath before he spoke.

"An Indian, you say? And one you are not prepared to discuss further."

"For good reason, sir. The man has saved my life."

The Mormon *pater patriae* seemed relieved and almost jocular as he continued. "A Lamanite is it, Captain? Well, we have our ways of dealing with these fellows, and it won't require the saber or the services of my twelve-shooter over on the wall either. No, the poor little beggar is probably just hungry and out of sorts on account of his wretched condition. A sack of flour and some inspirational words will change his mind, Captain, render him harmless as a housefly."

"I do not believe that will work with this one, sir."

"Oh? I did not know you were an expert on Indian affairs, Captain. Just in case you are not, allow me to inform you that the average Lamanite is in size and accomplishment on a par with your run-of-the-mill East Indian *ghorwalla*. I do not want to say that we brush aside such threats, but I can tell you that we treat other matters of security with far more concern."

"I am not an expert on American Indians, Mr. Young, but it takes no expert to know when to be fearful as Hobbes. I would move with great care. This Indian told me that a hard rain is going to fall. He is after your hair, and if he gets it, it will not be his first."

Mr. Brigham Young scoffed at this pronouncement and flicked his hand in the air as if dismissing a bothersome insect. His normal equanimity returned an instant later and he lightened the mood by skillfully changing the subject. "Oh, come now, Captain, we mustn't get too worked-up over such matters. Now, weren't we speaking of the fair sex? Why don't you come with me and I will introduce you to an eligible lady friend of mine. I think she will like you. Sister Sally Erb is a fine woman with the fire of Zion in her. Perhaps she can instill the spirit of the Saints within you too. There may be hope for you yet, Captain."

As troubled as I was about Mr. Young's dismissal of my warning, I must say that the prospect of meeting a young and available lady was enough to make me quickly forget the entire episode. The Prophet was a master at things of this nature. We left Mr. Young's office and walked a few blocks until we reached a very plain-looking cottage which was set quite apart from the others. Mr. Young knocked carefully on the door, and we were beckoned into an even plainer interior, consisting only of a very ordinary bed, a crudely built table, and a single chair. There seated was Sister Erb, unfortunately bathed in light from the dreary room's only window so that the extraordinary wretchedness of her person was in full display. Her hair and costume looked as if they had been rammed through a picket wire fence into a world of tribulation and woe. Her face was a cross somewhere between Staffordshire terrier and bullmastiff broken through stiff training.

Besides the distinct canine appearance, Sister Erb also had the misfortune of being one of those women who appeared to be sixty when she was, in reality, barely half that age. The expression on her mummified face was a reflection of her cheerless surroundings and she hardly showed signs of life when Mr. Young introduced me.

"Sister Erb, may I introduce you to Captain Burton? He is a visitor here in Deseret and has expressed a marked interest in our religion. Perhaps you could kindly receive him, and the two of you could discuss matters pertaining to the Saints." The Prophet turned to me and in a voice that could be described as a loud whisper said, "Sister Erb is a well-known expert on church affairs."

He indicated that the right woman may be able to bring me into the fold, and added fuel to the fire by declaring to her that special rewards are in store for those missionaries with enough pluck to convert ardent sinners like myself.

Sister Erb's mouth began to twitch. "Mission?" she said. "A mission right here in Salt Lake City, in my own home?" She knelt before Mr. Young and took his hand as if to kiss it. "I will devote myself to this task, Mr. President."

She turned to me. "Will you join me on your knees, Captain? Will you get down on your knees right now and accept the Lord Jesus Christ into your soul?"

I told her I would not. I told them both I was Hajji Abdullah, a mystic Sufi, a former Member of the Church of England, a drinker, a fornicator, an agnostic, an atheist, a committed and unrepentant sinner. I shouted there was no hope for the likes of me and bolted out the door into the street. I secured the nearest horse and rode like the wind until I was well away from the City of the Saints. I would sleep on the ground without shelter. I would forgo nourishment and personal safety. I would lose it all to be free of Sister Sally Erb and her mission of conversion. As I rode towards the mountains I realized that Brigham Young was right in the first place—I would not be a good fit in Mormon society. But on my word, I hold the man accountable for wrongfully telling me there were no old maids in Salt Lake City.

I was no more than thirty minutes away from town when there came a most urgent need to wash the trail dust from my throat and reconnoiter for an overnight camp. A grassy flat next to a bend in the stream caught my eye and I dismounted and headed for the cool water. As I contemplated the stream in preparation for my drink I was hit hard by a bone-jarring, flying tackle the likes of which are administered in serious rugby matches. My attacker held my arms fast to my sides and I panicked realizing I was unable to reach my revolver.

Then I realized I was being kissed, kissed all over the side of my face and on my neck, kissed on the ear and the nose. It was Love Eye, my wife, apparently overwhelmed by passion after not seeing me for less than a fortnight. She was squealing as she rolled me around in the grass and continued to administer her affection. When I was finally released, I saw Rifle Shot standing in the distance shaking his head and chuckling.

"Wah, Bur-ton, it has happened again. Stranger has surprised you in own camp. This time it is a squaw. You are like animal that keeps returning to same trap. Someday luck will run out. Smart animal watches for signs and does not get caught, stupid one ends up on fire."

We retired to a camp that the two sisters had made outside of town. Judging from the appointments, it appeared that the three of them had been in this particular spot for some time. Rifle Shot immediately went to his tent, fetched his breechloader, and began polishing it as we sat in front of the fire. This of course reminded me of his purpose to the Great Salt Lake. Considering my failure to impress the Mormon President of impending danger, I thought I might re-approach my friend with a mind towards reconciliation.

"I have met with Brigham Young; the man you wish to kill."

Rifle Shot nodded. "Mmmm, I know this."

I cleared my throat. "I noticed he has many bodyguards. He is not an easy fellow to get close to, and he also owns one of those new twelve-shooters."

The big Indian shrugged while studying the passage of a cleaning swab he was pushing through the barrel of his weapon.

"You know, it turns out that Mr. Young is not such a bad chap after all. He does not wish harm to Indian people. I think these Mormons just wish to be left alone, in peace, like all other decent people."

This comment took Rifle Shot from his business with the breechloader and he turned to me with a look of penetrating severity. "Mormons do not want peace any more than I do, or you, or any of the decent people you speak of. We all want what we want, and want to take what we need. Peace is just a word that sometime man puts in between. Is the hunter more decent than the rabbit he takes for his fire? Does the deer ask the wolf for peace? It is not the way of things. The only peace is death, when it is all finished the way it must be."

"But why must you be the minister of death. Why should you be the one to decide who is to live and die?"

Rifle Shot issued a rare smile. "Because I am the needy hunter, the wolf wanting the deer. It is the way it must be. The way it has always been."

There was no point in discussing this any further, nor was there an opportunity to do so, for Rifle Shot's squaw appeared at this juncture and unleashed a flurry of agitated comments. I could not understand a word of it and petitioned him for a translation after she left.

The big Indian filled his cheeks with air and exhaled in an upward direction. "She say I have no love in my heart, touch rifle more than her." He stood for emphasis. "Now there is not enough of *this!*" He rapidly thrust his hips back and forth simulating the *criso et ceueo.*[35] "Last moon, too much." He reseated himself and tried to regain his composure, but only succeeded in throwing his hands in the air. "Now she want me to move in tent with you, tells me she would rather live with her sister."

No sooner did he end this sentence than she re-approached us and directed some angry words at me. Her eyes were menacing and she wagged her finger dangerously close to my face. This latest attack prompted Rifle Shot to search the ground for the nearest "squaw husher," and he threatened to brain her with it until she retired into the shadows. A few last invectives came from the darkness and the big Indian finally pitched the rock in the direction of the angry words and added some of his own to follow.

"Wah, Bur-ton, she accuse you of sleeping with Mormon woman instead of her sister. Saw you coming from house of woman who look like dog."

"Yes," I said despondently. "Sister Erb. The ironic part is that I was actually running away from her."

Rifle Shot looked puzzled. "Ironic?"

"Yes, irony, my friend. It is a term that means things observed or said are sometimes an outcome of events contrary to what was or might have been expected, and maybe just the opposite. Like with

---

35 Latin technical terms for types of male and female reciprocating sexual motion. —Ed.

Sister Erb. I was leaving her house because I did not want to be with her, not because I had just finished making love with her."

The big Indian furrowed his brow and nodded. "Mmmm. I will have to think on this. But what does that have to do with how squaw sees things?" He shook his head. "I do not think they see this ironic. I think sometimes squaws see only what will make them angry." Rifle Shot began saying the word over and over as if practicing it, "Ironic, ironic. Is this just a man's word?"

"No, where I come from, women know this word and use it all the time."

"So." He held a finger before him and moved it between two imaginary spots. "They make this ironic invisible when they wish to fight?"

"I think that may have been used as a tactic once or twice."

"Mmmmm, ironic. I will have to remember that word. Maybe the next time I go, or do not go, to Three Trees, or when I want to give her the snake, or do not feel like it, I will tell her it is ironic. Maybe she will not get mad."

I told my friend that I did not think it was going to be that easy, and he complacently agreed. "No, Bur-ton. Not that easy. It is going to be the way I told you earlier."

"Earlier?"

"Yess, it is going to be the way it must be—the way it has always been."

September 19, 1860
Camp Floyd
Utah Territory

I ended that evening sharing a tent with Rifle Shot, a man whose reputation for snoring should be counted an equal match with his abilities for marksmanship and combat. Of course the sisters lodged together and talked throughout the night. I do not think I managed more than a half hour of fitful sleep.

At dawn I joined my friend as he squatted in front of the fire and excited last night's embers into this morning's flames. We did not speak for an unusually long period of time, and at length I had to ask if something were amiss. Rifle Shot took a brief look at me and then returned his attention to the fire. He poked at the ashes matter-of-factly and murmured, "Nothing to say. Day has yet to begin. Yesterday's words are over."

I suppose this was a fair enough answer, although over the years one does get used to a friendly greeting even after so short of a time as an evening's rest. At the risk of provoking an additional comment of that sort, I asked if he knew the way to a place called American Fork.

"Mmmm."

"Splendid. Then do you suppose you could show me the trail? I have some business there that I would like to attend to."

The big Indian narrowed his eye. "You are going to see Rockwell, the Mormon. That is where he stays." And after a long pause he announced that he would go along with me.

"Whatever for?" I said nervously.

"Business," he said with a malevolent grin.

Within the hour we were mounted and moving slowly along a trail that would, I was sure, lead to a rendezvous with bloody murder. He had painted his face once again and rode with his breechloader balanced across his lap and his pair of trousers carefully folded over his arm. Sometime just before midday, Rifle Shot stopped his horse and motioned for me to look behind us.

Through the ground heat distortion I could see a column of rising dust in the distance. It stained the air a yellowish brown and was quite noticeable against the brilliant blues and whites of the normal Utah sky.

Rifle Shot studied the cloud and announced that seven riders were approaching, maybe eight. He could not be sure. In either case he said they would catch up with us within the hour.

"Indians?" I asked.

"Worse. Only whites would make such a mess."

I queried him about what we should do, but he apparently did not think this question worthy of a response. He nudged his horse and continued on as before, seeming unfettered by his own discovery. After an hour of silence, and as if according to some mysterious schedule, Rifle Shot dismounted and spread his blanket on the side of the trail. There he sat and waited with his breechloader upright to the ground in one hand and the other resting in his lap. He was careful to position his trousers next to him so they would not be soiled, and also concealed under his blanket a very impressive scalping knife of considerable size and heft.

The tension was becoming unbearable as the dust cloud came closer. Naturally, the unflappable Indian displayed absolutely no sign of discomfort or anticipation even though we could now hear the horses as they approached around the bend.

The first sight of the strangers was that of Tree Jimboy and then a string of rider-less ponies tied in a line behind him. Of course, there were eight animals all told, just as the Indian had calculated from that distance more than an hour ago. The fleshy Jimboy was all but asleep on the lead horse, and when he caught sight of Rifle Shot on the side of the trail I worried that the fright of discovery might be enough to ossify his poor, overworked heart.

After the initial start and some jiggling in his saddle, Jimboy addressed the big Indian. His first words sounded something like, "Whelp, didn't think I'd be runnin' inta anybody 'long this route, not even an Injun. Don't you mine me, I means no harm, no sir."

When Rifle Shot did not respond, he carefully raised his voice a few octaves and said, "You speak American, mister? I say American, 'merican? Ahh, well then, *HOW*, mister! I say *HOW*. That's Injun talk, ain't it? Every Injun knows what *how* means, don't he?"

I thought it best for me to enter the picture at this point and I called Mr. Jimboy's name from the other side of the trail.

He nearly fell off his horse when he turned to answer. "Why, Mr. Burton! I wuz sort of wunderin' what become of you. You just sort of up an' disappeared back there at the Salt Lake City. I wuz suppose to lead you on to Camp Floyd and now here you come right on the trail. Foreign fella like yerself on this ol' trail. If that don't beat all."

Tree Jimboy struggled to dismount and was unable to completely do so without crashing to the ground. He picked himself up and addressed me in a serious tone and a lowered voice. "Ya know, Mr.

Burton, I don't think I didn't proper recognized that Injun right off, but now I do. Don't looks now but I believe that there's ol' Rifle Shot, the meanest most dangerous man in the Territories. Should have guessed it when I seen he don't speak none. They say he never speaked nor heared a word in his life. But you better watch out you don't cross this Injun, no sir.

"I should have knowed it when I seen them pants of his." Jimboy began to giggle, tried hard to suppress it, and then shot a glance over at Rifle Shot to see if he was paying attention. "Hee, hee, that crazy Injun's always carryin' his pants around instead of wearin' 'em. Ain't nobody can figure out why that is, but ain't nobody 'bout to ask neither."

I told Mr. Jimboy that we were on our way to American Fork, and he exclaimed, "With him?" He instantly covered his mouth with his hand in realization that he had perhaps spoken too loud. I told him that we were travelling together and asked why he was concerned about being overheard by a man who he believed was deaf.

"Oh, right, right," he whispered. "But, damn, I don't know if I'd even chance that with the man who kilt Lank Blacktower. Lank Blacktower was one tough son-of-a-bitch miner, way he worked an' drank an' fought an' all. Nobody thought he'd ever get done-up. No Sioux could ever do it, no sir, no white man neither. An' plenty of 'em tried. See, Lank didn't like most people; hated Injuns, soldiers, Mormons, other miners, you name it. Jus' the ornerest cus you'd ever see. One day he up an' kilt a Delaware named Little Moon, just up an' kilt him one day after he wuz drinkin'. No good reason, just cuz he wuz feelin' extra bad that day or somethin'.

"Well, seems ol' Rifle Shot over there took exception to that. Guess 'cause he's a Delaware too. He rode all the way up from Fort Laramie to do somethin' 'bout it and found Lank in the middle of one of his drinkin' fests; worst time anyone'd want to meet up with him. Rifle Shot wuz the biggest Injun any of us ever see'd 'round here, an' he walked right up to Lank, lifted up his breech cloth an' pee'd right on him. Didn't say a word, just pee'd all over him, an' turned an' walked away calm as he could be. Well, we all thought Lank would kill himself just tryin' to get up an' set out after him, but before he could git up straight, that big Injun whirled 'round, flung his knife, an' hit Lank square in the chest.

"Lank looked down to see what had happened to him, and when he did, he naturally commenced to collapse back into his seat. But before that man could sit back down, the big Injun had his rifle up an' shot-out both his eyes before you could say Jack Robinson. Two shots, two eyes gone quick as lightnin'. Just like that, perfect holes where them eyes should have been." Jimboy bit his lower lip and screwed his face into an awful visage, "Back of his head sure was a mess though."

Tree Jimboy mopped his brow. "I'll tell ya, there's plenty of folks what don't believe that story, but you go ahead and ask Doc Davenport or ol' Ned Woodside. They'll tell ya, they'll tell ya what become of Lank Blacktower." This story notwithstanding and despite Mr. Jimboy's fears, the three of us rode off to American Fork together; although I must say that the young man kept his distance from Rifle Shot and continued to lower his voice whenever he spoke of matters that may offend.

We were on the trail most of that day until in the distance I spied a small settlement consisting of a few modest but sturdily built structures and a horse stable. I turned and remarked to Rifle Shot that our destination was in sight, but when I did so the big Indian was nowhere to be seen. I asked Jimboy if he knew Rifle Shot's whereabouts, only to learn that he hadn't a clue.

"Why ask me?" he said. "I know better than to even look in his general direction and haven't even come close to doin' so since early this mornin'. He could've left three hours ago an' I wouldn't have knowed it."

So it was just the two of us and a string of ponies that pulled into American Fork Station that late afternoon. My purpose was to meet up with the notorious Orrin Porter Rockwell, the most celebrated Mormon triggerite and already one of the legendary figures west of the Mississippi River.

Immediately upon arrival, Tree Jimboy embarked on an urgent, almost desperate search for food. One would think he had not eaten in days when in fact that was all he did while *en route* from the Salt Lake. How one can, without stop, alternately eat salted rock candy, spoonfuls of marmalade and corn dodgers is a conundrum of the American frontier, but this is what Mr. Jimboy did until his stores of each were depleted. Now he was around back of the station making sweet words with a preparation chief in front of a mound of potatoes. His intentions were painfully transparent.

I entered the main station house which was occupied by a young lady engaged in a floor sweeping exercise and, I supposed, the shop-keeper himself who with back turned to me was stocking cans on a shelf. Neither of them acknowledged my presence, and so I reopened the door and shut it again in the hope that a more forceful closure would bring forth the desired results.

The young girl looked up from her broom and said, "James, there's a man here." The fellow at the shelf did not turn around at this announcement but rather took a side step in order to place himself in front of a mirror, and with this aid he looked at my reflection and delivered his salutation.

"Don't believe I've ever seen you in these parts before, stranger. How can I help you?" It was an odd thing to be engaged with a man whose back was to you, and especially to converse through the medium of a reflecting mirror, but these combined were not as odd as the high falsetto voice that issued from this grown man, nor the remarkably long blond hair which was plaited and pinned-up on both sides of his head.

I told him I was just arrived from Salt Lake City and was in need of rest and a few supplies.

"Moccasins are one American dollar and so's a lariat. A weight pound of tobacco is dollar and a half. Gallon of whiskey cost you thirty-two dollars. You can stay in the stable and feed your horse for fifty cents, and if you want to eat, you got to see the cook." I noticed his eyes narrow in the mirror. "And if you don't mind me asking, mister, what business did you have in Salt Lake City? You're not a miner or a soldier, and you carry no wares. You have the sound of a British pilgrim, but I not so sure about that. There's not the look of an English Saint about you."

"You are correct, sir, I am not of the Mormon faith, but I am acquainted with Mr. Brigham Young and have travelled here to be familiar with the State of Deseret and its people."

"Familiar is it?" The man turned from the mirror at that point and the first things I noticed were his striking pale grey eyes and that both of his trouser pockets were heavy with a revolver in each. Then I was even more taken aback at how badly matched his high voice was with the man now before me. This was no shopkeeper as sure as I am no Saint.

"Now stranger, tell me true—just how familiar are you with our President and Prophet Mr. Young?"

I described the man and my audience in detail—and Allah forgive me—even detailed my brief association with Sister Erb. Then, in my most polite voice, I apologized for failing to properly introduce myself. "I'm terribly sorry, sir: Captain Richard Burton, on leave from the Bombay Army. I am a student of anthropology and religion and have a great interest in the Saints."

The man considered this for a moment and announced that he was James B. Brown and asked, "What the hell does the study of ants have to do with religion?"

In the most delicate terms imaginable I informed him that anthropology has nothing to do with insects; it is the study of man, and because all men have religion, it was natural for me to inquire about the Church of Jesus Christ of the Latter Day Saints.

"Well, there's quite a bit to be said about that, mister. Suppose the first question I might ask myself is what the Saints think about assassins. I'll just go ahead and answer that one for you right away so we can get things straight from the git-go. There's been a history of people who come to the Mormons for no other reason than to bring trouble and death. I might inform you that our first Prophet, Mr. Joseph Smith, was assassinated in the state of Illinois. A mob of Carthage Grey's who done it, and you'd do well to know that a coward by the name of Frank Worrell and a few others paid with their lives for that act. Mormons have to naturally look upon strangers with suspicion." James B. Brown gave me a very staid look and said, "You wouldn't be one of them assassins now would you, mister?"

He came from behind the counter and approached me directly. "Appears to me you aren't really a student." He placed his hand on the left side of my face and ran his finger along the scar on my cheek. "This looks like somebody ran a spear right into your face. That doesn't happen in a schoolhouse. That's a memento from some wicked rough and tumble."

I told him the mark was left by the javelin of a Somali tribesman.

"Somali?"

"Yes. While on duty in Africa, Berbera actually. It was a very nasty affair. A good friend of mine was killed and mutilated, the rest of us horribly wounded and left to die."

"Africa, you say?"

"Yes, East Africa."

"Well, there you go, The Curse of Ham. Israel's in Africa, ain't it? That's where all the world's troubles began, so there's no surprise about you having problems there."

Mr. Brown assumed a slightly different attitude. He asked what I thought of Mr. Brigham Young and answered for me an instant later. "He is a great man. Oh, he is not Mr. Joseph Smith, but then that man was one of a kind. We had been friends for years, years before them heathens took his life. I'll tell you another heathen; that's that damnable Boggs of Missouri. You ever heard of him in your travels? Not if you're interested in religion, I'd suspect."

Brown was now heated to a full roll, and he was puffing around the room like a steam tug. "Goddamn son of a bitch don't deserve to live, Liliburn Boggs. Going to meet with a bad end if I got anything to say about it. I'm a Mormon in good standing myself, mister, except I can't seem to help myself from cussing and strong drink. That's two things that's just a part of me I can't do anything about—strong drink and cussing. Sometimes I think it's just plain good for the soul."

I told him that I was in full agreement about the strong drink part, and that was all that seemed necessary for him to call out to the floor sweep, "Mary, would you please go up to the house and fetch the Valley Tan?"

Until she returned with a whiskey bottle, I was not exactly sure what was going to happen. It seems every home product in Utah Territory is called Valley Tan because a tannery was the first technological process in the region. As a result, everything from the anti-Mormon newsletter to Sister Erb's needlepoint has the same sobriquet.

Mr. Brown's failing for strong drink was no boast. When the bottle arrived he filled two large glasses near to the top and insisted on "squars," i.e., no water or mix of any kind. As we lifted our first glasses in mutual salute he roared, "WHEAT," which I instantly recalled was the singular and favourite phrase of Orrin Porter Rockwell.

After two more rounds of the same "Mr. Brown" and I settled in and became somewhat better acquainted. We spoke easily and freely of Mormonism and various other topics of mutual interest. He had the look of a perfect ruffian, but I do not necessarily mean this in the pejorative sense. Rather, his ways were marked by a certain rawness that comes from years of hard and dangerous living; from men who have been close to perilous and fantastic events. I have seen the look in those eyes before—although surely not in the same hue—on the faces of veteran soldiers in the Crimea, Arab bodyguards in Zanzibar, Sikh sergeant-majors in the Punjab—they all have it: eyes that are owned by those who have seen wildness and death, and sometimes murder administered by their own hand.

But "Mr. Brown" had a twinkle in those eyes as well, and I soon learned that he was not as homicidal as advertised or as straight-laced as some of his brethren back at Salt Lake City. The first indication of this was when he gritted his teeth and said, "So, you've met Sister Erb, have you?" There was a cruel smile and then, "President Young took you over there for religious training and maybe a little matchmaking while he was at it?" He slammed his drink on the table. "Woof! That would take some doing. The only thing Sister Erb could make stand-up would be a cat's back, and that's only because she'd worry that old Tom near to death." He wiped his forehead as if to chase a worried sweat.

"It's a grisly thought, Captain. You better have another drink. Don't be shy when a man offers you drinking whiskey in these parts. I got another bottle just up at the house, and we can tuck right into that soon as this one runs dry. "Burrr," he said as if he were freezing, "Sister Erb, that's a shiver right there."

After a few more "squars" Brown confessed his true identity. "I won't be calling myself James B. Brown anymore. The name is Rockwell, Orrin Porter Rockwell, lot of my friends call me Port. Have to do something about my name when I meet up with strangers. Son of a bitch Lilliburn Boggs like to have me shot up for what happened back in Missouri, and just about anyone could be an assassin. So I have to be careful."

Although I knew some sketchy details of what had happened between the two of them back in Missouri, I felt obliged to allow him to tell his story, for it was obvious he was very keen on doing so.

"What? You never heard about that? Well, let me tell you something, Captain, that son of a bitch needed a good goddamn lesson taught him, and I've never been one to shy away from doing right when right needs doing. Especially when you're right. No man has cause to bring trouble to a peace-loving people like the Saints, and I don't give a good goddamn if he was the governor, or the president of the United States for that matter, no sir. That don't matter none to me. I might not be able to read or write a single word, but I know a home truth when I see it. And the truth was that Boggs had to go.

"When a decent man takes all he can take, then something has to be done. Well, that time came, and I set upon Boggs and was sure I ended his life right there with a single shot. But my hand must've been cold as a witch's teat, because it didn't happen. That son of a bitch lives to hunt me down to this day. That's why I got to be careful with strangers."

Rockwell pressed his lips together, shook his head, and then tossed back another squar. "Rickety shit! I believe that's the first time I ever missed my mark from that range, first goddamn time in my whole life. Well, Captain, bad as I feel about that, reckon I can say that one miss in a lifetime's not such a bad thing. Probably ain't a man in creation can say he ain't missed once."

I thought to myself that there is indeed such a man, and that he was somewhere outside at this very moment and just waiting for the right opportunity to blow Rockwell's head off. Rifle Shot meant harm to Rockwell just to clear the path for his primary mission. The very thought of the two of them engaged in a bloody altercation made my hands begin to sweat. This would be the pointless end for one or both of them and possibly extinguish the lives of two of the most extraordinary characters of the American west. Something needed to be done, but what? There was no chance of Rifle Shot entertaining any discussion on the matter, and if Rockwell ever found out that it was the murder of Brigham Young that was on the big Indian's mind, then it would be he who would be the aggressor.

Port Rockwell drained his glass and wondered aloud where the girl Mary had gone. The bottle was empty and he wanted her to bring another. "Ah, it's no matter, Captain. We can take a little walk to the house and finish up our drinking there. As a man of health I know a bit of Utah air is good for a man in between bottles."

All I could think of was Tree Jimboy's story about the besmirching and summary execution of Lank Blacktower and how that episode may be repeated as soon as we left the room. And there was no stopping Rockwell, who insisted that we repair to the house and start in on the other bottle.

Even considering my premonition, it was a horrific shock to see Rifle Shot standing on the path between the station and Rockwell's cabin. His breechloader was cradled in his arms and his expression was one of somber malevolence the likes of which I never hope to see again.

Rockwell stopped in his tracks as soon as he spied the big Indian, and I saw Rifle Shot's eyes widen and his gun shift position.

The next event was as strange as anyone could imagine. Rockwell hauled both pistols from his trouser pockets and rested them on either side of his feet, while Rifle Shot simultaneously bent and gently laid his breechloader on the ground before him. The two men then closed the distance between them and finally clasped each other's forearms in what must be some form of frontier handshake.

Rockwell turned back to me nodding, with a large grin on his face.

"Haven't seen this big critter in a dog's age. I'd come to think we'd never cross paths again, even thought that maybe he was one of them apparitions or some kind of angel."

The three of us walked together on the path to Rockwell's cabin and sat together outside on a blanket provided by our host. The Valley Tan was passed around, but the big Indian would have none of it. We did however all smoke from Rifle Shot's pipe which was filled with sumac leaf mixed with the peal of red willow.

For my benefit, Rockwell launched into the story of his initial and only previous meeting with Rifle Shot, which he reckoned to have taken place on a full-moon night some five or six years past. In his high-pitched voice, Mr. Rockwell admitted that he "was up to no good that evening and was where he shouldn't have been." As the story progressed, I learned that dressed as an Indian, he was in ambuscade awaiting a column of soldiers from Fort Laramie. He indicated that some of them "needed to be set right" for earlier transgressions against a group of Mormon settlers.

As Rockwell watched the cavalrymen approach in the distance, two Pawnee braves happened by, saw him crouching with his back to them, and by his disguise mistook him for a certain member of the Sioux tribe with whom they had a long-standing grudge. The two Pawnee set upon the costumed Mormon an instant later, and then began a furious struggle which Rockwell was hard pressed to sustain. He managed to dispatch one of his attackers, though in the process he was felled by a hard knock to the head which left him dazed and vulnerable on the ground. The remaining Pawnee scrambled to regain his war club, and after doing so, stood over Rockwell grinning and chanting some death song as he raised his cudgel and prepared to administer the *coup de grace*.

As fate would have it, Rifle Shot was the advance scout for the advancing cavalry column on that particular evening, and in that capacity he came upon the scene described above at precisely the right moment—at least as far as the helpless Rockwell was concerned. In the moonlight, Rifle Shot instantly recognized the trappings of a Pawnee warrior, and because that tribe is hated by the Delaware, he counted the man on the ground as his enemy's enemy and therefore a friend. Consequently, and without hesitation, he raised his rifle and discharged a single shot which passed between the Pawnee's arms (which by now were on the downswing) and crashed into his skull at the bridge of his nose.

"Such a shot I'd never seen," said Rockwell. "My savior must have been three hundred paces away from where I was laying and he hit that son-of-a-bitch spot-on with only the moonlight to aim with. The Pawnee fell square on top of me and took the air right out of my lungs. I was already dizzy as a hen before that happened, so when the shootist came and hauled that dead Pawnee off of me, well, I didn't know if I was looking up at some Lamanite guardian angel or if I had passed beyond and was looking at my own killer. As it turned out, I didn't have much time for these thoughts, because by now the army column had caught up to where all this was taking place and the sound of gunfire had brought a U.S. Calvary soldier charging up that hill.

"I guess all the soldier saw in the moonlight was a bunch of Indians, because he was now at a gallop with his saber bared and waiving up over his head. He was fixing to cut down the only man standing, and that of course was the gentleman who is sitting next to us right now. Damn fool didn't even recognize his own scout, just crazed with the idea of killing an Indian I guess.

"I still had my pistol in my hand when I was laying there on the ground and I saw in a minute that there was no chance for my friend to reload or in any other way repel the charge. Dizzy as I was, I picked up and fired a ball that knocked that cavalryman clear off his horse. Don't mind saying that was the second best shot of the night, and it damn near rivaled the first considering my fuzzy condition.

"So, in the space of maybe three minutes we had saved each other's lives. We both knew it and exchanged gifts. He gave me this here snakeskin band that I wear around my wrist, and for me, I went over to where I hid my ordinary clothes and gave him my trousers. Oh, I knew right away they wouldn't come close to fitting him, but I reckoned it'd be the first pair he ever had, and I knew how much Injuns like that sort of thing. We never said a word between us that night, never learned each other's name, and never saw each other until this day."

Rifle Shot sat taciturn through the telling of this story. What emotion he may have had was lost in the scrutiny of his pipe.

Rockwell tossed his head towards Rifle Shot. "Reckon this big fella has no English. Well, I can see he's a Delaware, that's for sure, and I think I still know how to speak a little of that language." The famous Mormon took a deep breath, postured, and in a stilted voice leaned over and began talking to Rifle Shot. He spoke very slowly and at an exaggerated volume."

Rifle Shot bent foreword to receive the words, and save for a weak grimace, made no response.

Rockwell again ventured into the linguistic wilderness and fired-off another volley of his badly crippled Delaware.

After looking deep into Rockwell's eyes, Rifle Shot turned to me and said softly, "He just asked if my sister's breast is too large for the canoe, and if yesterday's frog is barking."

Rockwell's eyes lit-up. He slapped his knee and threw back his head in a hearty laugh. "Well, Wheat. Turn me upside down. He knew the English words I was saying all along! My word. And all this time I thought he didn't understand." Rockwell flushed a bit, rubbed his chin, and chuckled. "Guess my Delaware ain't exactly what it used to be. Reken I need a bit of brushin' up."

September 21, 1860
Camp Floyd
Utah Territory

After a crazy night of drinking with Rockwell, I awoke the next morning with the unmistakable feeling that I was still drunk. Symptoms included a certain recklessness of disposition, a curious state of happy agitation, and an urgent want to lay carnal hands on any one of old Port's wives. I have only foggy recollections of the particulars of last evening, but I can recall the exchange of many stories and the opportunity for many lies. The big Indian's participation was limited to sober observation until, I think, Rockwell and I had finished off the third bottle of Valley Tan and it was around that time Rifle Shot disappeared into the shadows.

He reappeared some hours later, and we asked if he had changed his mind and was back to join us for a drink. He said that he was back to let us know that the evening was over and that the sun would be up in a few moments. He addressed us as one would a child. "You can never have last night's rest again, forever. You have made the bottles empty and filled them again with some of your sleep life. This is the death of sleep. Part of you has died." That was just before dawn.

I must have been shamed to sleep then for it was almost 10 a.m. when I awoke with the symptoms described above. Rockwell was already awake, or maybe he never went to sleep. He was loud and animated and was chatting up Rifle Shot in that high pitched voice using "wheat" as both adjective and adverb throughout every sentence. The big Indian listened attentively and seemed to be enjoying the stories.

I joined them at a table where we all sat and drank coffee. A short time after this an ashen Tree Jimboy entered the room cradling his ample belly. He complained of feeling queasy after what was described as a night filled with "a whole lot of raw potatoes smeared with lard." As an afterthought he also admitted consuming more than a dozen Bath Olivers.[36]

As the coffee began to clear my mind and overtake the residual drunkenness, I felt Rifle Shot was correct, part of me had died. I felt I was now rushing headlong into being a dead man, a dead man done in by the poisonous Valley Tan.

At this juncture, Mr. Jimboy announced that he was going to be sick, and sick-up he did without managing more than a step or two away from the coffee table. This enraged Rockwell who laid boot to Jimboy's arse and told him to pick himself up and clear the premises. This did me little good and was anyways too late, for acts such as Jimboy's are powerfully infectious, and especially so to someone in my delicate state.

Suddenly, I was overtaken by a panicky death rattle and an urgent need for immediate action. Unlike Jimboy, I was able to rush out the door and over to a patch of shrubbery where I collapsed in retching,

---

36 Sweet biscuits. —Ed.

gut–cramping horror as the poisons reached capacity in my cleansing organs and my stomach began to empty. An initial wave was followed by a second and then a third which left me so weak that I could do no more than sprawl exhausted in the shrubs and allowed myself to bake unmercifully in the midday heat. It was at that point I realized the shrubbery was in fact poison ivy and that I was breaking out into fiercely itching giant hives.

This was the nadir of my journey. Trying to match "squars" of Valley Tan with O. P. Rockwell was my undoing. I must have been out of my bloody mind.

Camp Floyd
Utah Territory

It is now two days since the American Forks episode and I am beginning to enjoy a measure of recovery. Tree Jimboy and I left Rockwell's station as soon as we were fit to travel and reached Camp Floyd's garrison just after sunset. I departed American Forks believing that Rockwell and Rifle Shot would work out some sort of agreement regarding the Indian's planned assassination of Brigham Young. At least that was my hope, and I do not see how I could have been of any more help in the matter.

I arrived to find that life at Camp Floyd had taken a bizarre turn which was coincidental with the arrival of the Danas. It all began that first evening, when Lt. and Mrs. Dana were invited to tea by the Commanding Officer's Wife, Mrs. Abbie Goodwin, as decent a Christian woman that exists in this world and a person devoted to the idea of bringing civility and decorum to Camp Floyd. I was asked to join the group at seven o'clock.

Although her husband and I arrived at the designated hour, Mrs. Dana's entrance was delayed because she had spent the better part of the day "liquorin'-up" at the post's most degenerate saloon in the company of an aging *vaquero* by the name of Mexican Jake.

Lt. Dana, who had been fidgeting in his best dress blues for the past hour, was in another room with the Commandant and had just about run out of excuses for his wife's absence when she finally burst through the front door. Not only was she near drop-dead drunk, but she had also dragged along Mexican Jake, who she insisted accompany her as escort for the evening.

The Commanding Officer's Wife clutched at her bosom as Mrs. Dana pushed past her, stumbled over to a tray of biscuits, and began eating with two hands. Abbie Goodwin stood aghast until she was obliged to jerk her head around in response to a lurid overture.

It was Mexican Jake, who had come up dangerously close to her and hissed: "*Buenas noche, Senora*, you are even more beautiful up close." He spied a golden cross on a thin chain around her neck. "Ah, are you a Catholic by chance, *Senora*? You know, I was going to be a priest. Yes, that's right, *Senora*, a man of God. Does that make you feel good, *Senora*? Does that make you feel like. . . ."

Mexican Jake lost his train of thought. His mouth hung open, and he somehow managed to open one eye much wider than the other. There was a long pause as he struggled to focus and regain his composure. "Please, *Senora*, you are too beautiful." The gray-stubbled *vaquero* attempted a courtly bow from the waist and reached for her hand with his protruding lips wrinkled and puckered into the kissing position, but he wavered forward at this point and had his *sombrero* knocked-off his head as its ample brim brushed down the front of Abbie Goodwin's blouse and skirt.

The Commanding Officer's Wife screamed and with the slightest bit of a push sent Mexican Jake face first into the floor. This brought Lt. Dana and the Commandant rushing into the room and simultaneously triggered a wild response from Mrs. Dana, who after seeing her escort in the horizontal position, immediately attacked Abbie Goodwin.

The two officers and I were trying to subdue Mrs. Dana, but this was not an easy task. She had Mrs. Goodwin's hair wrapped around one hand and the other in the Commanding Officer's Wife's mouth. Abbie Goodwin bit down, and in response Mrs. Dana reared back and attempted to kick her adversary into letting go. She missed, and instead delivered a stunning blow to the head of Mexican Jake who had by this time crawled up to the Commandant's wife's ankle, upon which he was attempting to land a slobbering kiss.

A sergeant at arms arrived and the four of us were able to wrestle Mrs. Dana to the ground and hold her until she calmed down. Mexican Jake was allowed to leave on his own, which he did after some crawling about on hands and knees before being able to stand. He was still very drunk and somewhat disoriented from the kick. He kept saying "Please, *Senora*, you are too beautiful." Poor Mrs. Dana; like the fly she has quit camphor to settle on compost.

XIX

ECCE HOMO: BURTON FINDS HIMSELF IN OTHERS AND DISSECTS MANKIND

September 27th, 1860
Salt Lake City
Utah Territory

The Camp Floyd reception spectacle was my parting memory of Mrs. Dana and the final scurrility of her former image. Her husband actually suffered a mild apoplectic stroke on account of the event, and as twisted fate would have it, ended up trapped in the camp's infirmary in a bed next to Mexican Jake. The crusty *caballero* had been collected from the dirt only a few feet from the Goodwin's front door and was being treated for alcohol poisoning and a concussion. For obvious reasons, the attending physician has forbidden any further conversation between the two for fear of worsening the lieutenant's condition. No one can say what has become of his wife. It is impossible not to sigh when contemplating the sin and sorrow of it all, this tale of the Dana's fate, this preposterous frontier drama and its quizzically melancholy ending.

And from that other American metaphor, Gaston La Mash, comes an equally fitting fare-thee-well. On my way to the stables where a new coach awaited, I paused in front of a saloon on Whisky Street after recognizing my companion's voice booming out from inside. He had cornered an audience and was in mid-delivery of a high volume rendition of the Flathead squaw story. I lit a cigar and leaned against the wall near an open window to get a last dose.

"So I give her back to that old chief, and don't you know a minute later her brother comes a whoopin' at me with a scalpin' knife over his head. Wal, I figured that was a sure sign they wanted me to keep her, but I'll be chewed-up before any man tries to make me do what I don't want to do. No sir! No siree Bob! Why that's all I live for, someone tellin' me what to do an' tryin' to take away my freedoms. I'll burst any man that tries. I'm the first cousin to Beelzebub in the American land of milk and honey, you can believe that!"

Yes, Mr. La Mash, this is indeed America, and it is a dizzying thought to imagine what will come from all those freedoms and the staunch efforts to protect them. Any man in this sweaty world who would suggest there is no excitement or merit in all this is an unblushing liar, but woe to the society that invites chaos through the headstrong pursuit of noble goals.

Enter now the barristers, bureaucrats and politicians, the missionaries, the money-mad, and other shielded sinners. It is a blood-chilling thing to contemplate just how many profligates this vast land could hold or where their varying interests may take it. In sum, it is a sad fact that Freedom also means one is free to be an insufferable and unmitigated bloody ass, and there is a fear that this wonderful and hearty land will not be conquered but rather will be ruined from within.

This journey has left me thinking about Man's natural genius for ruining things. Even loved and cherished things seem destined to be ripped apart, and often by those who love and cherish them. One need only recall the reburial of John Milton. A hundred years or so after the great bard passed, the population decided to dig him up and replant him under a proper memorial. When the adoring citizens got down into the grave they found three caskets, and the one on top was made of lead and sealed quite tightly. Everyone assumed that this was the one that held Milton, but they wanted to make sure, so tools were brought to peel back the cover of the coffin. Once it was hacked they indeed found John Milton himself in a great state of preservation.

So far so good, I suppose; but then it got nasty.

The Milton-infatuated populace who did this to preserve the man's honour went mad and began ransacking and insulting the coffin, grabbing in for his hair, bits of clothing and bone relics. And the woman who inherited the backyard that once was his graveyard then began charging admission so people could pay to see what was left—and that wasn't much after those who loved him all but dismantled him.

What is this about the human mania to ruin what we profess to love? Matrimony and money may be the first and greatest examples, but added to the sorry list may be friendships and nations, the animals that serve us, and the soil, water, and air that sustain us. We need not pretend that any place on earth is immune or that one society is less guilty than any other if given the opportunity; but if advancement equates proportionally to ruination, then we need only look to mighty and successful London, where one's clothes are covered and ruined with soot around the clock, where the air is unbreathable, the Thames an open sewer, and a place where otherwise healthy people come to die.

What to make of it all? This journey, which originated in a mud hut in Zanzibar and was forged by an enigmatic and even spiritual hunt for humanity, has cumulated in a realization that all of humanity is one and that the beast is a disease of the species and not particular to any people. Likewise the beauty that is in all men as well coexists somehow with the brute under the same skin.

As my laibon instructed, this trip was about being rather than doing. I can see that now. And I can see that witnessing, thinking, and the wisdom in setting my observations to page in a privy journal rather than in a formal travel book have all paid their dividends. Applied and careful thought are not matters for any kind of substitution (although there is much action in the world absent this process), and my private thoughts here have freed me from writing a book which would either be edited heavily by the censors or left unpublished—and if brought into print, destined for the indignity of being vetted by stodgy propriety.

The laibon predicted the freedom and security of writing the truth when he said that no king or earthly gods could suppress it. I celebrate being able to write without government, religious censor, or timid publisher destroying or hiding my words this time. And I cannot forget the happy street children of Zanzibar who sang out for "ink and paper" and the wealth they bring. Could they have been participants in this curious journey as well?

Having the pen replace the sword forced a mindfulness of the cadence of life and a chance to step back and have a deeper look into the performers on this stage—their actions, atrocities and affections, the way they interact with each other, with opportunity and adversity, and even their articulation with earth itself. At the moment I think this may be called the religion of existence.

Laibon Mbatiany directed me here to investigate Man, and in the process he hoped that I would find myself. He picked the right place, for America offered much in terms of diversity, exposed me to both the raw and the cooked, and along the way I think I did find myself. In the end I found myself in everyone else.

I confess to being John Hanning Speke—sober, stilted and solitary—and John Steinhaeuser—binged, benevolent and befriended. I am Col. Atkins Hamerton ground-down by the tropics and I am the tropics itself that feeds on life as greedily as a thirsty man drinks water. I am a sporting event and election with carefully constructed rules and formalities that fall before human chaos.

As the captain of a paddle boat on the Mississippi I am both the sternly religious Ezekiel Bibbs and the profligate Lester Beach. I am the resentful slave Kwomo and the man he became who delighted in having a slave of his own. In the same person I am the innocent and likable Pony Express rider and the Hunkpapa who couldn't help but murder him.

I am both the troopers and the Mormons, the hopeful settlers in the wagons and the Indians that had to end their dreams. I am the dead warrior Looking Bird without his necklace for the death journey, and I am the little boy who stole it from him. I am every Indian who ever hated another Indian, and I am Johnny Cotton and his son, and at the same time every poor soul in their wagon train. And I am Mrs. Dana.

Who I am, and who we all are, is not really a mystery to me at this point, thanks to my laibon. We are the animals who have coined the terms, "gentle as a lamb" and "the lamb of God" to capture in our minds the image of innocence, serenity, and peace; and the same animals that turn around and kill, butcher, and eat the very symbol of tranquility that we have created. Curious stuff. Yet we are also creatures of tears and unique compassion that is found nowhere else in the animal kingdom, and that makes it all even more curious.

What I learned about a few other things on this directed journey now captures my attention. This business with Laibon Mbatiany and the Marie Laveaus fascinates. Be it East African Shamanism or hoodoo in Louisiana Territory, I have seen with my own eyes that there is something to it that goes well beyond the pomp and ceremony that is a component of all yawning and conventional religions. I am not a proponent of the efficacy of prayer, but is not what I have witnessed a form of it?

There is an undercurrent to our perceived existence that reason and science cannot measure, a way of working that manifests itself in certain men and women who have found an ability to bring the extraordinary into the conventional. Magic—I want to know it and the world needs to want it.

Surely it is not the exclusive property of dark-skinned people, but so far it seems the white man hasn't found time to access the supernatural enchantments. Through their industry and genius they have given mankind much to make life easier, safer, healthier, better informed, better fed, and perhaps even a bit more beautiful; but I think they best relax and hope to use their talents to make their world a more intriguing and electrifying place.

I also wish to have a few words about Mr. Gaston LaMash. After a full exposure, I found his extroverted personality refreshing and perfectly emblematic of America. There is something to say for a man without pretensions, for in such cases one knows who one is dealing with and does not have to be troubled looking behind him all the time to try and find the other half. To be forthright is to compensate for much else, and creation would be a better place with more plain-spoken people, as well as nations.

Finally there is Rifle Shot, the stoic and storied introspective warrior, who knows enough of two worlds to find the truth in both. The man who "can shave the eyelashes off a wolf as far as a shootin' iron can carry a ball and put an arrow through a keyhole a hundred yards away" is also the man whose words echo over and over again in my head. It is this giant of a man who said, "But is it not the same in the land of the white man? Has it ever been any other way?" and "Mormons do not want peace any more than I do, or you, or any of the decent people you speak of. We all want what we want, and want to take what we need. Peace is just a word that sometime man puts in between. Is the hunter more peaceful than the rabbit he takes for his fire? Does the deer ask the wolf for peace? It is not the way of things. The only real peace is death, when it is all finished, the way it must be."

His introduction to the term "ironic" and in his struggle to adapt it to a universal and unsolvable domestic situation only adds to his brilliance. Although a man with potentials of vast personal panorama, he was always controlled and stayed within his good self. This is not an easy thing, and I have never met a man like him.

Mr. Frank Baker[37]
Athenaeum Club
London

Dear Baker:

This is strictly *entre nous*. I can't tell you how troubled I am over our growing misanthropic perception of the other fellow. It is nothing short of scandalous.

This realization of the human condition must be the saddest of all sad stories. Perhaps we should lay blame at the feet of the Christian God, for it is He who insists that all men are fallen before birth. Perhaps we should ask Him if simple baptism can really extinguish the curse of this original sin or how to deliver into the world a decent

---

37 Frank Baker was one of Richard Burton's favorite pen names. This was the last readable entry in the journal and was clearly a letter to himself. —Ed.

man with a lasting fair chance for civility. From all that I've seen—and I'm certain you agree—the response would be a disappointed and unequivocal blank stare.

While we have His attention, we might also inquire why pagandom owns all the handsome dressing, the greatest music and verse, and why the devil is in possession of the best sex. But to what end? We already know the answer. Blemished man is a hunter after life, love, and want of all else that suits him. This is the war we see both between nations and each other. Our religions are manufactured for charitable purposes and designed to help check the madness, but in the end they only serve to accelerate it. In fact, the more I study religion, the more I am convinced that man never really worshiped anything but himself.

At the very least, we may take sad succor in the knowledge that the glove which fits the disciples of Christ is also worn by the children of Jehovah, Buddah, Shiva, and Allah. We cannot seem to help but get in each other's way, and here is where the cloven foot shows itself. To lie about this would be a contemptible thing, Frank, but what to do about it?

This is our moral dilemma, and it is that for which no man has an answer.

We are the creator, the destroyer, the hero, and coward; at once both the prince and the pissant. Through the whirling complexities of circumstance we stand luckless as Basus, the Israelite who was given the much celebrated "Three Wishes."

The man's loving bride convinced him to use the first wish to make her more beautiful. When this was granted, her contumacious behaviour so infuriated her mate that he used the second wish to have her transformed to a bitch. With both of them thoroughly dissatisfied with the results of the first two wishes, the third was used to return her to the original state.

Mankind's first wish directs him towards the attainment of what seems right, but once this is granted we offend, we infuriate, we murder. The second wish is a war against the results of the first, and if we survive the struggle—the third wish fulfilled—we are back to where we started and unlucky enough to begin the process all over again.

I'll be the one to tell you, Frank, This is what makes the world go around. This is why the survivor's tale is the only and imperfect measure of righteousness. It really isn't fair but *n'importe*, true life is sung in a voice Divinely sweet and a voice no less Divinely sad.

I am sir, as always,

You

Richard F. Burton